A MILLION DIFFERENT WAYS

BOOK I OF THE HORN DUET

P. DANGELICO

Originally Published: March 2015

Reissued: June 2016 Fourth Edition

Cover Design: Najla Qamber, Najla Qamber Designs

www.pdangelico.com

ISBN: 9781495148743

ISBN: 9780692919675

ALSO BY P. DANGELICO

last words are read. If that's not a hallmark of a truly great author, I don't know what is. I highly recommend A Million Different Ways and certainly look forward to reading more from a very promising new author P. Dangelico in the near future!" *-Readers' Favorite*

Prologue

1985

Santa,
Hi. I am 6. I can rite becase I have a tuder.
Can you make my mom and dad like eech other. thanks
love sebastian

1987

Santa,
Hi its Sebastian. I live in texas and my parents dont
fite anymore. I dont see my dad much. my mom drinks
that stuf that smells can you help her?
Thanks you are grate.

love Sebastian

1988

Deer Santa,
My mom is in the hospitol agan!!!!!!! A boy in my class said
you are NOT REAL I really hope he is rong!!!!!!!!!! can you rite
write me back. I am not going to rite you anymore. I stil
still live in texas.

Love Sebastian

CHAPTER 1

GENEVA, SWITZERLAND 2012

Winter had worn out its welcome, dragging its feet well into April, but signs that spring had finally arrived were everywhere now. Daffodil stalks had timidly begun to sprout up from cozy beds of dirt, and a dusting of color covered the naked branches of the Platanus trees. The banks of the lake were packed with people emerging from hibernation. Their rolled-up shirtsleeves revealed skin as bleached as an uncooked baguette.

We sat on an old iron bench that faced the Geneva fountain, the Jet d'Eau, and watched it soar 138 meters into the clear blue sky. A watercolor rainbow appeared in the downturned arc of the spray.

"You can work at Yuri's nightclub if you want."

I glanced at Emilia and found her examining the cheese in her sandwich. "Don't take this the wrong way, Em—I appreciate the offer," I said in the most diplomatic tone I could muster. "But I'm not interested in getting out of a bad situation and into a worse one."

She wrinkled her slender nose at the cheese and picked it

out with long pale fingers. I devoured mine. I hadn't eaten a decent meal in days. On cue my stomach growled, nerves churning its paltry contents like a wash and rinse cycle. I placed my hand over it but only managed to reduce its angry roar to a low moan. Emilia stared at my stomach. An apostrophe between her brows marked her delicate features.

"How are you doing with money?" she asked in Albanian, our common language.

In an attempt to avoid her scrutiny, I kept my eyes on the bobbing masts of colorful sailboats tossed about on the windswept water. "Fine," I replied, a little too quickly. It was an egregious lie and we both knew it. Honesty had become a rare commodity between us in the last couple of months. Withholding the entire truth was the only way to be in each other's company without arguing.

My savings account was dwindling rapidly. I was reminded of it every time I looked in the mirror and saw the sharp angles of my cheekbones protruding, the dark depressions beneath my eyes. I couldn't afford to pay the rent on the tiny room off the Rue du Berne much longer. Just for a little while, in the span of time that it takes to eat a crappy sandwich, I wanted to forget my problems and lose myself in the breathtaking beauty surrounding me.

"Is there any way you can go back to the pub?" Her question caught me by surprise. Salt on an open wound. The burning sensation lingered as the memory of what had happened that evening came back to me in a rush...

It was our turn to close the bar that night and Pascal always seemed to forget something. The last time we worked the late shift together he had forgotten to lock the back door and the manager had threatened to fire us both.

"Did you lock the cash register yet?" I asked for the third time.

His dark eyes roamed over my rear end in approval. "Oui."

Pascal was considered attractive—he certainly never lacked female company—but if you asked me, he looked like the villain in a bad romance novel. His mouth had a perpetually smug tilt, and his black, deep-set eyes were framed by slanted brows that winged up at the ends.

It was past one a.m. Eager to close up and go home, I sat at the bar and divided the tip money while Pascal finished cleaning. It vaguely registered that he had been wiping the same spot on the copper top bar for ten minutes in mindless circles. My gaze nervously drifted from his powerful bicep, stretching the black t-shirt he wore, down to his meaty hand and calloused knuckles, the sight of which never failed to turn my stomach.

"Let's have a drink," he announced, his French accent coarse.

I paused from counting my share of the money and glanced up. Before I had a chance to respond, he had already poured himself a shot of tequila and knocked it back.

"Let's not," I snapped, too tired to even feign an excuse.

He wiped his mouth with the back of his hand and raked me head to toe with a blank stare. A flicker of something indefinable made me pause. All my senses coalesced, focused strictly on him. He moved behind me, to collect his keys from behind the bar, and I felt him purposely brush up against my rear end, his erection jabbing me in the small of my back. Pascal had been making sexual advances for months and had done so with all the girls. It never occurred to me that I was in any real danger.

A wave of confusion rolled over me. I stood there frozen in place while my mind questioned what my instincts were trying to tell me. When I finally gathered the courage to glance over my shoulder, I found him hovering disturbingly close, a predatory smile plastered on his face he did nothing to conceal. The realization didn't hit me all at once. It trickled in, collected in my gut, and slowly transformed into a feeling of dread.

"You know, my cousin works at the Department of Immigration."

"Yes, I know, Pascal," I curtly replied, unease getting the better of my self-control.

"For a well-educated woman, you're very stupid," he spat out.

There were a million things I wanted to say to him and none were particularly educated. This time, however, self-preservation easily prevailed over any impulse I felt to argue or defend myself. I grabbed my keys from beneath the cash register and stuffed them into the back pocket of my jeans. Not daring to turn my back on him, I slowly backed away.

"I appreciate the offer, but I can take care of it myself."

His eyes narrowed into aggressive creases and the air surrounding us instantly transformed—grew heavy with dark energy. I pretended not to notice his threatening glare and untied the black apron wrapped around my shrunken waist, throwing it onto my shoulder casually.

"See you Tuesday," I said, insincerity ringing loudly in my over-exuberance.

Escape was only an arm's length away, the door within reach when he spoke again. "Aren't you forgetting something?"

The delicate hairs on the back of my neck stood up straight. Dear God. My winter jacket was in the back office and I couldn't afford to leave it. The internal debate lasted only a second though. The look on his face made my mind up for me. "It's not that cold. I'll get it tomorrow." It wasn't even a small lie. There was still snow on the ground.

I gripped the doorknob and heard him moving, my hypersensitive ears registering footsteps over the heavy hammering of my heart. Time seemed to grind to a halt, reality collapsing into a singular, awful moment. I stepped out of the scene as if observing from some distant perspective and watched it play out frame by slow frame.

His thick, calloused fingers were splayed in front of me, holding the door shut. I could feel his hot, tequila-laced breath on the nape of my neck. His erection pushed against my rear end. My hipbones pressed painfully into the wood of the door. I couldn't hear myself scream; sounds seemed dull, wrapped in goose down. I struggled wildly but it was impossible to budge him. He outweighed me times ten. I realized my mistake much too late. I had calculated badly and hadn't anticipated his determination. I had grossly misjudged him and the cost was unthinkable.

In vain, I struggled to pry off the sweaty hand clamped over my mouth and nose. The pungent odor of his personal musk mixed with cleaning detergent and beer invaded my lungs, leaving no room for oxygen. Launched into a state of terror that was indescribable, any sanity I had a fragile hold on instantly fled.

"Shhh, you little *putain*. I'll make it good for you," he growled in my ear.

Then a bang as loud as a clap of thunder. It startled him, disrupting the violence. A group of young men stood outside the large picture window of the pub, pounding on the glass. They were obviously drunk and seemed in no hurry to move on. Pascal rocked back on his heels and relaxed his weight on the door long enough for me to react and jerk it open. I stumbled out into the icy night, greeted by a round of shouts and cheers. The young men rushed the door just in time to block Pascal from grabbing me again.

"*Va te faire enculer!*" he shouted, and the men replied with a few choice obscenities of their own.

I pushed through the crowd clutching the tiny gold cross around my neck for reassurance. Rubbing the warm metal between my fingers, I sent up a silent prayer of gratitude to whatever angel had delivered them. In the doorway Pascal stood eerily still, gripping the frame tight enough to turn his fat knuckles white. A blast of frigid air loosened the hold fear had on me, my body shuddering as I backed away into the dense black of the moonless night.

And then I ran.

I ran like the devil was at my heels. I ran even though the pain in my lungs felt like a sharp knife skewering me. I ran until I reached the safety of my little room, where a small immigrant woman with nobody in the world to protect her went to hide. I never went back for that jacket.

"There's a greater chance of me becoming the queen of England than going back there."

"Shit! That bad?!"

I picked nervously at the frayed hole on the knee of my jeans and tried to tuck the loose fibers back into the open weave but only succeeded in making it worse. "Unfortunately, yes."

A pair of elderly men walked past us at a snail's pace, arms locked behind their backs, bickering about the cost of living. One of them tipped his hat at me and I forced the corners of my mouth into a poor imitation of a smile.

"Have you heard anything from the hospitals?"

"Nothing...yet." My voice sounded weirdly high, my feeble attempt at optimism falling flat. I had applied for a residency position at half a dozen local hospitals months ago and hadn't received a single response. My three-month grace period had expired.

Originally signed in 1985, the Schengen Agreement allows EU residents to travel freely across borders without having to stop at checkpoints and show a passport. In 2008, Switzerland became the twenty-fifth country to join. More importantly, the law allows EU residents to obtain a temporary visa lasting ninety days within a six-month period. Unfortunately, that day had come and gone for me. And since Switzerland is notoriously strict about enforcing the limit—lawbreakers are routinely rounded up and deported after being subjected to enormous fines—I was constantly looking over my shoulder.

Thanks to the global economic meltdown, a blanket of hopelessness had settled over Europe. Not only was it suffocating growth and opportunity, it was also fueling an alarming anti-immigration movement. Previously fringe, far-right political parties were gaining momentum in Italy, Greece, Switzerland, and the Netherlands. Austerity policies had given birth to a destructive mentality of scarcity, a perfect breeding ground for hate and intolerance. Cracking down on immigration suddenly seemed to be the solution to every evil. No one wanted to acknowledge how closely it had begun to resemble a cycle of unpleasant history in Europe.

Italy had taken a big hit. The economy unraveled with each descending tick of the Italian stock market. By the time I graduated from the University of Milan medical school, funding for state-run hospitals had been reduced to the bare minimum. And since Switzerland's recognition of medical degrees from Italy is automatic, the decision to leave the relative safety of Milan, a city I had grown to love, was an easy one. I jumped on a bus headed north and three hours later found myself in a new country with a renewed sense of hope.

Geneva is a grande dame, an elegant lady, hosting a dinner party for friends from all around the globe. Arabic men dressed in traditional thobes are as common as young mothers pushing designer baby strollers in their workout spandex. Add to that bankers, students, and foreign dignitaries and what you get is a city filled with an eclectic mix of people who fit together as neatly as a colorful puzzle. I fell in love with her instantly. My shining city upon a hill. But as beautiful as she is, routinely ranking as one of the best cities in the world to live in, she also ranks as one of the most expensive. Financially, I was barely surviving, one paycheck away from total ruin.

"How are things with Yuri?" I asked out of habit. She brushed my concern away with a wave of her hand.

"Yuri isn't that bad. I can handle him."

I turned to look at her, an expression of disbelief plain on my face. "You can handle him?" Her eyes flickered away, scrupulously avoiding my glare. "Emi, he's involved with the Russian Mafia. It's no secret. I'm very worried for you. And what about your modeling career? Have you given up on that?" Something about Emilia triggered fiercely protective instincts in me. It had always been that way between us, since the day we met in grade school.

The pale skin between Emilia's arched, black brows puckered. "No." She stopped chewing her food and stared at the sandwich in her hand. "But I'm tired of starving myself, of getting up at four in the morning, of begging for jobs." She threw the rest of her sandwich away and crossed her arms. "Yuri takes care of me. Did I tell you he wants to buy me a brand-new BMW? It's red—my favorite color."

What could I say? I was exhausted, buried under a mountain of my own problems. I didn't have the energy to debate all the dangers she faced with this man. "Please promise me you'll be careful. No partying...no drugs."

Chastened, she studied her fingernails. Her pale jade eyes wouldn't meet mine. Beautiful Emilia. The fine-boned features and long legs did nothing for her self-esteem. There was also a new brittleness to her that I hadn't sensed the last time I saw her. I suspected she realized it couldn't last with Yuri, but was stubbornly trying to convince herself otherwise.

"What will you do now?" My eyes fell on the half-eaten sandwich she had discarded into the paper bag by her feet. I was so busy contemplating whether I should save it for later that her voice barely filtered in. "Vera?"

Reluctantly, I pulled my gaze away from the sandwich. "I don't know where else to look. The restaurants and the hotels won't take me without a visa." Emilia took one hundred francs out of her purse and handed it to me. I pushed it away and shook my head, my inconvenient pride protesting the indignation. "Emi, I can't."

She ignored me, shoved the money into my hands, and gripped them closed. A sympathetic smile softened her angular features. "When you become a famous doctor, you can pay me back...until then, don't."

Torn between shame and survival, I stared at the money and swallowed the bitter taste in my mouth. "You can count on it."

"I just remembered something." Emilia's expression was pinched in concentration. "One of the waitresses at the club said there was a position available at the Horn estate, outside the city, but they wouldn't take her because she doesn't speak proper English. It pays well and housing is included." Standing, she brushed the crumbs off her skinny black jeans.

"Kitchen or housekeeping?" I asked. Not that it mattered —I was ready to dig ditches in a graveyard if it meant being paid.

"Housekeeping, I think...maybe when you get there you can show them how well you cook."

I stood and wrapped my arms around her tiny waist, the height difference between us considerable. "I'll do anything they need me to. Thanks, Em, you know I love you."

"You're my oldest friend, Vera—my only real friend. I'd do anything for you."

The thinly veiled bruises on her soul were evident in her expression. I recognized those bruises, saw them in myself when I looked in the mirror. Liberty had taken its pound of flesh but we had survived.

"Horn. Why does that sound familiar?" I thought out loud. Emilia turned around and pointed to the majestic turn-of-the-century building. As the metallic letters glimmered in the sunlight, I recognized the name. Horn Banque.

CHAPTER 2

I wasn't surprised to discover that the only housing I could afford in Geneva was a small room in the red-light district. The windows of Pâquis embarrassed me. I always stared ahead when I walked past the barely dressed women in the store windows. As if in mutual agreement, they began filing their nails or checking their phones when they saw me, and resumed dancing suggestively as I walked past them. I pretended they didn't exist, even though the only thing that separated me from them was the thin glass between us. That and my education.

After my lunch with Emilia, I went to inform the landlady she needn't worry about fixing the small refrigerator. The sarcasm escaped her completely. It had been broken for months and no amount of begging had convinced the woman to replace it. The condition of the building was deplorable. Nevertheless, who was complaining? Not the tenants. Not a bunch of immigrants huddled together for some semblance of familiarity and safety, too scared to raise an eyebrow.

The apartment was a constant reminder of how low I had sunk in life. It was dark, cold, and the walls practically transparent. I knew exactly what time my neighbors left for work, who was having marital problems, when the prostitute down the hall was entertaining.

In a hurry to leave it far behind, I purchased a tattered valise in a secondhand shop and threw my belongings in without taking the time to fold anything. The valise had no wheels but I had learned to travel light. I had to be ready to pick up and move at a moment's notice. And I certainly didn't need another blouse; I was living the life of a Jesuit monk. I had been on one date in six years. Not that I was in any position to complain.

In hindsight, I never fully appreciated how charmed my life had been up until that fateful day six years ago. I was raised by a single parent who smothered me in love and support, indulged me in everything. My father taught me that I could do, or be anything I wished. I had grand ambitions and carefully laid out plans for my future—until my entire life was destroyed by circumstances outside my control.

There was no time to mourn. I learned to adapt quickly. My survival depended on it.

With only the clothes on my back and the little money I could get from pawning the few valuables I had, I fled, became a ghost, hiding in shadows and rejecting friendships and attachments of any kind. Because I was an accomplice to a crime, an expendable supporting character in a paperback thriller. I wasn't even the clever villain everyone hates to love. And the only thing I was certain of was that nothing would stop them from coming after me.

I flew down the stairwell, weaving around the children playing hide-and-go-seek along the dark musty corridor.

Their circumstances didn't diminish their joy in the game. They ran around me squealing and giggling, blissfully unaware of the dreariness of the place.

Halfway down, a loud shout and the thump of heavy boots drifted up from the ground floor, drowning out the melody of the children's laughter. I glanced over the railing and watched as a single file of police officers jogged up the metal stairs with purpose, weapons drawn. Panic stricken, I shrank back, pressed my spine against the wall. I had no intention of sticking around to find out whether it was a drug and prostitution raid, or a search for immigrants with expired visas. Doubling back through the door of my floor, I raced to the back of the building with my valise with no wheels banging against the side of my leg hard enough to leave a bruise.

People poured out of their apartments, the hallways crowded as they attempted to flee, the slow and weak being trampled in the process. A smothering wall of bodies blocked my escape, the reek of body odor and fear making it hard to breathe. With strength fueled by adrenaline, I bullied my way through to the emergency stairwell and ran out the service entrance.

The street was mostly empty. Only one young officer, smoking a cigarette, loitered on the corner. I wiped the nervous sweat off my brow before I walked past him, and rubbed the tiny cross around my neck in gratitude when he barely spared me a glance. As I walked to the bus stop, one of the children called my name, but I didn't turn around. I kept walking, away from the children, past the girls in the windows...putting as much distance between them and me as possible.

THE SMALL TOWN was just outside the city limits. I took three buses and spent ten francs I didn't have to spare to get there. It sat comfortably up the side of a hill, overlooking the shores of Lake Geneva; the charm of it fit for postcards and computer screen savers. Leaning my forehead against the cold bus window, I watched life fly by on fast-forward, as smears of intermittent color against the constant blue sky.

The landscape was dotted with neatly painted homes in different shades of yellow, white, and beige. The precise, geometric pattern of a vineyard stretched along the banks of the lake. Sidewalks that framed the winding, narrow roads were swept, flowerbeds neatly groomed, and grass looked trimmed with measuring tools.

After all these months, I was still dazzled by the natural beauty of Switzerland, the cleanliness, the order. I was homeless and financially hanging on by a thread. I should have been scared witless. Yet inexplicably, the tightness in my chest eased. And for the first time in months, I felt like I could breathe again.

When I stepped down from the bus, the sun made me squint and hide my eyes beneath the roof of my fingers. Across the street, an elderly man swept the front steps of his bakery shop. I asked him for directions to the estate and he kindly obliged while his wife stared at me suspiciously from behind the store window. I made slow progress down the single lane road. In an orchestrated rhythm, I switched my valise with no wheels from one sweaty hand to the other, dividing the painful task evenly.

My medical books made it ridiculously heavy. Actually, it must have weighed as much as I did. Between my unusually fast metabolism and not enough food to eat, I was scared to weigh myself. I rarely looked in mirrors. After running from the pub, I contemplated selling them, but decided to cut back on food instead. The books were the only things of any value I had left.

A small, yellow car sped by, barely avoiding me. Too tired to step aside, I watched the tiny car speed away while the driver waved an angry fist at me and cursed in French. Unbidden, an image of my father drifted in. I could see him shaking his head and raising an eyebrow at me. His *"princeshe."* I missed him. My father had been a man of influence in Albania. An intellectual, a visionary, a master of policy and diplomacy. That's how his friends eulogized him on that frigid day. I used to think he was the center of the universe, the source of all truths. Not anymore. Not for a long time.

I'm the one that found him swinging in his office. An image that wouldn't tarnish or fade. I could still see him in fine detail from time to time, when I was overly tired. His tall, lean form limp and swinging like a sack of clothes. The tinge of blue on the pale skin of his bare feet. The terrible sadness that would descend upon me shortly afterwards robbed me of breath and sapped all the strength from my limbs.

My sweaty hand was beginning to blister. The pain was a welcome distraction. I pushed thoughts of my father down and away, locked them up with all the other heartbreaking truths I did my best to ignore, and concentrated on putting one foot in front of the other.

———

WHAT STARTED as mild fatigue steadily grew into bone-crushing exhaustion. I was dragging my feet by the time I reached the driveway. Dandelions tumbled around me. Fat clusters of white, hairy seeds surfed the wind that kicked up.

One landed on my nose. And as I placed my bag down to scratch the itch, the estate finally came into view. I didn't recognize the sound of my own voice as a surprised bark of laughter erupted out of me. Somehow, I had been transported to a land of make-believe or a Disney movie. For a bizarre moment, I expected to see Julie Andrews come around the corner singing and dancing while Nazis stood on the front doorstep. I had anticipated something grand but this…this was unreal.

The manor was in the French style with lawn as tidy as a carpet extending out as far as the eye could see. It had a steep-pitched slate roof, chimneys shaped in pointed peaks, and slender windows capped with stone demi-lunes. A fuzzy vest of ivy clung to the golden limestone façade. And in the background, framing the breathtaking scene, sat Lake Geneva in all her splendor. In short, it looked like the home of a fair-haired prince. Except this was no fairytale. Well… not mine, at least.

I barely heard the rumble of a car approaching until it almost ran me over. Apparently, nobody in the countryside drives at a reasonable speed. The sports car raced past me without pausing. It looked absurdly expensive. All black and sensually sleek, the dark windows obscured the driver's identity. Gravel fired off under its tires like firecrackers on Bastille Day and kicked up a fog of silt.

I coughed at the dust billowing up around me, a white haze settling on my clothes. Add that to the list of injustices I needed to discuss with God on Sunday. I tried to brush it off but only succeeded in smearing it deeper into the wool of my navy cardigan.

By the time I stood at the service entrance, I was limp and dusty, and my toe was poking out through a large hole on the top of my canvas sneakers. Basically, I looked like a character in a Charles Dickens novel. Hunger and weariness made me impatient. I knocked several times, the blows growing more forceful, until a tall, elderly gentleman opened the door.

My eyes snapped up to meet his. He looked north of seventy years with olive skin and a neatly combed, thick shock of white hair. His expression and black suit made him look like an undertaker. I angled one foot over the other in a ridiculous attempt to conceal the hole.

"Yes?" His English had a subtle French lean to it.

"I was told you have a housekeeping position open at the house, sir," I answered with a shaky smile.

Thinly disguised suspicion lurked in his dark eyes. Looking through his horn-rimmed glasses, he inspected me closer. "How old are you?"

"Twenty-nine, sir. I'll be thirty in September."

A heavy pause.

"You have a very cultured British accent," he stated, although it sounded more like an accusation. Then he arched an eyebrow and dipped his chin, gazed at me from above his glasses, as if a better angle would uncover my ruse.

"I also speak French and Italian, sir," I said quickly, pressing my case before the door slammed in my face.

"Come in. We'll talk," he conceded with a sigh.

Spinning. Everything was spinning. I stepped inside and gripped the doorframe for support as a wave of nausea and light-headedness washed over me. "I'm Olivier Bentifourt. I have been the butler for the Horn family for thirty-five years." I don't remember what happened next, but I must have fainted because I suddenly found myself horizontal with the weight of the world sitting on my eyelids and strange voices surrounding me.

"She's so thin, the poor, poor girl," said a woman with a jovial French accent. "Charlotte, quick, get the pastries I made last night. She must have low blood sugar," there was a rustling sound, "and put some tea on the stove. She looks like that actress, you know the one, the American."

"Audrey Hepburn?" offered the butler.

"*Non*, Olivier. That actress," a snap of fingers, "I think her name is Natalie Porter."

"Portman," corrected a woman in a crisp British voice.

"Natalie Portman, *oui*. Thank you, Charlotte."

"She can't work here, Marianne. It doesn't look like she could lift a pillow." The butler's voice broke through the fog. I could feel the cool stone floor beneath me and a sore spot developing on the back of my head. I forced my eyes open and saw a halo of sparkling lights and fuzzy shapes, blinked repeatedly and still couldn't focus.

"I'm stronger than I look. I can prove it. I can lift at least twenty kilos." My voice sounded weak even to my own ears.

"Where's Bentifourt? Where the fuck is everybody?!" The deep, raspy male voice reverberated through the kitchen and echoed painfully in my head. Assertive footsteps drew closer, the ancient limestone walls amplifying every sound. I sat up with whip-crack speed and instantly felt dizzy again.

"Olivier, you should go, before he finds us in here," said the French woman. A minute later I heard the elderly butler's shuffle grow fainter. "Here, eat these."

My vision sharpened to discover a short, plump woman bending over me. She had a wide face, a crown of short blond hair, a gap between her two front teeth, and deep blue eyes as round as gum balls. Though probably in her sixties, she didn't have many wrinkles. Except for the fine laugh lines fanning out from the sides of her eyes. Resting in her chubby palm were three beautiful little pastries. After shoving them indelicately in my mouth, I shut my eyes.

Manna from Heaven. An explosion of flavors assaulted my

taste buds. Rich crème, fresh ripe raspberry, and flaky dough. A balance of sweet and tart married in perfect harmony. It was the most wonderful thing I had tasted in...well, in forever.

Her eyebrows lifted a fraction as she watched me shovel the third one in. "Better?" she asked with a warm smile.

"Much better, thank you." Mortification began to creep in, and the realization that I may have ruined the one good chance I had at a decent job. I scrambled to my feet. "*Madame*, I am so sorry, but I have been walking for hours and didn't notice..." My voice trailed off as she waved her pudgy little hand in front of my face.

"Shhhh, *c'est bien*. It's okay. I understand. You are here for the housekeeping position? I see you already came with your things."

Two sets of eyes fell on my pathetic valise.

"Yes," I answered meekly.

"Do you have a work permit?"

The moment of truth...I couldn't answer, just held my breath and prayed for divine intervention.

She considered me for a moment. "Do you know how to clean?"

"I clean very well, *madame*," I answered quickly.

"We will try for a week. If you cannot do the cleaning properly I will have to let you go. Agreed?" Her gentle eyes searched my face.

"I won't disappoint you. Thank you, so much. Thank you," I repeated, overwhelmed with relief.

"My name is Marianne Arnaud. I run the housekeeping staff."

I extended an ever so grateful hand. "Vera Sava, *madame*. It's a pleasure to meet you."

———

I followed Mrs. Arnaud up the stairs to the servants' quarters. She opened the door to a small room that had a twin bed dressed in crisp white sheets and a navy blue blanket, a pretty antique armoire, a picture window, and a small writing desk with a table lamp. It was perfect in every way. A spot in my chest began to warm, evicting the permanent chill that had taken up residence there since that night at the pub.

"The toilette is down the hall and your towels are in the armoire, along with fresh linens. I will send up your uniforms," she informed me as she walked over to the window. Pushing aside the linen drapes, she opened it up. *"Très jolie, non?* This room has a pretty view."

I walked over to the window and glanced outside. That was a gross understatement. My eyes beheld an explosion of color as if Monet himself held the paintbrush, beauty in its most profound definition.

Neat segments of rose cultivars grew in between a boxwood hedge shaped in an intricate pattern; flowerbeds of tulips and irises were artistically arranged by hue; Japanese cherry trees in full bloom framed the south border. And hidden among the lush vegetation, moss-covered statues of cherubs and naked nymphs peeked out. I was no gardening expert, but this one seemed elegant enough to rival Versailles or what I'd seen of Versailles in books and on the Internet.

"I'll leave you to get settled," Mrs. Arnaud said, closing the door behind her afterwards. I couldn't believe my good fortune. Rubbing my tiny cross, I made a mental note to call Emilia and thank her again.

"Sebastian!" The velvety female voice floated in from the garden.

I glanced from behind the linen curtain and noticed a tall

woman, her greyhound thin body encased in tight britches and riding boots, walking purposefully towards a very tall man. Leaning on a cane, he stood under a magnificent pergola covered by white, trumpet-shaped flowers that formed an otherworldly halo around him. He was too far away for me to make out his features, but the inherent grace in his posture and the refined casual clothes he wore spoke volumes about him. Wealthy and entitled—he was sure about his place in this world.

Heir to the throne.

The woman was clearly on a mission. She swung her hips provocatively and tossed her long blond hair over her shoulder like she was selling sex and shampoo. When she reached him, she placed her hands possessively on his face and kissed him. The kiss evoked no response from him. He stood completely still while she devoured his mouth. Weird, I thought. The lack of affection was noticeable from a distance. Though they did make a pretty pair.

The curtain ballooned up on a gust of wind and, at that exact moment, he lifted his face and looked straight at me. Startled, I stepped aside, my heart beating erratically as prickling heat crawled up my neck. The last thing I needed was to make a bad impression on my first day and my new employer had just caught me spying. I was about to flagellate myself when I was interrupted by a soft knock at the door.

"Come in," I called out.

The door swung open and a tall, curvy woman stepped inside. I judged her to be younger than me, probably in her mid-twenties. She had huge brown eyes and a full head of bright blond, curly hair pulled tightly in a bun. She raised her long, slim fingers to her hairline, where some wayward curls had escaped, and unsuccessfully tried to tame them back into place.

"Hello, I'm Charlotte Beckwith. I thought I'd introduce myself." She spoke with a very clipped British accent I recognized from the kitchen.

"Vera, it's nice to meet you. I'm sorry for the disturbance I caused downstairs."

"No worries. We need a little drama around here. I'm warning you, it's dreadfully dull most of the time." There was a devilish look in her eyes that made me instantly like her. "As a matter of fact, you'd be doing everyone a favor if you could take up fainting on a regular basis, just to break up the monotony of the day." Dimples punctuated her cheeks when she smiled. "There are thirty housekeepers, and I'm one of only two under the half-century mark until you came along," she continued, talking quickly.

"Thirty housekeepers?" I whispered. An army.

"That doesn't even include the groundskeepers. And tragically, not one attractive, eligible man in the five-kilometer radius." A crease formed between her golden brows. "Aside from the beast, of course, but he doesn't count."

My eyes widened. "The beast?"

"Oh, you haven't met him yet, right? Mr. Horn...Sebastian. Not that anybody would ever be that familiar with him."

Charlotte clearly had a predilection for drama. She came further into the room, plopped down on my crisply made bed without invitation and quickly moved into rapid-fire questioning.

Did I like live music?

What were my favorite books?

Did I speak French?

"Do you have a boyfriend? Maybe we could go out some time. There's not much to do, but there's a terrific café in town that has live music on Friday nights. Oh, they have this wonder-

26

ful..." she drawled, holding on to the word as if it belonged to her, "singer from Cape Verde with a gut-wrenching voice." She didn't pause for a reply so I pulled out the only chair in the room, sat down, and listened patiently as she chattered on. I noticed that she didn't offer any personal information, which was fine since I wasn't ready to share any of mine.

"Charlotte." I had to interrupt her or she would have continued indefinitely. "Why do you call Mr. Horn the beast?"

"Because it's more polite than calling him an arsehole." She picked invisible lint off my blanket. "Even though he is. Didn't you hear him when we were in the kitchen? Right, you were having a kip on the floor." I couldn't help but giggle. "He's awful. He never speaks, hardly ever, and when he does he's usually shouting. I don't care what happened to him. He's not a nice man."

"Is he dangerous?" My skin began to itch. I'd become hypersensitive to even a hint of danger.

"No, not dangerous...cold. Not in a malicious sense, rather like..." Her voice dropped to a whisper. "There's something missing, dead." As I contemplated her words, she continued, "Mrs. Arnaud says he wasn't always this way. He used to be funny and sweet. I find that a bit delusional. Although she swears that before his wife—" She stopped abruptly, a sheepish look appearing on her face. "Shit, I'm not supposed to gossip. Bentifourt will skin me alive." Her long legs swung back and forth beneath her, her effervescent energy spilling over her attempt to restrain it.

"Don't tell me. I don't want you to do anything that will get you in trouble." In no time I had become protective of this girl that was so eager to befriend me. I watched her lose the battle for self-control; her transparent face telegraphed every thought she entertained. She needed no encouragement from me to break the rules.

"Okay, I'll just hit the highlights. Three years ago he was married, and they were in a horrible car accident on the way to St. Moritz. It was a miracle they saved his leg."

The cane…right.

"And his wife?"

Charlotte paused before adding, "Died…and he was driving."

A somber silence settled between us. I had nothing other than sympathy for this man. It didn't take a medical degree to realize he was suffering from the loss of his wife. He must have loved her very much. "He's the only person that lives here?"

Charlotte nodded. "Alone." She hopped off the bed and walked to the door. "I have to get back. Mrs. Arnaud thought I was going for a smoke. When you're settled, I'll give you a tour of the estate. You start tomorrow."

The events of the day were starting to catch up with me. It felt like lead weights were strapped to my ankles. "Charlotte."

She turned to face me. "Yes?"

"Do I need a tour?" I asked, yawning.

A wide, bright smile stretched across her face. "There are eighty-two rooms in this manor. I still get lost." She laughed at the look of shock on my face. "Rest. I'll swing by when I'm done with work."

The door closed. I shuffled to the small bed and lay down. Too tired to take off my dusty clothes. Too tired to shut the window. I laced my fingers together on my stomach, watched the linen drape flutter as a chilly wind blew in, and fell fast asleep.

CHAPTER 3

I woke up abruptly, in the middle of the night. Confused and disoriented, it took me a while to adjust my eyes to the surroundings. Someone had turned the desk lamp on and a note sat next to it.

Vera-

Didn't have the heart to wake you when I came by at 6. You slept so soundly I actually had to check your breathing to make sure you weren't dead. Will stop by at 5 a.m. to do the tour. Mrs. Arnaud left supper for you in the kitchen whenever you wake.

Charlotte

I got up and pushed the curtain aside. The moon, hanging high, poked out from behind puffs of smoky clouds. It seemed to be around midnight, which meant I had slept for a straight ten hours. Remarkable. I couldn't recall ever sleeping so soundly. My stomach rumbled, taking the opportunity to remind me that it had been sadly neglected.

With my hair a mess, hanging loose down my back since I couldn't locate my only elastic band, and my clothes all crumpled by sleep, I padded barefoot down the stairs. Small sconces of dim light interrupted the darkness in the hallway. The perfume of food drifted up from the ground floor. I followed my nose to the kitchen.

On a long counter, I found an assortment of cheese framed by muscat grapes; a golden roasted baby chicken—the scent of which made my stomach cry in anticipation; fingerling roasted potatoes sprinkled with fresh rosemary; baby purple cauliflower diced into small triangles; and French string beans tossed with crunchy almonds. And lastly, the beautiful pastries that had brought me back to life from a fainting spell earlier accompanied a petit chocolate éclair and a delicate little fruit tart.

Robbed of grace and manners by deprivation, I shoveled everything into my mouth until I was so stuffed I could hardly breathe. The silence, disturbed only by the subtle ticking of an antique wall clock, wrapped around me like a security blanket. I sat back to study my surroundings as an ease I hadn't felt in ages came over me.

The large kitchen was dark and cozy, the ceiling vaulted. Gleaming copper pots and pans hung from a suspended wrought iron rack, and a large oak trestle table sat in the middle, its wood grooved from age and use. The smell of mouthwatering food mingled with the aroma of spices that were hung to dry near a window casement. It smelled of safety to me...like home.

I was dying to explore. After a lengthy debate with myself about the inappropriateness of it, curiosity still easily won over prudence. Unaware of where I was headed, I began walking down a seemingly endless corridor.

Despite how sound reverberated against the massive stone walls and the cathedral ceiling, the house was as quiet as a tomb. Along the way I came upon an enormous painting depicting a battle scene. The lights were too dim for me to be certain, but it looked like the work of an old master, in the technique of *chiaroscuro*. I had seen an exhibition of paintings similar to this one at the Uffizi. Apparently, this man had one hanging in some forgotten part of his house.

The corridor fed into a foyer that was large enough to house a small airplane. There was so much to take in I didn't know where to look first. An Austrian crystal chandelier dangled over me. I tipped my head back and circled around and around in awe at the sheer scale of it while an idiotic smile played on my lips. The dim light twinkling off the icy shards reflected onto the mosaic floor beneath me. I knelt down on hands and knees for a closer inspection.

A hunting scene. A terrified hare was trapped against a tree, pinned by a pack of hounds. Its vulnerable neck caught between the teeth of one the dogs. I reached out to stroke the silky pieces of polished marble when the air suddenly altered, vibrating with a charge that skimmed the surface of my body. The fine hairs on the back of my neck stood at attention. Instinctively, I knew that I was no longer alone in the room.

A pair of long, bare feet stepped into my line of sight. Male feet.

Startled, I fell back on my rear end and looked up. A large, dark form took the shape of a half-naked man. I heard a sharp intake of breath that I wasn't certain belonged to me, or him. As we stared at each other, time seemed to expand.

He was handsome—freakishly handsome—the kind that makes even the most conceited woman fidget. My mind began methodically cataloging his breathtaking face: large almond-shaped eyes with thick lashes. Check. High, sculpted cheekbones. Check. And a nose that made his face go from cold perfection to erotically masculine. It was gently sloped, aquiline, a perfect counterpoint to his sensual mouth.

He was tall, very tall, around 1 meter 92–6'3" if you prefer—with wide shoulders and a narrow waist. His chest was muscular and smooth, his abdomen cobbled. A path of hair traveled down from his navel and disappeared under the athletic pants that hung on his hips for dear life.

When my gaze descended past his waistline, it seemed he'd had about enough of my inspection. He pushed the wet hair off his face and arched a brow at me. His expression was opaque, cold, and fixed on me with an alarming intensity.

"Are you lost?" His deep voice was raspy, tumbled, with an easy American accent. A vague recollection of that accent crept in. I shook my head. "Then what the fuck are you doing wandering around my house in the middle of the night?"

A quick flame of humiliation colored my face, followed closely by a film of cold sweat covering every inch of my skin. I was never so grateful for the cover of darkness.

"The servants' quarters are in the west wing." He motioned with his long index finger, hostility oozing out of the space between his words. "I suggest you stay there if you want to keep your job." An annoyed smirk. "You do work here, don't you?"

Rendered mute by embarrassment all I could do was nod.

With a hitch in his step, he turned away from me and proceeded up the marble staircase. I stood up slowly and somehow managed to exert super-human control over the instinct to run for my life. My eyes briefly swept down to the mosaic floor and locked onto the image of the frightened hare. I knew exactly how that poor hare felt. I never looked back but I didn't need to. I could feel his intense glare burning me, singeing the delicate hairs at my nape.

As soon as I was out of his sight, I bolted to my room and jumped into bed. Pulling the covers over my head, I curled up into a ball and tried to catch my breath while my hand trapped my heavily pounding heart inside my chest. Charlotte had a point. He was foul-mouthed and angry. Radioactive angry. I needed to stay as far away from him as possible. I could do that, make myself small, fade into the background. Because I was absolutely certain of one thing—that man had nothing but contempt for me.

———

THE ESTATE RAN like a well-synchronized Swiss watch. Most of the servants lived in town and all of them arrived promptly for the spectacular breakfast served at daybreak. Maybe Mrs. Arnaud had discovered the secret to punctuality. Displayed on the long counter in the kitchen was a veritable buffet of delights. An assortment of fresh baked goods: steel-cut oatmeal sprinkled with fresh cinnamon and golden raisins, eggs cooked in three different styles, and café au lait powdered with a touch of Swiss chocolate. I sipped my café slowly, savoring every rich swallow of thick, foamy milk spiked with chocolate—my delight in it almost pornographic. The ever-present heavy suit of anxiety I dragged around had vanished overnight. I was flying so high I had to check to make sure I hadn't sprouted tiny wings on my feet.

After breakfast, Mrs. Arnaud led me to a series of rooms that needed to be cleaned. I was assigned the ones on the top floor of the west wing. The rooms were beautifully decorated with luxurious fabrics in pale colors and priceless antiques. The style was traditional French, and the décor was subtle and restrained in a way that only truly expensive things can be.

Mrs. Arnaud spoke with solemn pride as she recounted the history of the estate. The Horn family had called this fairytale place home since the early 1900s when Egon Horn purchased it from a destitute French industrialist. He was a descendent of something or other royalty, viscount or emperor of whatever—of Baden, I think. I didn't pay much attention to the title. I grew up in a country ruled by communist ideology for nearly half a century. Ambition was now acceptable, blue bloods never would be.

The affection she had for the current monster-in-residence was reflected in her eyes as she explained that Sebastian Clayton Horn inherited the property from his late father, Heinrich Horn, four years ago, along with the bank that had been in the family for nearly a century. *Who cares*, I thought. *The man has a filthy mouth and worse manners.* But I nodded respectfully and pretended to be impressed at the appropriate moments.

"He's American?"

"*Oui*, half American."

"Is there…a wife, madame?"

The purse of her plump lips suggested the topic was an unpleasant one. "There was." A pregnant pause. "She passed away three years ago."

"I'm sorry."

"She was barely thirty. A wonderful girl, very beautiful… there was a car accident." Her voice trailed off. Her fingers fluttered, unsure where to land. She seemed to want to say more but didn't so I remained quiet as well. In silence, she led me to a large closet that contained the cleaning supplies and left me to do my job.

———

I'M AN OBSESSIVE CLEANER. Nothing relaxes me as quickly as giving a bathroom a good scrubbing or organizing a closet. Exercise always seemed pointless to me when I could be cleaning instead, accomplishing a necessary task and discharging the inexhaustible nervous energy I often carry around. This job suited me perfectly. I threw myself into cleaning with vigor, desperately wanting to prove my worth to Mrs. Arnaud.

When Charlotte came to fetch me for lunch, I declined and asked her to leave a plate for me in the kitchen.

"I was worried about this. You're one of those over-achiever types. Did you hyperventilate in grade school when you got anything less than an A on a test?"

"No," I replied with a half-smile. "I never got anything less than an A."

"Figures. I'm warning you, don't make the rest of us look bad," she said with a mischievous smirk, her curly ponytail bouncing as she walked out of the room.

I stripped the beds and dressed them in luxurious Pratesi thousand thread count sheets, making sure that the intricate scroll embroidered at the edges faced up. I aired out the quilted coverlet and fluffed the pillows, smoothed the edges of the shams as sharp as a knife blade. I coaxed a reluctant shine from the antique dressers, washed and waxed wood floors, and dusted every flat surface until a sweat stain ringed the armpit of my uniform. I was on a tall ladder, working on a faint streak on the floor to ceiling window, when I noticed Mrs. Arnaud standing in the doorway.

She looked around with a satisfied smile on her face. "Vera, it's eight. You have missed *déjeuner* and *dîner*."

I wiped away the loose sweaty hair sticking to my neck. "I have a bit more to do, *madame*."

"These rooms have not been this clean and tidy since the estate was built in 1872," she said, a twitch of amusement on her lips. "We want our guests to be comfortable, but not enough to extend their stay. Come to the kitchen and eat."

"I can prepare something myself. I don't mind."

"Silence, silence…*allons-y*," she insisted, waving my reluctance away with her hand. Together we made our way to the kitchen.

———

I sat at the long counter in front of the La Cornue stove running the length of the wall. Completely engrossed, I watched as she placed the delicate handmade bowtie pasta in a dish, mixed in the broccoli rape, and drizzled it with olive oil. Somehow I managed to curb my impulse to dive head first into it. No small achievement, considering my raging appetite. My stomach had grown fond of having real food again.

We drifted into a comfortable silence while she watched me eat. Her pudgy elbows rested on the counter, her amiable face cradled in her hands. "Have you had this before?" she asked, twirling her finger at the pasta.

"*Oui, madame*," I answered between bites. "In Italy, I worked for a family that owned a restaurant and it's a popular dish there."

"But you are not *Italien*?"

"No, *madame*, Albanian…though I lived there for six years."

Her examining glance made me uneasy. I didn't want to lie to this kind woman who had essentially rescued me.

"How did you like *Italie?*" She sat on the stool across from me, and nudged over the plate with sliced heirloom tomatoes and fresh mozzarella cheese.

"I loved it. The Italians made me feel welcome, and there's a large Albanian community living there. The family gave me housing while I worked in the kitchen."

"*Vraiment?*" She sat up straighter, an alert look on her face. "Then maybe you can assist me in the kitchen as well. Mr. Horn refuses to hire another chef."

"But you cook so well."

"Cook, *oui*, but I am no chef. Delacroix was let go four years ago, when Mr. Horn took possession of the estate."

"Where did Mr. Horn live before?" The question tumbled out of my mouth inadvertently. My hand abruptly stilled from cutting into the mozzarella when I realized I had spoken out loud. I needed to do a better job controlling my curious nature.

"Texas." She emphasized the word in her heavy French accent. "Where the cowboys come from." I pressed a brief smile back down. "He came back to Geneva five years ago. He has an apartment in town." As I stood at the sink to wash my empty dishes, she continued, "I should warn you, Vera. Mr. Horn is a bit temperamental. He's not mean or spiteful, but he's endured too much in the last five years. He's still suffering, and I don't want you to think less of him if he behaves a bit...harshly. It's nothing personal."

I didn't bother telling her that I had already taken it personally. "I understand. Thank you so much, Mrs. Arnaud...for everything."

Her face revealed a warm understanding. Who knows what would've become of me without her mercy.

"Mrs. Arnaud."

"*Oui?*"

"Where does Mr. Arnaud live?"

"I don't know, *chérie*. He left for a beer thirty years ago and never returned."

"Oh…I'm…I'm sorry."

"I'm not," she replied, a strange twinkle in her eye.

"Good night, then."

"Bonne nuit."

CHAPTER 4

I craved tedium, anything that resembled monotony. For the first time in years my days fell into a comfortably predictable routine, absent of worry. In Milan, living and working with the Argentis had been an existence governed by high drama, every day an exercise in patience.

I dreaded going home after my university classes knowing I would be subjected to hours of Mr. Argenti's incessant complaining about the lousy economy. Pending doom—his favorite topic. If you paid attention to anything he said you would think we were in the middle of the great famine of 1315. My ears ached from the complaints, and my knees were scraped from praying for clients to fill tables. Most of the time we managed. On the nights we didn't though, the complaints escalated to cataclysmic proportions. The whole staff lived on pins and needles, drowning themselves in chamomile tea just to be able to sleep at night.

I awoke with a surplus of enthusiasm, happiness lingering on its smooth edges. My day only got better when I was assigned the dusting of the library. Even with the unholy temptation of thousands of rare books, I managed to be done by early afternoon. I went to the kitchen, to inform Mrs. Arnaud that I still had time to do another room, and found her fiddling with the blender. She repeatedly jammed different buttons with her chubby fingers, unable to get it to churn the ambiguous contents in the glass pitcher.

"*Merde!*" she shouted. My muffled giggle drew her attention. "Oh, Vera, can you please see if you can get this blender to work. I'm annoyed beyond annoyed, and Mr. Horn is waiting for his frappe."

I took the pitcher off the base and discovered the connection to the outlet had come loose. Exasperated, Mrs. Arnaud threw her hands up in the air.

"*Mon Dieu!*"

Once blended, she poured the suspect liquid into a tall, chilled glass. "Hurry to the *salle de sport* and give this to him."

Me?! Didn't Mr. Bentifourt do that sort of thing? Isn't that what butlers are for?

My knees locked, unable to move. I wasn't ready to face him again. Though, with any luck, I figured he would either not recognize me, or had forgotten altogether. So, determined to not let my emotions get the better of me, I placed the drink on a tray and proceeded to the gym, which I'd seen during Charlotte's grand tour. It could only be described as a faithful imitation of a medieval torture chamber, filled with strange machines and eerie looking straps hanging from the ceiling.

The closer I got, the clearer a woman's voice, speaking intimately, became. "*Oui*, like that…yes…yes…one more time." The thought of possibly interrupting his afternoon tryst made me sick to my stomach. My footsteps turned reticent, slowing to a crawl. When I finally reached the gym, I found the door wide open and forced myself to step into the doorway.

A woman dressed in skintight shorts and a tank top stood with her back to me. Her raven hair was scraped back in a high ponytail, her skin bronzed, and her muscles flexed and hardened every time she moved. Her attention was focused entirely on the large, male figure before her.

She stepped aside.

He was suspended in mid-air, hanging from the straps on the ceiling, while I stood paralyzed in the doorway, admiring him as openly as I would a piece of fine art in a museum. Or the statue of David I had seen in Florence...only better, bigger—definitely certain parts of him seemed to be. His face was tight in concentration. Not even the hardness of his expression could diminish the flawlessness of his masculine beauty. With sweat trickling down the suntanned skin of his bare chest, he lowered his body by slow inches, balancing only on his arms. Strained by the effort, those arms were bulging and rigid, trembling slightly.

There wasn't a hint of youth or softness anywhere on him, clearly scraped off by the sharp edges of life. The remains of those experiences were as evident from a distance as a neon sign blinking *Danger here! Proceed at your own risk!* As I watched him in a state of hyperawareness, something clicked into place. An insight. The truth of it absolute. This man lived behind an impenetrable fortress. He had locked himself up and thrown away the key. Although his body was still among the living, his mind had checked out.

The woman placed her hands on him. One on his corrugated abdomen, the other on his lower back. I couldn't tell if she was steadying or fondling him. Not that I blamed her—

that six-pack begged to be touched. She just needed to do a better job pretending she wasn't doing it for her sake.

My gaze traveled to the hair that disappeared under the black pants barely hanging on his hipbones. The end of his tan line was visible, marking the dip between bone and muscle. And then the oddest thing happened. An image flashed before my eyes...my lips on that bare patch of skin at the edge of his pants. A scalding heat swiftly rose up my neck, followed almost immediately by a mist of sweat collecting above my lips. I wiped it away with the back of my hand and bit the inside of my cheek hard enough to taste a faint trace of blood.

He suddenly looked up and a spark of recognition entered his eyes. *So much for him not remembering that evening.* His lids dropped to half-mast and his mouth turned sullen. Imprisoned in his intense gaze, my skin began to itch with an awareness that something unpleasant was coming.

He let himself down gracefully, careful to land on his good leg. The woman's eyes followed his and revealed a face as striking as the rest of her. Her wide, full mouth turned pouty when she saw me.

"I think that's good enough for today, Yvette." His voice was low and measured, his attention never wavering from me.

"*D'accord*, same time tomorrow?" Her expression managed to look both coy and adoring. I wanted to roll my eyes, though wisely refrained.

"No...let's do it next week," he answered while he motioned me forward with a flick of his arrogant index finger.

I took a deep breath, fixed my gaze on a point over his shoulder, and walked over to him. I could feel him examining me as he took the glass from the tray. I turned to leave when he stopped me again with that finger.

"Stay."

Stay?

He casually stepped closer to me, and it took everything I had not to take a giant step back. Every nerve ending in my body was on high alert. The size of him this up close and personal was overwhelming. The scent of him, expensive soap and clean male sweat, affected my body in ways my intellect couldn't even begin to understand.

The woman's gaze skipped back and forth between us. She was waiting for privacy, wanted the rude creature to herself. And I would have been more than happy to oblige her, but he wouldn't dismiss me. Instead, he took small sips of his putrid green drink and waited patiently for her to collect her gym bag. Her shoulders sagged as she walked towards the door.

"See you next week, Yvette."

I thought I heard amusement in his voice and glanced up. I couldn't have been more wrong. His face was unnaturally still, not even a blink to prove that he was in fact human. Yvette grumbled her goodbye in French. As she walked out, a desperate urge to beg her to stay came over me.

The second she disappeared the air between us grew thin, as if I were suddenly standing in high altitude, laboring for every breath. His heavy stare was all over me while he drank his witch's brew and dried the sweat off his chest with a small, white towel. Crawling through a pit of vipers would have been less unnerving. He was toying with me and we both knew it.

"Will there be anything else, sir?" I asked in my most condescending Miss Albright accent. *Dear Miss Albright.* I distinctly remember as a child wishing a tornado would take her away after seeing the *Wizard of Oz* for the first time. Now I couldn't be more grateful for all the relentless grammar and diction lessons she drilled into me.

He blinked at first, a touch of surprise in his expression. Then his eyes narrowed. "No."

I should cut off my tongue. I turned to leave.

"Actually, there is something." The chill in his voice stopped me dead in my tracks. Facing him, I don't know how I managed to remain composed. It felt as though a heavy metal band was playing a concert inside my chest.

"Have you been crawling around my house, in the middle of the night?" Adding in a velvet soft voice, "Like a thief."

He may as well have lit a bonfire under my feet because my entire body instantly went up in flames. It took a minute for me to remember how to make my throat work again. "No, sir."

"Good," he replied, then he turned his back to me as if I ceased to exist.

My nerves were so fried afterwards that my teeth chattered all the way back to the kitchen.

———

THE FIRST FEW days I lived in a food fog, indulging in all the food I could stuff into my tiny stomach. The Scottish salmon fillet was cooked to perfection. I licked the veloute sauce off my thumb and caught Giovanni, one of the gardeners, watching me. He quickly diverted his gaze as a stain of embarrassment spread on his cheeks. Across from me, Mrs. Arnaud prepared a dinner tray for François, a part-time driver and full-time caretaker of Mr. Horn's fleet of expensive cars. There was a weary tightness around her eyes.

"Mrs. Arnaud, let me do that please. You must be exhausted."

"Thank you, *chérie.*"

Outside, a cool wind caressed my skin. A blade of orange, the remains of daylight, cut the horizon in two while the edge of the sky dissolved into darkness. François was often busy tending to the cars around dinner time so we took turns bringing him his food. He was drying a black Mercedes SUV when he spotted me crossing the gravel driveway.

In his late thirties, he wasn't by any means classically handsome. It was the devilish sparkle in his hazel eyes, evidence of a wicked sense of humor and an easygoing personality, which made him attractive. He was medium height and cycling fit. I had seen him ride off a couple of times at dawn; his determined body bent over the handlebars, his legs pumping furiously beneath him.

He straightened and his warm eyes flickered over me, never staying in one place for more than an impersonal study. An inviting smile tipped up the corners of his mouth. He wiped his hands clean, and walked over to me. *"Merci, mademoiselle."* His French accent was smooth and soft. As he took the tray from me, our fingers tangled. A quick flash of heat appeared in his eyes, and his smile widened a touch. Normally that would've made my pulse hum nervously. And yet something about him felt safe, unthreatening.

"You're welcome. I hope I brought enough."

He was working up to something. I could read it in his lively expression, in the way he impatiently ran a hand through his wavy brown hair. He was nervous. "Would you care to join me in a glass of wine?"

I was considering how to gently decline when the bright xenon headlights of a sleek, black sports car came around the corner of the house, straight towards us. It pulled up next to

the Mercedes and the purring of the engine cut off. Spontaneously, my whole body went rigid. Much like what happens
to a gazelle on the plains of the Serengeti when it realizes it's
too late to run from the salivating lion crouching only a foot
away.

He stepped out of the car, gracefully unfolding his body
until he stood tall. The impeccable fit of his bespoke gray
three-piece suit outlined the extraordinary width of his
shoulders, and his French blue shirt accented his golden
skin. His tie had been discarded, and the top buttons of his
shirt were undone.

My eyes fell on the exposed skin at the base of his throat
and a film of sweat broke out on the back of my neck.
Having this reaction to him, of all people, was an unbearable
annoyance—not to mention a serious inconvenience.

Placing his forearm on the roof of the car, he rapped two
knuckles while his alert eyes skipped from François to me.
Some obscure, dark emotion crossed his face. I had no idea
what it meant. Then again, everything about this man was a
total mystery to me.

The atmosphere suddenly turned frosty. A deep flush
surged up from his collar. When his piercing gaze returned
to me, it was hard and filled with contempt. My mouth went
dry in an instant. It felt like he had just caught me stealing
the family jewels.

François greeted him but he didn't respond. He
continued to stare at me completely indifferent to the fact
that this farce was being played out in front of an audience.
And for a moment, it was just the two of us—all else seemed
to fade away. Until he slammed the door shut with enough
force to make me flinch.

Talk about anger management—he was a perfect candi-
date for mood-altering drugs.

With awkwardness I was certain I shouldn't be feeling, I turned to François and mumbled my goodbye. He accepted, looking as perplexed by Horn's behavior as I was, then, bless his gallant soul, he stepped in between the car and me. I wasn't about to stick around for another life-threatening glare, so I turned on my heels and marched back to the house.

As I reached the kitchen door, I heard gravel crunching under footsteps right behind me. My self-control took a nosedive, decreasing with every step drawing closer. I turned the doorknob in the wrong direction and tugged it hard enough to rattle the glass above it. He stopped disturbingly close. The man was a furnace. With my hair pulled back in a tight bun, I felt the heat radiating from him on the back of my neck or maybe it was his anger.

"Step aside."

The vestibule wasn't made for two people to fit comfortably. I almost tripped in my haste to move out of his way. Careful not to touch him in any way, I plastered myself up against the wall while his large hand gripped the doorknob and paused for an amount of time too long to be insignificant. When I looked up, I found him focused straight ahead, his brows pinched, his mouth set in a grim line.

"I advise you not to get overly friendly with the other members of the staff. They might get the wrong idea about you."

His wooden tone confused me. It took me a while to realize what he meant. But once it registered, my eyes snapped up to meet his blazing with righteous indignation. This man knew absolutely nothing about me. I had lived the life of a veritable monk these past six years. If I hadn't been so appalled, I would have laughed at the irony. Humiliation burned my cheeks as soft, angry words pushed up my throat. "I brought him his dinner."

He measured me with a faraway look in his eyes. "You've been warned." Jerking the door open, he entered the kitchen and disappeared down the hall with uneven footsteps while I stood there dumbfounded, watching his imposing form fade away.

I had no idea what it was about me that provoked such animosity. And the worst part was that I was naturally inclined to please and appease people. It never sat well with me to be disliked. And I had never been disliked this openly in all my life.

————

I DREAMED of him that night.

Startled and embarrassed, I woke up in a pool of sweat. Fragments of erotic images came flooding back to me so clearly that it seemed impossible they were only a figment of my imagination. In what dark part of my psyche had this sexual hunger been hiding? I barely had a pulse the last couple of years, and for it to be him to provoke it said nothing good about me.

My muscles felt listless, rubbery, as if I had been fighting something in my sleep. I got out of bed to change my nightgown creeping and groaning like a woman twice my age. Shoved in the back corner of a drawer, I found an old t-shirt I didn't remember I still had. Aleksander's t-shirt. The thought of Aleksander still left a bitter taste in my mouth, even though it was growing fainter with each passing year. That was progress, I guess.

I pushed the window open and a cool breeze drove the staleness out of the room. The air smelled of pinesap, clean and crisp. A full moon colored the silhouette of trees indigo. On the coattails of the scent of evergreens, a mist of sadness blew in. I leaned on the windowsill with my head in my hands and tried to will a feeling away that seemed determined to hang around. I needed a good cry, to get it out of my system, but I hadn't shed a single tear in six years and they refused to fall once again.

A tall figure emerged from the grove of trees. It was easy to identify him from the hitch in his step, his strides stiff and deliberate, as if he forced himself to take a longer step than was comfortable. In spite of his injury, he cut through the flower garden and reached the back door in half the time I would have. A leisurely stroll at midnight? I wondered what demons haunted his dreams. I'd be lying if I didn't admit I was a little curious about him. Okay, maybe more than a little.

The estate ran with ruthless efficiency. At first, I thought it was out of fear of provoking his nasty temper, though quickly realized that wasn't the case at all. On the contrary, the staff was unusually loyal to him. They never complained or criticized him in any way. I could see why. He was incredibly generous with them. We all ate the same quality of food he did and it was provided liberally. The pay was many times more than anybody else offered for the same position. And when someone became ill, he assumed the cost. One of the elderly housekeepers had enlightened me of that fact, along with the intimate details of her bunion operations, repeatedly—at least three times.

That's why it was close to impossible to ask anyone about him without earning a raised eyebrow, or a disapproving look. Anything I learned about him was from overhearing broken sentences whispered in dark corners.

"Here, place these in the mud room for Mr. Horn," Claire

said with a faint Irish accent. She handed me a pile of fluffy towels. "Likes to swim. Good exercise for his leg. Could've gone to the Olympics, you know. Don't tell nobody that, not allowed to gossip, you know."

Yes, I know!

In no less than fanatical pride, she volunteered that he was some kind of financial wizard, having made his own fortune before inheriting his father's. Not much was said about that man, except that he was nothing like his son. I got the distinct impression she meant worse—frightening to consider.

A financial genius and an Olympic athlete...hmm what next? Walking on water? Raising the dead? How about some common courtesy? Apparently that simple skill was too difficult for him to master. I almost said it out loud.

Even less was said about his wife. Mostly, it was about how beautiful she was. "Nice girl, beautiful" or "Beautiful girl, an angel." Those words, not necessarily in that order. I wondered what it was that made her so special. There had to be more to her to inspire such deep, lasting devotion from a man as hardened as Sebastian Horn. The absence of pictures still puzzled me though. Was he trying to erase her memory? There wasn't a single one to be found anywhere in the house. The only explanation I could think of was that the memory was still too painful for him. Then again, what did I know of devotion? I thought Aleksander had been devoted. That was a laugh.

His behavior towards me was still completely baffling. It wasn't just arbitrary rudeness; it was an explicit dislike of me. But why? What irredeemable transgression had I committed to inspire such disdain? I combed through every moment I'd spent in his presence as if the fate of nations depended on unraveling this Gordian knot and couldn't come up with a single, solid reason.

My head was pounding by the time I lay back down on the cool linen sheets. Staring at the ceiling, I searched for answers that weren't there. My eyelids heavy, somehow, slowly, I drifted back to sleep.

CHAPTER 5

The next day, Mrs. Arnaud discreetly asked if I would go tidy his bedroom. There was a strange, apprehensive look on her face when she spoke, as if she was about to explain further, then thought twice about it. When I reached his bedroom, I found the door shut. My nerves fluttered as I gripped the door handle, about to walk straight into the lair of the beast, but Mrs. Arnaud had entrusted me with the task and I would have done anything to please her. Pushing aside my reluctance, I opened the door and came to a sudden halt in lip-parting bewilderment.

The reek of stale alcohol permeating the room knocked the wind out of me. I ran to the tall French doors, which led to the balcony, and shoved them open. It was a disaster zone. Everything was either out of place, or tilted to the side. Empty bottles of hard liquor and beer lay scattered on the floor by a stuffed chair.

I would never have expected this of him. He was always so immaculate. For a moment, I speculated whether he was an alcoholic and discarded the notion. He didn't exhibit any of the typical symptoms of the disease. It wasn't uncommon for grief to provoke some kind of numbing addiction, but I seldom saw him drink and when he did it was always in moderation. Something must have triggered this binge. Although what, I couldn't imagine.

It took hours to sort through the destruction, longer than usual because I examined everything as I cleaned. All the furnishings were of the highest quality. Unlike the rest of the house, the design was clean, contemporary, almost monastic in its simplicity. The muted color scheme, a range of barely noticeable shades that played off each other complimented the design perfectly.

A Gerhard Richter painting hung on the wall above a tall dresser. One of his earlier works, it was done in photorealism. The subject was a mother cradling her baby, the infant trapped to her breast. Their faces were smeared horizontally, preserving their anonymity. The effect was startling. It could easily have been a dream or an old memory buried within my own mind. *What a shame*, I thought. Paintings like this belonged in a museum for everyone to appreciate, not in the corner of a rich man's bedroom among the remains of an all-night bender.

I couldn't tear my gaze away from the image. A swell of emotion rose up. My mother had died of a blood clot shortly after giving birth to me and I often wondered how different my life would've been had she lived, how different I would be. Not that I had anything to complain about; my father had been a wonderful parent. And a patient man, thankfully, because all the questions I peppered him with over the years would have driven an ordinary person insane. He would spend hours at night telling me stories about how much I reminded him of her. The only things I had left were those stories, a worn-out Polaroid of her at the beach, and a threadbare Hermès scarf. It wasn't nearly enough.

A subtle scent drifted up from the bed linens. My attention riveted on the impression his head had left on the goose down pillow, an unwelcome flush crept up my neck. Impulsively, I traced the dent with my index finger, the fabric cool under my fingertip. After a quick scan of the open doorway, I pressed the pillow to my face and inhaled deeply. Sandalwood, neroli, some other indefinable elixir that gave me goose bumps. *The man looks at you like he's surprised to find a pubic hair in his soup,* argued the voice of reason. A sobering thought. I dropped the pillow and finished making the bed, committing myself to cleaning until all evidence of his night of dissipation was erased.

———

BY EARLY AFTERNOON, I was done. As I was gathering the cleaning supplies, organizing them in the bucket to be put away for the day, I heard something move behind me.

"What are you doing in my room?" His raspy voice was low and quiet.

I snapped up straight, turned around slowly, and found him in the open doorway. Braced against the frame, he gripped it tight enough to turn his fingertips pale. His white dress shirt was taut against the swells of his chest, his tie loose, exposing the base of his throat. I watched his Adam's apple rise as he swallowed. His expression looked wary, all the muscles on his powerful body tense.

What was he doing here? He usually stayed in the city during the week. I could feel the pulse on the side of my throat humming. It took me a while to respond. Whenever he was near, my mind checked out, took a vacation, traveling over every small detail of him while I patiently waited for it to return to work.

"My job, Mr. Horn. I was cleaning." Oddly, his face relaxed at the bite in my voice. *Strange man.*

"You didn't break, or steal anything, did you?" he asked with cool candor.

My eyes must have been as large as dinner plates as I went through a list of scathing replies in my head. "No—and no," I said, after extensive editing.

I moved to leave, holding the bucket in front of me as a shield from more insults, but he remained in the doorway and continued to stare with that unnerving expression he always wore around me. It could only be described as fascinated disgust. I was about to blast him with a few choice recommendations on what he could do with that supercilious look on his face when he finally stepped aside, sparing me the pleasure. I walked out without another glance in his direction. And yet, I could feel his eyes glued on me all the way down the hall.

———

"CHARLOTTE...I have to tell you something."

In her bedroom, I found her sprawled on her stomach, her chin in her hands, her long legs kicked up behind her. Having worked at the estate for nearly two years had helped Charlotte save a considerable "little nest egg" that afforded her a television. She insisted I come watch one of her favorite shows after dinner and having learned how persuasive Charlotte could be when she got something in her pretty head, I agreed and saved myself the trouble of an argument. The situation was worrying me. I needed to talk to someone about it and Charlotte had proven herself a friend.

"What is it?" Her angelic face tilted quizzically as she patted the spot next to her. I sat down and started quietly, hesitantly. Things escalated quickly after that. I worked myself up into an indignant rage. Pacing turned into stomping. My murmur turned into a roar. And then I began to hurl unbecoming epithets like rocks at a sinner.

"His Highness asked if I was still crawling around his house like a thief!!! He's a bully and foul-mouthed...you-know-what without an ounce of class. He actually asked me if I stole something! And by the way, his room smelled worse than the crappy pub under my old apartment in the red-light district!"

Charlotte doubled over, howling with laughter. I didn't find it so amusing. In fact, the whole situation was giving me an upset stomach. And I wasn't certain if it was his contempt for me, or my mortifying attraction to him that was causing it. I was too ashamed to share that little detail with her.

"I told you he has a nasty temper. Although I've never seen him behave that badly before. I wouldn't worry about it."

Wouldn't worry about it? I was way past worry. "Charlotte, the man is making a sport out of humiliating me. He looks like he's about to throw up every time his eyes land on me. He hates me. I'm sure of it. It's safe to say, I should be worried."

"Okay, so he's a moody bastard, but he's never sacked anyone since I've worked for him. And once I dropped a bottle of Pellegrino on his brand-new computer." She made a gesture with her hands mimicking an explosion. "Destroyed it, so I know your job is safe."

"What did he do?!"

"Nothing, really. He stared at it, then told me to clean it up."

"That's all?"

"Yes."

It was becoming quite clear that his animosity extended only to me. How depressing.

After subjecting myself to twenty minutes of mind numbing stupidity, watching people on a deserted island try to outwit each other, I decided that counting sheep would be better entertainment. I was about to leave when she looked up from the screen.

"I meant to tell you that Isabelle is back tomorrow from vacation. Do yourself a favor and stay away from her." Pivoting her attention back to the show, she giggled at some absurdity that had just happened.

"I don't understand."

"She's a raging bitch and considers any attractive female in the country a personal threat."

"And what does that have to do with me?"

"Hello?? You're beautiful and Sebastian Horn is a gorgeous, rich bachelor." She waved me off, turning her attention back to the television as if it were silly to discuss the obvious.

"Charlotte, I don't know who this Isabelle person is or what she is about, but she's welcome to play *Jane Eyre* all she likes. I can't afford to lose this position, and I'm already on shaky ground."

A large dose of fear made it come out more harshly than I intended. Charlotte's expression softened. She got off the bed and hugged me. It felt sooo good, the warmth, the contact. I hadn't had a taste of it in years. "I didn't mean to upset you. I just think you should be careful. She always seems to get away with stirring shit up. Mrs. Arnaud and Mr. Bentifourt are oblivious to her ways."

"I understand. Night, Charlotte."

———

I SPENT the better part of the next day writing letters to the department heads of every hospital in Geneva. With a stiff back and cramped fingers, I crawled into bed earlier than usual and found myself staring at the clock I had purchased in town, growing angrier at every move of the large hand. By midnight I had to concede that reciting the periodic table in my head wasn't working. I didn't have any reading material in my room other than my medical textbooks, and those held no appeal whatsoever. The mere thought of all those wonderful books in the library made me groan. It was like waving a red flag at a bull. I really did try talking myself out of sneaking around in the dark, as I was rudely instructed not to do. I just couldn't make myself see reason.

The library was by far my favorite room in the manor. The high vaulted ceiling and aged patina on the walls made it both awe-inspiring and cozy. A long eighteenth-century table with high-backed chairs ran parallel to a carved stone fireplace. Holding an arrangement of fresh cut flowers from the garden, an important-looking Chinese vase sat in the middle. Rows and rows of carved bookcases stood on both sides of the room, extending out towards the windows, under which sat plush couches in cobalt blue velvet perfect for spending a lazy afternoon reading.

I tip-toed downstairs in my linen nightgown and bare feet and made sure to open the library door as quietly as possible, conscious that every sound was amplified by the stone walls. The faint scent of paper and lemon oil that greeted me made me giddy. Moonlight spilling in through the large windows lit my path, making it easy to navigate between the rows and rows of bookcases.

My fingers skated over the beautifully bound leather

spines. Some new, some ancient. The titles in various languages: English, French, even a little German and Latin. I wondered how long it took to accumulate all those books. Generations, I figured, some looked to be first editions. One title caught my interest. I pulled out an English copy of *Love in the Time of Cholera* and sat down, curling up on the floor cross-legged.

I was just getting settled when I heard muffled voices outside the door. Every muscle in my body turned to stone when a woman's voice became quite clear. *God, no, please don't do this to me.* My chest tightened, wringing every drop of air out of my lungs. I rubbed the tiny cross hanging around my neck and prayed for divine intervention. *Please keep walking, please keep walking, please keep walking.*

The doorknob squeaked and the voices entered the room. Apparently God wasn't taking requests at the moment. A lamp was turned on and the light cast a soft glow about the room. I plastered myself against the bookcase and tried to melt into the background by osmosis, my heart beating so violently I was afraid they could hear it.

"There is nothing to talk about, Paisley."

I knew that voice. He sounded bored and impatient. *I'm going to be fired for this. He is going to throw me out on my arse in the middle of the night!*

"Yes, there is, Scout," a woman replied with an American accent.

"Don't ever call me that again." His anger boiled up quickly, unmistakable under the veneer of his low voice.

"Or what? What will you do to me? Put your hands on me? Teach me a lesson? Shit, I hope so." Her brittle laugh echoed off the walls.

"What does your husband say when he sees those marks on you?"

Marks? What marks?

"He doesn't say anything. He doesn't care. Marcus has his own thing going on."

The curiosity was literally killing me. *Or at least, he will once he catches you.* The books were packed tightly on the shelves, obscuring my presence, thankfully, but also shielding them from me. I tugged out a skinny book wedged tightly in its place. Knowing how seriously I was courting danger, you could make an argument for temporary insanity.

As I spied through the narrow opening, I recognized the pale blond from the garden. She wore a red dress fitted closely to her slender body. I knew the designer (having lived in Milan for six years practically earned me a degree in high fashion). Azzedine Alaïa—outrageously expensive and extremely sexy.

She tossed her long hair over her shoulder and approached Horn, who was doing a great impression of a brooding male model with his arm resting on the fireplace mantle and his hip cocked. He stared into the vacant fireplace with his head tipped down. Although his posture was relaxed, there was an undercurrent of tension in his muscles that was evident to me. He began taping two fingers on the mantle, the rhythm quickening as she drew closer.

"I like it when you put your hands on me," she purred, "inside of me...when you leave your mark on my body, reminding me where you've been." She placed her hands on his chest and began petting him roughly, up and down his tailored white shirt, with an indifferent touch that made me want to smack her hands away. I wanted to explore every curve and dip slowly, carefully.

I really need to have my head examined!

Shame and fascination and a hundred other conflicting emotions battled for first place in my mind. I couldn't take my eyes off of him—as if he were true north and I was one of the many compasses that had no choice other than to be drawn to him.

Her one hand traveled lower until she was stroking the bulge that was steadily growing, straining the limits of his gray gabardine slacks. He ceased taping his fingers and squeezed the hand into an angry fist. The muscles of his jaw quivered from the strain of clenching it tightly. Ignoring the warning in his remote amber eyes, she continued to stroke him roughly. When she cupped him, however, his hand finally shot out and snatched her wrist, stopping her.

"I don't want you anymore. What part of that don't you get? Go back to Marcus."

"And how do you suppose I do that? Even if I wanted to, which I don't," she bit out.

His eyes held no humor as his lips lifted in an imitation of a smile. "Do what you always do, lie to him."

I could see the wheels turning as she deliberated her next tactical maneuver. I knew exactly when she decided to change tack when her face softened. "Scout, we were made for each other," she purred. "Who else is going to fuck you like I do? I know what you're doing, you're just trying to punish me for marrying Marcus, but that's history. We can be together now and—"

"Stop."

Her expression shifted from frustration to anger. She ripped her wrist out of his grip. "What's the matter, Scout? Can't you get it up? Is that what's bothering you?" Her perfect features contorted into an ugly sneer. "That you're only half the man you were before the accident?"

His face froze. I knew what that expression meant. I almost screamed in fear for her. A loud crash rent the quiet of the room. The vase hit the stone floor and shattered into a million pieces, the bouquet scattering in every direction. It took me a while to realize that he had her pinned face down over the table with her legs spread apart, his large body pressed up against her buttocks. Her hair was coiled around his hand, snapping her head back in a punishing grip, while the other pushed down on the top of her spine, trapping her completely.

"Is this what you want, you fucking bitch? I warned you never to call me that again." His voice sounded hollow, almost inhuman. I watched a strange, demented smile grow on her face. She laughed at him, a joyless, malicious laugh. Spurred on, he flipped her skirt up, reached under, and brutally ripped off her black thong.

Oh my God...they aren't going to...

He hesitated for a moment, his face revealing a mix of clashing emotions. Rage, lust, revulsion.

"Do it, you spineless asshole!" The scream earned her another violent jerk of her hair. His expression altered, became resolute. He fished a condom out of his back pocket, and, without slackening the brutality of his grip on her, unzipped and unbuttoned his trousers. They fell to his ankles, revealing black boxer briefs and an enormous erection tenting the fabric...he pushed them down.

I covered my mouth, swallowed a gasp. I should've had the decency to give them some privacy but it was beyond me. I couldn't look away if my life depended on it. I was mesmerized, entranced, and he was magnificent, built to scale and thrusting up powerfully.

A flood of sensation traveled from the tips of my toes to my hairline. I broke out in a full-blown sweat, a deep ache pooling between my thighs, every nerve ending painfully aware of him. I gripped my nightgown in a fist at the top of my thighs as my traitorous body responded against my will.

Never in my life had I experienced such a visceral reaction to a man. It was as if he held some secret code to unlocking my body that I was unaware of.

Jaw tight, he hissed, "I never met a woman so eager to be treated like a piece of garbage." A loud crack splintered the air, the sound echoing off the stone walls. The cherry stain of his handprint was visible on the white cheek of her rear end. He ripped the wrapping off the condom with his teeth, shoved her harder onto the table when she squirmed, and rolled it on. "I want you to remember this pity fuck, Paisley, because I'll cut my dick off before I ever touch you again."

With conviction born of anger and resentment, he kicked her legs wider and slammed into her in one powerful thrust of his hips. The table lurched forward, scraping the limestone floor loudly. He began viciously pounding into her, without an ounce of care, the slapping sound of their flesh drowning out her sensual whimpers and moans. As she climaxed, she screamed out a list of swear words that would've made a soldier blush, her short, red nails scraping the wood of the table.

His expression was pained, as if he was trying to deny himself. He didn't make a single sound, not even a soft exhale, when he came. The only visible sign was the slackening of his body, his shoulders slumping in defeat. Breathing heavily, he turned away to remove the condom. He didn't even finish buttoning his pants. They barely caught on his lean hips, a wet stain visible on the front of his underwear. With his head hanging and his shoulders bent, he leaned against the mantle and rubbed his eyes and brow with his thumb and index finger.

The aura of defeat surrounding him could be felt from afar. He looked...diminished somehow. And for some absurd reason, all I wanted to do was hold him, sift my fingers through his slightly too-long, silky hair, and tell him it would all be okay.

"Get the fuck out. We're done." His voice was low, weary.

She stared at his stony profile, stabbing him with her eyes. "You will always want me," she declared, smoothing her tousled hair back into place with long, bony fingers. "You will always take me back because I give you permission to do what no other woman will!" Snatching a compact out of her Chanel purse, she checked her work in the mirror. "We're not done. We're not even close to being done."

Stark silence. Her words didn't seem to warrant an acknowledgement from him. That sparked more outrage. Her blue eyes narrowed and her face reddened. She tossed the compact back into her purse and slammed it shut. And after an awkward moment spent waiting for an apology that never came, she stormed out of the room, heels clicking all the way down the hall.

He stood motionless for a long time afterwards, mastering his breathing, staring at the door with a faraway expression. As he tucked his shirt back into his pants, his large hands trembled, betraying his cool exterior. Then he took a small prescription bottle out of his pocket and tossed a pill into his mouth.

I was lost in thought, speculating about the pills, when his head suddenly snapped up. Wearing an expression that vacillated between bewilderment and anger, his perceptive eyes scanned the area. I froze, anxiety and fear converging in my gut. *Please, please, please go away!* He took a step forward and my mouth went bone dry. The moment seemed to last forever. But then, just as suddenly, he turned on his heels and stalked out of the room.

I sat there shaking for a full hour before I ran back upstairs and dove under the covers. It was impossible to sleep after that. All I could think about was the scene I had witnessed.

Who was that woman? The line for this man probably wrapped around the globe. So why was he sleeping with her? He threatened to cut off his privates for God's sake! What pills was he taking? And why did he look so lost when he thought nobody was watching?

I wanted to know all his secrets and he seemed to be hiding quite a few. And my reaction to him troubled me. I didn't understand where this strange attraction was coming from. I wasn't some stupid, empty-headed twit easily taken by superficial attributes. Adding insult to injury, there was no question that I had a profoundly opposite effect on him. After spending the better part of the night analyzing it to death and still finding no answers, sleep finally claimed me sometime around dawn. Only later would I realize that I never did get those books.

CHAPTER 6

Being a new employee I was obligated to work on weekends and holidays. I didn't mind. I never slept past six anyway. I never really slept well at all until arriving here. I opened the window and was greeted by a carpet of anthracite gray clouds that threatened to wash the day away.

A chill blew in that made the delicate hairs on my arm stand up straight. The gaunt, waif look I had been wearing for weeks was slowly fading. I could finally look in the mirror without being horrified by the dark circles under my eyes and the sharpness of my cheekbones.

Mrs. Arnaud made it her personal crusade to fatten me up like an Easter lamb. Daily, she plied me with enough gastronomic masterpieces to make the most committed ascetic lose their religion. I didn't have the heart to tell her that it would be a miracle if I could gain just a couple of pounds, having been cursed with an overly ambitious metabolism that incinerated anything I placed in its path, nor did I want to dampen her enthusiasm to feed me.

I gathered my long, straight hair into a high ponytail,

applied a little salve to my lips, and brushed the lint off of my navy uniform. Halfway down the stairs, I heard the low rumble of a familiar male voice and stopped mid-step. The air in my lungs left me all at once. Mrs. Arnaud had mentioned he'd gone to London on a business trip. I hadn't seen him since that night in the library, four days ago. Not long enough though. Still embarrassed at my reaction, I flushed just thinking about it. When his determined foot-steps echoed out of the kitchen, I continued down.

I found Mrs. Arnaud preparing a tray of paper-thin crêpes with fresh strawberry sauce, a few slices of honeydew melon, and a tall glass of the putrid, green drink. *"Bon jour,* did you sleep well?" she asked in her usual sunny timbre.

"Yes, *madame."*

Isabelle walked into the kitchen flipping her long auburn hair over her shoulder. While her cool gaze traveled from the top of my head to my feet, her mobile mouth curved into an insincere smile.

"Isabelle, put your hair up. This isn't a fashion show, *chérie.* It's unsanitary," Mrs. Arnaud ordered in a motherly tone. "Please take this tray to Mr. Horn. He's in his office." She looked straight at me. Stunned, the pulse on the side of my neck skipped a beat.

"I'll do it," Isabelle interjected, blocking me easily with her voluptuous figure. She bound her hair in a ponytail so quickly it almost made me laugh.

Thank God for aggressive women.

I had dodged a bullet—or something similarly unpleasant. I nodded, my pulse returning to normal. "She can do it," I said, cheerfully.

"Mr. Horn asked for Vera."

This was a troubling turn of events. Isabelle's frosty gray eyes launched poison arrows. Not exactly how I meant to begin with her, but I couldn't worry about that now. I had meaner dragons to slay. "Yes, of course, *madame*," I replied.

"Bon, hurry, before his frappe gets warm. It upsets him." *Heaven forbid*. I pursed my lips, afraid the words would slip out. Taking the tray from her, I practically ran out of the kitchen. I would've rather been drawn and quartered than give him a reason to complain.

When I reached his office door, uninvited erotic images of him flashed before my eyes. I shook my head to be rid of them. Shoving those wicked thoughts back into the dark recesses of my mind, I took a deep breath and knocked.

"Enter." His deep, raspy voice echoed off the walls.

Once inside the first thing that struck me was that the room was of a much smaller scale than the others. I hadn't seen it yet. I'd been rather studiously avoiding it like the plague. On the wall behind me were flat screen televisions of various sizes. The low sound of news and financial channels hummed in the background. A wide, mid-century desk sat in front of a small fireplace. On either side of it, windows stretched from floor to ceiling. The sunlight pouring through them obscured my vision. All I could discern was the imposing silhouette seated behind the desk. I could feel him watching me.

"You plan on standing there all day?" That loose American accent broke through the paralysis. I had to give him credit, it was hard to spark my temper but he managed it without any effort.

I stepped forward without making eye contact. After everything I had been through, I had somehow managed to survive with my pride intact. I wasn't about to give him the opportunity to trample it for his personal amusement. After placing the tray on his desk, I turned to leave.

"Where are you going?"

Turning slowly, I forced myself to meet his gaze for the first time in full daylight. Mistake. Big mistake. The beginnings of a slow flush prickled my collarbone. To stop its progress, I frantically searched for an image to distract myself with. *Dead kittens? Dead kittens. Dead kittens!*

"Did you say something?" he asked. The dismissive look on his face didn't fool me. This was a battle of wills and I wasn't about to be intimidated so easily.

"No." And then a staring match ensued. It would've been funny had I been on the outside looking in, had his contempt for me not equaled my attraction to him.

My senses converged acutely, bringing every aspect of him in high definition. To call him handsome would be like describing the Mona Lisa as a painting of a lady. His face was a perfect balance of symmetry and proportion with enough whimsy thrown in to make him completely unique. Those thick, spiky lashes were darker than his hair and excessive on a man. They set off the color of his almond shaped eyes, amber needled with green closer to the iris. High cheekbones balanced his aristocratic, thoroughly masculine nose. His mouth was wide, not overly full. His jaw firm. And it all ended with a soft punctuation mark on his chin. But it was so much more than the sum of the spectacular parts. What made him truly breath-catching beautiful lived beneath the surface. A smoldering pit of volatile emotion, an intense fire that blazed no matter how much he tried to cover it up. It was difficult to hold his gaze in the face of all that intensity.

His dark blond hair was a bit too long. It curled up at his ears and collar and fell over his eye. When he brushed it away, I swallowed—and hated myself just a little bit more for not being able to control myself. I had a sick feeling he had noticed. You don't become the head of one of the oldest banks in Switzerland at thirty-two years of age by being only a little perceptive.

My eyes drifted over his long fingers, on the white scars on the back of his hand, as he picked up the drink off the silver tray. He absentmindedly tapped his index finger on a leather-bound book. *Tap, tap, tap.* Pause. *Tap, tap, tap.* I could just make out the title...*Love in the Time of Cholera*.

My stomach plummeted to my feet. I couldn't feel my lips as anxiety escalated to an unbearable pitch. I waited for him to say something but he kept silent, torturing me by slow degrees.

"Marquez." *Huh?* "Do you like him?" My mind was slow to respond, like running through deep snow. "I guess you don't read. Do you speak?" he added rudely. No, I couldn't speak. I couldn't make a sound if I tried. "Forget it. You can take the rest of this shit away," he muttered and turned his attention to the televisions over my shoulder.

"I prefer *One Hundred Years of Solitude*." His sharp gaze returned to me. Staring and blinking. Blinking and staring. I took up the tray and turned towards the door. Relief washed over me. Somehow, I had just avoided a disaster.

———

WHEN I RETURNED to the kitchen with the food he had refused, Mrs. Arnaud pursed her lips. "He will waste away at this rate," she said, more to herself than anyone else in the kitchen. I thought it best not to point out that he was in no danger of wasting away, and was in fact rather deliciously in perfect shape.

By noon Mrs. Arnaud and I had managed to outline a menu for every day of the house party to be held at the end of the month. We worked effectively together. She was the butterfly, her mind wandering in all directions, full of creative ideas, and I was the net keeping her on track and organized. She handed me a glass of freshly squeezed orange juice, and sat back down at the trestle table where our strategic plans were laid out.

"Do you have a *chère ami*, Vera?"

The question took me by surprise. "No, *madame*."

Her nurturing eyes searched my face. "Don't let time pass you by."

"I was engaged once...back in Albania." I shrugged. "Anyway, it didn't work out." I hadn't meant to confide so much, but her gentle, soothing manner had me singing like a canary.

"Are you still in love with him? Is that why you're alone?"

Alone? Yes, very alone. "No, not for a long time." I was about to list all the valid reasons for choosing to be alone— fear of getting arrested and deported being the most significant—when something entirely different came out of my mouth. "I guess I'm alone because I haven't met anyone that interests me enough."

She smiled knowingly. "I see, a romantic."

"Me? No, not at all. I'm a very practical person, but I have to feel something." I thought of Aleksander. His betrayal had been devastating, although, in hindsight, a necessary evil. I had been so naïve, much too open and trusting.

Mr. Bentifourt walked into the kitchen sneezing.

"Ninety milligrams of zinc, olive leaf extract, and at least a thousand milligrams of slow release Ester C...you'll be over it in no time," I casually suggested while my eyes remained on the seating arrangements.

"I haven't asked you, though, have I?" His brusque reply spawned a series of uncharitable thoughts I kept to myself. His pocket rang and he retrieved an iPhone from it. Raising it closely to his face, he grumbled, "Bloody phone. I can't read the bloody thing."

"That's because your glasses are on top of your head, Olivier," Mrs. Arnaud reminded him, all warm tolerance. He rolled his eyes and placed his glasses on, his eyebrows rising comically high as he read.

"Vera, Mr. Horn would like a bottle of Pellegrino. Bring a chilled glass with you." *Me again?* I almost huffed. "Do hurry, he doesn't like to wait."

I grabbed the Pellegrino bottle and a glass from the refrigerator, refrained from slamming it shut, and stalked out of the kitchen muttering a series of vulgar words under my breath that I rarely, if ever, use. I worked myself up into a juvenile fit of temper as I walked back to his office. My knuckles rapped loudly on the door.

"You don't have to break the damn thing down. Come in!"

For the first time in ages, I choked down a laugh. "You rang, sir?" I knew I was asking for it and I didn't care one iota. I actually managed to keep a totally impassive expression as he glared at me. I stepped closer to the desk, his eyes following me the whole time, and handed him the frosty glass, then the bottle. He took one look at the glass and scowled.

"Why is this chilled?"

Is this a trick question? "I don't know."

"Go back and get me another glass. This will leak all over my paperwork. And if you're not smart enough to get it right, send somebody that can."

It was as if he knew exactly what to say to turn my mind black with rage. His eyes returned to his paperwork, dismissing me. After a deep, calming breath, I walked out.

Back in the kitchen, Mrs. Arnaud cocked her head in

confusion when she noticed the glass I held up. "He doesn't want it chilled."

"*Absurde*, he always has it chilled."

When I returned I pounded on the door again. It was beyond my capacity to behave where he was concerned. The dogged, bullheaded facet of my personality beat reason and intellect over the head and seized the controls. "Come in, damn it!"

Good. I was glad he was irritated. The little voice of reason spoke up, begged me to back off. *This is not a man to be toyed with*, it screamed. So of course, I ignored it.

Inside his office I found him standing in the middle of the room, leaning on his cane, his other hand casually resting on his hip. What checked me wasn't the subtle tension in his shoulders, it was the volatile energy lurking beneath the stillness. I looked up into the beautifully severe face that loomed over me and held out the glass. My hand hung for what felt like a long time. He didn't take it, just narrowed his eyes, indicating that retribution would be forthcoming.

"Put it on my desk," he said, his voice so calm it bordered on mockery.

I walked around him, giving him a wide berth, and placed the glass next to the bottle. "Will that be all, sir?"

"No." His tight smile didn't reach his eyes. "I want you to go get a lint cloth and dust all the TV screens."

When I explained it to Mrs. Arnaud, her smile fell. "Unbearable...what's wrong...don't understand," she grumbled, banging drawers open and shut in her search for a dust cloth. That sparked a satisfied twitch of my lips. *Good. Let her be annoyed with him too.* "Here," she said as she handed me the cloth, "let's pray he's in a better mood the rest of the day." I stalked back to the office and opened the door without knocking.

"Aren't you a quick study," he drawled, his sensual lips curving sardonically. I was ready to wave the white flag. He had won this round soundly.

He sat in a club chair facing a wall covered in flat screen televisions, his injured leg stretched out straight, the other bent. I ignored him, held my tongue; one of us obviously had to be the adult. I began to dust the sets with quick, gentle strokes, stretching up on my toes and bending forward to reach the top of them. All the while I could feel him watching, scrutinizing every inch of me. My ears burned in embarrassment.

"To the left more."

In a moment of temporary insanity, I fantasized about slapping the cold, arrogant look off his face, then kissing him...and then I wanted to beat myself black and blue just for thinking that. "Did I miss anything?"

"No. You can go," he mumbled. His voice was tight. I turned to get a better read on him and found his color high, his eyes downcast. He scowled at the carpet and the hand on the armrest clenched and released repeatedly.

Not smug at all. Huh, strange. How in the world had his wife put up with him? This mystery required a stiff drink or a lobotomy. I stood there anticipating another snide remark but none came. When he looked up again, his eyes were shuttered, closed for business.

"You can go," he said quietly.

So I did.

CHAPTER 7

Touch, vital to life yet so easily taken for granted. I had been denied that basic human need for six long years. I hadn't missed it, hadn't even noticed its absence with all the other needs taking precedence. Now it was storming back with a vengeance.

By the time I dragged by achy body into the shower, it was late in the evening. I turned the water on as hot as I could bear it and bent my head, allowing it to beat down my neck. As I closed my eyes, a catalogue of fuzzy images elbowed their way to the forefront of my tired mind. Scruff on a lean jaw the color of summer wheat. The dense crowded edge of a fan of lashes. A pair of brandy colored eyes.

No. No...No.

Desperate to purge the images, I flipped through my memory bank in search of a distraction. Aleksander. All dark handsomeness and subtle charm. He had a way of carrying himself that made him seem more worldly than everyone else around him; a quality that most women didn't fail to notice. I certainly didn't. His features were perfect, almost pretty for a man, and he knew it. He used his assets with the lethal precision and skill of a trained predator. He was flirting with a girl with long, blond hair when I first saw him. She hung on his every word, staring as if she had just discovered the sun. He leaned in to whisper something in her ear, looked across the university courtyard, and our eyes tangled. Stunned, I couldn't look away, trapped by the charismatic glint in his obsidian eyes. Then he winked at me and returned to seducing the blonde. I wanted him as I had never wanted anything or anyone before. I thought we were destined for each other. Destiny, however, had other plans.

I tried to hold onto the memory of Aleksander's face but the harder I tried to reach for it, the quicker it slipped away. As soon as my head hit the pillow, an image of long blunt fingers sweeping through tawny hair appeared. Too tired to fight them off, I let them all tumble in. The tiny scar on his top lip. The trail of dark blond hair that started at his navel. The set of his broad shoulders.

My hand slipped under my nightgown, caressed the tip of my nipple until it pebbled hard and sensitive. I pulled it between my fingers until I could feel the gentle tug coalescing heat and desire between my thighs. My palm skimmed the warm surface of my taut belly and traveled lower, searching for that neglected place that needed attention. I turned onto my stomach, my arm beneath me, and bent one leg, hitching it up. My hand moved in a steady rhythm, opened the folds, brushed over that tender nub where all feeling converges. A fever was growing. I quickened the pace picturing those delicious hipbones, the valley next to them, the cobbled muscles of his stomach. And then a wave of bliss so powerful broke over me that I almost cried with relief.

It must be the long stretch of abstinence, I told myself. I hadn't been touched in ages. Maybe it was time I considered finding a nice man to spend some time with. The thought wandered away as I drifted off to sleep.

———

ANY PRETENSE of decorum or courtesy quickly disappeared. We began treating each other with open hostility, going at it like the Serbs and the Croats. Well, maybe not that brutally, but it still managed to shock the rest of the staff into incoherent gasps and wide-eyed stares when they witnessed it. He didn't seem to be troubled by it, not one bit. On the contrary, he seemed to relish the opportunity, though the my knee jerk reactions to his taunting did not speak well of me either. He also lingered around the estate more. That was annoying. He seldom slept at the manor during the week when I first arrived, electing to stay at his apartment in town because of its proximity to the office. Now every time I turned a corner, he happened to be there. If I didn't know better, I might have thought he was purposely seeking me out to antagonize me.

A few nights ago I was asked to bring a glass of whiskey to his office. Entering quietly, I stopped short when I found him speaking on the phone. The dim light casting a glow around his profile made him look like a gilded icon. The fact that I could actually entertain such a ridiculous thought made me want to punch myself in the face. His long body was sprawled out on the plush, coffee colored couch, paperwork everywhere. His chin tipped down and the cold glare of the laptop resting on a side table illuminated his face. That's when I realized how tired he looked. His hair was messy, like he had run a worried hand through it repeatedly.

For some demented reason that I can't explain I had the overwhelming urge to smooth it back into place for him.

"What are the margins? I think we need to sell. I don't give a shit, Tom, stop stepping on your dick and do it. I'm in no mood to fuck around...what else...I'll decide what's below the bar...we'll hash out the details tomorrow."

As the call ended, he glanced up at me. For a split second I thought I saw the beginning of smile, but it disappeared just as quickly. His intense gaze immediately snapped back to his paperwork, the sight of me too unpleasant to bear apparently. I placed the glass of amber liquid on the side table and waited for him to say something.

"You know...Switzerland is paying illegals to repatriate." He continued to stare at his paperwork while I stood there frozen in disbelief, stunned by how easily malice fell from his lips. It took me a while to gather my wits and walk out. Unlike him, I was an amateur at mental warfare and did a poor job pretending that his jabs didn't leave a mark. And for the life of me I couldn't understand why he didn't fire me if he wanted me out of his sight bad enough to suggest I should leave the country altogether.

A day later, as I walked by his office, I heard Isabelle's throaty French accent floating out of the wide-open doorway. I turned to look and found her bent over him, her large breasts a short distance from his face as she arranged the lunch tray on his desk. When our eyes connected, I saw him flinch. Surprisingly, a deep flush developed under his tan. I stood there basking in his discomfort while satisfaction shaped itself into a sly smile on my face. The feeling of triumph was fleeting though. And as it faded, all that remained was an empty sadness.

We passed each other in the hall later that same day. Turning a corner, I almost bumped into him. His hand shot out to steady me for only a moment before he quickly pulled it back, as if I had some incurable disease he didn't wish to be infected with. His eyes wandered over my average breasts. "You can always buy yourself a pair," he muttered.

I stood there slack-jawed while he walked away. He always did get the last word.

I was living on an emotional tight wire. It was exhausting and, worse, sucking up precious energy that I needed to focus on my career. The problem was that as soon as he managed to convince me that he was the devil in the flesh, he did something that shocked me into believing there was still a scrap of humanity left in him.

Shortly after the "we'll pay you to leave the country" incident, I overheard the muffled sound of crying coming from the kitchen. I didn't want to interrupt someone's private moment so I stood at the bottom of the staircase, out of sight, and listened as Mrs. Arnaud gently consoled Claire. "Don't you worry, Claire, we're all here for you. If you need money to pay Jack's legal fees, we'll all chip in." Another muffled sob from Claire.

"It's the damn drugs, Marianne. They've ruined his life, you know. I don't know what to do any more."

"He's only twenty-five. He can still turn it around if he wants to," Mrs. Arnaud tried to assure her.

"What the fuck's going on? I called the kitchen phone and nobody answered."

My heart skipped a beat. He sounded irritated and impatient. In other words, his usual self. There was a heavy pause of silence before Mrs. Arnaud spoke.

"It's Claire's son, Jack. He was arrested again."

All I could do was pray he wouldn't be cruel to Claire at a time like this.

"I'll call David. He'll bail him out. We'll get him out of this mess."

"David is the best lawyer in the country, Claire. You see— it'll all be fine."

If a unicorn had suddenly trotted into the room, I would have been less astonished.

"Claire, can you convince him to go to rehab? I'll pay." he asked in a soft, low voice.

"I don't know. I'll try."

I stepped further into the kitchen, still unnoticed.

"Try real hard," I heard him say. And then his eyes snapped up and found me. For a moment I felt something soft, a silken tentacle, reach out for me but it was gone in an instant. His gaze darted away. Then he turned and walked out, leaving me to sort out what had happened for hours.

I couldn't put him in a box, label it heartless monster, and throw it away. That's what messed with my head worse than anything. So I did what I always do. I forged on, tried to put a brave face on even though I was completely demoralized.

I was in the kitchen, slicing fresh zucchini and contemplating how to extricate myself from this quagmire, when Mr. Bentifourt rushed into the kitchen holding the arm of one of the gardeners.

"Marianne! Marianne! Giovanni cut himself. I need the first aid kit!" he shouted, grave concern etched on his face. Servants poured into the kitchen, the loud commotion stirring everyone's curiosity.

Giovanni was short and stocky, around thirty years of age. The smile almost always fixed on his boyish face had begun to sag with the loss of blood. He had a dirty towel wrapped around his forearm. Mrs. Arnaud toddled as quickly as she could on short legs to a cabinet and unlocked it. Visibly shaken, she squinted at the labels on the vials as she tried to read without her glasses. I peeked inside and found a small refrigerator well stocked with vials of anesthetic and antibiotics.

Years of education and instinct propelled me into action. I coaxed her aside, her expression a mix of confusion and anxiety as she watched me grab everything quickly. Antibiotics, anesthetic, a package of sterile needles, syringes, and thread. "I know what I'm doing, *madame*. Trust me." Consenting with a quick nod, she stepped away and gave me room to work.

"Charlotte, I need clean towels, and grab the cotton and bandages I have here." Charlotte scrambled forward and I dumped them in her arms. We moved towards the table where Giovanni, his usually florid countenance turning sallow, looked close to passing out.

Bentifourt stepped in front of me before I could reach for Giovanni. "Now see here, young lady—"

"I have a medical degree, sir." It must have been the pronounced note of authority in my voice because, although he did it apprehensively, he moved out of my way.

I lifted the bloodstained towel and inspected the wound. It was deep, but it appeared that no major vessels had been cut. When I looked up, Giovanni gave me a wane smile. "Someone needs to hold on to him," I said, looking around. "He's going to hit the floor in about ten seconds."

Two young men I recognized as gardeners grabbed his shoulders. They held Giovanni steady while I cleaned the wound, disinfected it, and stitched the jagged cut that wrapped around the top of his forearm. As I finished wrapping it in surgical cotton and securing it with medical tape, I glanced up and found a devilish glint in Charlotte's eyes. Her lips parted into a bright grin. Mrs. Arnaud still hadn't recovered from the flurry of activity, her pudgy hand clutching her chest while it rose and sank with each agitated breath she took.

"I would never have consented to such a thing, but there was so much blood and I thought"—Bentifourt sighed—"an artery had been cut. I must say, I'm relieved, the nearest hospital is an hour away." His voice was weak and stressed, reminding me of his age.

"He's not in any danger. Nevertheless, he may have cut some ligaments. I'm not an orthopedic surgeon. He needs to be checked out."

Bentifourt motioned to the two young men holding onto Giovanni. "Theo, David, take the truck and don't speed." As they escorted him out, Giovanni turned to me with a wobbly smile. *"Merci, mademoiselle."* I was just happy to have been of service. It was a rush, being called into action, doing what I was meant to do in life. I glanced at the staff members crowding the kitchen. There was a newfound sense of respect in their open expressions, even a bit of excitement to have discovered something special tucked amongst them.

I was flying high when I felt his presence. I could always feel him, a soft touch on my skin. I looked over my shoulder and found him standing in the doorway, his features carved in stone, eyes fixed on me as if he were seeing me for the first time. Servants scattered as if someone flipped a light switch on a colony of roaches. Bentifourt walked towards him and drew his attention, disrupting the current between us. He blinked out of a trance and abruptly left the kitchen.

Would he be furious with Bentifourt? I didn't want him bearing any anger on my behalf, even though the old man hadn't exactly made me feel welcome.

"What a day! It seems we have gotten quite a bargain with you, Vera," Mrs. Arnaud burst out, herself again. Relieved, I smiled. Nothing meant more than what Marianne Arnaud thought of me.

"That was bloody awesome!" Charlotte paced back and forth, gesticulating theatrically. "It was like an old episode of Gray's Anatomy. Blood and guts everywhere. The patient comes in clinging to life and then, when the tired, old head surgeon fails, the young resident steps in"—she wheeled around—"and saves the day!"

"Charlotte, really?" I bit my lip, suppressing a goofy grin. "I feel the need to point out that no one was clinging to life. No guts anywhere, thank God. And I have never once saved the day. I might have ruined a couple though."

She rolled her eyes in a comically exasperated fashion. "You're such a bloody stickler for details."

"But you do have medical training?" Mrs. Arnaud cut in.

"Yes, *madame*. I have my medical degree. I graduated with honors." I whispered the last part. "But I still have to complete my residency." Mrs. Arnaud regarded me thoughtfully. "*Madame*, I hope I didn't do anything to get Mr. Bentifourt in trouble. Mr. Horn looked angry. Not that that's uncommon—" Mrs. Arnaud shook her head, stalling my words.

"*Non*, Olivier has handled Mr. Horn since he was a child. There is nothing for you to worry about." She picked up the bloody rags and handed them to Charlotte. "*Chérie*, take these to the laundry room please." As soon as Charlotte left the kitchen, a heavy silence fell. I glanced up from the table I was busy disinfecting and found Mrs. Arnaud watching me. "I'm going to tell you something, Vera. Not because I'm making excuses—because I believe you will understand." Taking a seat, her shoulders slumped, deflating with a heavy exhale.

"I was thirty-five when I came to work here. I wasn't

doing well...mentally. My husband had left me without a word, not even a note. Sebastian was a little boy, only six, and always alone." A tender smile tugged at her lips. "He would sit in the kitchen with me and help with whatever I was doing. Mostly, he just kept me company. We became friends instantly, even if we didn't speak much. He hardly ever said anything. It saved me from my own misery...he saved me." Lost in the memory, she glanced over my shoulder with a troubled look on her face. "His mother was either out having a good time or tending to her own needs. And her husband was far from a good parent. He was extremely demanding...never saw him hug the child once in all those years." When they returned to me, her eyes were filled with an earnest strength. "I know he can be harsh, but try not to judge him too harshly. That man has had very little in his life to be happy about. And may I remind you that all that glitters is not gold."

I shrank from the slight disapproval in her voice. And although I wasn't about to forgive his behavior towards me, I had to agree that I had been quick to judge him. Would I have made more allowances for him if he'd been ugly and poor? Probably. I would've looked for excuses for his behavior. And pain would have been an obvious one.

———

I RETURNED to my room by early evening and found the door ajar. I paused, contemplating whether I had shut it firmly when I left that morning, and decided that I had. An insidious fear sprouted up. The impulse to flee made my heart beat in a ramshackle rhythm. I fought it—surely I was safe here, I thought.

Pushing the door open, I quietly stepped inside and

noticed my desk lamp turned on, the curtains moved aside. Dusk had fallen. The lavender glow cast smeared shadows on the walls that made the room look eerie and unfamiliar. That's when I noticed him sitting in my chair, his cane propped against the wall, my medical book in one hand and his head bent over it. He wore a simple white t-shirt and an old pair of Levi's, a complete departure from his usual *lord of the manor* look with his expensive suits and air of invincibility. He raked his long fingers through his hair absentmindedly. He looked almost human, relaxed and approachable when at ease.

His head rose and the eyes that met mine were not the same shuttered ones I had come to know so well. On the contrary, the eyes staring back at me now were warm and curious, filled with yearning—the feeling profoundly familiar. I reached for it but it pulled away, leading me dangerously near the edge of something big. Scared of what I might find, I took a cautious step back and the spell was broken.

The warmth leaked out of his expression as he retreated behind the walls of his fortress. He closed the book and placed it on my desk, grabbed his cane as he stood, shrinking the room with his overpowering form, wielding his size as a weapon.

"Medical books." The sensual rumble of his voice reached inside of me and triggered things I didn't want to feel for him. Like a tuning fork, my body responded immediately. Heat accumulated below my waist and a pulsing need settled between my thighs. I was petrified he would realize my attraction to him so of course the devil in me chose that moment to make an appearance.

"What are you doing in my room?"

"She speaks." There was a smile in his voice, though his

face gave nothing away. That kindled my anger. I refused to be something he toyed with for his amusement.

"I shouldn't have to say anything to you. You shouldn't be here." When he stepped forward, I instinctively moved back, crashing into the cool, stone wall. Adroitly, he'd trapped me, only a slice of light left between us.

I refused to satisfy his ego and meet his gaze. I simply stared ahead, pretending to see nothing and feeling too much. The heat radiating from him warmed my clammy skin. His distinct scent, soap mixed with expensive cologne, invaded my senses. It was intoxicating. I wanted to lean into it so instead I pressed my spine up against the cold stucco and flinched as it dug into the thin skin of my back.

"Thank you for taking care of Giovanni." The warm puffs of his breath near my temple made my hairline tingle. The vibration of his rough-hewn voice danced on my skin. "The surgeon said you did an adequate job with the stitches." *Adequate job?? Those stitches were perfect!* "Don't do it again. I keep a helicopter here for that exact purpose."

The taunting had the desired effect. My eyes snapped up and resentment made me glow the color of good Chianti. I caught him searching my face and realized much too late that it pleased him to shock me. And I'd played right into it like the overwrought, lusty idiot I had become. "Please leave, or I will scream." He stared back unfazed by the threat. But he was wrestling with something. I could feel it as distinctly as the heavy thumping of my heart.

The loud shrill of his cell phone broke the stalemate. He pulled it out of his back pocket and briefly glanced at the screen, his amber eyes returning to me quickly. He wasn't done with this conversation. The unspoken promise hung between us. Then, without a glance backwards, he stalked out of my room.

When the door shut, I sagged against the wall, trying to recover from the drain of energy that follows an adrenaline rush.

The longing I had detected in his eyes must have been a pathetic figment of my imagination, years of abstinence having damaged my ability to judge anything regarding the opposite sex. The pheromones in my blood were running amok. This man had no warmth left in him, no empathy whatsoever. Charlotte said he lacked something. She was right. Perhaps when his wife died, the best parts of him, the human parts, had died with her.

CHAPTER 8

The next few days were unseasonably warm. We began spring cleaning, starting with the drapes in the great room. I dragged them outside and beat the dust out of them until my arms were reduced to two useless rubbery appendages. Mrs. Arnaud shook her head when she saw me stumbling through the door, buried over my head in heaps of costly Italian silk. Shortly afterwards, Theo came in and helped me hang them back up.

With his assistance, I was done by early afternoon. And the weather being agreeable, I decided to go into town for some shopping. I needed to buy a new pair of sneakers to replace the ones that had disintegrated on the road to the estate, and more of the body oil the apothecary had mixed especially for me. Bulgarian white roses with a woodsy note of light musk. It was the one small luxury I allowed myself.

The charming town had one of everything: a bakery, a butcher, a church. I had spent hours walking through the narrow cobblestone streets trying to get lost. It was impossible. No matter which direction I walked in, I always found myself back in the center of town, the piazza, where old men sipped their espressos and winked at me as I walked by.

In the distance, the sky signaled fair warning of an approaching storm. A ribbon of delicate pink, blue-gray, and mandarin orange trimmed the horizon. As I hurried across a front lawn as tidy as a putting green, I spotted Giovanni spreading mulch on a flowerbed of flaming red geraniums. He paused to tip his wide brimmed hat at me and I waved back, afterwards continuing down the long gravel driveway at a brisk pace. Pushing the sleeves of my t-shirt up over my shoulders, I let the sun heat my pale skin. The air was crisp, rife with the scent of fresh cut grass, inviting me to take deep breaths.

Overwhelmed with gratitude, I sent up a silent prayer to whatever guardian angel had led me here. So much had changed in the past few weeks. There was still that dreadful second when I awoke, expecting to find my face plastered against the scratchy polyester pillowcase of the bed in my old apartment. Yet nothing was sweeter than the relief that washed over me when I realized it hadn't been a dream.

I was floating on cloud nine when a familiar black car turned onto the gravel driveway. Instantly, I came crashing back down to earth. It slowed as it neared me. I didn't look in its direction. Pointless, really. First, the windows were an impenetrable black. And second, I knew exactly who was driving. He was going to trample all over my good mood. Of that, I was certain.

The dark window slid down. He paused a beat before removing his silver aviator sunglasses. Arrogance incarnate. Nina Simone's soulful voice drifted from the car speakers. *"Sinner Man." Hmm, how appropriate.* He stared at me with a displeased curiosity—not unlike how one would inspect a new mole or a gray hair. His gaze did a subtle head to toe inspection of my person, and a small v appeared between his brows. With a heavy sigh, he turned down the music.

"Where are you going?"

His audacity never ceased to amaze me. It didn't even sound like a question, more like a reprimand. "Into town."

I walked past the car. A moment later, I heard it moving again. The car pulled up next to me, slowly keeping pace. The passenger window slid open.

"Get in the car. I'll give you a ride."

I tried to refrain from looking horrified. Not sure I succeeded. "That won't be necessary, but thank you."

"That wasn't a question. Get in the car."

I stopped and turned, gaping in disbelief. The arrogance of this man was beyond comprehension and I'd had just about enough of it. I put my hands on my hips and blasted him with a scowl of my own. Although, I think, not nearly as terrifying.

"I'm certain you consider yourself lord of all you survey. But last time I checked, I was not sold into slavery. So contrary to what you may wish, I am walking into town."

His narrowed eyes reminded me of a sleepy tiger, right before it pounces on some poor unsuspecting baby elephant. "There's a storm coming. Get in the car, or I will get out and put you in the car myself." *He couldn't possibly be serious?* He raised an eyebrow. "Don't doubt it for a minute." He was serious. I was also pretty sure that he could, and would do it. This was not a man who made idle threats. There wasn't a soul in sight to ride to my rescue so I did the only thing I could—I got into the car.

The door barely made a whisper as it sealed shut, enclosing me in absolute luxury. My wandering eyes drank in every detail. The instruments were all black and sleek, the trim was gleaming exotic wood, the cognac leather interior hand stitched. It was immaculate. I felt terribly out of place, afraid to touch anything.

"Good girl."

I turned, leveling him with a nasty stare. "I see that it has escaped your keen power of observation that I am not a girl, nor am I a dog to be commanded to stay or to come."

"It hasn't escaped me…trust me," he muttered cryptically. "Lord of all I survey?" The side of his sensual mouth curved up in a brief smile, a glimmer of amusement on an otherwise stony expression.

"Yes, Your Highness." Then a muffled laugh he covered up with a cough. I'd never heard him laugh before. Not once. It took me by surprise.

Each second we drove in silence seemed to last an eternity. I sat there upright and stiff as a corpse, fuming with resentment, feeling his perceptive gaze take in my shoes, my clothing—every detail about me. The contrast between us was startling. Everything I wore was either worn out, old or mended. He, on the other hand, was perfectly groomed, draped in thousands of euros worth of clothing. I stole quick, surreptitious glances in his direction, and like a beggar at a banquet, there was so much my greedy eyes wanted to take in that I didn't know where to begin.

He had removed his jacket. Daunting for his custom-made suits to contain all that testosterone no doubt. And his shirt still looked fresh. *Really? His clothes won't even wrinkle on him?* A silver Rolex with a lapis blue face sat on his wrist. Silver cufflinks carved into delicate knots winked at me from the French cuff of his silky cotton shirt. The seductive scent of laundry detergent and his expensive cologne mixed with the smell of new leather was subtle enough that I wanted to follow my nose in search for more of it.

Inadvertently, my gaze landed on my worn-out jeans

and the ugly truth smacked me in the face. I was a woman far beneath his notice, undeserving of consideration or civility. My vanity kicked and screamed. My pride bristled at the injustice. I didn't want to be here. I didn't want to be anywhere near him. I didn't begrudge him his magnificence, but I hated how it made me feel...inferior, unworthy.

The thump of his thumbs on the steering wheel drew my attention. My eyes traced the curves of the silver B stamped in the middle. Absently, he stroked and tapped the polished wood. White, asterisk shaped scars covered the back of his hands, starkly evident against the golden tan skin.

The accident. An image appeared in my mind's eye. My lips, on his hand...kissing every one. Disgusted with myself, I tore my gaze away and focused straight ahead, my jaw clenched tight enough to shatter glass. I never fully understood irrational compulsions before I met this man. Humbling, to say the least.

"Why would you wear those shoes to walk three miles?"

His voice interrupted a slew of self-recriminating thoughts. Glancing at my striped espadrilles, I replied, "I didn't have any choice."

He was quiet for a while, brooding, making me uncomfortably aware of the escalating magnetic charge between us. *Why this man?*

The road suddenly seemed endless. When he spoke again, his voice had dropped a couple of octaves and had softened at the edges. "Where did you study medicine?"

"Milan."

"What was your specialty?"

My gaze flickered over to him. The casually bored look he often wore had been replaced with an attentive one, his eyes sparkling with curiosity. "Family medicine. Oh look, we're here," I said with mocking cheerfulness. "Well, thanks for the pleasant ride."

He drove up to the storefront and parked the car. I felt a pressing need to get as far away from him as possible. Opening the door quickly, I was about to step out when he clasped my wrist. My heart raced as I stared at it. Everything about that moment seemed amplified times ten; his warm grip firm but gentle, the electric current skating on my skin. The pads of his fingers found my pulse. I couldn't breathe, paralyzed by his touch, by all the feelings it evoked.

"Vera, I..."

My eyes lifted to his. There was an unexpectedly contrite look on his face. I panicked, scared that he would recognize what was on mine. Desire. "I have to go." I tugged my wrist and he released me.

The thunderheads were already over us. Fat teardrops splashed on my nose, my mouth, my cheeks. My heart hammered wildly. I ran into the store and stopped just inside to catch my breath. The skin on my wrist felt burned, branded. I rubbed it in a desperate attempt to erase the feeling. How could just a touch have me this undone? But it wasn't just any touch—it was his touch that had thoroughly destroyed my composure.

I was angry at myself. Mostly for falling prey to lust. Most importantly for possibly jeopardizing my personal and financial security. I stood before the items packed on the shelves fighting to regain some control over my wayward emotions. Absentmindedly, I grabbed a couple of things and went to pay.

"Oh," I frowned. "I'm...sorry. You can remove these three items," I said in French to the store clerk.

An herbal laxative.

Hemorrhoid cream.

And men's deodorant.

Through the store window, I could see the rain coming down in buckets. The sky had turned angry, as dark as pitch. I stepped outside and found his car still out front. Stranger yet, I wasn't surprised. The passenger side window slid down halfway and our eyes met through the blur of water.

"Get in," he shouted.

I shook my head. Weakly, I argued, "I don't want to get your car wet."

"I don't give a fuck-all about the car. Get in!"

It was futile arguing with him. I would only get "more wet" and stood a very good chance of being struck by lightning. Quickly yanking the door open, I jumped in and the window sealed shut.

The icy mask did nothing to conceal the pent-up emotion blazing in his eyes. "What would you have done? Walk home in the dark? In the middle of a thunderstorm?"

"I'm ruining your beautiful car." That was an understatement. I sat there a bedraggled, soaked lump, my clothes plastered to me indecently, dripping all over the fine leather upholstery.

He reached into the back seat and grabbed a clean white dress shirt. "Here," he said, handing it to me. It was perfect and beautiful and probably cost a fortune. "Take it," he insisted.

I'd heard that implacable tone before. He was thoroughly intimidating when he was like this, and I was too baffled by his reaction to put up a fuss. When our fingers touched, he pulled away quickly. I patted my face and throat, soaking the super fine cotton, and caught a trace of his delicious scent still clinging to it. *Dear God, this is torture.* The craving to bury my nose in it and inhale deeply was almost unendurable. I placed the shirt on my lap.

Visibility being near zero, he drove slowly as the heavens opened up and unleashed the worst of it. The only sound in the small space was his steady breathing coupled with the hiss of the windshield wipers working frantically to keep up with the heavy downpour. There was something perversely reassuring about the sound of his breath. It reached deep into my bones and chased the chill away.

"It wouldn't be the first time I walked home in the rain," I mumbled.

"Are you trying to piss me off?"

He wouldn't look at me as he spoke, glared at the road instead and gripped the steering wheel with two hands tight enough to turn his knuckles pale.

"No. I...I don't really understand why you are. And can you please stop using that language around me," I demanded, clutching the shirt to my throat as a child would a safety blanket.

He turned towards me with a probing glance. The anger dissipated and amusement appeared in his brandy colored eyes. Exhaling slowly, the tension drained out of his shoulders and his grip on the steering wheel relaxed. "What's wrong with my language?"

"I don't care for profanity. It's the tool of an undisciplined mind."

His lips quirked. "Who said that?"

"I did." When I glanced at him again, I found him watching me with an intensity that made me quickly avert my eyes.

We pulled up to the back entrance of the house a short while later. The worst of the storm behind us, only a few scattered showers remained as the sun struggled to break through the wall of steel blue clouds. He put the car in park, brooding silently, while I sat there perfectly still. My nerves raw. All my senses completely locked on him. Prey in the presence of a predator. *Except you want to be caught*, the dark, deranged part of my psyche taunted.

I waited for him to say something but he kept staring ahead, his eyebrows pinched together in deep concentration. *If we could find some middle ground and coexist amicably.* I tried to bridge the uncomfortable gap between us. "What does the B stand for? Bossy? Belligerent? Bellicose?"

"Bentley."

"Oh…I'm sorry about your car. Can it be fixed?"

"Enough about the damn car. Promise me next time you want to go anywhere you'll get a ride from Theo or one of the guys."

"If they're not busy."

He turned to me with such a withering glare I'm surprised I didn't turn to stone on the spot. "Let me be perfectly clear. If I find out they let you walk again, they will all be looking for new employment." The last words were uttered in a deadly calm voice that left no room for doubt.

"Fine," I replied in a petulant tone. I tugged on the door handle several times without success. My gaze slowly slid back to him in question, trying to gauge what it was that was happening between us, and found his attention still focused forward.

"Are you scared of me?" he asked, his voice so mild I almost didn't hear him.

"No." I was much more scared of myself, of the feelings he provoked in me.

"Then why are you desperate to escape?"

I almost laughed. *Where…do I…begin?* "You mean, apart from the fact that every time you speak to me you are either appallingly rude, deeply insulting, or an arrogant jerk?"

From his profile, I could tell he was fighting to keep a smile off his face. "You're right."

I finally heard the click of the doors unlocking and pushed mine open. I ran towards the back door, trying to escape an uncomfortable feeling nipping at my heels, and paused in the vestibule to watch him. He held the white shirt I had used to dry myself with as if it were the shroud of Turin, staring at it with an unfathomable expression. That uncomfortable feeling nipping at my heels parked itself in the pit of my stomach.

As I walked into the kitchen, Mrs. Arnaud caught the sight of me soaking wet and gasped, "*Mon Dieu*, get changed before you catch a cold."

"Yes, *madame*."

Fifteen minutes later, I was soaking in a hot bath, the water line just below my nose and the scent of white Bulgarian roses drifting up from the steam. Every minute of the day's events played over and over in my mind while my toe fidgeted with the waterspout. I made a mental list of possible explanations:

One: he saw me as some kind of charity case. That did not sit well with me. My pride huffed and puffed. Two: he didn't want to see me run over by a car. *People do drive aggressively around these parts.* He probably didn't want the bother of having to identify the corpse of one of his wayward employees. I could see him trying to explain it to the police. A handkerchief over his nose as he inspected the remains…

Yes, that's her. Well what do you expect? The idiot walked to town wearing those ridiculous shoes.

I even contemplated the possibility that he was trying to somehow make amends for his appalling behavior in the past, but quickly discarded the notion. So once again, I was left scratching my head about him, unable to dislodge that haunted look on his face from my mind.

After work the next day, I went to my room to change out of my uniform and found a sleek, silver object sitting on my desk. There was no note. I stared at it for what seemed like an eternity before touching it.

A brand-new Apple laptop.

It had to be from him. There was no other possible explanation. And I wasn't about to go around asking. I couldn't keep it, of course. That would imply something, and none of it good. It crossed my mind more than once that this might be some kind of test, because I didn't trust anything that resembled kindness from him.

CHAPTER 9

It was my day off. The sun finally made an appearance in a sky painted cerulean blue and I planned on spending it entirely outdoors. Two days prior, I had taken a bus into the city and got caught in another sudden downpour. Soaked all the way through to my underwear, I didn't exactly make the best of impressions as I walked from hospital to hospital, dropping off the packets that contained my query letters. In any event, all I could do now was hope for the best and wait for a call.

Grabbing my book bag, I headed out to find a soft patch of grass as far away from the manor as possible. Mrs. Arnaud insisted on packing me a basket for lunch, afraid that any lack of attention to my diet would cause her to lose any progress she had made in her quest to fatten me up. Charlotte found me as I was about to walk outside.

"Prison break tonight. Let's go listen to some live music."

I hesitated, not quite feeling like I could let my guard down yet and indulge in some fun. When you've been living hand to mouth for so many years, old habits are hard to break. "I don't know, Charlotte. I don't want to walk home late at night—" She held up a hand, stalling my excuse.

"Theo promised to come pick us up." Theo being the eighteen-year-old gardener who was completely infatuated with her. I sighed and smiled. "You might as well agree now because I'm prepared for any and all arguments," she added. That was one of the things I loved most about Charlotte, her inexhaustible enthusiasm for life. It was refreshing.

Resigned to my fate, I capitulated, "All right, tonight it is." She jumped up and down with glee. I couldn't help but laugh at her unabashed joy, her spontaneity; something I lacked altogether, life shaping me into someone measured and deliberate.

"I'll be by your room at nine," she yelled as I walked away.

I cut through the garden, marching past the tulip and iris beds. I kept walking until I reached the well-worn path behind the conservatory and the manor was well out of sight, until I came upon a wisteria tree that belonged in a fairytale book. The base of the trunk was knobby and wide, a dark burnt umber color. It twisted around itself and reached up into the warm, blue sky. The branches held long columns of clustered lavender blooms that hung down like the tumbled curls of a little girl. With a ridiculous smile on my face, I stepped under the enormous canopy and closed my eyes, the columns of flowers brushing against my head and shoulders. An overwhelming sense of excitement raced through me as I stood under that magical tree. I couldn't shake the feeling that something big was about to happen.

I kicked off my espadrilles, and spread the blanket at the base of the tree. Flopping down, I yanked on the elastic holding my ponytail together and my hair fell silky and straight below by breasts. I needed a haircut. One of the many things that had been neglected over the last couple of years.

Inside the basket were sandwiches stuffed with full crème Brie and smoked Parma ham, a cluster of red grapes, and a couple of freshly baked madeleines. I popped a grape in my mouth. Bursting, it spilled its sweet treasure on my tongue. I flipped open my book with every intention of reading a couple of chapters as a refresher, but as I lay down with my knees hitched up and my feet on the ground, a lazy feeling stole over me. The wind whispered a lullaby in my ear and sunlight broke through the canopy of flowers, dappling my face. Swaddled in a deep sense of serenity, I closed my eyes and floated somewhere between fantasy and reality.

I'm not sure if I heard him or felt his presence. In any case, my eyes crept open to find him a few paces away, standing rigid, his face taut with apprehension. Even from afar, I could tell he was struggling with something. My stomach sank with a thud as all hope for a peaceful afternoon fled.

He was wearing a white v neck t-shirt that outlined the power of his broad shoulders and the width of his chest. However galling, I had to admit his beauty seemed to increase exponentially every time I saw him...and his virility. My newly resurrected libido snuck that one in. When he stepped forward, I scrambled to sit up and banged my leg against the trunk, flopping around as graceless as a fish out of water. He came close enough that I was forced to look up. Shoring up my defenses, I pressed my back up against the tree and wrapped my arms around my bent legs.

"I didn't mean to wake you," he said, looking up at the tree, his eyes narrowing at the sunlight peeking through the canopy. His silky hair rustled in the wind and fell over his eye. Deep in the back of my mind, where the dark, shameful part of me lives, I saw myself pushing it aside with my fingers.

"You didn't. I was only resting my eyes." I looked away, a flash of heat tickling my neck.

"Is that what you call it?"

He was exceedingly good at obliterating my self-control. Good sense would dictate that I did not get into yet another argument with the man who paid my salary, but why start using good sense now—that train left the station the minute I met him.

"Shouldn't you be at the office? What are you doing skulking around the property? Or are you so obsessed with provoking me that you walked all the way out here to get your daily quota in?"

The side of his sensual mouth curved up briefly before he trained it back into a firm line. "I do own the property so I'm not sure you can call it skulking. I'm working from home today. And I didn't have to come all the way out here to provoke you, I could've just waited 'til you came back to the house."

The silence stretched on. Neither one of us hurried to fill it. And yet, instead of it being awkward, it felt...strangely comfortable. I noticed he was leaning a little more heavily than usual on his cane. He tipped his beautiful face up towards the sun and closed his eyes. There was an extra tightness around them that indicated his injury was causing him pain.

An overwhelming urge came over me. I wanted to take his pain away, soothe him.

"Did you leave an Apple laptop in my room? I can't keep it." I kept my eyes on my bare flexing toes as I spoke.

"Why not?"

"Because it's beyond inappropriate. I'm not in the habit of

accepting expensive gifts from strangers." Gathering my hair quickly, I tied it back in a ponytail, readying myself for battle.

"I'm not a stranger—I'm your employer." His voice was unusually bland. I didn't let that fool me.

"Or employers."

"That would be stupid." His anger percolated quickly. "Those books are outdated. You need a computer."

"You make perfect sense, but I still can't accept it. It'll be in your office tonight." I doubted anyone ever dared to disagree with him, not if they valued their welfare. His eyes assessed me shrewdly. His jaw tightened and he raked his fingers through his hair. He was working up another argument, as apparent on his face as if he had shouted, "Pistols or rapiers?" Surprisingly, though, he pivoted and walked away with ground-eating strides. Needless to say, I was relieved, although unsure if the issue had been settled.

The cane must have sunk into a soft patch of grass because I watched him lose his balance and crumple to the ground. Instinct thrust me forward, towards him. He was clutching his knee when I reached his side. I knelt down closer and discovered his face twisted in pain.

"Should I go to the house and get somebody?"

"No!" he barked out. "Give me a minute." Reaching into the pocket of his athletic pants, he pulled out a prescription bottle. I snatched it out of his hand and read the label.

"These are very strong. When was the last time you took one?"

His eyes briefly darted away from me, then returned weary and cautious. "Four hours ago."

"You're not due for another hour," I said as gently as possible. Unlike him, I gathered no pleasure seeing him brought low.

He stared at his leg and didn't respond. When he finally did look up, the mask was gone. His eyes were two deep pools of emotion, allowing me a glimpse of his pain and frustration, beseeching me to understand.

Wordlessly, I walked back to the basket and grabbed a small bottle of Pellegrino. His large hand trembled as he took the bottle from me. I wrapped mine around his, to steady it, and felt him flinch. Was I that repulsive? I couldn't even begin to understand this man.

His athletic pants were loose at the bottoms. Before I realized what I was doing, I had reached down and pushed the hem up his calf. He stiffened immediately and gently covered my hand with his own, the warmth of his palm unleashing a swarm of butterflies in my stomach.

"Don't," he murmured.

"It's okay," I whispered, holding his gaze as I watched him wrestle with it. This may help until the pill starts to work."

He reminded me of a great wounded beast, guarding himself, ready to strike out. No sudden movements. Talk softly. It must have been evidence of how much pain he endured that he let me touch him at all. He released my hand and my practiced fingers went to work, moving up his leg until his pants were pushed high up his thigh. I looked up briefly and found his features frozen. He was holding his breath, his eyes wide and focused on me. A light mist of sweat glistened on his forehead. He looked almost... frightened.

The scar was an angry snake wrapped around his leg. My fingers alternated pressure around the kneecap. Massaging, soothing, stimulating. I gently kneaded up and around the knee, to the lower thigh, then down the calf; the scars sometimes smooth, sometimes rough under my fingertips. He flinched a number of times, but then subtly pressed into my touch instead of pulling away. I inspected the thick scars where the skin grafts pulled over bone and sinew and discovered they didn't prevent any mobility. The root of the problem must have been elsewhere, where the titanium pins held bones together.

I glanced again in his direction and found his expression had completely transformed. His eyes were closed, his breathing deep and steady, his nostrils flaring. The grooves around his sensual mouth had relaxed. What a sight—even more stunning than when he was neatly groomed and master of himself. A real flesh and blood man, not the unfeeling sculpture he usually resembled. His dark golden scruff glinted in the sunlight. My gaze fell on the tiny scar at the top of his lip, the one I wanted to trace with my tongue.

"What were you doing walking this far from the house?" I asked, my ears burning in shame. When he didn't open his eyes, I thought he hadn't heard me.

"I come out here to think."

"I'm sorry. You wanted some privacy and you found me hanging around." The tension in his muscles had eased, his color was returning. The thick fringe of his lashes fluttered open and revealed slightly dilated pupils. He caught me staring and with quicksilver speed, his expression shifted. The wounded creature transformed into a predator. A full-sized tiger.

"Good for me that you were." The sensual murmur made my scalp prickle and my throat tighten.

"Were what?" I mumbled, my train of thought derailed by the spell his smoldering eyes and voice were casting.

"Hanging around." How could two simple words sound so indecent? Everything south of my navel tingled.

Very slowly, he reached out and caught a lock of hair that had escaped my ponytail. I held my breath as he coiled it around his index finger and tucked it behind my ear. Shocked and confused, I remained perfectly still when his hand didn't leave me immediately. The pads of his fingers grazed the tender skin of my neck, under my ear, and lingered there, happy to stay forever.

When his focused attention landed on my lips, however, I finally came to my senses and stood up. It must be the drugs, I told myself. The drugs made him forget who I was for a moment.

"I should get you back to the house." I couldn't keep the anxiety out of my voice. It sounded high and far away.

He wouldn't look at me as he planted his good leg on the ground, underneath himself, and offered out his arm. I braced myself to counterbalance his weight, more than twice my own, but as he levered himself up, the momentum carried him forward and his body slammed into mine. Mistake. Big mistake. It was unbearably intimate. My hair stood on end. I could feel his body as if the clothes between us didn't exist.

I looked up and found him gazing down with an unapologetic sensual smile on his lips. I tried to pry loose, tried to escape the lure of it, but he held on, gripping my shoulders tightly while the hard evidence of his virility pressed against my stomach and a flood of sensations screamed through me.

Step away. Step away right now!

It took the self-control of a Sohei warrior monk to peel myself away and search for his cane. "Let me help you get back," I said in a timid voice, as I handed it to him. He agreed with a slight nod, his eyes boring into mine with super-human intensity.

There was no way to avoid touching him again. Cautiously, I gripped him around the waist, placed my shoulder under his armpit for support, and began walking towards the house.

"You're stronger than you look," he murmured.

I couldn't answer, my wits deserting me. I forced myself to concentrate on the task at hand, careful not to steer him onto any irregularity in the grass. All my senses were on high alert, my body vibrating with too much awareness. His blistering body heat. The heavy weight of his muscular arm draped over my shoulders. That addictive scent. It was a miracle that I managed to resist the urge to snuggle against him. Considering the significant height difference, we fit together rather perfectly.

"Can you please keep the computer? Nobody has to know about it." I had never heard his voice this gentle, intimate. *The voice of a lover.*

"I can't keep it because I can't explain it to Mrs. Arnaud, and I would never lie to her."

"A woman with scruples." He barked a joyless laugh. "How original." I pretended not to hear that, wasn't about to open that can of worms.

Maybe it was the beautiful bucolic setting or the crisp, fresh air. Or maybe it was the heat and hardness wrapped around me. In any case, the tension transformed into something pleasant, companionable. We walked in silence until the house came into view. But I could feel him thinking, strategizing his next move.

"I could tell her that I loaned you a computer for your studies." I knew he wouldn't back down. He was clearly a man accustomed to getting what he wanted. Somewhere in the back of my mind that knowledge made me pause uneasily.

"Fair enough. But I'll return it to you when I leave."

"Leave? Where would you go?" His expression remained inscrutable while his grip on my shoulder tightened.

"Anywhere I'm accepted in a residency program." I felt his steps slow fractionally, looked up and found him deep in thought. "Why do you drink so much?" I bit my lip when I realized I had voiced it out loud. He met my inquisitive gaze with apprehension.

"Who says I drink too much?"

"I do."

He blew out a deep breath and stared ahead, avoiding eye contact. "It's under control."

"You can't drink with all the medication you're taking," I said softly.

"I know—trust me, I know." There was a sad resignation in his voice that made my heart ache for him.

Up ahead, one of the groundskeepers, a tall, muscular man named Daniel, spotted us. He rushed over and took the other side, supporting Sebastian's weight easily. We were close enough to the house that other servants came pouring out to help. I was pushed aside in the shuffle, stood watching as they carried him away. Then, just as he was about to disappear inside, he turned and our eyes locked. *Were we friends now? Did he want that too?* I wasn't sure what had happened, however, something had changed between us.

CHAPTER 10

"I'm going to the bar to get another drink, we'll never get service here." Charlotte cupped her mouth as she spoke. The noise level was deafening. The air was thick with smoke and body heat.

"What?" I screamed back.

She laughed and motioned theatrically with her hands, miming her words. "ANOTHER DRINK???"

"No, I'm good." I laughed again.

It was the most fun I'd had in ages. The singer was indeed as good as Charlotte said she was. Towards the front of the room, dancing broke out, causing a chain reaction that ended with a number of young women being hoisted up on the tables. Charlotte and I were pressed against two brothers, one too short and the other too young. The short one was starting to annoy Charlotte as he kept pushing up against her, staring openly at her breasts when he spoke. The young one blushed every time I looked at him.

Not having much choice in clothing, I decided on my ivory silk blouse, my best jeans, and the only black high heels

I owned. I had removed my mother's Hermès scarf and placed it in my handbag. The place was a sauna, my clothes soaked in sweat.

I turned to see if Charlotte had managed to muscle her way to the bar when something caught my eye. My body reacted before my mind did. There was a knot in my stomach and goose bumps swept over my skin from head to toe. Way in the back, leaning up against a wall...I saw him. He was looking straight at me with his usual penetrating stare. His arms were crossed in front of him, making the pale blue dress shirt he wore strain in all the right places.

I blinked, not trusting my eyes, and when I looked again, he was gone. For a moment, I wondered whether I was far more drunk than I realized, and decided to analyze the mystery later. I refused to let him ruin my evening.

Charlotte finally resurfaced with her drink. We ended up sharing the cold beer and continued dancing until a little after one, until exhaustion and the pain in my feet took over. It was a refreshing change to be tired from joy instead of worry.

A thick bank of fog met us as we walked out. The reflecting light from the street lamps made the night sky glow with a heavenly incandescence. The chill made me shiver and cross my arms tightly, trying to hide the puckering nipples evident through my wet blouse.

Theo pulled up in an ancient Citroën that sputtered to a stop. Laughing, we piled into the car quickly while Theo held the door open in a gallant attempt to impress Charlotte. As he tried to put the car in gear, it lurched forward and stalled, rattling my teeth.

"Are you sure we wouldn't be safer walking home?" I whispered to Charlotte.

Theo looked over at me with thinly disguised annoyance.

"I'll have you know this car is a classic," he blurted out in French, right before the tail pipe practically exploded. Charlotte and I exchanged skeptical looks and swallowed the impulse to laugh out of mercy. I pressed my forehead to the cool window as Theo reversed.

That's when I detected a familiar dark sports car parked down the street. My breath caught when the headlights turned on and the car sped away. Glancing sideways, I found Charlotte flirting with Theo. She hadn't noticed a thing.

"Charlotte, have you ever seen Mr. Horn out? In town, I mean."

"Fuck no, never. Mr. Sunshine-N-Rainbows only goes to the most exclusive restaurants and parties."

"He's not that bad. He can be a good sport when he's in the mood," Theo added.

Charlotte arched a perfect blond brow at him. "What does that mood look like? Because I've never seen it."

———

WE ENTERED THROUGH THE KITCHEN, taking turns giggling and shushing each other. I felt carefree, relaxed, and thankful that Charlotte had insisted on going out. I needed that, someone to force me to loosen up. Charlotte, yawning loudly, bid me good night and carried herself to bed. I grabbed a water bottle from the fridge, and made it halfway to my room when I realized I had left my mother's Hermès scarf on the kitchen counter.

As I stepped back into the kitchen, my pulse jumped, my heart registering the charge in the air. I turned my head and there he was, with his back to me, dwarfing the stool he sat on. His posture was graceful, of relaxed elegance, his injured leg straight and the other bent, an expensive driving moccasin perched on the bottom rung. My eyes moved appreciatively over his broad shoulders while they had the opportunity to indulge themselves, taking in every detail.

The pale blue dress shirt was half tucked in his jeans, as if he'd dressed in a hurry. His elbows rested casually on the counter, making the breathtaking swells of his wide shoulders stretch taut the silky fine cotton. His interest was fixed on an object. I leaned in to get a closer look and realized he was holding my scarf, playing with it, pulling the worn silk through the circle of his index finger and thumb.

Mesmerized, I watched him do it again and again, wondering what it would feel like to have those big hands on my body, caressing me the same way they caressed the silk. He suddenly looked over his shoulder and found me standing there. I caught the flicker of surprise before he quickly concealed it.

"Mr. Horn?"

He turned in his seat to face me. "Maybe we can dispense with the formalities since you've already had your hands on me." His voice was low and measured, but something in his tone made me uneasy, penetrating the dulling effects of alcohol. My smile faded. Pouf. In only a fraction of time all the ease we had shared earlier in the day evaporated.

"My scarf, please." I held out my hand. It hung between us vulnerable and alone while he stared at it. I didn't feel up to another sparring match with him so I pulled it back. We were dancing around something I was in no condition to deal with. What did he want with me anyway? Certainly a man with his looks, power, and wealth didn't go lusting after housekeepers. It seemed ridiculous to even consider. Still, I couldn't deny that inexorable pull between us. It was present as always, getting under my skin, unsettling my nerves, and making a general mockery of my self-control.

"Come get it," he murmured, "I don't bite."

My eyes widened and irritation loosened my tongue. "Yes, you do. You can get quite vicious actually."

His lips quivered, though there was no amusement in his eyes. The dim light did nothing to conceal all that smoldering intensity. That didn't bode well for me. "Did you enjoy yourself tonight?"

"That's none of your business. But as a matter of fact, I did," I answered curtly.

He stared back silently for an excruciating amount of time. When he spoke again, his voice dropped lower. "You enjoy making a spectacle of yourself? Rubbing up against men you don't know like a cat in heat?"

I sucked in a breath, shocked by his outrageous comment as if he had slapped me. My entire body flushed crimson. *Ground control, we have a direct hit.*

His cynical smile vanished when he noticed the horrified expression on my face.

With my eyes fixed on the kitchen floor, I held out my hand again because I would have rather died than let him see that he had this kind of effect on me. "My scarf," I demanded, forcing out the words past the lump of anger and embarrassment stuck in my throat.

Before I knew what hit me, he had wrapped his palm around my wrist, yanked me forward into the unforgiving wall of his chest, and trapped me securely between his thighs. His fingers raked through my hair, gripping the roots tightly while his other hand cradled my neck. I felt the lightest brush of his thumb along the edge of my jaw right before his mouth crashed onto mine.

Maybe it was the aftereffects of the alcohol. Maybe it was the shock. Whatever it was I didn't move a muscle for a full minute trying to decipher what was happening. Then my instincts finally kicked in. I squirmed and struggled to get loose. My small hands pushed against the uncompromising hardness of his shoulders, but it was like trying to budge the Matterhorn, an exercise in futility.

The kiss was at first painful, desperate. Then, catching himself, he backed off and began seducing me with a gentle insistence that disarmed me completely. A nip, a dry brush. He slanted his lips in search of the perfect angle. His mouth caught at mine, teasing me until I succumbed to the temptation and stopped fighting him. It didn't take much for me to surrendered and kiss him back, everything about him was a siren's song I had zero power to resist.

He stood slowly. One hand left my face and traveled down my back, coaxing me flush against the hard swells of his body. The heat radiating from him erased any lingering contrary thoughts. I lost dominion over myself and melted into his touch.

There was no awkwardness, and no hesitation. There was also an odd sense of familiarity present between us that I couldn't explain. My hands, moving of their own volition, stroked his shoulders and traveled up his neck. As I raked my short nails through his hair, he breathed out a relaxed sigh and pulled me tighter. The hand on my lower back pushed me up against the erection straining against his soft, worn jeans. My hips, having plans of their own, hitched up and pressed against him, striking me in just the right spot. I shivered as a bolt of lightning raced through my attention-starved body and a low moan rose up my throat. *God, how embarrassing.*

He broke the kiss, and my eyes fluttered open. A wicked half-smile curved his perfect lips. That smug smile jolted me right out of the alcohol and sex-induced spell, fury exploding within me. I pushed away and slapped him hard. The loud crack echoed in the kitchen.

I had never struck anyone in my life. One, it's not in my nature. And two, I'm a physician, the Hippocratic oath and all that. However, the satisfaction I felt seeing his startled expression was obscene. The bewilderment on his face, though, quickly transformed to cool mockery.

"Is this how you get your kicks? Screwing around with the help?"

"Not usually." He sounded bored, as if he didn't particularly care one way or the other for what he had just sampled. That ratcheted up my sense of outrage.

"I was hoping for some civility," I bit out, right before I wiped my mouth with the back of my sleeve. "I see now that's asking too much of you. I haven't got a clue what you're about, or what game you're playing, but don't ever touch me again!"

And then he smiled. The first genuine smile I had ever seen on him. It was a ridiculous, blinding thing, all American white teeth and scorching sensuality. And thank heavens he never used it because it reduced my brain into a useless pile of gray matter within seconds. He barked out a laugh when my scowl slipped. He actually laughed *at* me. So I did the only thing I could, I gathered up the tattered remains of my dignity, turned on my heels, and stalked out of the room.

By the time I reached my bedroom, the happy buoyancy I had felt earlier in the evening had long vanished. In its place there was an anchor sinking me to a level of self-loathing I had never quite experienced before. I felt like the biggest fool, cringing as I thought of how easily I had succumbed to his seduction. For a horrified moment, I contemplated what could have happened if he hadn't broken the kiss and smiled at me. I had to stay as far away from him as possible, because

I wasn't sure of anything anymore. Least of all, my own judgment.

———

I DIDN'T SEE him for days after the incident. Mrs. Arnaud mentioned in passing that he had stayed at the apartment. I assumed he was choosing to avoid me. He never stayed in town anymore, to my everlasting regret. Maybe it was about work. Regardless, I wasn't prepared to face him. I was living in a state of high anxiety. I didn't know if I should say something, or let time smooth things over. I just hoped we could both pretend it never happened and things could go back to normal. His constant taunting and insults paled in comparison to how his kisses messed with my head. I almost longed for those days.

Thoughts of him consumed my every waking moment, distracting me to the point that it was interfering with my work. I misplaced things, burned the coffee twice, and put fabric softener into the washing machine instead of detergent. Every time I thought about that night, I turned hot and restless. My entire body flushed and a heavy ache took up residence south of my waist. I was sure I wasn't the first woman to swoon at his feet, but I had no desire to be part of that overcrowded club.

I had just finished organizing the linens and towels for the guests arriving for the weekend when Mrs. Arnaud sent me on one last errand. She handed me five wooden hangers draped with his beautifully tailored shirts. They were all creamy white, except for the simple, tiny monogram sewn in a midnight thread on the cuff…SCH.

"Vera, bring these up to Mr. Horn's closet. Make certain they face the same direction as the others, and organize them by color. It upsets him when it's not done properly so please be careful. And then you're done for the day. You worked way too late yesterday, you can't keep pushing yourself like that."

"Yes, *madame.*"

I didn't bother explaining that I had to push myself to stop from remembering the feel of his hands on me, the taste of him. Fuzzy, lust-filled images would flash through my mind at the worst possible moments. Earlier that day, while eating lunch, François was speaking about his daughter, I think—I was barely paying attention—when suddenly I could feel the curved planes of *his* chest against my breasts, *his* hands kneading my rear end...the feel of the hard column of his sex. When my eyes met François', my face burst into flames. His curious expression turned heated, then a slow smile stretched across his face. That's all I needed, more complications with men I had no business getting involved with. I turned away abruptly while he was in the middle of a sentence and probably left him wondering whether I had lost my mind.

I stepped into his bedroom and looked around nervously before making a beeline for the closet. The size of a small apartment, it was elegantly styled with built-in furniture made of lacquered, exotic wood and nickel hardware. A silk Tibetan carpet in muted tones covered the hardwood floors, and a contemporary crystal chandelier cast sparkles of warm light that bounced off an oversized mirror. His clothes hung like perfect little soldiers, evenly spaced apart, ready to be called into battle. After placing the shirts in their proper place, I paused to stroke the luxurious cashmere of his Kiton suits. My eyes fluttered, closing shut as I basked in the sensation of the kitten-soft fabric brushing across my cheek.

When I opened them, I found him standing in the doorway, staring. I wasn't surprised to find him there. It seemed like we were on some unavoidable collision course. The masculine slashes of his brows momentarily creased in question. Then I watched the realization wash over him, that we were alone in the cocooned silence of his personal items. Reading my intensions perfectly, he quickly covered the doorway with his body.

"Wait." His voice was gentle, another about-face from him.

"Please move," I demanded, managing to keep my voice steady even though I was anything but.

"I just want to apologize."

I stood with my arms crossed and watched a mix of emotions move swiftly across his face. He did look rather uncomfortable. "Was that painful? Did you almost choke on that word?"

The side of his mouth melted into a disarming, boyish grin probably unleashed on scores of defenseless women with absolute success. I almost smiled back. Almost.

"I guess I deserve that."

"So you're apologizing for kissing me?"

"No."

"No?"

"I'm apologizing for insulting you," he said in a soft voice, his eyes fixed somewhere far away. "That was…uncalled for. My anger got the best of me."

"As it often does, seems to be your default setting."

He cocked his head as he contemplated my words. "You slapped me."

"You deserved it."

His lips twitched in silent mirth. "I liked it."

Huh? "You're a strange man." The silence remained for a moment too long. I couldn't hold his bold gaze, the intensity of it heating my neck. The charge between us gathered momentum. I rushed to fill the silence. "Apology accepted. Although I still don't understand why you would be angry with me."

He treated his shoes to a thorough inspection. A heavy sigh escaped him. "When I saw you dancing...with that guy." He shook his head. "It made me mad."

What? Wait...what? "I don't understand."

"Don't you?" he murmured. His amber eyes lifted and met mine, glowing brightly with a soul deep yearning. It was suddenly hard to breathe. I was shocked by how openly his emotions stared back at me, and shivered with an acute awareness that we were at a crossroads and he had made his choice.

He stepped closer while I stood frozen in disbelief. He was more agile than I anticipated because I found myself pinned between the warmth of his chest, and thousands of euros worth of custom Italian suits. My heart raced and heat rushed over my collarbone.

"We can't do this...you...you shouldn't. You have to stay away from me," I pleaded.

His reply was almost inaudible. "I can't." He tugged at the elastic that held my hair in a tight ponytail, and raked through it with his long fingers as it fell loose down my back. My eyes fluttered. I should have stopped him, should have made more of an effort to resist...but it felt soooo good to be touched, my entire body coming alive with the sensation.

His warm lips came crashing down on mine, then gentled when he realized I wasn't resisting. His fingertips cradled my face and traced its contours. I swayed into him, pulling him closer as I gripped his finely tailored shirt for balance. His harsh exhale thrilled me. Slanting his mouth, he deepened a kiss that tasted of peppermint and lust and a desperate frustration that surprised and confused me. I kissed him back, matching his intensity.

Overcome with desire…it was the only way to explain my behavior.

"Wealthy financiers don't fall in love with immigrant house-keepers!!" that soft voice of reason suddenly shouted in my ear with a megaphone. The doubt found purchase. He felt me pull away, and he redoubled his effort.

"Vera, I…let me…please," he muttered between kisses. He knew exactly where to touch me to bend me to his will. With gentle persuasion, he wiped away the remains of rational thought, replacing them with a surfeit of feeling. I let go, followed his lead without further objection, and let him do as he wished.

The kiss was tender, artful, giving me just enough that when he retreated, my tongue chased his. He discovered the sensitive skin of my throat and licked and grazed it with his teeth while his nimble fingers unsnapped my uniform. His thumb stroked the dip near my collarbone and ran along the line where my demi bra and breast met.

He seemed to know every sensitive point on my body, branding the skin where his magic fingers had been. As my hands wandered over his chest, I felt him quiver beneath my touch and heard his breathing grow rough and deep. His eyes squeezed shut. Pain or pleasure? By the look on his face, I wasn't certain.

His fingers hooked over my bra cup and pulled it down, popping my small breast out so smoothly I barely noticed my state of undress. He grazed my painfully sensitive nipple with his hot palm and teased it between his fingers, tugging rhythmically until the tide of pleasure building had me squirming and panting, and made me completely forget that we could've been discovered at any moment. And he was equally lost in this thing that had ignited between us. In a primitive act of ownership, I felt him sink his teeth into my trapezius muscle, his hand skate between my thighs. His other palm caressed my rear end, squeezing, urging me closer. My hips hitched up, my body molding itself to his perfectly. I needed more of him, a lot more. And I wasn't about to stop until I got it.

We both heard it at the same time, the other servants moving around outside. We broke apart, panting loudly. In a panic, I covered myself up and raced out of the closet without sparing him another glance. I caught my reflection in the massive Regency mirror in the hall. My mouth fell open in shock. I didn't recognize the person staring back. My pale skin was flushed. My hair was a teased mess. My full lips were an unseemly red from the bruising kiss. I looked like a teenager that had been thoroughly shagged in the back of a car—except I wasn't. I was a grown woman who didn't know how to resist the proverbial forbidden fruit.

Gathering my hair in a messy ponytail, I rushed back to the safety of my room to regroup. I was taking the stairs by two when I looked up and found Isabelle staring at me with a lethal look in her eyes. Her scrutiny made me uneasy.

"Vera—"

"Can't talk." I walked around her with my head down in an effort to avoid eye contact. If she suspected anything she could cause me a world of trouble, if not outright disaster. The one thing I had going for me was that she had personally witnessed the skirmishes. She was aware of the antipathy Sebastian and I had, or seemingly had, for each other.

I locked my door and fell face first on the bed. For whatever reason this man awakened something in me that I scarcely recognized. Desire. Having to scrape by for so long had worn me down, obliterating any need for intimacy. It was an after-thought. Except it hadn't entirely vanished. It was just buried deeply, waiting for him to come along and play archeologist.

I was way out of my depth. I wasn't about to fool myself about that. You could fill a teaspoon with what I knew about carrying on an affair, and the risk incalculable. One bite of the apple could certainly ruin me. I wondered whether once the physical need was satisfied, sanity would return and life could resume as usual. The little voice of reason insisted there was a flaw somewhere in that theory. This seemed more than a passing curiosity. It already felt like a full-blown addiction. At least, it did to me.

CHAPTER 11

Over the next few days the estate was buzzing with nervous energy. The gardeners were in a state of frenzy over the pruning of the rose garden, Mrs. Arnaud was arguing with the butcher over the size of the lambs she had ordered, and the cleaning wasn't even close to being done.

I was bestowed the privilege of wiping down all one thousand of the crystal glasses and goblets. Needless to say, I never wanted to see another piece of stemware for the rest of my life. And Charlotte, after her fingernails had turned black from polishing the silver, felt equally disgusted about flatware.

I was grateful for Charlotte. She was a good friend to me. I felt unbearably disloyal keeping what had happened with Sebastian a secret from her. But I couldn't risk it and I still couldn't explain it, even to myself.

I hadn't seen him in three days. He had slept at the apartment. Maybe he regretted it, thought twice and found me lacking. How depressing. Now that I'd had a taste of it, I wanted him with an urgency that was shameful. In any case,

I would know soon enough where we stood. There was no avoiding each other once the guests arrived.

The Horn family hosted a house party at the end of spring every year, a tradition that had been handed down from generation to generation. We would all be pressed into service attending the whims of bankers, socialites, and investors. Since some of the guests would require extreme patience—Bentifourt actually said "the patience of a saint"— he admonished us to be on our best behavior. Charlotte, never missing an opportunity to offer her opinion, rolled her eyes theatrically while I pushed down the urge to giggle. We were all in the kitchen, wiping down an infinite amount of china when Mr. Bentifourt walked in.

"Marianne, Mrs. Redman will be joining us as well. Make the arrangements."

Mrs. Arnaud pursed her lips. *"Merde."*

Well, that said it all. I leaned in closer to Charlotte. "Mr. Horn's mother," she whispered, "very high maintenance. And he gets even crazier and nastier whenever she's here—as if that's possible," she added with another comically wide-eyed stare.

"What are you gossiping about, Charlotte?" Isabelle interrupted in a snide tone.

"We weren't gossiping, you meddling bitch."

Mrs. Arnaud eyed her sternly. "Charlotte."

"Mrs. Redman?" I asked.

"The name of her fourth husband, *chérie.*"

———

WAY PAST MIDNIGHT, I was busy playing with the laptop. It had been a long time since I was connected to the world. Cell phones, the Internet, all the technology we take for granted these days, I had learned to do without. I had pawned my computer and cell phone years ago. Besides, there was no one left to stay in touch with.

It had been weeks since I had dropped off the query letters at the hospitals and still hadn't heard anything. A bit demoralizing, even though I knew persistence would eventually pay off. Filling their requirements wasn't the issue. My medical school grades were impeccable, and the University of Milan was well regarded. I spoke fluent English and Italian, had a working knowledge of French. German would have given me an added advantage, but there weren't enough hours in the day. Besides, the Swiss German spoken in some cantons is so harsh and unique that even native speaking Germans have a problem understanding it. There was no question that being a foreigner was a disadvantage, I just wasn't certain how much.

In the meantime, I'd decided to expand my search to include hospitals in Zurich, and was busy researching each one when an iMessage bubble popped up on my screen addressed to VSava@mac.com.

SCHorn@Horn&Cie.com
   "You're up late."

I froze, my fingers suspended over the keyboard, while my emotions took a hairpin turn from confused to appallingly thrilled.

VSava@mac.com
   "How do you know my email address?"
   SCHorn@Horn&Cie.com
   "I set up an account for you when I bought the computer."

I hadn't thought of that. And now that I did, I wasn't certain I liked it.

VSava@mac.com
"I'm writing letters to hospitals in Zurich."
SCHorn@Horn&Cie.com
"Why Zurich?"
VSava@mac.com
"I can't afford to be picky. I'll go anywhere I'm accepted."

The silence was deafening. Then I heard the bling of an incoming message.

SCHorn@Horn&Cie.com
"You can't leave Geneva."

What does that mean? It wasn't even a question.

VSava@mac.com
"Of course, I can. There's nothing keeping me here."

No response. I wanted to end it on a good note so I rushed to fill the silence.

VSava@mac.com
"Why are you up this late anyway?"
SCHorn@Horn&Cie.com
"Couldn't sleep."
VSava@mac.com
"Pain?"
SCHorn@Horn&Cie.com
"No."

I waited patiently, hoping he would explain. God knows why I cared, but I did. Then I heard the bling.

SCHorn@Horn&Cie.com
"Thinking of you."

I felt blindsided, at a loss as to how to respond. Before I could spontaneously combust from nerves, the bling of an incoming message sounded.

SCHorn@Horn&Cie.com
"Good night, Vera."
VSava@mac.com
"Good night, Sebastian."

It was the first time I had called him by his name. Another invisible line crossed. Concentrating on the letters after that was impossible. My mind wandered, my fingers wandered. I hit the Safari button and stared at the cursor until my fingers started moving without consent.

"Sebastian Horn"

Don't do it. Do not do this! This was wrong. Every intelligent cell in my brain screamed for me to stop. I hit the enter button anyway, followed by the images icon.

-Sebastian at a charity event for Sudan, Bono standing next to him.

-Sebastian on a sailboat.

-On the beach in St. Barth with some model.

-In Aspen, with a tall, blond TV reporter.

…and then I saw it.

-Sebastian and India Horn.

I clicked on the picture. They were on a sidewalk, outside a hotel. The caption read: *Four Seasons, New York City.* He was dressed in a sleek black coat, a gray scarf wrapped around his neck. Only his stoic profile was visible as he pulled her along with his fingers laced through hers. Turning towards the cameras, she wore a wide, bright smile on her delicately beautiful face, her pale blue eyes sparkling with joy, her long, chestnut hair flying behind her. Tall and thin, they were a matched set. She looked blissfully happy…and in love.

I was crestfallen. My stomach sank down around my feet.

Somehow, I knew what I would find. The evidence of what had been nagging me for some time. *Why me?* Generally, I find myself attractive. I'm considerably intelligent, although not brilliant. I'm a reasonably good cook. I'm an excellent housekeeper. I'm loyal but sometimes impatient. I'm stubborn like hell but not quick to get mad. In other words, I'm an ordinary woman. I couldn't fathom why he wanted me.

It was common knowledge that this man was considered the catch of the century. Wealthy, successful, intelligent, beautiful–beautiful beyond compare. He could have anyone just by pointing. Why me? I couldn't work it out and the reason was before me in vivid detail. They looked like they belonged together. Birds of a feather, if you will. Two magnificent swans. I'm more of a sturdy mallard than a swan.

I clicked on an article about the accident. It happened in January, on the road to St. Moritz. He was driving a Range Rover. The roads were icy, though it hadn't snowed in weeks. The writer speculated that an oncoming truck caused Sebastian's SUV to career over the side of the mountain. The Rover hadn't dropped far, but it had landed on the passenger side badly, killing her on impact.

Phantom tears stung my eyes. The real thing still refused to fall. When she had been an anonymous, faceless specter, I hadn't given her much thought—anyone willing to work in medicine needs thick skin and a strong stomach. After seeing that picture, though...so much joy, so much hope. I knew what that felt like. I also knew what it was like to have it ripped away. I closed the computer and crawled into bed. This couldn't be anything other than a passing whim on his part, a sexual curiosity. The question was, what was I going to do about it?

———

THE GUESTS BEGAN ARRIVING EARLY on Thursday. I watched a metallic blue Porsche pull up to the entrance from the window of the upstairs den. A man, handsome and well-dressed, stepped out of the car and handed Bentifourt a Louis Vuitton duffel bag. He was extremely fit, evident by the cut of his jacket, young, around thirty, and he was handing a seventy-year-old man his bags to carry. This was going to be a long weekend. A woman stepped out of the passenger side and my eyes widened. Paisley. That would make him, Marcus, the husband; all the details from that scandalous night indelibly branded on my mind. She threw her arm around his shoulders and gave him a quick peck on the lips. They disappeared inside while Bentifourt slowly trailed behind, weighed down by their luggage.

I raced downstairs to see if I could help. Ignoring his objections, I managed to wrestle some of the bags away from him.

"Is Sebastian here?" Paisley asked no one in particular while she nibbled on the end of her sunglasses, looking inconvenienced. Then she turned to me. "Be careful with my things. And put us in the east wing—near Sebastian. We don't want to be near the other guests."

I watched Bentifourt's expression turn weary. Sighing, he drew himself up. "We have the best guest room ready for you, madam."

"It's okay, Paisley, whatever. Who cares where they put us," Marcus interrupted in a placating tone.

The door to the office banged open and Sebastian walked out. He looked furious. His eyes skipped from me, to Bentifourt, then to the bags we were holding while Paisley gave him a cat-that-ate-the-cream smile.

"What the fuck, Paisley," he growled, his narrowed eyes full of unmitigated disgust.

Marcus stepped forward. "Sebastian, it's okay. We'll take whatever room, really, it's not a problem."

"You're here ten minutes and you're already turning my household upside down. Bentifourt show them to the guest wing." And with that, he walked back into his office and slammed the door shut. For a horrified moment, I thought it would fall off its hinges.

She whined the whole way up to her room.

By six all the guests had arrived except for one, Mrs. Redman. I would be lying if I said I wasn't incredibly curious about her. Charlotte was right. He was bent out of shape worse than ever. He slammed every door he opened and closed, shouted for Bentifourt more times than I could count, and wouldn't come out of his office to greet his thirty guests. Each of who gave Bentifourt a weird curious expression when they inquired about him and were told he was not seeing guest until dinner.

A half an hour later a bright red Rolls-Royce Phantom pulled up. Charlotte and I followed Mr. Bentifourt out to help him unload the car. The driver opened the passenger door and a long, slim leg poked out. She stood up and scanned the open doorway, her well-exercised body wrapped in a clingy, pale blue dress. She had golden blond hair cut in a chin-length bob parted to the side and her makeup was flawless. She didn't appear to be a day over forty-five, even though she was more than ten years older.

"Where's my son?" Her voice was girlish and her vowels elongated, an American drawl I had only ever heard on TV.

"He's in his office, madam," Mr. Bentifourt answered.

On cue, Sebastian walked out of the open doorway and stopped at the top of the landing. He was freshly shaven and dressed in a tailored white shirt open at the neck, no tie—his stark masculine beauty needed no adorning. The fit of his shirt made his shoulders look exceedingly broad and his waist narrow. The slim gray slacks hugged his hips and emphasized his long legs. He leaned on his cane, his other hand tucked casually in the pocket of his pants. The relaxed pose belied an air of unease about him that was plain to me. Eyes shuttered, the bored aristocrat was back.

"Diana."

"Sugar, the least you could do is give your momma a hug." She walked up to him and threw her willowy arms around his neck. With her Louboutin platforms on, they were almost eye to eye. He didn't embrace her, just removed his hand from his pocket and patted her back in a wooden, stilted gesture, the awkwardness palpable.

On close inspection, one could tell they were related. The physical similarities were certainly there. The shape of the eyes (although hers were green), the arch of the brow, the soft dip in the chin. But where her beauty was fragile and cold, his was robust and sensual.

He looked over her shoulder and caught me watching them. The bored expression lifted for a moment, his eyes examining me thoroughly. Then he scowled. "Diana, you're only here for four days. Why are they unloading five suitcases?"

Noticing my struggle to lift the two bags up the stairs, he grabbed one from me as if it weighed nothing. I couldn't fight him for it; I didn't want to make a scene. Charlotte and Bentifourt were right behind me and would have certainly noticed.

"A woman should always be prepared."

"For what, exactly?" The bitterness in his tone had no effect on her.

"To always look good, sugar," she replied with a playful smile.

Again, I tried taking the bag from him as we followed her inside, and still, he ignored me.

"Is there Fiji in my room? You know I can't drink Evian, too soft, makes me go to the bathroom. And what about the lavender sachets? I need those. They relax me. I haven't been sleeping well lately. Make sure everyone knows not to knock on my door before ten."

Staring at her with a fathomless expression, he held up the bag. "Here, Mother." The word mother laced with mockery. She looked at him as if he had offered her a dead rodent.

"Don't be silly, Scout. That's what the help is for."

Mrs. Redman turned on her heels and headed up the marble staircase. Bentifourt grabbed the bag and the three of us, following closely behind, marched up the stairs like a bunch of pack mules. I glanced briefly over my shoulder and found Sebastian standing in the foyer, staring after her with a distant look in his eyes. Something about that look made me sad. *Scout.* The name Paisley had called him that night in the library, the name that set him off in a rage—the significance of which I couldn't even begin to understand.

CHAPTER 12

C ocktails started at six in the sitting room. One of the largest rooms in the manor, it was formally decorated with yards of Italian silks, hand painted De Gournay wallpaper, and a platoon of settees and love seats. Charlotte, Annabel, and I passed around fluted glasses of Crystal Rosé and tiny canapés while the guests chatted amicably. There was a comfortable vibe in the room. Probably because they all seemed to know one another. They, no doubt, traveled in the same social circles. Sebastian hadn't made an appearance yet. The only small awkwardness. I noticed Mr. Bentifourt repeatedly check his wristwatch and exchange commiserating glances with Mrs. Arnaud.

Balancing a loaded tray of crystal flutes, I squeezed between the bodies of young financial warriors dressed in ultra-expensive suits. They all had an air of ruthlessness about them, a barely contained aggressive energy as they jockeyed for position around the attractive, super-skinny women in the room. Actually, I had never seen so many beautiful women assembled under one roof. And yet the men seemed more interested in competing with each other than with the prize. I noticed Paisley overtly flirting with two of them and wondered where her husband was.

As I passed by a sharply dressed elderly man, he invited me over with a wink and a mischievous glint in his powder blue eyes. Although he must have been around eighty, he vibrated with the snappy energy of a much younger man. "I know you have strict orders not to serve hard liquor. Bentifourt gets tetchy about such things. However, do you think you could do an old man a favor? Could I tempt you to be bad?" I couldn't resist the silky British accent or the devilish twinkle in his eyes.

"What may I get you, sir?" I asked, smiling.

"What a darling girl you are, beautiful too. If I were five years younger...Macallan—55, if he has it."

"I'll see what I can do."

When I returned to the sitting room with a crystal glass of the extremely rare vintage balancing on my tray, Mr. Bentifourt grabbed my arm. "Who's that for?"

"The man in the navy, double breasted, sir."

His grip on my arm relaxed. "Charles Hightower, yes, alright. But no one else."

"Pardon, sir, but who is he?"

"The late Mr. Horn's best friend. Also an important client of the bank."

I located Mr. Hightower near the fireplace, holding court with a couple of young bank employees, and handed him the glass. "Beautiful and resourceful. I like that in a woman."

After managing to unload another tray of champagne glasses at record speed, I went to stand next to Charlotte against a wall on the other side of the room. "There's that bitch sister-in-law," she said, tipping her blond head towards Paisley.

Startled, I asked, "Did you just say sister-in-law?"

"Yes, her husband is Mr. Horn's stepbrother."

Good God, he was sleeping with his sister-in-law! This would require excessive analysis at a later date.

"She makes my life a living hell every time she's here," Charlotte whispered. "Last time she had me pick the chocolate chips out of the mint chocolate chip ice cream—no exaggeration." It was almost impossible for Charlotte not to exaggerate.

These people inhabited a world so far removed from mine. Sleeping with your sister-in-law was way outside the norm of decent behavior in my book, the stuff soap operas were made of. I glanced at Paisley and found her in an animated discussion with Mrs. Redman. They were obviously well known to each other. And so alike in their dress, their appearance, their mannerisms they could have been mother and daughter.

Looking bored and restless, her husband, Marcus, sat opposite them in a spindly Louis XVII chair with his ankle resting on the opposite knee and his thumb tapping the armrest. He scanned the room impatiently until his gaze settled on me. His chocolate brown eyes traveled from my face to my feet in a subtly appraising manner I didn't care for. Unfortunately, when he motioned me over, it was too late to pretend I hadn't seen him. "May I get you something?"

His index finger rested on his full lips as he deliberated. "Are you British?"

"No."

He motioned for me to come closer. I braced with apprehension for a moment, before bending down.

"Did anybody ever tell you that you look a lot like Natalie—"

"No, never," I interrupted.

And of course, His Royal Highness chose that exact moment to make an appearance. When he stepped into the room, a collective silence fell over the crowd and all eyes turned to him. He was magnificent in a lean navy suit. His soft white shirt was cleaved by a deep purple tie of thick silk and a double Windsor that few men could wear without looking ridiculous.

Heir to the throne.

Unfortunately, his gaze was elsewhere, fixed with laser precision on me. I immediately knew there was going to be trouble when Sebastian's eyes narrowed. Not that he had any right. Regardless, by now I knew how irrational he could get when that look came over him. And there I was, bent over and flushed, with Marcus' dark head dipped and his eyes trained on my breasts.

Snapping straight, I hurried away. Sebastian's scrutiny followed me until Charles Hightower approached him, his face softening as they exchanged friendly pats on the back. There was genuine affection between the two and for whatever absurd reason it pleased me. He always held everyone at a distance.

Except when he's kissing you, the devil in me spoke.

For a man that was so often closed off and alone, he was a born leader. People naturally gravitated towards him. He moved gracefully about the room, making friendly conversation and shaking hands with his traders and clients. My eyes were not the only ones that followed him everywhere. Aside from Paisley, the wives and girlfriends of a number of the guests stared with undisguised hunger, some brazen enough to openly flirt under the noses of their dates. One in particular, dressed in an elegant white sheath dress, devoured him with her pretty blue eyes and stalked him around the room.

When he finished making his rounds, his gaze connected

with mine. I walked to him balancing a tray of champagne flutes. He took one, though didn't drink it. The silence expanded between us, fraught with tension. My composure began to wane under the power of his intense stare. I looked around for a lifeline, any excuse to walk away. My rescue came in the form of the woman in white. Over his shoulder, I spotted her heading in our direction and turned to leave.

"Wait." Though barely a whisper, the singular word carried a force that stopped me in my tracks. Conscious that there were people watching him closely, I faced him and tried to remain as inscrutable as possible. "What did Marcus say to you that made you blush?" The pretense of indifference in his blank stare did nothing to mask the anger in his voice. I watched *Miss Blue Eyes* push past some of the traders that tried, without success, to catch her attention.

"I can't remember. Can I get you anything else?"

He sighed deeply, annoyed to be disobeyed. "Since you won't answer that question, I have another." His face gave nothing away. "Did you enjoy watching me fuck Paisley that night in the library?"

There was a buzzing sound in my ear, followed immediately by the heavy hammering of my heart. My mind locked up. I drew a perfect blank, trying to process what he had said to me. When it rebooted, a scalding heat rose swiftly from my toes to my hairline.

"There you are," the blue-eyed woman cooed. "I've been looking all over for you." She placed her hand on his bicep and his jaw tightened imperceptibly.

"Caroline, it's good to see you. How was New York?"

"Sugar, didn't you break the one hundred freestyle record as a freshman at UT?"

Both their heads turned in the direction of Mrs. Redman's voice.

"The butterfly," Sebastian casually replied.

Paisley, eyes wide in triumph, turned to Mrs. Redman and shrieked, "I told you, Diana." But Mrs. Redman's attention was elsewhere, trained on me with a look on her face I had seen before on her son.

Humiliation made me cower and shrink. I don't know how I got my legs to work. All I know is that I felt myself automatically retreating backwards, away from her unwanted interest. Sebastian didn't spare me another glance. He continued to speak amicably with the woman in the white dress as if nothing of great consequence had just occurred. Left alone to struggle with my disturbed thoughts, I backed out of the scene, made myself small, and disappeared. Any warmth I felt for him died a quick and sudden death at that moment. My healthy pride wilted for the first time in years. And a small bud of resentment blossomed in my heart.

———

Dinner was served at 8:30 in the dining room. Hanging from a ceiling painted with clouds and flying cherubs, the massive chandelier was dimly lit, casting a romantic glow about the room. Tall, silver candlesticks dotted the hand-embroidered white linen tablecloth. Low arrangements of spring flowers, including bright pink peonies and white hydrangeas from the garden, separated a dining table as long as a runway, and glints of candlelight bounced off the angles of fine cut crystal glasses.

The room was filled with the sound of enjoyable company, cheerful laughter, the low buzz of conversation. The staff stood to the side as each delectable course was served and removed for the next one. The conversation flowed as easily as the expensive vintage. Sebastian hadn't said much. He sat at the head of the table, a sullen king slouching in his chair with his head resting on the triangle of his index finger and thumb. I caught him staring at me more than once. His gaze, however, darted back to the tablecloth or the glass he was holding when our eyes met. I was seething with anger. What kind of man took pleasure in mocking and harassing an employee? A housekeeper so far beneath his station she wasn't worth noticing.

The woman called Caroline was sitting to his right, practically bending backwards to get his attention. She looked like his type: beautiful, wealthy, elegant. You could sense her infatuation from across the room. There was a desperate quality to her wide-eyed stare that made me feel sorry for her. *He isn't worth it, trust me*, I wanted to scream. Every time she spoke to him, she touched him: his forearm, his hand, his shoulder. I watched him stiffen, flinch subtly, and I was glad for his discomfort.

"Caroline, I almost didn't recognize you. You've lost so much weight since I saw you at the Fashion Council Awards in New York." Paisley's irritating voice, with her pronounced disingenuous sweetness, pierced my anger for a brief moment. Seated a few chairs down from them, her eyes were fixed on Caroline and Sebastian all throughout dinner. Lying in wait for the right moment to attack apparently.

Caroline blushed and blinked before finding her voice. "Thanks, Paisley, but I haven't lost any weight."

"Really? Then it must be that beautiful Carolina Herrera gown you're wearing. I tried it on at Bergdorf Goodman. You need wide hips to wear it well. Didn't fit me at all." Conversations around the table suddenly hushed, everyone's attention turning towards the head of the table.

"I ran into Robert at *Daniel*. His new fiancée looks fifteen."

Caroline smiled sweetly and replied, "We're divorced. He's free to marry a goat if he wants."

Sebastian wasn't nearly as gracious. He impaled Paisley with a vicious scowl that was nasty enough to shut her up. I found that distastefully hypocritical seeing that he had essentially done the same thing to me. My esteem of him sank even lower. As I cleared his dishes away, he looked up at me with a repentant expression, a silent plea in his eyes. I turned away abruptly. Hell would freeze over before I would let him see how affected I was by his words.

I was returning from the kitchen, having dropped off a tray of crystal glasses that needed to be rinsed, when I saw him striding purposefully towards me. In no mood to deal with him, I turned on my heels and fled in the opposite direction. I thought I'd safely gotten away when I felt his strong grip on my upper arm.

"I need to speak to you," he said quietly.

I turned around and tilted my chin up, resentment written all over my face. "Let go of me, right now."

"There's something I gotta say first." His pained expression had zero effect on me. I wouldn't have thrown him a lifejacket if he were drowning.

"Sebastian," a woman's sweet voice chimed in.

I peeked around his arm and realized it was her again, Caroline. The woman was relentless. She stood down the hall craning her slender neck to see whom he was talking to, but I was well hidden by his powerful frame.

"You promised to show me the painting—the Goya?"

His lips flattened into a grim line. "Give me a minute, Caroline. I'll meet you in the dining room." He looked harassed and frustrated. *Good.* I hoped she didn't leave his side all night.

"Yes, Sebastian, go show your girlfriend your *Goya*," I mocked, ripping my arm out of his grasp.

"She's not my girlfriend." His jaw pulsed, his voice tight. "We need to talk later."

"I'm not interested in anything you have to say," I replied, head shaking.

Eyes narrowed, he raked his fingers through his hair. "I'll find you." And before I could argue again, he turned and walked away.

By midnight most of the courses had been served. Mrs. Arnaud dismissed the first shift, including Charlotte and me. The tension wrapped around my head like a medieval torture device had produced a blinding migraine. I walked out to the garden in desperate need of some fresh air. The chill of night chased a shiver up my back and a sharp pain pierced my lungs. Whether it was the cold air or despair, I couldn't say. I felt alone, disconnected from the world, even myself. My force of will had deserted me. For the first time in six years I didn't know what I was doing anymore.

I marched towards the gazebo covered in climbing roses. Inside, I sat with my head in my hands. The constant attacks on my character...the unwelcome desire he ignited in me. It was too much for me to process at once. I was on a roller coaster ride in hell, my emotions rising and falling with every meaningful moment shared between us. It was tearing me apart and worse yet, making me doubt myself. Tears began to pour out of me. The first tears in six long years. I couldn't stop them any more than I could understand why they were starting to fall now, of all times.

The sound of approaching footsteps suddenly intruded.

"Go the hell away." My voice cracked. I never cried in front of other people, but my composure had been annihilated. I looked up, my face ruddy and leaky, and found his concealed in shadow. He moved swiftly, lifted and wrapped me in the heat of his body, his powerful arms fastening us together. It was impossible to budge him, which only made me cry harder.

"I hate you! Let me go!"

"I'm sorry, shhh…please don't cry. I'm an asshole. A real shit heel. Forgive me, Vera. Please, forgive me."

I was trapped, forced to accept his comfort. He kissed my neck, licked the trail of salty tears. Shifting to my face, he lightly brushed his lips on my closed eyelids, on the pulsing vein at my temple. In my weakened state, fighting the magnetic current between us was impossible.

He sat down and arranged me on his lap. His hands cradled my face possessively. The light from the garden sconces revealed his regret. His eyes, wide and solemn, gazed back at me so reverently that I almost forgot he was the reason I was so wretched. I couldn't look at him. I was mixed up, hurt, and on some shameful level relieved that he had found me.

He kissed me. One, two, three brushes of his soft lips, coaxing me to accept his apology. I resisted him for all of a minute before I gave in. However, the part of my mind that could still reason insisted I would hate myself later for it, so I turned my face away.

"I want to know why?"

"Why what?" he asked softly.

"Why does it please you to humiliate me? What have I ever done to you to deserve such wrath? I don't understand you, and quite frankly, I'm tired of trying." I stared at my hands, my fingers laced together on my lap.

There was a long pause before he spoke. "It's not wrath…

it's...you didn't do anything. I just..." He blew out a deep breath and raked his fingers impatiently through his hair. "You make me feel things I don't want to feel. But I promise you that I won't take it out on you anymore. I don't want to hurt you, I want..." He looked into my eyes with such longing that it made my throat close up. "I definitely don't want to hurt you," he murmured, his voice soaked in remorse.

I had recognized the intense desire simmering under his schooled features before. Even when the armor of self-control he always wore put an ocean between us, kept me safely at a distance. In the silent shelter of the gazebo, however, for a fraction of a moment, he let his guard down, revealing more than lust, revealing something profound and important and way more than I was equipped to deal with.

He kissed my swollen lips again, ran his thumb along my cheeks and wiped the dampness away. The kiss transformed the moment I wrapped my arms around his neck. Less comforting, more urgent with need. When I raked my nails through the hair at his nape and tugged it, he broke the kiss and closed his eyes. A small smile played at the corners of his sensual mouth. I had never seen him look so unguarded. It was utterly fascinating.

He hauled me astride his lap, my skirt bunching up. I could feel him as if our clothes didn't exist. He was hard as stone. Every time he rubbed against me, sharp sparks of pleasure ignited, burst forth. His long fingers stroked the rungs of my spine and traveled lower to my bottom. Cupping my cheeks, he pressed me closer until there was no air left between us. Pushed beyond my limits, I could no longer fight my desire. Frantically, I tugged the back of his shirt out of his pants in search for the hot skin of his well-muscled back. He gasped at my touch and squeezed my butt cheeks in return, encouraging me to meet his hard, pulsing thrusts while he devoured my mouth.

There was certainty in the way he touched me. Like he knew what I needed, knew things about me he shouldn't. It was so easy to relinquish all control to him, to place myself in his skilled and capable hands without reserve.

On a last powerful thrust, he pushed me over the edge of a fierce orgasm. I gripped his hair even tighter as my body clenched and released in shockwaves that seemed to go on forever. A warm and heavy bliss spread all the way to my toes and fingertips, a haze of euphoria making me drowsy.

"But you..." I gasped.

"Not now. It's okay," he said, exhaling harshly.

He placed tender kisses on my nose, my eyebrow, my cheekbone. One after the other. As if he couldn't stop himself. I bumped against his still painfully hard erection and sucked in a breath.

"You go inside first. I need some time," he mumbled. He helped steady me as I got off his lap on shaky legs. Still, I didn't move. I didn't want to leave him, feeling vulnerable and unsure about how things remained between us. It seemed like every time we reached some kind of under-standing, some semblance of peace, it would quickly blow up in my face. The emotional push and pull was exhausting. I worried my bottom lip, wondering if I should say something, when his eyes, catching every detail about me, flared.

"Go now, or I won't let you go all night," he added, punc-tuating the order with a quick hard kiss.

All night? I ran out of there as quickly as I could on weak, uncooperative limbs.

I spent the rest of the evening analyzing everything that had transpired until I was going in circles. I could still feel his body imprinted on mine; desire coursed through me just thinking about it.

I made him feel things he didn't want to feel. I guess I couldn't fault him for being honest. I could understand how lusting after a housekeeper would be an inconvenience. I certainly didn't want to be attracted to him either, but I had resigned myself to the fact that there wasn't a damn thing I could do about it.

Whatever was happening between us would be exorcised with sex. All I could hope for was to survive the aftermath. After all, I was a prisoner of my past. I couldn't risk him finding out what had caused me to leave Albania, and he had the world at his feet. It was only a matter of time before he would tire of me. I would take the pleasure and nothing more. I accepted that and found solace in the fact that the rules of engagement were clear. I wasn't a young girl who believed in fairytales. No prince was riding to my rescue. I had always rescued myself—and I wouldn't want it any other way.

CHAPTER 13

"Sorry, sorry. didn't sleep well," I mumbled. Charlotte kept studying me with a quizzical expression. I yawned for the ten thousandth time as we loaded the serving cart with drinks.

"Were you out at a rave all night?" The side of her rosebud mouth kicked up in a half-grin. I returned a blank stare, my mind not having caught up with the question yet. "Joking. Jesus, you are out of it today. We need to take these to the south lawn. They're shooting this morning."

"Shooting? Animals?" I asked, horrified.

"No, clay pigeons."

"Thank God."

We exited out onto the expansive blue slate patio that wrapped around the back of the manor. A carpet of green rolled out for acres, stretching all the way to the shores of Lake Geneva, the grass sheared with such precision it may have been cut with a pair of scissors. Vibrant beds of irises lined the path that led to an elegant navy and white striped tent erected a week prior. The invigorating effect of the crisp, clean air woke me up. Also, the fact that I couldn't help being a little nervous. I wanted to see him, to see if the fragile alliance we had formed the night before remained. Or if we were destined to continue this seemingly endless cycle of three steps forward, two steps back.

Charlotte and I wheeled the loaded cart down the slope to where a group of the guests had assembled. Mr. Bentifourt stood next to the bar overseeing the setting of the table for lunch with his knobby hands clasped behind him. Nearby, a number of the groundskeepers worked with a metal contraption, loading terracotta disks inside of it while the other half worked with some spooky looking shotguns, inspecting each one closely before placing them side by side on a table.

Alcohol and guns. What a pleasant mix.

A group of the women stood under the tent hiding from the unusually strong morning sun while the men checked out the guns. A shrill of forced laughter drew my attention. Paisley stared into the face of a handsome but cold looking bank executive, laughing at whatever quip he had whispered in her ear. Marcus watched his wife with brooding interest. The vein in between his brows pulsed. I realized then that whatever Paisley had told Sebastian that night in the library —about Marcus not caring—was very much a lie.

Mr. Bentifourt spotted us as we approached and came to help steady the overloaded cart. After unloading it, we immediately started serving cocktails. The three of us, working quickly, could barely keep up with the demand.

"Vera, if you don't mind fetching more ice?"

"Certainly, sir."

I cut across the blue slate patio and entered through the French doors. A familiar raspy voice, talking quietly, caught my attention.

"My guests are waiting, Diana. What is it?" he snapped.

"I see the way you look at her…What do you think you're doing?"

I stepped behind the voluminous silk drapes, out of sight, my curiosity getting the better of me.

"What the hell are you talking about?"

"That girl with the big brown eyes. The one that looks at you like she just seen Jesus…the housekeeper. You can't save them all, sugar. This one needs more than a wing mended, or a bone set."

I felt my chest compress painfully. Me. She was talking about me. My pride roared in outrage. *Look at him as if I had seen Jesus?!* I needed to stop spying on him. Hadn't I learned that painful lesson yet? This was beyond humiliating. And what the hell did she mean by saving this one?!

"You, of all people…" he said in a sinister drawl, "giving me advice…I'm 'bout to laugh my ass off. I'm the one that found you in the barn with that groom's head between your thighs. What was he…fifteen? Maybe sixteen years old?" His voice was low, controlled, but the underlying rage was as conspicuous as an albino elephant.

"Oh, Scout, that was almost twenty years ago. When are you going to forgive me?"

"When you change," he sneered. He was ruthless when angered. His angry footsteps faded away.

I could hear Diana Redman breathing harshly as she stepped through the French doors and exited. Peeking out from behind the heavy silk drapes, I made sure the coast was clear before I ran to the kitchen. By the time I reached the lawn party with the ice, Bentifourt was scowling in open displeasure.

"I'm sorry. I'm not feeling a hundred percent today."

"Maybe you're catching a cold?" *Thank you, Charlotte,*

always looking out for a friend. She winked as Bentifourt inspected me closer.

"You do have some dark circles under your eyes." Bentifourt leaned forward, squinting. "Can't have you serving guests if you're sick."

"It's nothing, I'll rest later today before we serve dinner."

Diana Redman walked towards the tent wearing black Jackie O glasses. Her face was ruddy, puffy, evidence of tears present. As soon as she sat down next to Paisley, Charlotte offered her a bellini. Taking the glass, she tipped it back and drained it in one swallow.

Sebastian stood with the men inspecting the guns. This was obviously not new to him; he looked at ease and in control. He picked up a shotgun that had one barrel over another and loaded the weapon expertly. Then he stared down the muzzle and lifted it skyward. "Pull," he yelled.

The groundskeeper activated the machine and flying disks shot out at different angles and speeds. In seconds he had fired the weapon twice, the sound loud and violent, and struck both dead center. The shattered remains of the clay pigeons flew in every direction. He repeated the exercise two more times. The guests clapped a tad too enthusiastically if you asked me. There was a subtle sense of awe when they spoke to him, and about him. The formality in their voices was even more telling. It wasn't just respect, there was a hint of fear there too.

Paisley screamed and clapped her hands disproportionately louder than everyone else. If she was trying to get his attention, she succeeded. Sebastian narrowed his eyes at her and stalked over to Bentifourt.

"How many drinks has she had?"

"Three already, and no food."

Sebastian turned and caught my gaze, his eyes glowing

with warmth and anticipation. I knew what he was asking. I smiled briefly, afraid that someone might notice, and watched a subtle tenseness leave his shoulders.

"Cut her off," he murmured in a low voice to Mr. Bentifourt. Mr. Bentifourt responded with a brief nod, and Sebastian returned to the group of men taking turns shooting, none being as proficient as he was.

When Charles Hightower stepped forward for his turn, Sebastian was by his side immediately, instructing him with whispered words of encouragement. Mr. Hightower missed the first couple of shots. Although, undeterred, he ended by striking the last four. Smiling proudly, he pated Sebastian's cheek, and Sebastian reciprocated with a warm smile. It was sweet to watch the open display of affection between the two men. Clearly, very little of it existed between him and his mother. The pain and resentment between those two ran deep.

After the shooting, everyone sat for a casual lunch. Paisley kept ordering more Bloody Marys, and Mr. Bentifourt kept refilling her glass, pretending there was alcohol in them. Caroline took the seat on Sebastian's right again and resumed her heavy petting. I almost felt sorry for him. He looked impassive to everyone at the table, but I knew better. To me, he looked like a trapped animal.

"I'm told there are plenty of quail to hunt around here," said one of the associates to no one in particular.

"My stepbrother has a firm no-kill policy on his estate, John," Marcus informed him, derision underscoring his words.

"Really?"

Sebastian's keen power of observation never seemed to fail. He looked sharply in their direction.

"Yes, Sebastian's famous for finding small injured animals

and nursing them back to health when he was a kid. His nickname was Boy Scout. By the time my father married his mother, he had moved on to saving larger animals, of course." Marcus buried a sly smirk in his champagne glass.

Sebastian's jaw pulsed with barely contained anger. "Marcus." The hard-edged reprimand drew everyone's attention. At first Marcus stared back defiantly, the tension escalating, but he inevitably submitted to the threatening glare of the larger predator at the table. Sebastian's cautious gaze darted quickly in my direction, measuring how much of the conversation I had heard.

Nursing small animals? I tried to picture Sebastian as a sweet, little boy with floppy, sandy hair, tried to reconcile that with the man I knew now. The one heavily armored, locked behind a fortress. I could see only glimpses of that little boy. He hid him well, protecting what was left of him. I wondered what Marcus meant by larger animals and earmarked it for later analysis.

"I never did see the sport in killing a tiny bird that flies badly." Sebastian's eyes were hooded, shuttered. The bored aristocrat had come to lunch.

"I didn't mean to imply. I mean...I don't really hunt. I was just told..." He reduced the poor man into a stammering idiot with one phrase.

Diana Redman found her voice after two bellinis and a half a bottle of Haute Brion. "Sugar, you should show everyone your pets later."

"Are you still keeping red tails?" Mr. Hightower asked. He swirled the Bordeaux in his glass before lifting it to his lips.

Sebastian turned his attention to Charles Hightower and his gaze shifted from detached to warm in an instant. It was amazing to watch. I wondered if anyone else noticed, although it didn't seem so.

"Just the ones I rescued," Sebastian answered.

"Fearsome creature, the red-tailed hawk, also hardier than the peregrine."

"Yes, as you know my father preferred peregrines."

"Your father resisted progress in many ways. I have no doubt that you'll do what it takes."

Sebastian didn't answer immediately. "My father didn't understand the pace that the financial world operates in today. But I'll give him credit, we may not have grown exponentially, like some other institutions, but we also aren't stuck holding a large share of Greek debt. And we never bought into the derivatives scam. Our reputation worldwide is intact...I owe that all to him."

Charles Hightower raised his goblet of wine in the air and tapped the glass gently. "A toast to Heinrich. May he rest in peace knowing he left the Horn family legacy in skilled and capable hands. To another hundred years of prosperity."

———

ONCE THE TABLE was cleared and all the contents of the bar were safely put away, Mrs. Arnaud insisted I rest. As I made my way to my bedroom, I heard uneven footsteps echoing down the hallway and noticed Sebastian up ahead, his gate stiff. Something didn't feel right. Without a second thought, I followed him into the library, watching him grimace with every step he took. He entered and immediately turned left, walking past the rows and rows of bookcases to where the cobalt blue couches sat under a wall of windows. It had started raining shortly after lunch and was still coming down gently, tapping on the glass, filling the room with a soft rhythmical lullaby. I shouldn't have followed him, but I knew he was in pain and too proud to let anybody see him in that condition. I just wanted to reassure myself that he didn't need any help.

By the time I reached him, he was spread out with his injured leg resting straight on the couch and the other foot flat on the floor, his arm covering his face. I bit my lip, uncertain if I should disturb him. "Sebastian?" His arm came down. The spark of surprise in his eyes turned thoughtful. "Can I get you anything? Your pills?"

He shook his head. "Come here," he said. When I hesitated, he held out an outstretched hand. "Please."

My steps were tentative as I walked over and sat on the ottoman in front of the sofa. He took my hand, gently stroked my knuckles with his thumb, and placed it on his injured knee. I looked up into wide, pleading eyes and a thousand unspoken words crossed between us. He couldn't bring himself to ask, yet trusted me to understand what he needed—the moment exponentially more intimate than if he had kissed me.

Shifting, I sat between his legs, closer to the injured one, and began massaging it. His lashes fluttered before his eyes closed. I felt his hand come to rest possessively on my knee, completing a circle, anchoring himself to me.

"The recoil of the gun," he said softly. "You have to stand with your knee bent and absorb the force."

"And naturally you had to take more turns than everyone else." His lips twitched in amusement. A fiercely competitive man, there was no way he would have let anyone outdo him, even at a considerable cost to his health. The tension drained from his muscles as he relaxed into my touch. I watched his expression transform from tense to blissfully serene and felt a surge of triumph, knowing I could do that for him. I liked that he needed something from me. No need to examine that too closely. "When did you last take your pain medication?"

Eyes still closed, he sighed deeply. "An hour ago."

"Oh."

Brandy eyes met brown and held. "This is better than the oxy."

"You're building tolerance to this dose too quickly."

"I know." The hand resting on my knee started to travel higher up the inside of my thigh. I covered his hand to stop him, and the corners of his mouth crept up in a sexy smile.

"I see you're feeling better," I scolded, fighting a grin of my own. "I should be going. They're probably wondering where I am."

He grasped my wrist to stop me. "Not yet." The boyish whine in his voice was impossible to resist.

Then the door opened and voices entered the room. My anxious gaze snapped to his relaxed one. Panic stricken that we would be discovered, I tugged on my wrist but he wouldn't let go. The shameless seducer knew I was in no position to make a fuss. Pulling me closer, he pressed his index finger to his lips and shook his head. He wrapped one arm around my waist when I came crashing down on top of his chest, shoved the other hand in my hair, destroying the neat arrangement of my bun. A huge white grin spread across his face as I struggled in vain to push up, no match for his strength.

I tried to evade his marauding hand but it was futile. It fell in disorderly clumps over my shoulders. His laughing gaze roamed over my features, absorbing every detail. When it landed on my lips, his expression turned serious. His eyes grew heavy-lidded and his soft lips reached for mine. He nibbled my bottom lip, licked the seam until I opened for him. Every part of me melted under his tender ministration. And as he deepened the kiss, I suddenly didn't care who walked in on us.

"The DOJ is being very thorough."

Marcus. I pulled back and glanced at Sebastian. He continued stroking my spine with unhurried care while his eyes narrowed and his attention pivoted to the conversation.

"We have nothing to worry about. Sebastian has everything under control," Mr. Hightower responded. That silky accent was unmistakable.

"Yeah, but do you have control of Sebastian?"

"Relax, Marcus. Take the poker out of your arse."

"I'm not the only one that's nervous, Charles."

"Let me handle them. You, on the other hand, need to pay more attention to your wife. I saw her stumbling around the living room a short while ago."

"Fuck!" Determined footsteps walked out of the room, followed a minute later by slower, softer ones.

"What was that about?" I whispered. Sebastian's gaze was far away, thoughtful.

"I'm not sure but I intend to find out."

"What's a DOJ?"

His eyes returned to me bright and smiling. "Curious little thing, aren't you," he murmured. "U.S. Department of Justice. They're going after tax evaders."

"Oh," was all I could think to say because my mind was quickly going numb, lulled into a relaxed, sensual fog by the rise and fall of his chest. The heat emanating from him soaked into my body and turned me boneless. The comfortable silence between us slowly morphed into something else altogether. His eyes, sulky, smoldering with naked lust, drifted to my kiss-bruised lips again.

"I want you." It was one of the sexiest things I had ever heard, full of unabashed confidence and naked honesty. I drew back, feeling trapped and unsure. Although my body didn't share that uncertainty—it knew exactly what it wanted. The feel of his rock-hard shaft pressed against me was enough to send every ounce of blood in my body to that area. He wouldn't let me squirm away, held me steady in his warm embrace, and nudged me with his erection while he stroked my bottom in lazy caresses that had me aching for him.

"Come to my room tonight. Be there by eleven."

"I can't," I said, shocked back to reality from the pheromone fog I was drifting in.

"You will," he said, burying his knowing smile on the side of my neck and kissing me softly, "because you want me as much as I want you."

When I pushed off, he let go and tucked his hands neatly behind his head. I stared at his sexy, confident smile and attempted to herd my scattered thoughts. It rankled that all my resolve and good judgment crumbled in the face of his charisma. "We can't," I said in a shaky voice. He didn't say another word. That smug smile on his face said more than enough. So I did the only thing I could, I bolted out of the library, putting as much distance between me and temptation as possible.

CHAPTER 14

I lay in bed watching the minutes tick by on that blasted clock and debating whether I should get up and chuck it out the window. Unspent desire was making me restless and irritable. I slipped out of my underwear and kicked off the covers in a fruitless effort to cool off the heat beneath my skin. I tried everything to find a comfortable position, but every time I closed my eyes I saw him. That sexy smile playing on those soft lips. The sensual flare in his eyes.

I turned on my stomach and my hand sank down below my belly, over the soft worn linen pressed up against my enflamed skin, lower still to the place that felt empty and achy. Sensual images tormented me. Those eyes, warm and fiery one moment and fathomless the next, tempting me to join him in a dangerous game. The gilded silky skin of his muscular chest. Those pants hanging precariously, baring his hipbones.

Because you want me as much as I want you.

And I did, I just didn't like being an open book. That made me cringe. He already had scores of women panting after him, to count myself among them was aggravating, and that he knew it was worse.

Jumping out of bed, I pushed the curtains aside and opened the window. At the edge of the garden, a dark figure disappeared into the copse of trees, a familiar hitch in his step. I knew then what I had to do, what I couldn't resist doing if my life depended on it. I raced out of my room without a second thought.

I followed him across the north forest, straining to keep up with him. Considering his injury, he was surprisingly quick on foot. When we reached the lake, I hid behind an old oak tree and stared with eyes wide in wonder as he ripped his t-shirt off and pushed down his pants, exposing the muscular globes of his delicious backside. Mentally, I traced the dents on the side of the muscle. *The good Lord spared no expense making this man.* I gripped the bark tightly, not even feeling it dig into my flesh.

He dove into the water with uncommon grace. I expected him to be a skilled swimmer but I wasn't prepared for the power and beauty of him cutting across the width of the lake. Poetry in motion, every stroke efficient and dynamic, like everything else he did. After four laps, he swam back to shore.

In the water, he was all grace and elegance but when he stepped on dry land, he faltered a bit as he reached for the cane propped up against a large rock. Less Greek God, more human being. He made no attempt to cover himself, stood naked and dripping wet, daring me to take a good look. And what I saw took my breath away. He was hard, thrusting up proudly.

Holy shhh...

"I think you know how much I want you." His deep, raspy

voice ripped through the silence of the night. How could I possibly miss it?

I stepped out from behind the ancient oak—it seemed silly to pretend I wasn't there—and stood fidgeting with my nightgown, nervous and ridiculously turned on. My eyes swept over him. Moonlight bounced off his broad shoulders and spilled down the slopes of his smooth chest. My gaze followed the ragged, angry scar that snaked down from his hipbone, around his thigh and knee and ended abruptly at his ankle. But his erection...it was perfect. Long and thick and thrusting towards his flat stomach. Every ounce of blood in my body converged below my waist.

When my gaze returned to his face, I found his lids at half-mast, eyes blazing with hunger. "How did you know?" I asked. Tipping his head to the side, his lips quirked. I was a foregone conclusion basically. I rolled my eyes, more at myself than at him.

"Come here," he purred, his American accent making him sound casual and unassuming even though he was issuing a command. My body knew what it wanted far before my mind was ready to concede defeat. My feet obeyed without hesitation, carrying me to him. He reached out slowly, clasped my forearm, and pulled me flush against his naked body; heat, lust, and water soaking the front of my linen nightshirt. My nipples puckered at the abrasive feeling of the wet fabric while the rest of me buzzed with anticipation as his sex pressed against my stomach. All heat and hardness. I gasped at the feel of it.

He held my face as his soft lips descended onto mine, brushing back and forth until I let him in, teasing me to join him in equal measure. I'd never been kissed like this. Like time meant nothing, and there was no reason for kisses but the kisses themselves. Lazy, rich kisses. To Aleksander every sensual act was a means to something else, something more. Skill was a tool to get what he wanted. With Sebastian every sensual moment was suspended, with no beginning or end, making me all the more impatient to have him.

"I've wanted this…" he whispered, his lips hovering close enough to mine that I could feel the sound on my skin. "For so long."

When I gazed into his amber eyes, illuminated by the crescent moon, they revealed much more than lust. There was plenty of that, but there was also a recognizable wariness, as if he was one step removed from really being there.

The pads of his fingers traced the contours of my face: the bridge of my nose, my cheekbones, my eyebrows. "Beautiful," he murmured. His thumb stroked the fullness of my bottom lip, seeking entrance. My lips parted for him in welcome. I watched his nostrils flare when I sucked on it. Then I bit down hard.

"Jeeeezus." In an outburst of unbridled passion his lips came crashing down on mine, insisting I surrender to him. The hard truth was that he had been undeniably in control since the start. I was his to do with as he wished, a mindless slave to his erotic charms. And I was tired. So tired. Tired of being good, tired of being strong, tired of being defensive. I wanted him to take me. I wanted to relinquish everything to him.

I reached for his smooth chest and he trapped my hand over his heart. Covering it with his own, he slowly coaxed it lower, over the landscape of his hard muscles, the ridges of his abdomen, and onto the smooth heat of his erection. "Say my name."

His beautiful sex pulsed in my grip. Firmly under his spell, I whispered it. "Sebastian."

He guided me up and down the hard column. His girth

was impressive, a little too impressive. A pang of unease hit me as I began to wonder how my body would be able to accommodate him.

"Trust me." He exhaled sharply as my grip tightened. Did I trust him? Inexplicably, I did. His other hand wrapped around my waist and coasted down to my rear end, caressing, petting. His eyes widened. "No underwear?"

I shook my head, too embarrassed to admit that I had been touching myself to the thought of him before I followed him out here. A trace of a knowing smile touched his sensual mouth. My thumb stroked across his swollen crown, precum spreading across the velvety slit, while my other hand cradled the heavy weight of his sac and squeezed gently. His forehead furrowed and the muscles on his jaw pulsed.

"Stop. I'm too close," he mumbled, his voice strained as he pried my fingers loose and kissed my palm.

He sat on the flat surface of a large rock and pulled me in between his spread legs, gripping my hips possessively. My fingers wove through his silky hair as his mouth found the tight, pink nipple pushing through the wet fabric of my nightshirt. I could feel the warmth of his tongue, the scrape of his teeth before he sucked hard. A jagged burst of energy shot to the apex of my thighs, and my toes curled.

I hardly noticed when he grabbed the hem of my nightshirt and pulled it up over my head, leaving me completely exposed to his unambiguously hungry gaze. I thought the blanket of night would loosen me up. No such luck. Modesty returned in a heartbeat. I immediately became self-conscious, hiding my small breasts in my hands. It had been ages since anyone had seen me naked.

"Don't," he said, as my eyes met his. "Don't take away my pleasure."

His pleasure? I would've given him anything he asked for.

He had the power to enslave me with one glance. I lowered my hands and he pulled me closer, spreading soft kisses on my breasts while his skilled fingers found the slickness between my legs. My nails dug into his shoulders while he played with me, stroking deeply until my legs threatened to buckle.

"Christ, you're wet," he muttered. "Say it, say you want me," he commanded.

When I didn't answer right away, his mouth feasted on my breasts, turning my body against me.

"Yes."

"Yes, what?" His fingers stilled and I practically mewled.

"Yes, I want you," I said impatiently, and his fingers mercifully resumed their wicked assault.

"Beg me." Another command. I should have been annoyed, but I was too turned on to care.

"I beg you, Sebastian. Please. I want you, you know I want you."

"Only me. Understand?"

As if anyone could even begin to compare.

"Yes! Yes!" I was rapidly descending into a state of sexual insanity—if there is such a thing—trembling with need, blinded by lust. He petted and teased, tugged on my nipples with his sweet mouth in an orchestrated rhythm that had me on the verge of disintegrating. When he pulled his skilled fingers out, I heard myself scream, "Nooo!"

He placed me standing on top of the rock. Before I had time to think, his sweet mouth was on me again, tugging gently in a pulse, caressing me with his hot tongue. An intense spike of pleasure screamed through me and a veil of sweat broke out over every inch of my skin. Bouncing between pleasure and pain, I was on the verge of splintering apart.

"Don't come yet," he had the audacity to command while every muscle in my body tensed. His voice was gentle, even though this was no suggestion. I desperately wanted to please him so I fought it, biting the inside of my cheek in an effort to distract myself. "Kneel." I was suddenly standing on solid ground. His shirt fluttered down and I lowered myself in front of him without hesitation. He was circumcised. How American, I thought. The utter perfection of his manhood was mesmerizing. I couldn't wait to worship it. I wanted to make him lose his mind like he was doing to me.

I grabbed him firmly at the base and heard a quick intake of breath. The muscles of his thighs turned to stone. He tasted clean, a trace of soap and his own unique male musk. I started sucking strongly on the sensitive tip, scraping gently with my teeth as my hand moved up and down with a slight turn of my wrist. He caressed my hair with such gentleness it was a credit to his superior control. His breathing grew rough, erratic. I pressed my tongue on the frenulum and his jaw locked, his brows pinching together in concentration. On a deep thrust, he slammed into the back of my throat and my eyes watered.

"Thank you," the words said so softly that I almost didn't hear them. His head was thrown back, eyes shut, the look of pure ecstasy on his face. I felt a surge of triumph when he moaned. This was a man quiet in passion. All of a sudden, he gripped both my arms and hauled me up like I weighed nothing.

"I have to be inside of you," he demanded, breathing roughly. Then punished me with a bruising kiss. For what? For taking away his control? I nipped his bottom lip and drew blood. Startled, he pulled back, wiped the blood off with his thumb and inspected it. His expression transformed instantly. A predatory smile split his face and the air around him crackled with a charge. I stepped back, aware that I may have unleashed something I was too inexperienced to handle.

I felt the cool scrape of rock on the backs of my legs, my shoulder blades grinding into the rough surface as I lay back. Bracing his weight on his muscular arms, he bent over and kissed me passionately, lifted my hips to his and positioned himself. I wrapped my legs around his waist, mooring myself to him. Before I could feel his invasion, he paused and looked into my eyes with an expression I didn't understand, couldn't fathom. The moment expanded, filled with meaning. His gaze held mine as he sank into me, the thick slide of his manhood filling me until I couldn't take any more.

"Jesus Christ…you have to get used to me," he said, a trail of slurred words I could barely understand.

My body yielded slowly to his. Though every inch of him felt excruciatingly good. He teased me mercilessly, rocking deeper each time, withdrawing almost all the way. I grabbed his rear end, my short fingernails digging into his smooth skin, and pulled him closer. He shook his head, denying me. As I was on the verge of shedding tears of frustration, he hauled me up onto my feet and turned me around. "Put your damn hands on that rock and don't move them."

There was a hard edge to his voice that made my spine tingle in excitement. His warm body cradled me from behind and his possessive hands held me closely. Reaching around, he sifted through the soft patch of curls, and touched me where I was aching for him. I came undone in his hands, my body no longer my own.

"Is this what you want?" The question didn't necessitate a reply. He thrust his hips quickly and held steady, ripping a scream of satisfaction from my throat. My long hair wrapped around his hand, he pulled my head back until I could feel the warmth of his breath near my ear. "Is it?" he repeated in a seductive whisper, licked my throat and sank his teeth into the curve of my neck.

"Yes!"

Withdrawing all the way, he entered me slowly this time. The pads of his skilled fingers stroked me with certainty, with dexterity that comes from experience, even in my present state, something I didn't fail to notice. I was bunched up, desperate for release, but he kept it from me, just out of reach.

"You can come now, Vera." His whispered words reached through the drift of pleasure.

Knowing what I needed better than I did, he drove his powerful body into me hard and deep, buried to the root. It shattered me, the orgasm so intense I blinked repeatedly, pushing back tears. On a harsh exhale, he dug his fingers into my hips and pulled out, his cum spilling onto my lower back.

I was listless in his arms while he held me tightly, both of us quiet. Only the sound of our heavy breathing filled the air. He kissed the side of my neck and placed his cheek on my shoulder. I leaned back into him replete, and more at peace than I could ever remember feeling.

We stood like that for a long time, until he turned me around and searched my eyes with a seriousness that made me uneasy. What was he looking for? Signs of distress? I was too emotionally and physically drained to think straight. "Come on." Another demand, although his voice had softened. Taking my hand, he pulled me into the lake and proceeded to wash the evidence of his lovemaking off of me with such tenderness I could hardly breathe, a heavy weight suddenly sitting on my chest. I felt him trace the rough scratches the rock had inflicted on my back. "Does it hurt?" he murmured.

"No," I answered, meeting his gaze over my shoulder. "It feels good." Because it did. I felt alive, anchored in my body.

"You're coming back to my room."

I blinked in disbelief. "Have you lost your mind? There's a house full of people, somebody could see us."

The relaxed sated look of a man well pleasured vanished. In its place there was an imperious scowl. He grabbed my hand. I tried to resist but he held on firmly and tugged it to his lips. His eyes never left mine while he kissed my palm, each knuckle on each finger, and bit my thumb. I sighed, my legs trembling as heat converged bellow my waist again.

"You'll come back to my room, or I will follow you to yours. And, Vera, I promise you, I won't be quiet."

CHAPTER 15

We snuck in through the French doors of his office on high alert, padding through the halls like a couple of amateur thieves. When I stepped into his bedroom, it started to hit me; what we had done, what I had started. I turned around and found him leaning up against the closed bedroom door, his arms tucked behind him, bringing all the well-developed muscles of his shoulders and chest in startling relief. A smile teased the corners of his mouth and his eyes were hooded with a sensual sulkiness.

My God, you...are...stunning.

"You look nervous. Having second thoughts?" he asked, dry amusement in his voice.

"Second, third, fourth. I shouldn't be—"

He pushed off the door and reached me in two strides. Lifting me off the floor with ease, he held me tightly to the solid mass of his chest and hid his beautiful face in the curve of my neck. He was breathing hard. "Nothing has ever felt more right to me."

My body started a slow slide down that outlined every

swell and curve of him, and brushed against the impressive erection tenting his athletic pants. He gripped my head and held me in place for more of his passionate kisses, trying to convince me with his body and his mouth of how he felt. Dazed by lust, I barely noticed when he grabbed my much-abused nightgown and lifted it over my head. I followed without objection as he pulled me towards the bed. But when he sat down and his glazed eyes roamed over my nakedness with an all-consuming hunger, I stiffened self-consciously. I felt vulnerable, at his mercy. He held all the cards and I had declared myself along for the ride when I followed him to the lake.

"Please turn the lights off."

His gaze returned to mine, measuring my discomfort. "Why are you embarrassed with me? I've never seen anything so beautiful. I could stare at you forever."

There it was...the absolute truth, shining openly in his eyes. And it robbed me of the ability to speak. This man had enough women lining up for him to wrap around the planet. It seemed absurd that he would choose me. I know I'm attractive, but I'm also a particular type. Too skinny, large eyes and hips sometimes too large, depending on my weight, to be considered classically beautiful. So if one likes that "look," then I'm your type. And if not, then I'm as far from attractive as the Sahara is to the Amazon.

He gripped my hips and pulled me between his legs. Instead of kissing me, though, he closed his eyes and placed his lean cheek on my chest, over my heart. It shocked me. I stood there with my arms suspended in midair, unsure what to do. I was prepared for scalding, take-no-prisoners sex from him. This vein of tenderness however...I didn't know where it was coming from. There was a stabbing sensation in my stomach and a dull ache near my heart. I wrapped my arms around him. One hand grazed up and down his spine while the other scraped gently through his hair. He squeezed me tighter and shivered under my touch.

"I've been wanting to do this since I found you crawling along the floor of my house," he said, exhaling deeply.

My smile wouldn't stay down. "This? Really?"

"Among other things."

"As I recall, you weren't too pleased to find me 'crawling around your house.'"

"Darlin', I found you on hands and knees. It's a good thing it was dark or you would've seen exactly what I was thinking." His loose American accent had an immediate effect on my female parts.

"Sebastian?"

"Hmmm."

"How did you know...I was in the library that night?"

A long pause. "Roses. But something deeper, sexy."

"You could smell me?"

"Hmmm, it's been making me crazy, couldn't work, couldn't sleep at night thinking about it. What is that stuff anyway?"

"Body oil. It's just...body oil."

I could feel his smile on my skin, the soft shadow of his beard brushing my breast, the warm suction of his mouth on my nipple. I inhaled sharply. "Are you sore?"

"A little."

He lay down on the soft quilt and pulled me down with him, my pliant body sprawling on top of his. I stared in wonder while he played with my hair. Who was this affectionate man? I didn't recognize him at all. "How long has it been?" He held onto my chin while his eyes searched mine. He wouldn't let me look away, leaving me no place to hide. I was an easy read for him.

"A long time."

"How long?"

"Long enough that I'm a little sore."

"How long?"

The bossy aristocrat was back. At least it was the kinder version. I blew out a resigned breath. "Six years." The last time I saw Aleksander, before he boarded the train for Brussels and left me at the mercy of a pack of wolves. Sebastian's hands stalled on my shoulder blades.

"Vera...how many lovers have you had?"

I struggled and tried to escape the steel circle of his arms, but he was an immovable force. "How dare you. That is none of your business. Let me go! Thousands! How many have you had?!!"

He had the effrontery to chuckle as I struggled in vain. "Too many to count—and it is my business. You are my business. Besides, I already know you're inexperienced," he claimed with a hint of smugness in his voice. His sensual lips returned to the delicate skin of my throat, soothing me into submission until I ceased to struggle. Frankly, I couldn't resist him if I tried. One touch, one sweet word, and I was putty in his hands.

Breathless, I asked, "How do you know that?"

"I've never seen anyone blush so easily."

I couldn't help rolling my eyes. "Great."

"Makes me hard as a rock. If you had any idea what I want to do to you every time I see it, you'd run out of here screaming."

His audaciousness made me laugh, and his expectant gaze coaxed an admission out of me. "One...before you," I grumbled. Nothing I was proud of. I was practically thirty years old, for goodness sake. Clearly, I had quite a bit of living to do.

"So...I'm two?"

"Yes." The heavy silence that followed had me wondering if it bothered him.

"I'm honored."

I glanced up again and found him staring with the same profound intensity that always made me shrink away, afraid that he could read my thoughts. He captured my lips before I could and kissed me until sense and desire stopped waging war in my mind.

"I need you," I said, practically whining. He worked me up quicker than I wanted to admit. Until I was begging him to ease the emptiness before I actually expired from it.

"Shhh," he whispered and let the weight and warmth of his body calm my nerves. "Slowly, or you won't be able to walk tomorrow." There was no arrogance in his tone, only tenderness and concern. When he flipped me onto my back and pried my thighs apart, I tensed, instantly shy again.

"Let me."

This was no request. After that, it was impossible to hold onto any sense of modesty. He arranged me spread open for his inspection, tasted me in licks, and nibbled the tender skin inside of my thighs as he worked his way north to where a fever of epic proportion was growing. His skill and stealth chased away all rational thought, all my awkward-ness. My muscles tensed and bowed as he feasted on me, licking and blowing on the sensitive nub still tender from all his attention earlier, and finally drew an orgasm out of me so violent I thought my heart would stop, my uninhibited scream echoing throughout the room. I heard a drawer open and close, the sound of foil ripping. My eyes fluttered open to find him standing with his legs spread apart and his erec-tion jutting up. He looked larger than life, determined... hungry.

"I need to be inside of you," he said as he rolled on a condom.

It was a simple statement of fact. Absolute. As was his need for oxygen or water. There was no negotiating and no doubt. *Yes, yes,* my mind begged silently. I breathed a sigh of relief when he positioned himself between my thighs. Pieces clicked into place naturally. A familiarity that comes from time shared we didn't have. I wanted to melt into him, disappear altogether. I felt strangely complete. Odd, because I'd never noticed that part of me was missing. He shunted deep and exhaled harshly, my aroused body welcoming him.

"I don't want to hurt you."

"You won't," I reassured him, urging him on with a nudge of my hips.

His lust-filled eyes squeezed shut for a brief moment. He rocked his hips gently, gradually increasing the force of his thrusts. I wrapped my legs around his waist and pulled him deeper. His eyes, drunk with pleasure, watched me closely, capturing every twitch and moan. "Open your eyes. I want to see you when you come for me," he purred. The intoxicating sweetness of his lovemaking made it impossible. Every time my body quivered, on the brink of rapture, he held steady, leaving me coiled tightly on the edge of release. "Don't come yet," he ordered. I was strung out, exhausted. A tear escaped my eye and ran down my temple. He kissed me and licked the tear away. "Mine," he whispered in my ear.

"Sebastian, please."

Driving into me deep and steady, he pushed me over the edge. I broke apart with indescribable pleasure, my body vibrating from a seismic climax. In an unguarded moment, a look of amazement swept across his face. And then he joined me, reared up and came hard, the sinuous muscles of his backside turning to stone under my fingertips.

"Holy shit," he gasped between loud pants, "holy shit," he repeated, before he buried his bewilderment in the curve of my throat.

I wrapped my arms and legs around him, held him tightly. Because I knew what he meant. This was more than incendiary sex. This was something else altogether. Something I didn't want to contemplate. I was so spent I almost fell asleep with him still inside of me. He kissed me tenderly: my eyelids, the tip of my nose, my lips. When he pulled out, the sting made me whimper. I knew I was going to ache a whole lot more the next day. And in the drowsy afterglow, I didn't care.

———

THE BACKS of my knees were...sweaty. Hanging in the air was the primitive scent of sex and sweat. A large muscular body pressed up against my back, branding me with scalding heat. *Sebastian*. It was all coming back to me now. His sex was wedged against my rear end, and a muscular arm thrown over my waist. I could feel the puffs of his deep and even breath against my hair. He shifted and pulled me closer.

Surrounded by him, I had never slept better. However, I needed to get back to my room before the house woke up. I picked up his wrist and squinted at the large face of his Rolex. The darn watch had no numbers on the dial. Although, the large hand looked to be...

"What are you doing?" His voice was deeper and raspier than usual.

"I can't believe you let me fall asleep." His rumpled hair and relaxed expression made him look young and outrageously sexy. "I worked you over pretty good," the side of his mouth kicked up, "seemed like the polite thing to do."

"When have you ever been polite to me?" I was only teasing but his face fell, grave all of a sudden.

"Vera...I...that's over. I need to explain." When I struggled to get up, he hugged me closer, his sex springing to life. My eyebrows shot up. "Be still," he muttered.

"I have to get back to my room!" I whispered forcefully. "What time is it?" Anxiety made me restless to get going. He checked his watch.

"Three."

The stiffness left my muscles, my fretfulness momentarily allayed. I swung my legs off the bed and almost immediately found myself on my back, pinned under two hundred pounds of aroused, hot-blooded man. His fingers cradled my skull and his erection pressed against my abdomen. My eyes fluttered as he shifted and hit me squarely where I needed him. *Good God...*He knew where all the buttons were. In one night he had mastered my body, knew it better than I did. I watched him struggle with something before he spoke.

"I behaved like an asshole because...I didn't like the way you made me feel."

My stomach sank, the euphoria fading fast. "Yes, I've heard this before," I said with a touch of indignation in my voice. "You didn't like finding yourself attracted to the housekeeper. Quite an inconvenience, I get it."

"No. That's not it. Vera, look at me." I turned my head and held his gaze. The disappointment was evident in my eyes. "I wanted you from the first moment I saw you. At first, it was just a physical attraction. I figured sooner or later it would just...I don't know...go away, as I got to know you."

"Let go of me," I insisted and tried to push him off to no avail.

"Be quiet and listen—it didn't. I wanted you more than I've ever wanted anybody." He exhaled sharply. "I...I couldn't stay away. I tried. I just couldn't do it," he admitted, shaking his head as if it still bothered him. "I hated myself for it so I took it out on you for making me feel...weak...out of control."

His voice trailed off. I saw what that confession cost him. His eyes darted away. When they returned to me, however, they were open, reflecting the depth of his feelings. There was wonder and desire present, a flicker of hope. But what stirred my curiosity was the large dose of unease.

"Like pulling pigtails?"

His lips twitched. "Something like that...I'm sorry," he said softly, stroking my hair back. "Can we start over?"

I would forgive him anything if he kept looking at me that way. "Yes," I replied, the word pushing past a lump in my throat.

His eyes brightened, and a spot somewhere around my heart ached. I liked seeing him happy. I wanted to make him happy, and that scared me half to death.

"I have to go," I whispered.

"Okay...just one more thing," he murmured before he kissed me again and again.

———

Yawning loudly, I looked up and found Mrs. Arnaud's large eyes fixed on me with pointed interest. My hand stilled from stirring the béchamel sauce.

"Are you getting enough sleep, *chérie?*"

My smile was tight as I replied, "Yes, *madame,* maybe reading a little later than I should." *May God forgive me.* I was waiting for a bolt of lightning to strike me down where I stood. Satisfied with my answer, she turned and rifled through the refrigerator.

A moment later Sebastian walked into the kitchen and I noticed two things. One: Mrs. Arnaud treated him to the same inquisitive inspection she had given me. And two: the man looked as fresh as a winter breeze. That was entirely unfair. He was wearing a white t-shirt and jeans, a baseball cap with an S over the rim that caused his hair to curl up at the sides, and a large dose of mischief was present in his bright eyes. The air around him was light and relaxed. I was glad for that. He was always so serious.

I felt him brush up against me, as he walked by, and my eyebrows shot up. My scolding glance only earned me a playful leer. It was a dangerous game. Even though Mrs. Arnaud's head was still buried in the refrigerator, thankfully unaware.

"What were you reading that was so interesting?" he asked in a mocking tone.

I'd like to read you your last rites at the moment, I replied with my glare. The impossible man winked at me. I bit my bottom lip to school a smile that refused to stay down. Having finally located the butter, Mrs. Arnaud turned and waited with warm interest for my answer.

"Umm, *A Thousand Years of Solitude*, I mean *One Hundred Years of Solitude*," I muttered, blushing madly. It certainly had felt like a thousand years before last night.

"Really?" he asked with innocence worthy of an Oscar nomination. I promptly answered his query with another glare of warning. "I prefer *Love in the Time of Cholera*," he continued, undaunted. Then directing his attention at Mrs. Arnaud asked, "I'm taking the guys to the lake for some fishing, Marianne. Could you please pack some drinks and sandwiches?"

"*Bien sûr*, I will send Vera down around noon?"

Sebastian's face split in a satisfied grin. "Perfect. Oh, Ben called this morning. He's coming to stay for a while. He should be here by tonight."

"I'll make up a room for him far from the other guests."

After thanking Mrs. Arnaud and directing a salacious glance my way, out the door he went. I immediately got busy, afraid of being studied too closely. I've never been good at keeping secrets, and beneath Marianne Arnaud's sweet façade lurked a deadly quick wit. I directed all my energy at washing the eggs Charlotte had brought in earlier, meticulously examining them to make sure all the feathers clinging to the shells were removed. It seemed to work. She returned to mixing the ingredients for the crêpes.

"Mrs. Arnaud, who's Ben and why does he need a room far from the other guests?" I asked offhandedly.

"He's a very dear friend of Sebastian's," she answered. The fact that she called him by his first name caught my attention. Strange, that. "The poor, poor boy has night terrors. He can get quite loud. Always requests a room far from everyone else. I think it embarrasses him. He was in the American military."

"How awful. I can only imagine."

"Vera, you mustn't let him upset you."

Of course—nothing escaped her. "He has a gift for doing that."

"He hasn't been the same since the death of his wife. He doesn't know how to manage his emotions very well."

I guess it was better that she thought we hated each other. A pang of guilt hit me. Still, she had just handed me the opportunity to ask about things I was burning to know, so I took advantage of it.

"What was she like?"

"She was lovely." Her gaze swung out the kitchen window. Pensively, she added, "A bit fragile but sweet. They were only married a month before the accident…he was devastated." In the pause, her brow furrowed. "I'm not certain he will ever recover completely."

The fragile bud of joy that had bloomed within me overnight withered and died on the vine. My heart throbbed with a dull pain. Somehow, in my delusional mind, I had stopped thinking of him as still in love with his beautiful dead wife. I had completely blocked it out. What an idiot. I needed to hear this, needed to remind myself daily that this was only about sex.

"And it's not like he had an easy childhood," she added. "There's only so much a heart can take."

Her voice snapped me back to the present. "How bad could it have been? He grew up in the lap of luxury," I responded, a bit more curtly than I'd meant to.

She examined my face closely before she spoke. "*Chérie*, growing up in a palace does not protect you from misery."

"What do you mean?" I mumbled.

"His mother is the kind of woman that should never have had children. I'm certain you've noticed. They were headed straight for a divorce before she got pregnant. Anyway, she used the boy against his father. It got quite ugly, saw that myself."

"How?" My heart was suddenly pounding in my ears, and my throat struggled to squeeze out the word.

"Imagine a little boy never getting an ounce of love or affection from his mother unless she's putting on an act in front of his father. The boy knew—he was always clever and sensitive—he knew," she finished in a whisper. Her words hung in the air while her attention returned to the batter she was mixing.

I thought of the love and affection I grew up with. Never in doubt. Always available. I had been smothered in love.

What could it have been like for a child to never have felt wanted or loved? Emotions I was not comfortable with began leaking out of my heart. I tried to stop them, but it was a finger on a gunshot wound—it did more harm than good. I was already in serious danger of loving this man. And that, I could not allow.

———

AROUND NOON I drove the golf cart down to the lake. A long canoe bobbed on the water. It was filled with men doing too much talking and not enough fishing––probably already having scared most of the fish to the other side of the lake. The other was on shore. Sebastian had been waiting for me. My heart skipped a beat as I watched him approach with a playful smile on his handsome face. I parked the golf cart and began unloading the baskets of food and beverages. I wouldn't meet his eyes. They had too much power over me.

"Hey, what's wrong?" he asked in a soft voice.

"Nothing's wrong. Excuse me, I need to unload this cart."

"Let me help," he murmured, taking a basket from me. Together we walked towards a giant oak where chairs and a picnic table sat in the shade. "Why won't you look at me?"

I looked up, my expression blank. "I'm busy. I have work to do." I thought I caught a flash of pain in his eyes before I turned away, though maybe I was imagining it.

Working quickly, I arranged the food and the container of iced beverages while an awkward moment of silence stretched out between us. He stood aside, studying me as if I were one of his balance sheets, a discrepancy that needed to be solved. I did my best to ignore him. As I finished setting the table, he reached out and almost touched me before he pulled his hand back and glanced over his shoulder. We both turned to watch the men pushing the canoe onto dry land.

"Come to my room tonight." His voice was sweet, supplicating. It made me ache for him.

"No, I can't," I whispered.

I heard him sigh. The heavy air surrounding him was back. I could feel it. After a beat, he walked away. I stared at his retreating back and fought a strong impulse to run after him and throw myself into his arms. It was better this way. I had to keep myself as emotionally detached as possible.

CHAPTER 16

A postcard sunset turned the sky a kaleidoscope of colors. Cerulean to radiant violet. Magenta to cadmium orange. Lost in thought, I leaned against the stone column of the doorway and stared absently at the horizon. I couldn't even enjoy the stunning show Mother Nature was putting on. What Mrs. Arnaud had revealed had thrown me off balance. Now I wish I hadn't asked. We were one day into it and it had already gotten complicated. I hated complicated, complicated was messy.

A black Mercedes sedan approached and pulled up to the front entrance. The passenger handed the driver some bills, opened the door, and unfolded his large body out of the back of the car. When he stood, he was not quite as tall as Sebastian and more heavily muscled. There was a bit of dangerous air surrounding him. You could sense it even at a distance. A quick appraisal revealed that he was handsome: a straight nose, a firm jaw, black hair cut efficiently short. Both arms had sleeves of tattoos that started at his wrists and disappeared under the short sleeves of his gray t-shirt. He definitely didn't look like the rest of the bank's clients.

Holding the garment bag over his shoulder, he jogged up the stairs rather gracefully for a man his size. He moved slowly, smoothly. Something told me that there was a powerful force behind those languid movements. That's when he glanced up with eyes of the most unusual color, a pale smoky gray with rims a silvery blue-green. The color of a blue spruce pine. I couldn't stop staring. Against his suntanned skin, the effect was shocking. And he was obviously accustomed to women having this reaction to him because his sensual lips shaped themselves into a knowing smile, two dimples on his lean cheeks further punctuating the matter.

"Hi, I'm Ben Winters," he said in a deep baritone.

I pushed off the column and stood straight. "Hello," I answered, offering a polite smile. "Mr. Horn mentioned you were arriving this evening."

Following me inside, he ducked his head to hear me better. "Where is the sunuvabitch—I mean, is he in his study, ma'am?" he drawled, his expression charmingly unrepentant. Mr. Winters was a lady-killer. I didn't need to see or hear any more to know that. A voice called to me from somewhere down the hall.

"Vera, where are you sneaking off to?" The snickering voice drew closer. "Is that Daniel you're going to hide in a corner with? Oh, Daniel," she teased. I turned to face the owner of the snickering voice. Charlotte walked up with her hands on her hips, ready to poke fun at whomever I was with. Meanwhile, Mr. Winters turned around. They stood before each other as if someone hit the pause button on a video. I stifled a laugh. Charlotte's face was frozen, eyes wide and astonished. I'd never seen her speechless before, didn't even think it was possible. Mr. Winters, on the other hand, was doing a great impression of an ice sculpture. The only sign of life was the rosy glow visible on his sharp cheekbones.

"Charlotte, this is Mr. Ben Winters. He's a guest of Mr. Horn."

Crickets. Until the door to Sebastian's study swung open and he stepped out. His eyes jumped from me, to Ben, to Charlotte.

"Ben?" Sebastian's voice broke the spell. Mr. Winters turned around and the two men hugged, pounding each other on the back. There was enough testosterone in the room to fuel the western hemisphere.

How in the world did they not break bones doing that? Amazing what men mistake for affection. When the pounding finally ceased, Sebastian slung an arm around Mr. Winters and turned to face me. A bright smile stretched across his face. My knees almost buckled. His face transformed to a whole new level of gorgeous when he smiled like that.

"Vera, this is my best friend, Ben," he announced cheerfully, slapping poor Mr. Winters on the chest as he spoke.

"You mean, your only friend." Mr. Winters smirked.

My attention jumped back and forth between the two men before me, the contrast between them intriguing. Mr. Winters still had the casual, rough edges of an American, his handsomeness rugged and raw, while Sebastian had honed all that into strict, lethal masculine elegance. Mr. Winters was all easy smiles and open charm. Sebastian, on the other hand, kept everyone at a distance, not welcoming female attention in any way. Beneath the stunning façades, though, there was a common virtue—both men were profoundly comfortable with who they were.

I grinned like the village idiot. "Pleasure to meet you, sir."

His large hand engulfed mine. "Call me Ben, please."

Charlotte still had that deer-in-headlights look about her.

"And may I introduce Charlotte," I reiterated.

Mr. Winters' face turned grave as he grasped Charlotte's hand and shook it. I glanced at Sebastian and found a quizzical look on his face. Our eyes met and I shrugged, unsure what to think myself.

"Come on, Ben. We have a lot to catch up on."

Grabbing Charlotte's elbow, I steered her towards the kitchen. Behind me, I could hear Mr. Winters trying to reduce his deep baritone to a whisper.

"Jeeezus H, how do you not walk around here with a constant hard—" I looked over my shoulder and Mr. Winters caught me watching. His eyebrows lifting a fraction, he muttered, "Never mind," before the door to Sebastian's study closed.

———

IT WAS JUST PAST ELEVEN. I knew that because I'd been glancing at the clock every fifteen minutes while I read a French version of Jane Austen's *Persuasion*. Well, I was attempting to read it. I kept finding myself on the same page over and over again, not remembering a single word. It had taken every ounce of willpower I possessed to stop myself from going to his room. And I was paying the price for it now. I was unfocused, I was in a horrible mood, and my body ached for him.

The door creaked. I held my breath. Until Sebastian stepped inside and quietly closed it behind him, locking it afterwards. A pang of relief shot through me, quickly followed by barely contained excitement. He leaned back against the wall with his hands tucked behind him. My undoubtedly hungry gaze did a slow perusal of his long body. Starting at his bare feet, my eyes ran up the black track pants hanging on his lean hips, over the stunning breadth of his bare chest. Just looking at him altered the chemistry of my body.

A storm was gathering strength in his eyes. He was mad, and I couldn't have cared less. He looked so good it took everything I had not to leap on him and cover his sullen mouth with kisses. Then I remembered I wasn't dressed for a visit. I looked down and cringed. I had my worst old linen nightgown on, and my hair was piled on top of my head in a messy bun. Not exactly a temptress. I did a mental check of what underwear I had put on after my shower and decided it wasn't the pair with the hole in it. Thank God for small miracles. Not that I had sexy black g-strings hiding in my wardrobe. Still, I didn't want to scare him away.

He smirked when my eyes zeroed in on the large erection tenting up his pants. My nightwear didn't seem to be damp-ening his desire. A prickling heat started at my toes and spread through my limbs, making me restless and my skin painfully sensitive. The soft nightgown I was wearing was suddenly made of pins and needles. He walked over to my narrow bed and sat on the edge, facing me. Without a word, he took the book out of my hand and placed it on the desk.

Thank God, you're here. "You shouldn't be here," I mumbled. I couldn't take my eyes off his thick shaft. My entire body lit up at its proximity. He cupped my face, his thumbs brushing my cheeks. His gaze, hot and molten, drifted from my mouth to my throat.

If you don't touch me soon, I'm going to pounce on you. "Your friend seems nice." I knew I was babbling but there was nothing to be done for it. When he stared at my lips with that sensual threat in his eyes, it scrambled my thoughts and destroyed my composure.

You're in serious danger of being raped if you don't hurry up. "You shouldn't have introduced us, Sebastian. I'm just the housekeeper," I rambled on while lust and need carried on a completely different conversation in my head.

His eyes softened. He leaned down and kissed me gently, brushing my lips with his. Once. Twice. "Not to me, you're not," he stated quietly. His tenderness crushed any lingering remains of doubt I may have harbored.

I wrapped my arms around his neck and kissed him back. Potent alchemy. The kiss turned wild in a flash. Everything happened quickly after that. I was dragged onto his lap. He tugged at the elastic that held my messy bun together until it broke and my hair spilled down my back. Coiling it around his hand, he pulled my head back to feast on my neck. His kisses became more demanding, almost desperate. Ablaze with desire, heat flooded the farthest reaches on my body. In record time, he had me turned on and tuned into him so completely that I wouldn't have noticed or cared if somebody had walked in on us.

The curtains were wide open. He turned off the lamplight, and a full moon bathed the room in blue shadows. Eyes locked on mine, he stood in front of the window and pushed down his pants. My heart skipped a beat. The moonlight traced the silhouette of his nakedness as if he had stepped out of my dreams. Imperfect—though perfect to me. The magnificence of the moment stole my breath away.

He pulled me out of bed and grabbed the edge of my nightgown, lifting it slowly over my head, deliberately drawing out the sensation of his warm fingers grazing my cool skin. Hooking the sides of my not-so-bad panties with his fingers, he pulled them off. When he was done, we stood before each other naked, two people not wanting to need one another yet wanting each other desperately. I knew then I was in serious trouble.

His passion-filled eyes never left mine as he sat in the chair and guided me to stand between his thighs. I wove my fingers through his hair and scratched his scalp with my short nails. His thick lashes fluttered and a relaxed sigh escaped his lips, the hardness gone from his features.

"You're so fucking beautiful...all I think about is being inside of you." The murmur rippled across my skin. With deliberate patience, he kissed a path from my navel to my nipple, circling the distended tip with his tongue and blowing on it, clamping down hard enough to send a jolt of pleasure racing to the peak of my thighs.

I bit the inside of my cheek trying to stifle a moan. My lids grew heavy. I struggled to keep my eyes open as my attention-starved body soaked up every bit of sensation. With infinite patience he stroked the seam of my sex and dipped into my body, urged me closer with a gentle caress of my rear end. A finger slipped between my cheeks unannounced, brushed over the highly sensitive area. A thrill of sensation shot through me. I grabbed his erection at the base and stroked him. A slow hiss escaped his lips as my thumb spread pre-cum over the sensitive crown. Wrapping his hand around mine, he stopped me and handed me a condom fished out of his pants.

With warm anticipation, he watched my trembling hand roll the condom on. I straddled him and slowly sank down, the heavy penetration stretching me until he was so deep I could barely move.

"Let me," he whispered.

My eyes glazed over from the overwhelming sensation. His hands cradled my face and his lips caught at mine.

Only him. Nothing else existed. The way he felt inside of me, the sound of him, the taste of him. It was all-consuming. And he was equally present in the moment, making me feel needed and treasured, my pleasure his only concern. It destroyed me—an arrow to my Achilles.

He began rolling his hips in hard, shallow thrusts, grinding against me. When I matched his effort, he buried a harsh grunt into the curve of my neck. I urged him on but he forced me with his body to submit. Until his lips command silently. *Now, Vera. Now!* Teetering on the tipping point, I couldn't quite get there, sweet oblivion maddeningly out of reach.

"Sebastian—" His thumb skated lightly over my swollen clit and pleasure shot outward to every point in my body. Placing his hand over my mouth, he muted my scream. Then he gripped my hips and brought me down hard, shoving himself even deeper. A tremor subjugating his powerful frame, at last, he found his own release.

We sat entwined and held each other tightly for a long time afterwards. Neither one of us wanted to break off the intimacy. *Don't let go*, I wanted to say but didn't. Instead, I hid my face in the curve of his neck and breathed in his comforting scent while his fingers stroked the rungs of my spine. A wave of wistfulness broke over me. Besieged with all this closeness, my resolve was crumbling fast and caring for him filled me with dread. I was petrified of what would become of me once it was over. I wiped my face of emotion before I looked at him.

"Come back to my room with me," he softly pleaded. I shook my head and his expression hardened instantly. "Vera..." He could even make a whisper sound menacing—so mercurial, my tender, despotic lover.

"No. I mean it, Sebastian. You have to go." *I'm scared. I'm in danger of losing myself.* I tried to get off his lap, but he held onto my hips.

"Why are you doing this?"

"I'm not doing anything. I have to get to sleep."

His solemn eyes studied me as if he could find a secret back door to my mind that would reveal all my thoughts and intentions. Instinctively, I knew that if I yielded, he would be forever riding roughshod over me. I held his gaze until his hands rose in surrender. When I stood, a burning sensation made me wince. His imperious scowl made its first appearance of the night.

"Honeymoon fever," I explained. "Happens when you haven't had sex in a long time...then have a lot of it." My smile did nothing to temper his irritation. He jerked the condom off.

"Come to my room and take a bath," he said in a voice tight with concern.

"Go," I ordered, his pants hanging from my extended hand.

We stared at each other in a silent battle of wills. I could practically see the wheels spinning, his predatory mind calculating the cost to profit ratio. He was clearly not accustomed to being told no, or accepting it as an end. His lips thinned and his eyes narrowed. He sat down on the bed and shoved his pants on without care.

Suddenly feeling shy, I turned my back to him and slipped on my nightgown. Before the unease could find traction, he was holding me. His arms wrapped around me from behind and pulled me into the shelter of his body. Relieved, I leaned against him, closed my eyes, and savored the quiet comfort of his arms.

His soft lips hovered near my ear as he spoke. "When these people leave, you and I are going to have a long talk."

"There's nothing to talk about."

He placed his hand over my mouth and slapped my rear end, a muffled yelp jumping from my lips. "You bet your sweet, sweet ass there is," he stated with total certainty.

After planting a loud kiss on the side of my throat, he let go. I was instantly cold and lonely, already missing his touch, before he even closed the door behind him. Alone in the moonlight, I stared at the door and rubbed my stinging rear end, wondering how I ever thought I could manage this man.

CHAPTER 17

M rs. Redman entered the bedroom as I fluffed the last of the pillows on the bed. She stood in the doorway wearing tennis whites and a scheming gaze. Large, dark sunglasses sat on top of her head, forgotten. It may have been my imagination, but it felt like the temperature suddenly dropped about 30 degrees. An arctic chill seemed to follow her everywhere she went.

"Oh good, I was wondering how long it would take you to get around to my room."

I stiffened at the backhanded remark. "I came as soon as I was told, madam. I was busy with the other rooms, and there was a lot to do." It had taken me more than two hours to restore some order to her bedroom. Clothes were strewn about everywhere, as if a tornado had ripped through. The tornado was currently inspecting me from head to foot in a not-too-subtle manner that made me uneasy. Actually, she made everyone uneasy, including her own son. I couldn't get out of there fast enough and moved towards the door to exit.

"What's your name, sugar?"

I paused. No way to avoid this. "Vera."

"Vera, what a sweet name. How long have you lived in Switzerland?"

"Six months."

"You're here illegally."

It wasn't even a question. The blood in my veins turned to ice. I didn't answer right away. She waited me out with a fixed, disingenuous smile on her line-free face.

"I have a medical degree. I'm waiting to hear back from hospitals about their residency programs."

"Isn't that charming, but you're still here illegally. Am I wrong?"

I could hear my teeth grinding. "No."

"You seem like an intelligent woman, so I'll get straight to the point. I see the way you look at my son and I don't care for it."

"I don't know what you mean." Even though the heat crawling up my neck demonstrated, without a doubt, that I did.

"Oh, I think you do, and I don't blame you, not a bit. He's stunning. You'd have to be as blind as Helen Keller not to notice."

"I have quite of bit of work to do," I said, moving forward.

She smiled at my brusque tone. "I certainly hope you don't have designs on my son."

I flushed an especially deep shade of scarlet. "I have no idea what you're referring to, Mrs. Redman. Now if you'll excuse me."

"Let me spell it out for you then. He's beautiful and richer than forty other billionaires on the Forbes 100. He is out…of your…league. You two don't even belong on the same planet. My son has a bleeding heart. He needs protectin' from someone like you."

My stomach sank to my feet. *Someone like me?* I tried escaping before she could land another blow. To no avail. As I passed her, she wrapped her bony, manicured fingers around my arm in a surprisingly firm grip.

"Leave him alone."

I jerked my arm out of her grasp. "I've never done otherwise," I argued. My voice was surprisingly steady, considering everything else was in turmoil. I forced myself to measure my steps all the way down the hall. But once I was out of her sight, I bolted downstairs, my feet moving as quickly as the thumping of my heart.

Luckily, everyone in the kitchen was too busy to notice my distress. I wasn't in any condition to lie convincingly. In search of a dark place to lick my wounds, I exited through the kitchen door and marched towards the planting garden, stopping only when I reached the stone wall bordering the tomato plants, the one well out of sight from the house. Leaning against it for support, I closed my eyes and tried to rein in the tumult of my emotions. My limbs felt like dead weight. The shot of adrenaline wore off, replaced by nausea and a growing sense of dread.

I could feel the stain of emotion on my neck and tried to rub it away. My father always said criticism could never hurt unless you agreed with the one doing the criticizing. He was right, as he often was. The audacity of that woman. The worst part was that I did agree with her. What was I doing? We didn't belong together, not in any rational sense anyway. I was taking all the risk, and I was the one that couldn't afford to gamble. Of course she thought I was interested in Sebastian's money. Little did she know. His money was a major complication, the one thing that really stood between us.

"What are you doing out here?"

I jumped at the sound of his voice. Lost in thought and self-pity, I hadn't heard him approaching. "Getting some fresh air." I started fidgeting under his intense scrutiny. I didn't have the energy to lie. Even my smile was shaky. He stepped closer and dipped his head to kiss me. But when he noticed the mark on my neck, he stopped short, his eyes narrowing at the evidence of my discomfort.

"Why the hell is your neck all red? What happened?" he asked, suddenly alarmed.

"Sebastian, please. Let it be. I don't want to discuss it." I could see the flare of concern in his eyes. He wanted to badger me about it. He stepped closer and lifted his hand to my throat, caressed the splotch on my neck tenderly, outlining it with his fingers. The feeling exquisite. I wanted to sink into him, bury my face in the curve of his neck, and let him chase all thought away.

"I'll let it go for now. I want to show you something. Come." He held my hand and dragged me beyond the wall, towards the boxwood hedge.

"No, I can't…really, I shouldn't."

"Yes, you can. It won't take long."

I shook my head, dug my heels in. "Where are you taking me? Mrs. Arnaud will be looking for me."

"Relax, I told her you were helping me with something." He held up a plastic bag.

"What's that?"

"Chicken."

We walked until we came upon a little house with bars on the windows. "What is all this?"

"It's called a mews. It's housing for my falcons." His eyes lit up on that last word, a lopsided smile growing on his heart-stopping face. *Be still my beating heart.* His smiles were so rare they felt like sunshine after a nuclear winter. I would've done anything for one of those smiles. "Next to it is the weathering yard. That's where they exercise."

He rummaged through a storage bin and pulled out a long suede glove, slipping it on before he opened the mews door. The bird stepped onto his arm and perched there. It was large and admittedly scary. It had a plush coat of white feathers speckled with brown on its breast, and a long red tail that fanned out at the bottom. Its eyes were penetrating, watching me as if it could read my mind and discover all of my secrets.

"Isn't she beautiful?"

My head whipped around. "It's a she??!"

Grinning at my bewilderment, he explained, "Falcons are female. The male is called a tiercel...and much smaller." I stared in wonder at the impressive animal: her sharp talons, the proud breast, the sharp look in her eyes. "Well, what do you think?" he asked, watching me closely. I didn't miss the moment of uncertainty in his gaze. He looked like a little boy offering to share his favorite toy. *I think you're killing me, you beautiful, sweet man.* He might as well have taken a sledgehammer to my heart because the wall I was trying to erect crumbled at once.

"The females are bigger than the males? I like those odds. Is there a reason why?"

He paused, a sly grin shaping his sensual lips. "There's an evolutionary theory that the females over time chose smaller, less aggressive males to provide for her and the young. So she could...dominate him more easily."

"Hmm, makes perfect sense to me. Clever creature," I replied with a grin of my own.

His eyes turned sulky. "That only works with red tails, darlin'. In the real world the larger, more aggressive male always wins."

With all this heat between us I'm surprised I didn't go up in flames. "How did you get into this? Your father?" His expression hardened instantly. His jaw twitched as he placed the bird on her tall, wooden perch. All the lightness and fun erased with a casual question.

"Did I say something wrong…Sebastian?" He stared at the bird with an absent look on his face. "Tell me," I whispered. I had to fight the urge to hold him and kiss that look away.

"After my parents split, I spent summers here with him. He thought living with my mother was making me soft." A bark of joyless laughter surged out of him. "On my way back from feeding his birds one day, I found a fledgling, a young bird that had been thrown out of its nest." Turning to face me, his bleak gaze held mine briefly. "I took it back to the house and showed it to my father. He told me to put it back where I found it, that Mother Nature would take care of the rest…I just couldn't do it," he admitted, his head shaking. "I hid the bird in my room. Marianne helped me build a nest." His face swung away, his eyes searching for something in the distance before they returned to me.

"A couple of weeks later my father found me upstairs, feeding the bird. He grabbed it out of the box and snapped its neck before I knew what hit me." A horrified gasp rushed up my throat. "Said I had to learn that life was cruel and some things aren't meant to take up space in this world," a weary sigh filled the pause, "so the answer is no. I didn't learn this from him."

My hands were shaking. Gripping them closed, I hid them behind my back. I couldn't imagine any parent doing that to a young, impressionable child. It was obvious the pain from that phantom wound was indelibly burned onto his soul. And intuitively, I knew he wouldn't find comfort in pity or sympathy—he was too proud a man.

"If the Buddhists are right, then the only justice is that he comes back as an unsuspecting field mouse in his next life." The clouds in his eyes parted and his gaze turned warm. A brief smile touched his lips. "Does she have a name?" He smirked awkwardly while I studied him. "Spit it out. What is it?"

"Only if you swear never to repeat it," he said in all seriousness.

"I swear, now what is it?"

A beat of silence followed.

"Beyoncé," he said in a low voice.

My eyebrows nearly reached my hairline. "Beyoncé? This fierce creature's name is Beyoncé?"

He scowled, staring at something by his feet. It must have been the roller coaster ride my emotions were on all day because my body began to spasm from the effort to contain the laughter. Tears started streaming down my face.

"Good, great. Got a good chuckle out of it...okay...get it all out now...are you done?" He looked annoyed and embarrassed, and utterly kissable. "Can we feed her now? She's hungry."

"Of course...of course." The giggles left me a little at a time. I handed him the chicken, and watched as the bird grasped it with her sharp beak and flipped it into her mouth. "Why doesn't she hunt for food?"

"She was injured when she was young. A larger raptor tore her wing. I put her back together, but she won't ever fly in the wild again."

"Oh...then I'm glad she has you." I smiled at the loving way he stroked her breast, with the back of his fingers.

My son has a bleeding heart... I shut her voice out of my mind, determined not to let her mar this intimate moment.

He turned to me with the same alert expression I saw on the bird.

"She reminds me of you."

"The beak?" he murmured.

"No, I think your nose is beautiful. That's not what I meant. She's self-contained, innately noble, and that intense focus in her eyes...it makes me feel like she could look into my soul." I shrugged and averted my gaze, afraid I had said too much.

He stared back at me as if I had just performed a slight of hand trick he couldn't quite figure out. The falcon walked down his arm and back into the mews. He shook the glove off, letting it fall at his feet, and closed the distance between us. Reaching for my hand, he brushed his thumb over my knuckles, and hauled me into his arms. There was so much emotion burning beneath the surface of his skin. I could feel the heat of it. He was quiet as he held me, cradling my nape with his warm hand. I pressed myself closer and he kissed the top of my head.

This feels right. I tried not to ruin the moment by reasoning. "Isn't there another one?" I mumbled into his shirt.

"Yes. The boy who takes care of them when I'm busy fed her earlier."

"What's her name?" I absently asked. A long pause, a deep sigh. "What is it?"

"Lady Gaga," he answered in a resigned voice. I burst out in laughter, and he held me until the tremors subsided.

———

IT WAS EARLY AFTERNOON. Most of the guests had either departed for the golf course with Sebastian, who'd promised not to walk the course or had gone fishing. Paisley and

Marcus had chosen to stay behind and had taken one of Sebastian's smaller jet boats onto Lake Geneva. We didn't see each other the night before. Every attempt Sebastian made at sneaking away from his guests was thwarted. First, by Caroline Pruitt, who insisted on speaking with him at length about the investments Sebastian had made with her trust fund. And later by Charles Hightower who insisted on playing poker until an uncivil hour. It was around two by the time he made it back to his room. I was sound asleep by then and never heard the incoming email.

Mrs. Arnaud encouraged us to take a break. We would be serving another formal dinner that evening and would be up late, so I knew I wouldn't be able to rest. I've never been the type of person who can take a nap in the afternoon—too much nervous energy. The bathrooms on the first floor needed a thorough cleaning. I figured this was as good a time as any.

I had just finished polishing the faucet when the door swung open, and a large male body bumped into me. The powder room wasn't large enough to accommodate two people. Startled, I bounced off the wall and teetered forward as I lost my balance. A hand grasped my forearm to steady me. I looked up and found Marcus standing inside the tiny room, his fingers still wrapped around my arm.

"Didn't mean to scare you," he said, smiling blandly.

He had a neat, boyish appearance, handsome in a clear-eyed way, but I sensed some artifice in his mild manners. When I pulled out of his hold, he remained in the doorway, and I was stuck with nowhere to go.

"I'm done cleaning this one. Feel free to use it." A prickle of unease crawled up my spine when my gaze met the fixed, unnatural smile on his face.

"You never answered my question." He cocked his hip

casually and extended his arm, blocking my exit. My stomach clenched a little. I didn't ignore it. I'd learned to trust my body's survival instincts.

"What question?" My voice was purposely cold.

"You said you weren't British. Where are you from?"

"Albania."

"Albanian." His mouth twisted in a sly, sarcastic smile. "Albanians are known to be tough, stubborn, right?" He leaned his hip into the doorjamb and crossed his arms, making himself more comfortable. I was growing more anxious by the minute.

"That's a stereotype, but I'll take it as a compliment. Now, if you'll excuse me, I have more cleaning to do."

"Sebastian is a hard taskmaster, I take it. Keeps you… busy?" The lascivious tone in his voice turned me rigid. I banked my emotions, trying desperately not to go into full-tilt panic. Had he realized the situation between Sebastian and me, or was it my own paranoia?

"Mr. Horn doesn't concern himself with what the staff is doing. Please step aside."

His face impassive, he studied me for what felt like an eternity. I stepped forward, determined to push my way through, and he grabbed the top of my arm. "Hold on, we're not finished." Without enough room for me to get any leverage, it was impossible to break out of his hold. An epic scream worked its way up my throat.

"Is this bathroom available?" The smooth baritone brought me to a halt mid-struggle.

Marcus immediately loosened his grip. Scooting out immediately, I found Ben Winters standing in the hallway. His body was tense, barely containing a violent, tangible force. If I thought him untamed before, he looked positively savage now. His eyes were two shards of ice in his austere face. The lady-killer was gone. All that remained was the killer.

It took only a moment of the wordless debate between the two men to make Marcus retreat. A small part of me felt thrilled, vindicated. Marcus gave Mr. Winters a nonchalant shrug before he stepped inside and shut the door. When Ben looked down, his whole body softened, his eyes filled with concern. "You alright?"

I must have looked more shaken than I felt. He placed his large, warm hand on my shoulder, and patiently waited for my response.

"Yes, I'm fine, Mr. Winters. Thank you." The tight, crisp note of unease in my voice disagreed.

"Ben, please," he insisted in a gentle voice. My hand came up to smooth back hair that was already smooth. I wasn't fooling him. He could tell I was still jittery.

"Thank you, Ben. I'm fine, really. I should go."

"Ben?!" Sebastian's edgy shout reverberated down the hall. He stood with his hands on his hips, glaring at us. This afternoon was going from bad to worse. As far away as he was, I could see him scowling at Ben's hand resting on my shoulder. The crazy possessiveness needed to stop. I couldn't have him pawing the ground like an enraged bull every time someone of the opposite sex spoke to me.

The corner of Ben's wide mouth crept up. His hand fell away from me. "I got this. You go on."

I wasn't in any condition to deal with another altercation, still too strung out from the last one. I watched him walk towards Sebastian and then fled in the opposite direction, seeking the sanctuary of my room.

CHAPTER 18

The chattering of birds woke me. One eyelid curiously crept up. My window was wide open, and the room was washed in gold by the afternoon sun. I had lain down for a minute–my head throbbing with the aftertaste of adrenaline and stress–and must have fallen asleep. I was surprised Charlotte hadn't come to fetch me. We were serving the last formal dinner that evening, and there was still a lot to prepare. In any case, I couldn't remember opening the window.

A rustle of movement in the corner caught my attention. Still wearing his golf clothes, he sat in my chair, dwarfing it. His large body was bent forward, his elbows resting on his knees and his fists under his chin. He was staring with a quiet intensity that made me want to squirm and hide. Our gazes locked and I watched a mix of indecipherable emotions cross his face. A sense of relief stole over me.

I'm so glad you're here.

"How long have you been sitting there?" I asked, sitting

up and rubbing my eyes, my voice raspy from sleep. I hadn't bothered to take my uniform off. It was a wrinkled mess. Without a word, he came to sit on the small twin bed and cupped my face with such gentleness that it almost made me cry. "Don't you look like the lord of the manor," I teased, trying to lighten the grave mood.

Ignoring me, he closed his eyes and placed a sweet, tender kiss on my lips. "Are you okay?"

I wasn't sure if I wanted to crawl onto his lap and lay my head on his shoulder, or push him away and tell him to get the hell out. I couldn't bear the kindness or the concerned look on his face. It was a drug, addicting and dangerous for me.

"Yes, I'm fine. Why would you ask that?" The snappy tone in my voice made him pause. His hand dropped back down, leaving my face cold and lonely where the warmth of his palm had been.

"Ben told me what happened with Marcus. I'm sorry. That won't ever happen again. They're gone. I threw them out."

My eyes widened, the last traces of sleep evaporating. He'd thrown them out? "What did you say to him?"

"I told him that if he ever looked at you again, I was going to make sure he tripped head-first into a wood chipper."

My mouth gapped open. "You're joking…right?"

"I'm deadly serious about keeping you safe. He's right to be scared of me."

Words deserted me. How was I to respond to that? His expression was hard and remote, a current of violence emanating from every fiber of his being. I needed to bring him back to me, to restore some sanity. I placed my hand over his heart and petted him gently in slow circles, working the anger out of his muscles. My hands traveled around his head, coaxing him closer. When I ran my short nails over his nape, he let out a deep sigh. Sensing his acquiescence, I kissed him, teasing his lips apart until he softened and kissed me back. I don't know how I knew what he needed from me. I just did, as he knew where to touch me.

"Will you come to the lake with me tonight?" It was the first time he'd asked, instead of issuing a decree. That was progress.

"I don't know. We'll be done late with dinner this evening."

"Meet me in the woods by midnight."

Okay, well, baby steps.

"Go now. I need to change my uniform."

He gave me a curt nod and smacked my lips with a quick kiss, then stood and quit the room. I stared at the door as it closed behind him, his words still ringing in my head. *I'm deadly serious about keeping you safe.* His behavior in the past was starting to make sense now. He was worried for me. Sweet, beautiful man. And the look on his face…it had been so long since anyone was concerned for me. I was in serious danger of losing what little grip on reason I had left. There wasn't even the smallest doubt that I would meet him at midnight, and we both knew it.

———

HE PULLED me through the woods that led to the north side of the estate, where the small lake was located—Lake Geneva being too dangerous and cold for midnight swims. The moon concealed itself behind a carpet of clouds. It was so dark I could barely see a foot ahead of me. All of a sudden, a warm gust of air pushed them aside, and a shaft of light fell on his flexing shoulders. I stopped abruptly, my hand yanking out of his grip, and he turned with a questioning glance. He was so beautiful my heart hurt. Probably because I knew he would never really be mine.

"You're beautiful," I whispered.

His sharp gaze softened and his mouth curved into a lopsided smile. Moving swiftly, he pushed me up against the rough trunk of a sycamore and kissed me, driving my head back with his passion. He grabbed my rear end, his fingers digging into the soft flesh of my hips, and lifted me up without any effort. I wrapped my legs around him and held him tightly.

"I need you," he said breathlessly, between kisses.

I had unleashed a monster. He'd never been this impatient, demanding. He devoured my mouth, his tongue in deep penetration. There was nothing I could do but submit. He fumbled with his athletic pants, trying to free his erection, and roughly shoved himself against the thin linen of my nightgown, hard and hot against my sex.

"I want you," I murmured. I was so worked up I couldn't stop the words from spilling from my lips. He cupped me, stroking impatiently. When he pressed his fingers inside of me, he discovered just how much.

"God, you're wet," he whispered, the rasp in his voice more pronounced. He positioned himself and let my body sink, fully impaled by my own weight. My short fingernails dug into his shoulders. My teeth scraped the delicate skin of his throat, making him gasp and press closer.

The feeling of utter fullness, of possession, was mind-blowing. He was everywhere. He began thrusting up hard and sure, the sensation so acute that I came in a sharp, explosive climax that had my body closing around him in a vise-like grip. He kept pounding into me until he allowed himself the same relief, my name ripped from his throat in a shout loud enough to echo through the woods—he wasn't quiet in his passion anymore. Sagging against me, he buried his face in the curve of my neck, his chest rising and falling rapidly as he struggled to breathe.

Reality returned in an instant. With it came the sting from the scrapes inflicted by the ragged bark. My throat pinched from the swell of emotion boiling up. He snuggled closer. Ever so delicately, with care reserved for precious things, I stroked the nape of his neck and sifted my fingers through his hair.

Things were so good between us. Why this man? This man I could never have.

"No condom...Jesus," he said between choppy breaths. "When are you due for your period?"

That hit me like a thunderbolt. I was never irresponsible. Never.

"I don't get it regularly. Mostly, I don't get it because of my weight. There's little chance anything happened. My mother had a hard time conceiving."

His gaze lifted to mine and found absolute truth. He placed me back on solid ground and my legs wobbled, incapable of holding me up. Before I could stumble, he pulled me into his arms and anchored me to his solid frame. "You should probably be on birth control, just to be safe. God knows I have no control around you."

He was right, of course. I wasn't even going to pretend that I didn't love it when he lost his vaunted self-control with me. I replied with a simple, "Okay." And realizing that there wouldn't be any argument, he grabbed my hand, laced his fingers through mine, and led me to the lake.

I WATCHED him swim the width of the lake twice before he swam back to me. The graceful line of his body cut through the water with ease. For a moment I wished I could have seen all that power at full throttle, before the accident, then quickly abandoned the thought. This is who he was now— my imperfect, perfect lover.

"Will you at least try?" he asked with a teasing smile. His face transformed when he was playful, glowing as if lit from within.

"No. I'm not exaggerating when I say I'm not a good swimmer. I keep paddling and never get anywhere."

We were treading water close to shore. He kept touching me, his hands roving over me unconsciously, pulling me closer. I wrapped my legs around his hips, and his large hands stroked my rear end and squeezed.

"Sebastian…" His fingers sifted through my intimate curls and tugged. I yelped and laughed, swatting his hand away.

"Hmm, nothing sweeter than my name on your lips."

"Someone said that you were supposed to be on the U.S. Men's swim team, at the Sydney Olympics. What happened? How come you didn't go?"

His expression sobered, his smile flattening into a grim line. He rubbed his face, his wide palm brushing water drops off his thick lashes. *Blast it.* I hadn't intended to ruin the good mood. My smile disappeared, too. When his hand lifted, he looked at me pointedly.

"You really want to know?"

I felt awkward, like I had stepped over some invisible line. "Only if you want to tell me," I answered softly.

"I've never told anyone before." He seemed surprised at himself, feeling the words out on his lips.

"You don't have to," I mumbled.

Soothing the awkwardness, I reached out and ran my hand against the bristle on his cheek and jaw. He grabbed it, turning his face into my palm, and kissed it.

"My mother overdosed the night before the Olympic trials. She was in a coma for three weeks."

"How?"

"Valium, Percocet, and vodka. The official story is that I pulled a hamstring. The family called in favors to keep her name out of the papers and the hospital records—my mother's family is in the oil business, and very influential in Houston."

The water was suddenly cold. My teeth chattered. "I'm sorry," I said while I held him and cradled him with my arms and legs, unwilling to let anything separate us.

"It's old news." He stroked my bottom again and gripped my hips. "Time to get out. You're shivering."

My heart ached for him. It was obviously not old news. It was clear he still harbored a good deal of anger and resentment. What a sacrifice. To train all those years and have it taken away from you by no fault of your own. I could certainly empathize with that. A clear picture was coming together about his ambivalent relationship with his mother and it wasn't pretty.

We took our time walking back to the house, shrouded in silence, accompanied by moonlight. I couldn't stop staring at our entwined hands, imprinting my mind so I could cherish the memory someday. I had tried my best to remain detached and failed, lost that struggle a while ago if I was honest with myself. I was no expert at handling illicit affairs. He was steadily pulling me into the deep end of the emotional pool. My willpower was no match for the depth of feeling I had for him. It was a demoralizing discovery because, eventually, he would move on, and I would be left to patch up my shattered heart. Aleksander's betrayal had taught me a harsh lesson. I could never allow myself to need someone again, to depend on anybody. Self-preservation trumped everything, even love.

"We need to lay some ground rules if we're going to continue this...this affair."

He stopped and turned, his eyebrows hitching up at my clinical delivery. "Ground rules? Umm. Okay. How do you usually conduct these things?" he asked with a shade of sarcasm just this side of anger.

"I don't usually conduct anything, as you well know, but I think we need to draw some clear boundaries."

"I'm all ears." He released my hand and raked his hair back off his face.

"First...the alcohol and the painkillers scare me."

He looked pensive. "I've been thinking about that. The drinking isn't a problem. I don't know about the oxy...maybe with your help..." His voice trailed off, his expression turned cautious. I couldn't see the beautiful mask anymore, the ruse that everyone else saw when they looked at him. All I could see was the uncertainty in his eyes. Had anybody ever been there for him?

"Of course, I'll help. All I ask is that you try." A flash of amazement appeared in his eyes before he hid it. He hadn't taken anything for granted. "Second, I want this to remain private, between us. I don't want anybody at the house to ever know." His brow pinched. Clearly, he wasn't in agreement, so I continued before he worked up an argument. "I have a ridiculous amount of respect for Mrs. Arnaud. I don't know where I'd be without her kindness, and I would be mortified if she knew."

"Marianne is an extremely understanding person."

"I don't want her to know," I interrupted, my voice rising. I wrapped my arms around myself, holding down a nervous tremor.

"Okay, easy. We'll keep it between us, for now."

"All we have is now. I didn't expect this to happen, but it has. This is about you and me now. No past and no future."

He stared out towards the house, brooding. When his eyes returned to me, they were apprehensive again. "So this is about sex. Is that what you want?"

Stay strong. I braced myself, even though my stomach clenched painfully at the wounded look on his face. "Yes. And when it's over, when you're ready to move on, we won't ever speak of it again." My voice sounded hollow, disembodied. My short fingernails dug into my palms.

"How do you know I'll be the one to walk away?"

Bitterness underscored his words. He would run, not walk, if he ever found out about my past. "You will," I answered, as I began walking away.

———

"ALL I NEED IS six more eggs. Just cooperate and I won't bother you again for a couple of days." I reached under one of the hens tentatively. She wasn't having any of it. "Ouch! That's the third time. I'm warning you!"

"If you want to get under their skirts, darlin', you gotta sweet talk 'em. Not threaten 'em."

My back snapped straight and my head whipped around. Ben Winters stood outside the gate in long shorts that reached his knees and a sweat-soaked, white t-shirt that molded itself to the bulges of his chest so indecently I had to force myself to look at his face.

"Good morning, Mr. Winters. Out for a nice jog?"

"Yes, ma'am. Need some help?"

"Are you a hen expert, Mr. Winters?"

His eyebrow hitched up and his lips curved into a devilish smile. "No...but I know something about getting under skirts." His shameless smirk made me burst out in laughter. *Lady-killer.*

"Be my guest."

He entered the large pen that housed the exotic chickens and handed me his iPhone. "Call me Ben, please."

"Your accent—I had no idea Americans really spoke that way until I started working for Mr. Horn." He glanced at me sideways with an amused expression. I got the distinct impression he knew more about my relationship with Sebastian than I wanted him to.

"Not Americans, Texans." Circling the chicken coop, he studied the hens from different angles.

"I think you have to just go for it," I encouraged.

He stood with his hands on his hips and his eyes on the hens, his brow creasing thoughtfully. "Sebastian's pretty much lost most of it."

"You've known each other a long time?"

"We've been best friends since the fourth grade." Gingerly, he tried to sneak his hand under the hen. She pecked him before he had a chance to remove it. "Ouch."

I bit back a laugh. "Too slow, Ben, too slow. She's deadly quick."

"I didn't exactly look like this in the fourth grade."

"You don't say."

"Na, I was real skinny. Malnourished. I had a tough upbringing." My face fell when I realized he was no longer kidding. "One day, after school, a bunch of older boys started picking on me. Beat me up real good until Sebastian stepped in and set them straight. I think one kid lost a tooth. Then he took me home with him. I lived there for two months before anyone figured it out."

"Two months?"

"We've been best friends ever since," he affirmed with a boyish grin.

Still reeling from the story he'd told, I watched Ben try to gently push the hen off the nest with his forearm. The hen only flapped her wings and made a fuss, scowling at him. That's when Charlotte marched in with purposeful strides, a cigarette rakishly hanging from her lips. She stuck her arm under the hens and extracted six warm eggs like she was strolling down the dairy aisle at a supermarket. Handing me the eggs one by one, she directed a haughty glare at Ben. There was a confusing undercurrent of hostility between them. I made a mental note to ask her about it later.

His eyes narrowed at her self-satisfied smirk. Suddenly, he snatched the dangling cigarette from her lips and ground it out under his sneaker. "Disgusting, filthy habit," he grumbled. Then, pivoting on his heels, he stalked out of the chicken pen.

"How dare you!"

"I dare," he shouted over his shoulder.

We both watched him walk away, his muscles flexing and rippling under the wet t-shirt with every step he took. I turned and pinned Charlotte with an assessing glance. "Is there something you're not telling me?"

"What makes you say that?" she replied. She tugged anxiously at the loose curls that had escaped her ponytail. I raised a disbelieving eyebrow. "It's nothing," she added, feigning innocence poorly. It was clear to a blind man that it was indeed something. "Nothing I can't handle, at least." The resigned tone of her voice nagged at me. As I watched her march back to the house, I made a mental note to get to the bottom of it.

CHAPTER 19

The next day guests began departing at dawn. It was a long process of preparing meals, counting bodies, and dragging luggage to the landing in front of the house. The entire staff was overworked and exhausted. The last remaining guests were his mother and Caroline Pruitt, the name I heard whispered about. Apparently she was an American steel heiress.

We caught sight of each other in between meals and departures. Caroline, ever present by his side, yapping at his heels like a rat terrier. His eyes were dim, withdrawing. I didn't blame him. I knew he was hurt. As much as I was an open book to him, I had gotten very good at reading him as well. Still, it had to be done, for both our sakes. We both needed to stay grounded in sober reality.

Diana Redman had been watching me with the same marked interest as one of Sebastian's falcons eyeing its dinner. She made sure that he and I weren't left alone for a single moment. Little did she know, I had done a good job of that all on my own. He hadn't approached me once. I caught him staring a couple of times but he turned away as soon as our eyes met.

I had just finished wrapping the leftovers from lunch when Sebastian walked into the kitchen looking every inch the "lord of the manor." Not a hair out of place, wearing a closely tailored white shirt of silky cotton, a pair of lean cut linen pants, and Italian driving moccasins. The very picture of ruthless power and elegance. The mask was back on, fixed firmly in place. The fact that I had done that to him made me excruciatingly uncomfortable.

Mrs. Arnaud reached into the refrigerator and pulled out a container filled with small pieces of chicken. I started drying the silverware with quick, firm strokes while my eyes flickered back and forth to his. He wouldn't look at me. It hurt, even though I deserved it. Over the last few days I had grown accustomed to seeing him brighter, happier. Now the solemn expression was back and all I wanted to do was kiss him until I banished it from features too perfect for his own good.

"Can you give me a hand with this?" His gaze, still elsewhere.

"Yes, of course."

We walked past the vegetable garden and through the woods without saying a word. He stared ahead and kept his usually long stride in check. Even with that hitch in his step, I had to push myself to keep up with him. I wanted to scream. All the easy comfort between us had vanished. And with a few calculated words, we were back to where we had started weeks ago.

Without thought or consent I reached for his hand and laced my fingers through his. His eyes snapped to our joined hands. Surprise flashed briefly. Then I felt a gentle squeeze and his brandy colored gaze lifted to meet mine. He was waging an internal battle. I could see it blazing in his eyes, and knew immediately which side won when I heard the bag he carried hit the soft grass, felt his arms sweep around me in an unbreakable hold. A tremble bounced off of him when the hard planes of his chest impacted my soft ones. His fingers found their way to my hair, dismantled my neat ponytail in seconds. His other hand roamed up the skirt of my uniform and kneaded the small cheeks of my rear end. Pulling me closer, he shoved the unmistakable evidence of his passion against the soft curve at the top of my thighs. An electric jolt branched through me, my moan swallowed by his desperate kiss.

I would have laughed at his impatient seduction if I didn't know him better. He had totally lost control of the volatile emotion he kept tightly leashed. Some dark, greedy part of me loved that I could get him this undone. It was exhilarating, a potent aphrodisiac. The part of me that still managed to reason, however, counseled me to be careful. I wasn't certain if I had a tiger by the tail, or it had me.

Before I could object, he had me pressed into the sun-soaked ground among wildflowers and tall fescue, his large body cradled between my thighs. He pressed impassioned kisses up and down my throat, scraping the thin skin with his teeth in a carnal show of possessiveness. He exhaled harshly. It turned me pliant, amenable. Thoughts of resisting melted away, replaced by disjointed images and sounds strung together like rosary beads. Reality bled into a dream.

The rustling sound of the oaks. A white butterfly floating drunkenly above us. Chirping from a far-away bird. The too-close buzzing of a bee. His hands stroking, caressing my breasts. The smell of starch on his shirt and that scent, that scent that was distinctly him. He ground his erection against

my sex. My hips hitched up to meet him in consensual agreement. Whispers escaped in between kisses and nibbles.

"Need you," he muttered. "Can't wait…" His fingers
gripped the top of my pantyhose and began pulling, determined in his goal. I reached down and covered his hand.

"We can't. Not here," I whispered, then unmercifully
licked the sensitive skin below his earlobe.

"Now!" The command loaded with raw emotion. "Have
to be inside of you," he mumbled. He redoubled his effort,
and in his haste shredded the hose in two. He was breathing
hard, the remnants of control snapping visibly. Impatiently,
he fumbled with his linen pants. I tried to help but he shoved
my hands aside. His erection finally free of his boxers, he
shoved the wet tip against my aroused and eager body and
pushed against that swollen, tender spot that made me see
stars.

"Sebastian, condom," was all I could get out in sharp fits
and starts.

"Shit! I'll pull out."

Words of reason and admonishment got caught in my
throat. He slid deep inside and filled me with unbelievable
pleasure before I had a chance to think twice. A relaxed sigh
escaped his lips, the mere act of being joined giving him
incomparable relief. I wrapped my legs around him and held
on tightly. I could feel him everywhere, as if this beautiful,
virile man were made just for me. With every sweeping
thrust, the pleasure built. The rhythm bold, surging out with
luscious slowness, then thrusting deep and sure. He held me
down securely, easily dominating me. I was powerless
against such strength. Gladly, I relinquished all control, and
the thrill of it pushed me closer to climax.

"Now, Vera. Now!" Jaw clenched tightly, he forced the
words out, his face contorting from the effort it took to

hold back. On a powerful thrust, I exploded, my body clenching and releasing in a rolling orgasm that squeezed him tightly. He shouted, a guttural oath following my name, and pulled out. The look of unadulterated bliss swept across his face before his head dropped to the curve of my neck.

His grip on me didn't loosen. "Don't let go," he whispered. It was almost inaudible. But I heard it nonetheless.

————

WE WALKED BACK to the house tucked up against each other, our strides turning lazy and reluctant the closer we got. He plucked a pretty wildflower with five broad petals stained in bright pink, and twirled the stem in between his index finger and thumb with such tender care I was becoming jealous of a tiny flower. I looked up and discovered a playful grin hanging on his face. He wiggled his eyebrows at me and I burst out in laughter. *You make me so happy*, I wanted to say but didn't.

I tried to push away from him, but he held me firmly against his chest. "Where do you think you're going?"

"Away from you. You're a terrible influence." I couldn't stop giggling, his affection coaxing a reserve of pure joy out of me that I didn't even know I possessed.

"Never," he whispered seductively. "Never," he repeated, his expression serious this time. My smile slipped, the spell broken. He tucked the flower behind my ear and silenced my mind with a kiss.

A loud crack split the sound of trees rustling in the wind.

Before I realized what had happened, I was on the ground, caged by two hundred-plus pounds of muscle. Eyes blinking, ears ringing, it was all a mass of confusion. A moment later, my mind registered the wild look on his face, and just as abruptly, the sound returned.

"Vera! Vera, are you okay?! Have you been hit?!"

Hit? I certainly hit the ground hard enough when he tackled me. I couldn't understand what in the world he was shouting about. Why was he so alarmed and angry? My line of sight shifted slightly to the right. That's when I noticed the blood stain spreading on his shoulder.

"Oh my God! Sebastian, you're bleeding!" I struggled to get up.

"Don't move! Someone's shooting at us!" he shouted, pinning me firmly.

"Shooting? Who could be shooting at us? Why would they be shooting at us?"

A strange stillness had fallen over everything, the forest, and wildlife all holding a collective breath.

"I don't know. Could be—" His face grew pale, his eyelids heavy. He shook his head, trying to stay conscious. All emotion fled, and my mind sharpened to respond in lightning-quick decision-making, unlike anything I could accomplish under normal circumstances. I have always been at my best when a crisis arises. Some people lock up and freeze, others get overly emotional, overwhelmed with anger or fear. I turn as steady and dependable as a U.S. dollar bill.

He was too weak to protest when I rolled him onto his back and ripped his shirt open. The bullet wound had grazed him on the outside of his bicep. It had cut through muscle. Thankfully nowhere near any bone or important blood vessels. I tore his shirt apart and tied a punishing knot around the wound, staunching the bleeding. He grimaced as I thumped my fingers hard and fast on the top of his breastbone in an attempt to keep him awake.

"Sebastian, you've been shot. It's not serious. I've stopped the bleeding. But I need your help to get you back to the house—unless you want me to go get help."

"No…no. I'll get up. Give me a hand."

I threw my shoulder under his uninjured arm and levered him up. We had been here once before. Except he was no longer an adversary or a stranger. He was the man I…I cared for him. Of course, I did. How could I not? He was so easy to care for. That thought was a lead marble rolling around in my stomach–or a bullet.

As we approached the house, I began screaming for help. People poured out of the woodwork. They ran towards us, shouting instructions at each other before they lifted Sebastian's weight off of me and pulled us apart. Unwilling to let me go, he reached out with his uninjured arm and our fingers tangled. Ben Winters grabbed my shoulders and shook me gently, making me tear my gaze away from Sebastian.

"Vera, what happened?" he asked in a steady, soothing voice.

"The falcons. We went to feed them…we were walking back. I heard a crack. Sebastian was bleeding…bullet went through clean." I only heard bits and pieces of my own story told in a weak voice I didn't recognize.

"You're not going to faint, are you?"

That snapped me out of my daze. "Of course not! I'm a physician for heaven's sake. I have to go dress the wound before they take him to the hospital."

His eyebrows hitched up at the unexpected sound of authority in my voice. "Okay. If you can make it back to the house on your own, I need to check something out."

"Ben, please be careful." His eyes landed on my small hand, resting on his forearm, and the stern set of his mouth relaxed.

"This is what I'm trained in." He squeezed my hand before removing it and stalked off into the woods.

———

"VERA! WHERE IS SHE, DAMN IT!" I could hear him bellow from downstairs, his raspy voice echoing down the hall. At least he wasn't fading out of consciousness again. I made my way up the marble staircase at a brisk pace.

A group of servants hovering outside his bedroom door parted to let me enter, a question mark hanging over their heads. Charlotte, in particular, studied me closely. Caroline Pruitt stood inside his bedroom doorway. She narrowed her eyes at me when I walked past her, turned to inspect Sebastian, then me again. I avoided her watchful gaze purposely. With the way Sebastian was carrying on you'd have to be obtuse not to notice that there was something highly irregular going on.

I found Sebastian sitting up in bed, his expression a mix of worry and frustration. Aside from the dried blood painted on his bare chest and the strip of shirt still secured around his bicep, he looked to be in good form. His body sagged into the mattress when he caught sight of me. The tension left his face by small degrees with every step I took walking around to his side of the bed. His eyes, bright from the flood of adrenaline, followed me the entire distance.

Mrs. Redman sat on the edge of the mattress flipping her hair and generally making a nuisance of herself. *A selfish creature to the core,* I thought with unmitigated disdain.

"You have no idea how scared I was when I was told that you'd been shot, Scout. My nerves can't take any more surprises like this." She turned to face the staff. "Can somebody get me a goddamn martini like I asked for five minutes ago?!"

I noticed Mrs. Arnaud was busy inspecting her nails, Mr. Bentifourt quietly conversing with François. He caught my attention and his head tipped in the direction of the dresser, where he had placed the medical supplies.

"There are too many people in this room," I declared, my critical gaze directed straight at Mrs. Redman. I wasn't about to make any allowances for her rudeness because she had given birth to him. I waited patiently for her to get up. To no avail, she sat there watching me with a mulish expression that provoked me further.

"*Allons-y, allons-y.*" Mrs. Arnaud clapped her hands, herding everyone out the door and down the hall. Caroline Pruitt paused in the doorway and glanced at us pointedly before leaving. A shiver of unease rippled across my skin.

"Mrs. Redman, your son," I paused meaningfully, "has endured a considerable amount of blood loss and pain. I need to clean the wound. Kindly remove yourself." My gaze met Sebastian's and a sympathetic understanding passed between us. It was mind-boggling that she could be so oblivious to the fact that her son was injured and in pain. I couldn't even begin to imagine the horror of growing up with a woman like that.

Her bright, green eyes transformed into two slits. After what I had been through, it would take a lot more than her poisonous glares to intimidate the likes of me. "Who do you think you—"

Bentifourt stepped forward, interrupting the list of insults she was about to hurl at me. "Mademoiselle Sava has a medical degree, madam." I was so surprised by his unexpected gallantry that I turned to stare. A strange twinkle lurked in his dark eyes.

"Diana," Sebastian added in his imperious tone. That must have been the magic combination of words because she left in a huff.

"I've brought up all the necessary medication. Should I call for the helicopter to be readied?" inquired Bentifourt.

"No!" Sebastian shouted. "It's a fucking scratch."

Bentifourt didn't even blink at the outburst. I placed clean towels under his arm and removed the binding gingerly.

"It's hardly a scratch, Mr. Horn. Stop moving or you'll start bleeding again. You need antibiotics and you need to be seen by a doctor."

He gave me a cynical smirk at the sound of the formal address, then his gaze darted back to Mr. Bentifourt. "Call Dr. Schultz. He'll come to the house," he grumbled like a petulant teenage boy. After a subtle nod, Bentifourt walked out of the bedroom, leaving us alone.

"I'm flushing out the wound now…you almost fainted," I stated, cleaning it with Betadine solution.

"I know," he muttered, his eyes downcast while he smoothed a nonexistent wrinkle on the bed cover. He was embarrassed and ridiculously adorable. I bit the inside of my cheek to curb a smile. He wouldn't find it amusing. When he looked up, concern was written all over his breathtaking face.

"Are you okay? I fell on you pretty hard." Gently, he tucked a stray lock of hair behind my ear. I quickly scanned the open doorway before meeting his eyes again.

"I'm fine. Who would have done this?"

"I don't know. The police are on their way." His eyebrows pulled together.

"Could it be a hunting accident?" The silence caused me to glance up. His face was stony, unreadable.

"Could be," he answered, nodding absently.

"You don't look like you believe that."

"I'm not sure yet. Did Ben go check the woods?"

"Yes."

"He'll figure it out. I don't want you to worry."

While I wrapped the wound in sterile cotton, he placed his hand possessively on my knee, squeezed and held on tightly. He did that often. It was such a small gesture. But nothing Sebastian did was gratuitous, everything he did held purpose and meaning. My eyes darted back and forth to his hand as I worked, contemplating what it meant. And then it hit me...

He held on to me as a child would for reassurance—afraid to let go. Shocked by the discovery, my breath stalled and a sudden sinking sensation gripped me. How in the world could a man at the top of the food chain, possessing power and prestige in abundance, feel this alone? My gaze lifted from his hand to his solemn, brandy colored eyes. I sighed. Unknowingly, he had just stolen another piece of my heart.

CHAPTER 20

"The police wish to speak to you, Vera," Mr. Bentifourt announced.

I looked up from slicing the chanterelle mushrooms for the risotto we were preparing for dinner and cut my index finger. Wincing, I dropped the bloody knife and it fell, clattering loudly onto the stone kitchen floor.

"Vera, you're bleeding!" Mrs. Arnaud ran over with a paper towel and wrapped it around my finger, keeping pressure on it.

Would they ask for papers? I immediately broke out in a nervous sweat.

"They only want to ask about the events this morning. There's nothing for you to worry about. Mr. Horn and Mr. Winters are in the living room with them," Mr. Bentifourt reassured in a sympathetic tone—another surprise. He was rarely sympathetic, or reassuring.

A warm and comforting hand squeezed my shoulder. "Go, *chérie*, Mr. Horn won't let anything happen," Mrs. Arnaud said in a super gentle voice.

I went to the sink and washed my hands, using the time to pull myself together. I could feel my heart pounding in my throat and it wouldn't be wise to meet them with a guilty expression that could be read from across the room. When I reached the door, I took a deep, calming breath and knocked. Once inside though, I went rigid under the intense scrutiny of four men. My eyes promptly searched for Sebastian. He was sitting in a stuffed chair, his posture casual. The warmth and encouragement in his gaze released a subtle tension I was unaware I was holding in my solar plexus.

Two men sat on the couch opposite him. One of them was young and hard looking, the other, middle aged and thick around the belly. The young one sat on the edge of the couch full of alert energy. The older one kept stuffing his face with Mrs. Arnaud's freshly baked madeleines and licking his fingers.

"Vera, Inspectors Duebel and Tribolet need to ask you a couple of questions about this morning." My eyes lifted to the sound of the deep voice. Mr. Winters stood close to the window with his arms crossed over his wide chest. "It'll only take a minute." I walked to the empty chair next to Sebastian, gripped by an overwhelming urge to touch him. For once, I was the one in need of reassurance.

"Please have a seat, mademoiselle," said the older inspector without looking at me. He reached for another cake, his fingers dangling over them, his attention entirely absorbed by the selection process. He was either incredibly sly or incredibly stupid. Either way I wasn't taking any chances so I sat perfectly still, perched on the edge of my seat with my hands in my lap, trying to remain as inconspicuous as possible.

"My name is Duebel," he informed me. Crumbs spilled from a mouth that reminded me of a carp's. "My associate here is Tribolet." He waved a crumb-covered hand in the general direction of the man next to him. Then he brushed them together, dropping crumbs on the antique Aubusson rug under our feet. My eyes fell on those crumbs and narrowed.

In the periphery of my vision, Sebastian forced down a smile. When I looked up, I found Inspector Tribolet inspecting me with pointed interest and felt, rather than saw, Sebastian stiffen.

"Let's move this along, shall we." His brusque tone earned the attention of both the inspectors, his intense focus now completely trained on the younger man.

"Yes, of course, Mr. Horn," said Deubel. "Mademoiselle, you were accompanying Mr. Horn on an errand through the woods on the north side of the estate? Correct?"

"Yes."

"And on the way back, about"—he checked his notes— "one hundred thirty meters from the house, you heard a loud sound, a crack?"

"Yes."

"What happened next?"

"Mr. Horn pushed me to the ground. I had no idea what had happened at first. Then I saw the blood on his bicep and quickly inspected the wound to discover that he had been shot. I took off his shirt and secured it around his arm to stop the bleeding."

"You were able to ascertain that you were no longer in immediate danger?"

"No. I guess that was ignorance on my part. I thought it might have been a stray bullet."

"And then you walked back to the house? You heard nothing else?"

"Correct."

"Your last name, mademoiselle? For my records," Tribolet cut in.

"I think you have enough for your records, Inspectors. Mr. Winters will show you out. Please keep him apprised of any developments," he announced in his usual *heir-to-the-throne-and-I-own-you* voice.

Tribolet didn't take too kindly to it. His eyes narrowed and the side of his mouth curved up slightly in a creepy grin. Deubel gave Tribolet a quieting glance and motioned towards the door before the bulls locked horns. Both men stood and proceeded to walk out with Mr. Winters bringing up the rear. Before exiting, however, they paused in the doorway.

"Thank you, Mr. Horn. May I call if I have any more questions?" Tribolet asked, his tone bordering on mockery.

There was an explicitly tense moment of silence as Sebastian's glare warned Tribolet to heel. "Of course, Inspector. I'll help any way I can." The touch of something sinister in the smile that followed gave me goosebumps. I never saw this side of him.

As soon as the door closed, Sebastian manacled my wrist and pulled me onto his lap. I flopped down against him and tried, without much effort, to squirm loose; I wouldn't risk bumping into his wound. "Are you crazy? Anyone can walk in!" The forceful whisper was completely useless in distracting him. He held me close and placed a string of sweet kisses up my throat, followed by an assertive scrape of teeth.

"No one is walking in except for Ben, and he knows about us."

"How could you?" Empty words. I was sighing in pleasure while I said them. The devil knew exactly how to disarm me.

"He's my best friend, Vera." His warm palm started

228

moving up my inner thigh, closer to... A knock at the door startled me. He held on firmly with his good arm while I struggle to get off his lap. Ben walked in, glanced at us with a blank expression, and threw his big body down on the couch with his long legs spread apart.

I would have laughed were I on the outside looking in. The two men started talking casually as if it was an ordinary thing for me to be sitting upright and rigid as a corpse on Sebastian's lap, my eyes as round as buttons, heat flashing up my neck. My fingers found the edge of my apron and fiddled nervously with it.

"Did you find the shell casing?" Noting my unease, Sebastian pressed my hand flat and laced his fingers through mine.

"Yeah, .300 Winchester Magnum." Ben's eyebrow twitched up. "Not likely anyone's hunting big game around here."

They were both quiet for a while, an icy chill suddenly permeating the room. Sebastian sighed deeply. I turned to study his face and didn't like what I found.

"What does that mean?" My voice was high and tight. I waited patiently while Sebastian and Ben exchanged knowing glances.

"It means that maybe this was no hunting accident," he answered grimly and squeezed my hand.

"Someone is intentionally trying to hurt you?!" Now I was legitimately worried. Cupping my face, he forced me to meet his eyes.

"Look at me. There's nothing for you to worry about."

"Vera, I'm going to have three of my best guys here by morning. Sebastian will be well protected until we can figure out who's behind this," added Ben.

"Your guys? I don't understand. And what are the police doing about this??!"

"Ben runs one of the most respected private security firms in the world. If anyone can figure this out, he can."

"Private security?" I was so inundated with information and raw emotion that I found myself repeating everything like an imbecile.

"Yeah, all my guys are ex-Special Forces, ex-Mossad. They're the best at what they do."

"And what is that?" I asked, genuinely intrigued.

"Hunt people down," he replied, shrugging.

Goose bumps popped up on my skin at the calmness of his reply. "What do they do once they've found them?"

Ben's eyes were glacial when he spoke again. "Whatever is necessary."

I had never seen such total lack of emotion on a human face. It was terrifying.

———

FOR THE NEXT few days I lived on pins and needles, worried for Sebastian, worried that *Inspecteur* Tribolet would get a bug up his rear and start snooping around. It wouldn't take much to find out I was undocumented.

As promised by Ben, three men arrived the morning after the shooting. Two of them looked like they were straight out of a Hollywood movie—large, brawny, and covered with tattoos that included Bible verses and skulls. An interesting combination. The larger man was bald, sporting a dark goatee, presumably to make him look even more menacing. The other was classically handsome, every feature perfectly symmetrical, and had a bored, unflappable look about him. And yet, out of the three, the less physically imposing one was indisputably scarier. He had a hyperaware look in his black-as-midnight eyes and a sardonic tilt to his mouth. Tall and slim, I couldn't deny that he was handsome in a villainous way. He reminded me of a picture I once saw in a textbook of a black mamba snake. Unremarkable and completely deadly.

I had been summoned to Sebastian's office and found him leaning against the back of his desk, gripping the edge. A king addressing his knights. As he made the introductions, I stood silently, organizing my thoughts. I needed to strike a delicate balance, communicating my apprehensions without undermining him in any way.

"Vera, this is Bear Mahoney, Justin Luck, and Gideon Hirsch. They will be on duty until the situation is resolved."

I shook the bald one's hand. "Bare, as in naked?"

His face split with a perfect white grin. "No, ma'am, as in the animal."

Mr. Bored and Handsome merely nodded, couldn't be bothered to extract his hands from his pockets. "Ma'am," was all he said.

Mr. Hirsch took my hand and surprisingly placed a brief kiss on the back of my fingers. The word "assassin" flashed through my mind. I didn't have to look to see Sebastian stiffen and frown. Luckily, that's all he did. In the silent moment that followed I glanced at him and our gazes locked, a thousand questions self-evident in my eyes.

"They need to know that we're together. Their job protecting us depends on it." His tone brooked no argument.

He knew me so well, better than anyone had ever known me, and in such a short time. Unsettling, to say the least. The three knights watched me expectantly for my agreement, I suppose. I was trapped in a prison of my own making with no escape. I could only hope that their professionalism extended to keeping secret affairs secret.

"Miss Sava, I assure you that you have nothing to worry

about," Gideon Hirsch coolly stated. He seemed to be the brains of the outfit. "We will do our best not to get in the way but I advise you to check in with us whenever you leave the premises—as a precaution." An intriguing accent. His Rs were soft, not quite rolled as with a French accent.

A dull ache was developing between my eyes. Pinching the bridge of my nose, I said, "I'm sure Mr. Horn has confided in you that...umm, that...our relationship is not public knowledge...and I would like to keep it that way. How is this going to work? I don't see why I need protecting. They aren't after me."

Gideon Hirsch's eyes were hooded when he spoke again. "The quickest way to hurt someone is to target the people they care about." I stiffened and kept my gaze pinned on Mr. Hirsch, too much of a coward to witness Sebastian's reaction. "I'm sure you wouldn't want to do anything to jeopardize Mr. Horn's safety?"

"Of course not," I said, chastened. That was an understatement. I would've taken the bullet for him if it were possible. I left shortly afterwards, after what felt like a scolding by Mr. Hirsch. As I paused outside the door, I heard words that weakened my knees.

"What do you know about her? I'm running a full check."

"No, you won't, Gideon. I know all I need to know."

"For fuck's sake, Sebastian. Let me do my job."

"I mean it—she's off-limits."

My heart was pounding as I walked back to the kitchen. I didn't doubt that with Gideon Hirsch's resources, he could uncover in an hour everything I was so desperately trying to hide. All the years of sacrifice...I had forsaken friendships, a social life, and anything that would reveal my identity. I had been a ghost these past six years, and now it was all in jeopardy because of one misstep. Never once did it occur to me that desire would be the instrument of my undoing.

———

A DAY later Sebastian found me in the library, one foot perched on a stepping stool, the other wedged on the bookcase I was dusting. I didn't see him the night prior. A message from him popped up on the computer screen around midnight. I lied about having a migraine and begged him not to come to my room. I knew it took a lot for him to obey my wish. And yet he had. I was fighting an uphill battle not to fall into a comfortable routine spending every night making love until I barely had the energy to crawl back to my room. It was dangerously easy for us to be together.

"I'm staying at the apartment tonight. I have a late business dinner, but I'm taking you to Geneva tomorrow afternoon. We'll stay there overnight."

"Absolutely not."

"Be ready."

"I can't get the time off!" I replied in a shouty whisper.

He wrapped his arms around my waist, buried his face among the folds of my skirt, and bit my rear end.

"Ouch!"

"That's what you get for arguing." His devilish fingers coasted down my waist and up my skirt. My legs trembled.

"I will fall and split my skull if you don't stop that immediately!"

He caressed the inside of my thighs, cupped my sex, acute sensation lingering everywhere his skilled fingers had been. My hands curled into tight fists in an attempt to hold onto the feeling as long as possible. He rubbed me in an achingly lazy rhythm with the nail of his thumb running along the seam of my sex, over the pantyhose. When my legs failed, he placed me on solid ground and nudged my body forward. My sweaty palms landed on a wall of first editions and my head dropped, my heavy breathing matching his. Trapped between his tall, muscular body and the bookcase, the heat emanating from him was all around me, the weight of him deliriously arousing. The sensation of being completely overpowered, dominated, was so exhilarating that it shocked me.

Where had this part of me been hiding the last ten years? Never once, in all my time with Aleksander, did I ever feel this overwhelming desire to be taken. I always thought my taste conventional when it came to sex, almost staid, and this new discovery shamed me. There had to be some perfectly good Freudian explanation for this...or maybe it was Jungian. Regardless, this was not who I thought I was.

I pushed back against the erection tenting the front of his gabardine slacks and heard him exhale harshly. It turned me on, knowing I had as profound an effect on him as he had on me. He bit the side of my neck, driving me to distraction. Caught unaware, my stockings were at my ankles before I realized what had happened. It jolted me right out of the pheromone-induced daze.

"Are you mad? Someone could walk in!" I struggled to turn around but he held me in place.

"Then we better be quick."

"Quick? You don't know what the word means!"

A burst of laughter was muffled on the side of my throat. Then he shut me up with his expert touch, petting me over my underwear, cultivating my desire for him. It didn't take much. I was slick the moment he touched me. Truthfully, it started as soon as he walked into the room, my body so attuned to him. Slipping his fingers inside, he nudged me with his erection from behind until he had me worked up in a frenzy of need...needing him.

Yes. Yes. Soft. Ready. Willing. Those were the only words my body ever spoke to his. Never a *"no."* Never even a *"maybe."*

"You're wet. Tell me how much you want me," he whispered in that raspy voice that drove me wild.

"You know I do."

I heard his trousers unzip, the tear of foil. He pulled my underwear to the side and pushed himself inside of me. A slow delicious friction into the welcoming softness. My short fingernails dug into the leather spines of the books and left tiny crescent marks. He pulled out and buried himself again and again. One large hand gripped my hip while the other wrapped around and stroked my clit. Imprisoned between two points of pleasure, I gave up all resistance.

"Tell me."

"I want you, only you, desperately," I said, my voice reedy and breathless. He thrust and held himself perfectly still inside of me...the bloody tease. "Oh Christ, Sebastian, please, please. I'm begging you!"

Something occurred to me in the sensual fog I was drifting in. He needed me wild and mindless for him. It drove him, and he wouldn't stop until he had me at his mercy. When he started moving, I began climbing again, rapture within reach. Then we both heard it.

Voices. Just outside the door.

My whole body turned to stone. "Stop, we have to stop," I whispered.

"Shhh." He thrust quick and deep, slamming into me at just the right angle, and placed his palm over my mouth in time to stop a primal cry from exploding out of me. Mindless and at his mercy. The voices faded. His fingers found me again, circling the tender, swollen nub, plucking gently. The tight coil unspooled. My muscles collapsed around him so firmly it triggered his release. He muffled a grunt into my shoulder and rolled his hips, milking his pleasure.

"Holy shit," he said, gasping. I couldn't have said it any better myself. I felt his forehead fall onto my back and listened to him fight for air. He kissed my neck and squeezed me tight before stepping back. I was incapable of anything that resembled movement, my body a loosely assembled pile of limbs. He straightened my clothing before restoring his own.

I turned around, expecting to find him as shattered as I was, and discovered His Highness the picture of relaxed elegance instead. Not a hair out of place, a sated smile on his handsome face, his graphite gray suit wrinkle-free. How the hell was that even possible? I was certain I looked as thoroughly worked over as one of the girls in the red-light district.

"Geneva tomorrow afternoon. I don't care what you tell her. Tell her you're visiting a sick friend, for all I give a shit. You don't need to bring anything. Meet me at the café in town if that makes you more comfortable." When I failed to respond, rendered stupid from an epic orgasm, he arched a brow and gifted me with one of his *Adonis-in-the-flesh-and-you-are-powerless-to-resist-me* smiles. "Good girl." Then he placed a peck on my lips, patted me on my behind, and left me standing there, contemplating whether this man had robbed me permanently of my ability to reason.

CHAPTER 21

The piazza was deserted. An old tomcat with one eye stared at me suspiciously from his lofty spot on a low wall. He knew what I was up to. As instructed, I waited patiently for him at the café. Worrying the nail bed of my thumb with my index finger, I finally clasped my hands in my lap in an effort to stop them from fidgeting. I had already torn three perfectly clean paper napkins to bits. The guilt of lying to Mrs. Arnaud about visiting a sick friend made my stomach churn. All of a sudden, that second latte had been a bad idea.

The black Mercedes SUV was parked across the street, a literal and metaphorical shadow following me everywhere. As I paid the bill for the café au lait, Sebastian's Bentley GT pulled up. I looked around like an inept spy before I stepped inside. With a relaxed smile on his handsome face, he leaned in and kissed me. I felt shy, out of my comfort zone. I tried pulling away but he held my chin and deepened the kiss. "You look nice."

I looked down at my clothes: my ivory silk blouse, my

best jeans, and my black heels. I looked far from nice. Unlike him, though, I didn't have any choice. My eyes did a slow and slightly annoyed perusal of His Majesty. Freshly shaved and dressed in beige linen pants and a white shirt, he looked nice, he always did. An alligator belt and Italian driving moccasins put an exclamation mark on his terribly expensive and extremely understated attire.

"What's that look for?" he asked, mild amusement on his face.

I was sulking. I couldn't help it. It also wasn't his fault that being near such sophistication made me feel a little homelier, a little less of everything good. "Why do we have to leave the estate? You look splendid by the way." The small, juvenile whine in my voice couldn't be missed. I turned to stare out the window while the car sped down the country road. He grabbed my hand and rubbed my knuckles.

"Splendid, huh?" His lips twitched, his warm eyes smiling. Then he kissed each knuckle and bit my thumb. I pursed my lips and gripped my knees together. This man had a direct line to my libido. "I just want us to spend some time together without having to sneak around. I have something special planned for tonight." There was something wicked in his voice, alluring.

"I need to ask you something," I said matter-of-factly, and looked over.

"What's on your mind?" His expression turned guarded.

"Paisley...she's your sister-in-law."

He had the grace to look a little guilty. When he continued to stare ahead, I thought he was going to dissemble.

"Paisley and I dated in high school," he said and exhaled deeply. "When she got tired of waiting for an engagement

238

ring from me, she seduced my stepbrother and married him instead."

Exactly like a soap opera. He looked over to gauge my reaction. I couldn't hide my surprise.

"Maybe my ego was a little bruised at first. But it's not like I was in love with her. I got over it quickly…she never did," he claimed. "She was unfaithful to him from the start. Although, from what I hear, so was he. By the time I moved to Geneva, Marcus was doing extremely well as a currency trader." I shifted in my seat to face him and he placed his hand on my knee, his thumb lazily stroking back and forth. Again, that vital link. "So when he called asking for a job, I hired him. Right about that time, Paisley decided she wanted to stay Mrs. Redman more than she wanted to stay in Texas."

He paused for a while, unsure how to continue it seemed. When he began to speak again, his voice grew quieter. "After my wife died…I…I was in a very bad place, for a long time. It wouldn't be fair if I blamed Paisley entirely for taking advantage of the situation, but that's when it started." His eyes darted back and forth from me to the road.

"Are you attracted to her?"

"No."

"Then why her?" Another deep exhale told me he wasn't entirely comfortable with the question, and neither was I.

"She likes it rough, Vera. Very rough. What you saw in the library…that was nothing. Let's just say I was happy to slake my anger out on her." He searched my eyes for disapproval and found none. Who was I to judge him?

"Thank you for telling me."

I noticed the almost imperceptible way his muscles relaxed at my words, the way his breathing changed. "Honesty cuts both ways," he replied. I shrank away from his searching gaze.

———

WE PULLED UP TO AN ELEGANT, turn of the century building across the street from Lake Geneva. The Cologny district was the most exclusive in the city. I wasn't even inside yet and I already felt as out of place as an atheist at a Christian summer camp. It was quiet, no Vespas speeding by, no honking of horns or traffic congesting the streets. We parked in an underground lot and took the elevator up to the penthouse. As the elevator doors shut, Sebastian pulled me into the shelter of his warm body and pressed me closer, until the stiffness was gone from my spine. I sighed as he cradled my face in his large hands and kissed me slowly. He was such a tactile man. When he touched me, everything felt right.

We entered the apartment with a set of codes on a panel. The carved maple door opened, and as I stepped inside, dim lights automatically turned on to reveal the beauty and elegance within. A mixture of contemporary and antique furniture struck the right balance. All clean lines and rich, luxurious materials. Inviting, comfortable instead of formal. Biedermeier pieces in pale wood, oversized down couches in a palette of soft neutrals. However, the view stole the show: an entire wall of windows that overlooked the city and the shoreline of the lake.

I could feel him watching me closely, measuring my reaction. No one had ever expended so much energy trying to gauge my thoughts. My eyes came across a large squeegee painting hanging at the end of a hallway and my breath caught.

"Is that a Gerhart Richter painting?"

"Yes, do you like his work?"

"Very much. I mean what I've seen online." I knew the Tate in London had one, and so did Sebastian, apparently.

"What do you think?" There was a sweet, uncertainty in his eyes. I wanted to launch myself at him and kiss that look away. A nervous laugh escaped my throat instead.

"It's breathtaking."

"It's mine. I bought it and had it renovated long before I inherited the estate, or the bank...this is really home for me."

"You don't feel at home at the estate?" I was surprised by his confession. He played lord of the manor quite naturally.

"It's my father's house." With his hands buried in his pant pockets, he shrugged. "That's how I'll always think of it." His expression had turned a little too somber. I reached up and petted his chest until his gaze returned to me with a smile.

"You want to talk about it?" I asked gently.

"Not tonight. Come." Grabbing my hand, he pulled me through a bedroom and into a walk-in closet where women's clothing hung neatly spaced apart. It felt like I had been dropped from a fifty-story building, my stomach bottomless. "These are for you. I'm pretty sure I got the size right," he casually explained.

Oh...

"The first dress is for dinner. Then we'll come back here and change for a party we're going to."

Speechless, I picked up the hanger and inspected the first dress, running my fingers over the soft, light wool. Roland Mouret. It was constructed and sleek, a deep burgundy color; perfect for my pale skin and dark hair. The other was a floor-length, black gown of silk jersey. It had a halter top and a knife pleated skirt with a slit that split the side. A small tag with gold lettering was visible. Gucci. I could feel him watching me.

"Did you pick these out?" Our eyes met and he replied with a quick nod. "I love them. Thank you, Sebastian." His earnest, shy smile made something inside of me come loose. My stomach fluttered.

"I'll leave you to get dressed."

I watched his steps as he walked out, and couldn't detect any extra stiffness. I had come to know the way he carried himself so intimately that I could tell when the pain started to break through the oxycodone, even when he tried his best to hide it.

"Sebastian..." He turned and looked at me, sweet expectancy on his face. I wanted to tell him how much I appreciated him, how much everything he did meant to me...how much he meant to me. "Nothing...I'll be ready soon." His smile faded and guilt made my gaze swing away. I had never thought of myself as a coward, but apparently I was.

Inside the closet, I found two shoeboxes. The first one was a pair of platform black, kidskin Christian Louboutins with a peep toe. I inspected them like they were priceless artifacts, a weeks' worth of salary I reminded myself. The second contained a pair of Sergio Rossi black high-heeled sandals that had thin straps crisscrossing all the way up to the knee. They were incredibly sexy and tasteful. There was also a tiny pink shopping bag from Agent Provocateur that contained a few pairs of silk thigh-high stockings. I was a bit disappointed to discover that there wasn't any sexy lingerie. My practical cotton bra and panties weren't exactly seduction material.

The bathroom attached to the bedroom was as beautifully decorated as the rest of the apartment. I sat at the vanity to do my makeup. Staring into the Queen Anne mirror, I wondered how many times she'd sat here doing the same thing. His beautiful, dead wife...whom he was still in love with. The bathroom had a feminine quality to it. Did he have it decorated for her? My spirits sank just thinking about it. The more he disclosed about her, the more I wanted to know. His confession about having been in a dark place after her death elicited a range of emotions that ran the gamut from empathy to jealousy. A novelty for me. Why did she so thoroughly own his heart?

Once done with the makeup, I undressed and placed my neatly folded clothes in the closet. I took my time rolling on the stockings, enjoying the feel of them on my skin. The silk was gossamer thin. They had a wide band of lace at the top and some type of adhesive rubber that made them stay in place. Slipping on the platform Louboutins, I walked into the closet to fetch the dress. The image in the tall mirror startled me. I didn't recognize the person standing there. My legs looked shapely in the sexy stockings, my lips plump from kissing, and my eyes were full of sparkle.

A vague memory of my engagement dinner crossed my mind. I was laughing at something Aleksander had said when I caught my reflection in a mirror. The same lively anticipation stared back. The situation was entirely different back then, there was promise in the future. All I had with Sebastian was the present. I couldn't delude myself into thinking there was any future for us. That door was firmly shut. I could play pretend for an evening, but I was not Cinderella. There would be no marriage to any prince in this story, no happy ending.

The Roland Mouret dress fit as if it were made for me. It was sleeveless and fell just above my knee with an interesting pattern of folds all over, like origami. I left my hair down. Parting it to the side, it fell over my shoulder.

I was securing one side with a pretty black comb when Sebastian walked in and came to an abrupt halt. An uncontrollable smile spread across my face. Effortlessly elegant, he wore a pale gray gabardine suit with a crisp white shirt. His face was unnaturally still as we stared at each other.

"You look..." he whispered. Reaching me in two long strides, he pinned me against the full-length mirror before I could blink. "You look too good to stay home, or you'd be underneath me right now," he mumbled between kisses that trailed down my neck. Two strokes of my bottom and his hands stilled, his eyebrow raised in question. "What's this?"

"My underwear." He pulled his lips between his teeth, fighting a smile.

"I'm aware of that. What I meant was, why are you wearing them?"

"Why wouldn't I?"

"Take them off." I stared back, blinking. Was he serious? "Now."

A shiver raced through me, quickly followed by a blast of heat. Not accustomed to wearing such high heels, I had to grip his arm for balance while I stumbled out of my trusty underwear.

"The bra."

"Sebastian—"

"Turn around," he ordered, removing my bra with the dexterity of someone who was practiced at it. The memory of his hot palm remained on my skin as he zipped me back up. It was mortifying how quickly he could reduce me to a puddle of need. "Come." Another order.

Hastily, he dragged me from the room and out of the apartment. In the elevator, he quickly enfolded me in his arms. He couldn't keep his hands off me any more than I could resist touching him, my desire feeding off of his. He placed kisses on my nose, my temple, and my mouth between mumbled words I couldn't discern.

When the elevator rang and the doors opened, we broke

the kiss panting. A busty redhead stood before us staring openly, her overfilled lips pursed. She was dressed in a white, banded dress that brought her cleavage front and center. Sebastian's expression transformed immediately. His Royal Highness was back. She stepped inside the elevator while her eyes raked up and down Sebastian's body in flagrant appreciation. I didn't care for it one bit.

Mine.

"Sebastian?" Another American.

"Lucinda." His tone was cool, standoffish.

"You look...well." She did nothing to mask the surprise in her voice. When her gaze settled on me, her dark blue eyes immediately turned icy.

"Never felt better. You?" he asked with no real interest, his attention still on me.

"Just got back from L.A. I didn't know you were in town."

"I've been busy," he murmured in a blatantly lascivious tone that, I won't lie, I was delighted to hear. The elevator reached the parking garage and the doors slid open. Sebastian threw his arm around my shoulders and pulled me out. I stole a quick glance behind us and found Lucinda slack-jawed.

"Good seeing you, Lucinda. Say hi to Patrick for me." He was a consummate actor. All the little nuances of his expressions, the ones he thought he hid so well, had become a native language to me.

"Slow down. I can't walk in this dress."

His lips quirked. "I won't let you fall, lover."

"Lover?"

"We're lovers, aren't we?"

I was grinning like a fool again. He did that to me, often. "Yes, I guess we are."

Once I was inside the car, he buckled me in. I never had a

man buckle my seatbelt before. It was strange and endearing at the same time.

"Hungry?" he asked as he turned on the ignition, his door whispering shut.

"Very."

"Good."

We pulled out of the garage and onto the road. I looked in the side mirror and recognized the black Mercedes SUV right behind us.

"Are they going to follow us everywhere?"

"That's their job. Why? Does it bother you?"

"Not if it keeps you safe."

"Us safe." He turned and pinned me with an alert glance. "You're with me now."

I didn't want to darken the mood with an argument, so I let the comment slide. "Who was that woman?" I could tell by his mixed expression that he didn't want to discuss it. "Is she an ex?"

"No. But not because she hasn't tried." His brow creased and he gripped the steering wheel tightly.

"Why do you dislike her so much?"

"How do you know I dislike her?"

"You're not the only one with the power of observation, lover."

He gave me a brief smile and sighed deeply. "That's a conversation for another night. I don't want to think about her right now." Cupping my small hand in his, he raised it to his mouth and kissed it.

"Okay," I answered, because I knew better than anyone that some topics were poisonous and I didn't want the smile to fade from his lips.

CHAPTER 22

W e pulled up in front of a building covered in ivy, a brass plaque reading Le Chat Botte next to the mahogany door. Sebastian put the car in park and Gideon Hirsch suddenly appeared, holding the driver side door open while he scanned the area with a razor-sharp focus in his dark eyes. After Sebastian helped me out, he settled into the driver's seat and drove away. We navigated around the rows of Rolls-Royces, Porsches, and Mercedes that lined the curb outside the restaurant typical of Geneva.

Inside, the bar area was richly styled, all dark wood and dim lighting. As soon as we walked in, a whole crowd of heads swiveled in our direction. I stiffened, my steps growing stilted. Sebastian looked back with a questioning glance, and when he noticed the tight look on my face, smacked a quick, hard kiss on my lips. He pulled me along, exuding that aura of superiority he always wore in public, and parted the sea of people that filled the bar without any effort. I followed in the wake of his magnificence with my chin down. Not even the expensive clothes helped stifle the overwhelming feeling that I was an imposter, a fraud playing at something I was poorly suited for. I wanted to shrink into a ball and roll away.

The maître d' greeted Sebastian with an indecent smile on his mobile, carnal lips. He caught me glaring at him and pressed those lips into a forced smile. "Mr. Horn, how wonderful to see you again. Your table is ready."

Eyes all over the dining room continued to follow us as we were led to an intimate table in the corner, near the windows. It had a breathtaking view of the city. Night had fallen and the Jet d'Eau was lit up. The maître d' sat us across from each other and continued to devour Sebastian with his eyes—not that he noticed, suddenly absorbed in the wine list.

"That'll be all, Jean. We're taking our time tonight."

Jean finally unfastened himself from our table, albeit reluctantly.

"How do you do it?"

His gaze lifted from the menu. The ghost of a smile lingered on his sensual mouth. "Do what?"

"Innocence doesn't suit you," I counseled. He chuckled, looking young and carefree for once. "How do you put up with the fawning masses?"

His eyes turned sulky, smoldering. "I'm only interested in one person fawning over me."

"I think we can safely say that I've been fawning over you since the day we met."

"That's not true," he replied, shaking his head. "I've had to work very hard to get you to fawn over me." I fought to keep a straight face, but I just couldn't do it when he was being so unabashedly sexy and charming. I must've fallen down a rabbit hole because two month ago I was contemplating eating my best friend's discarded cheese sandwich, and now I was dining at the best restaurant in the city with this glorious sex god.

"Wine?"

"I'm allergic, order whatever you like." Nothing gave me a blinding headache faster than a glass of wine.

"How about champagne then?"

"Yes, please."

Sebastian looked up and Jean was at his side in a heart-beat. When his gaze returned to me, his eyes were devilish crescents, a smile in them that made me burst out in laughter.

"Jean, we'll have the Krug '88."

"Of course, two glasses?"

"No, just one for my lovely lady," he replied, and Jean promptly scampered away to do his bidding.

"You're not having any?"

"Driving." Of course, the oxy wouldn't mix well with the alcohol. I was proud of him. He was trying, as he had promised.

"Don't people like you have drivers? Or permanent security detail?"

"I have security when I travel, but not at home. Draws too much attention. Besides, I like privacy, can't have any with too many people around." His pointed gaze held mine. "I've got a question for you."

"About what?" I did the best I could to sound relaxed, under the circumstances. I hated being under the microscope. He was too perceptive, saw too much in me. When Jean suddenly surfaced with the bottle, I was grateful for the reprieve. He poured and let Sebastian test it before serving me a chilled flute.

"Your British accent."

"Oh." I heaved a small sigh of relief. "Miss Albright—my

nanny until I was thirteen. She was a very stern, very proper British nanny with a degree in child development. Mr. Whitehurst was my tutor until I went to university. He was Oxford-educated. My father was a big believer in education," I replied, praying he would leave it at that. Needless to say, I was in rare company, having access to nannies and tutors in my country was unheard of. I took a refreshing sip of the rare vintage.

He leaned his head on the triangle of his index finger and thumb, his expression thoughtful. "Have you ever been?"

"To England? No. America was my obsession. All I did was watch old American television shows when I was a kid." He nodded, a sweet smile playing on his lips. "I told my father I wanted to move to Malibu and be a lifeguard when I was thirteen. He didn't think it was a good idea. Shocking, I know." The old memory made me smile into the champagne glass. "I'm certain I wouldn't have filled out the red suit quite like Pamela Anderson. And seeing that I'm not a very good swimmer, medicine was the better choice."

"I'll take you there. I have a good friend that has a house on PCH in Malibu. We can watch the sunset with a nice bottle of champagne."

My smile faded. "Don't say that."

He cupped my face and kissed me, licking a drop of champagne off my top lip. Self-consciously, I glanced around and noticed curious stares skipping back and forth between us. The heat from their collective attention made my cheeks burn.

"Why not?" he said in a low, sexy drawl. "There's so much I wanna share with you."

My discomfort growing, I tried to pivot away. "I never hear you speak that way to anyone else."

"Lost most of it at Stanford. Only comes out when I'm drunk...or turned on."

"You're always turned on."

He shook his head. "Only around you. I'd love to see you in a little red bathing suit," he added, cleverly maneuvering me back.

"As I recall, someone suggested *I could buy a pair.*" It was a casual remark tempered with a smile. And yet, his whole demeanor changed instantly. A flush crept up his neck and a scowl darkened his features, his gaze dropping to the water glass his long fingers held.

"I'm sorry," he murmured. "You should know that I think you're perfect just as you are."

I felt guilty for teasing him. He wouldn't look at me. He kept staring absently at the water glass, twisting the stem around and around. I cupped his face and raised his lips to mine, trying to persuade him with kisses to soften.

"Hey, I was teasing you. Come back to me."

His mood took another sharp turn. He grabbed my face and kissed me back passionately. A little too passionately for public consumption. A forced cough rang above us and we startled apart.

"I'll order for you. Any other allergies?"

I should have been irritated, but I wasn't. I knew better now. His drive to control and dominate came from fear, from this irrational impulse he had to guard and take care of me. For whatever reason, he needed it and I gave it to him willingly.

"Yes." Surprised, he glanced up from the menu. "To over-bearing men," I said, my eyebrow arching. It was just a brief smile, and it disappeared just as quickly, but I caught it none-theless.

Jean took the order, standing much too close to Sebastian

if you asked me. In the meantime, my eyes took the opportunity to indulge themselves. And there was so much to take in, every small detail about him a precious jewel I wanted to secretly tuck away so I could admire it later, in the privacy of my thoughts. Where it hurt no one to dream of what could've been if I weren't me, if we were just two ordinary people that had met in an ordinary way.

"You never mention your family."

His question sucked me out of my thoughts. My hand stopped abruptly from reaching for the champagne glass, my gaze sliding up to his. "My mother died in labor and my father passed away six years ago. There's no one left." Sipping the champagne slowly, I hid my unease in the glass. His scrutiny remained on me though.

"That must be difficult," he said, brushing my cheek tenderly.

I pulled away, too unsettled to meet his perceptive eyes. My gaze slid to the window. "I'm used to it."

"Is that why you chose medicine? Because of your mother?"

The reflection of the streetlights sparkled off the Jet d'Eau. "I suppose...I don't care to look at it too closely," I admitted. "Let the dead bury the dead." Even though it was a soft murmur, spoken more to myself, he must have heard me because his gaze grew startling in its intensity, the meaning of which, I couldn't even begin to fathom.

We started with a course of marinated sea bass, fleur de sel, combawa, with an infusion of spider crab and Indian verbena. The aroma floating up from the artistic presentation made my mouth water and my stomach grumble. Sebastian's eyes were focused on me as I savored every bite. It made me terribly self-conscious.

"Is Marianne not feeding you enough?"

I blanched. "What do you mean?"

"I heard your stomach growling."

"She's been nothing but kind and generous. It's me. My metabolism is in overdrive all the time. I can't keep weight on."

"I want you eating more. Promise me."

"I'll try."

"Promise me, or I'll speak to her myself."

Worry ripped through me. "No, please don't. I promise."

When the main course of Dublin prawns rolled in kadaïf arrived, I scrambled to change the subject. By now, I'd learned that arguing won me nothing and only caused him to entrench more firmly. "Do you like what you do? Running the bank, that is." For a moment, he looked confused. "Hasn't anyone ever asked you that before?"

"Actually, no," he answered, mild amusement in his voice. He gathered his thoughts before adding, "I don't know if I would say I love running the bank. It's the game, I love."

"The game?" He poured me another glass of champagne. I savored every rich swallow, the delicious vintage making me loose and easy.

"Trading is a zero-sum game," he explained. "There's no gray area. Someone wins, someone else loses." An aggressive glint sparked in his eyes.

"How did you get into it?"

"I started as an energy trader. I told you my mother's family is in the oil business." He shrugged casually. "The rush is addicting."

"It wasn't about the money?"

"Money is just the scorecard. The rush comes from winning. And trust me more people lose than win. Anyway, I was always expected to take over the bank." This was a side of him I rarely saw, unless he was barking orders or swearing at one of his people on the phone. I was separated from that part of his life. The real part.

"Do you still trade?"

"No. I have too much responsibility. Keeping an eye on my guys handling the billion-dollar portfolios is a full-time job."

I tried to act blasé at the figure but failed miserably. "Billion?"

"Multi-billion," he corrected, his mouth curving into a roguish smile. He was so cocky, so sure of himself when it came to his work.

This was exactly why I didn't want to leave the safety of the estate. There, I could pretend we were just two people desperately attracted to each other. Here, I was faced with the uncomfortable truth that we were worlds apart. The word "imposter" kept popping up in my mind. His brows pinched together when he realized what my mind was chewing on. Grabbing my hand, he raised it to his lips and kissed the palm.

"Don't do that. Don't pull away. It's just money."

A dry laugh surged up my throat. "Says the billionaire. Rich people are the only ones that ever say it's *just* money."

"It means nothing between us. And I won't apologize for it. You'll learn to live with it."

It was so easy for him to let his imagination run wild, to consider the possibilities. He didn't have a clue what I was hiding. I didn't have that luxury. And I would do anything to keep him from discovering the truth.

"I don't have to learn to live with anything. The only place we belong together is in your bed. And when it's over, you'll go back to your world, and I'll stay in mine."

His eyes were intense, burning with pent-up emotion,

and his breathing had quickened. He was struggling to control himself. "Are you done?"

"Yes."

He signaled for the check. "We have somewhere to be."

Jean picked up the pace when he realized the air hanging around the table had suddenly turned frigid. Once the bill was paid, Sebastian pulled me out of the restaurant. The tension surrounding him was palpable. I knew something was coming. As soon as we hit the street, he dragged me into a dark alley, around the corner, and pushed me up against the side of a building. Before I could take a breath, he grasped my face and his mouth came crashing down in a brutal kiss.

I took it. I took all of it. His frustration, his desire, his need to dominate, to make me bend to his will. He bit my bottom lip hard enough that I could taste the metallic tang of my own blood. He squeezed my breasts roughly and my body bowed into his hands, rather than shrinking away. His reckless passion stoked mine to a fever pitch.

"You need to do a better job listening." I felt a scrape of teeth on the delicate skin of my throat. The sting lingered. "Who do you think is calling the shots here?" he asked, his voice descending into a primitive growl. I was pretty sure it was a rhetorical question.

He shoved his stone-hard erection against my sex and slipped his hand under my tight skirt, hiking it up forcefully. With the heel of his hand, he brushed my clit just enough to drive me wild. Struggling to get closer, I ripped the shirt out of his pants to stroke the muscles of his lower back.

"Do you want me?" Two fingers secretly slipped inside of me. "Do you?"

"Yes!"

"Good." The wall of heat was gone in an instant. He

pushed off of me abruptly, leaving me utterly aroused and unfulfilled, cold and alone where his touch had been. I wanted to scream. His eyes were hooded, sulky, daring me to challenge him. When I didn't respond, the flat line of his lips curved in victory. Grabbing my hand, he pulled me onto his side. "Let's go."

Good Lord, this man was mercurial. His need for ownership should have worried me. But it didn't. If I was being honest with myself, I had to admit that part of me liked it. Having been on my own for so long, it was a relief to relinquish control to someone stronger, more powerful, more worldly. I was tired. All I wanted to do was drift and let the inexorable force of this stormy control freak take me—for a little while, at least.

Gideon popped out of the driver's seat and scanned the area. I slipped into the car and Sebastian snapped my seatbelt on. He was quiet and brooding all the way back to the apartment, the air between us heavy with the tension radiating from him. Any attempt at a civil conversation was pointless. He was an unbridgeable island when he was like this, an ocean away.

On the elevator ride up, he yanked me into a rough embrace. The guardedness had crept back into his eyes. He barely paused to look at me when we entered the apartment. "Get changed. You have ten minutes."

Talk about hot and cold.

I went back to the bedroom and slipped out of the beautiful shoes, the stockings, and dress, tucking them safely back in the closet. I laced up the high-heeled gladiator sandals that reached my knees and went to fetch the Gucci dress. The silk jersey was fine enough to pass through a wedding band. I could barely feel it, the fabric whispering on my skin as it fell down, over my body. The slit exposed my bare leg up to the thigh. I felt naked. Between the shoes and the dress, there was more of me exposed than I was comfortable with.

Sebastian walked in wearing a slim tuxedo with a laydown collar, a fat bowtie skillfully tied. Even more devastatingly handsome than usual, he looked like he had stepped out of the pages of Men's Vogue.

"Nice tux. Who's your tailor?" I tried for cool indifference. His lips quirked. At least he wasn't brooding anymore.

"Tom Ford. I'm glad you approve."

As he stalked towards me, his liquid fire gaze traveled from my unpolished toes to my hair in a slow, sensual inspection that made my skin burn. Gripping my neck gently, he bent his head and brushed his soft lips back and forth on mine until I leaned in and kissed him back. When his lips lifted, I opened my eyes and caught him wearing a small, unreadable smile. He brought his other hand out from behind his back and held out a navy leather box with the word JAR written on it. Curious, apprehensive, I looked up and found him regarding me attentively.

"I...I..." I wanted to explain that in no way was I accepting jewelry from him but words deserted me.

"I want you to wear these."

He opened the box and my hand lifted involuntarily, floating in midair before landing on my throat. Nestled inside, on a leather pillow, was a pair of exquisite chandelier earrings. They were designed in a delicate floral pattern with cascading petals, the tiny pave stones colored in shades of white to lilac.

"The wisteria tree?"

There was a smile in his eyes. "Do you like them?"

"They're amazing but—"

"You'll wear them for me," he interrupted, crushing further discussion on the topic.

He took them out of the case and gently placed them on my earlobes. Then he grasped my shoulders and spun me around to look in the floor-length mirror. My hands flew to the earrings.

"I don't want to ask but…but I have to ask…these are real, aren't they?"

"You don't have to hold them up," he said, his lips quivering in amusement.

My hands wouldn't stay down. They kept flying protectively back up to my ears. "I can't wear these. I'm already petrified of losing them."

"Then I'll buy you another pair."

I laughed nervously. "You're joking?"

"I'm not joking. Look."

He moved to stand behind me and motioned to the image of us reflected in the mirror. My cheeks were flushed and my mouth was the color of summer raspberries. Sebastian's eyes sparked appreciatively, all sorts of erotic promises dwelling there. He wrapped his arms around me and pulled me into the warm shelter of his body. Nudging me with his hips, his impossibly hard sex twitched as it pressed up against my rear end. My body instinctively pushed back in answer.

Wet. Willing. Ready. Always, for him.

His body heat danced on the bare skin of my back. My lids grew heavy, drunk on lust, while a pleased sigh worked its way up my throat. I felt his smile on the side of my neck. His practiced fingers slipped under the flimsy silk jersey and skated lightly over my breast, tugging, teasing me into a state of blissed-out incoherence.

Take it. Take anything you want. It's yours.

The devil knew me better than I knew myself. He had stolen behind my rigid wall of protection and seized what he wanted with no objection from me. As he continued the tormenting of the damned, our eyes met in the mirror. I couldn't guard myself from his perceptive, amber gaze any more than I could say no to him. I could feel him looking into my soul and finding my weakness for him. That was the dark irony of our story. He hated himself for his, and yet I was just as powerless to resist him. Maybe more so because I risked a hell of a lot more than he did.

His hand slipped inside the slit of the dress and teased back the folds of my sex. He played with my body like he owned it, working his magic, annihilating me with his patience. The experience was a master class in seduction. I screamed his name as I came, my head falling back onto his shoulder in total surrender.

"Look at me." Our eyes met in the mirror again. He held me possessively, my breast, my sex. "You belong to me," he affirmed quietly.

Those words sank deep inside of me and caused a riot, my heart simultaneously rebelling and rejoicing. A strong instinct for self-preservation insisted I pull away, but he released me before I got the chance.

"Come on." Once again, I was dragged out of the apartment. My head was swimming. Between the orgasm and the conflicting emotions, I could barely string two words together by the time he had us both buckled into the Bentley.

"Where are we going?" I asked, my voice small and unsettled.

Glancing briefly at me, he answered, "You'll see."

What I couldn't fail to miss was the calculated sharpness in his eyes.

CHAPTER 23

W e walked down a dark, deserted alleyway. No place I would be found without a well-muscled, two-hundred-pound sex god standing next to me to protect me. Gideon had taken the Bentley at the corner. The building looked industrial, and a mountain-of-a-man wider and taller than Sebastian guarded the entrance. He was dressed in a black suit, and had an earpiece he pressed with his index finger. As soon as his eyes landed on us, he moved to open the iron door. I glanced at Sebastian and watched him nod to the doorman. Clearly, they were not strangers to each other.

We stepped inside a dim, narrow corridor lined in deep purple velvet. It went on forever, leading into a small jewel box of a chamber. It was octagonal and covered in etched mirrors all the way around. Sconce lights sparkled off the mirrors, giving it a romantic luminescence. I stared at the different angles of our reflection with an odd feeling of detachment. As I watched Sebastian's hand stroke up and down my bare back, it occurred to me that we looked like two people in love, two people that belonged together. If only.

The door opened, and a woman dressed in black with a veil covering her face stepped forward and handed us two masks. They were Venetian and covered the entire face. Mine, white. Sebastian's silver. The woman turned around and motioned us forward.

"Put it on for now," he whispered in my ear. Reluctantly, I did as I was told.

We followed the woman into a large room that was lavishly decorated with heavy drapes in burgundy brocade silk, mahogany antiques, Persian rugs, and Impressionist art. An enormous fireplace with a carved stone mantle anchored the center of the room. The whole place had a dark, gothic sensuality about it, beautifully decadent. It was also crowded with people lounging, drinking, and talking. All the women wore black gowns, and all the men wore tuxedos. Everyone wore identical masks.

Elegant anonymity. My stomach fluttered, and my pulse picked up an unsteady beat. I grabbed Sebastian's lapel and drew his ear to my lips. "Is this somebody's home?"

"No."

I heard the smile in his voice but didn't have time for a follow-up question. The veiled woman was leading us down another corridor. As we stepped inside a small, narrow room, she turned and closed the door behind her, leaving us alone. Confused, I looked around, searching for clues. One wall was covered in padded velvet and the other was black glass. It was empty except for a delicately carved, high-backed chair that resembled a throne. Sebastian took off my mask before taking off his own.

"Where are we?" My heart was beating rapidly, my body more aware than my mind. Sebastian's eyes were sulky, glazed with desire. He picked up the chair and pushed it against the velvet wall.

"I want you to do something for me," he said in a silky voice.

He was playing the part of the lover again, the possessor receding into the background. He kissed me gently, licking the seam of my lips until I opened for him, his tongue dancing with mine. The touch of fear in my blood, mingling with desire, put me in a state of hyperawareness, every sensory experience amplified.

"Anything."

He stepped closer, pushing me backwards until my bare back was flush up against the soft, velvet nap. In front of me, he was all heat and hardness wrapped in soft wool, while behind me, the velvet nap was silky and cool. He nestled between my thighs, his sex hard and ready. I sighed with pleasure. The pads of his long fingers charted a path from my throat to my breasts, followed by lazy kisses on my jaw, my throat, and my collarbone. He pushed the flimsy fabric of the halter aside and grazed my nipple, then palmed it, teasing until it formed a little peak.

"I want to know what you thought when you saw me fucking Paisley—no, don't tense up. Talk to me. I want to know your thoughts as well as I know your body. I want every part of you." The vibration of his low, raspy voice played on the thin skin of my throat. Igniting like a trail of gasoline, the feeling led straight to my sex. "Did you like watching?" he whispered. "Tell me." Pushing aside the skirt, he stroked me with the heel of his hand, torturing the words out of me.

"Yes, I liked it." My voice was breathy, barely audible.

"Tell me," he repeated, casting his incantation with the lethal skill of a snake charmer. He sucked on my neck, scraped it with his teeth then licked the abrasion in an obvious declaration of ownership.

"I thought you looked magnificent."

Another tug, another stroke of my clitoris. My body chased his hand when he left me.

"Go on."

"I watched you take her, overpower her and...and I got wet just watching you." I didn't like the sound of my own voice. It reeked of desperation. Smiling against my throat, his wicked fingers circled the sensitive nub, never quite hitting it. I spread my legs wider.

"More," he crooned.

Yes! Yes! More, please, my mind was screaming. He bit down on my trapezius muscle and I felt it below my waist, a heavy ache, a relentless need to be filled up. "I wanted it to be me so badly. I was jealous and ashamed because I wanted you to take me. I wanted you to push me down on the hard stone floor and push yourself inside of me."

Two fingers slipped inside, tormenting me, rewarding me. I couldn't keep the moans and pants from surging up. I almost whined when he withdrew his fingers, licked them clean, and placed me standing on the chair.

Suddenly, the black glass came alive. The lights turned on and revealed a bedroom with a massive four-poster bed on the other side while we remained cloaked in darkness. Glancing down, I discovered Sebastian's eyes twinkling wickedly. Before I could say a word, he dug his strong fingers into my hips and held me steady as his head dove between my thighs. His warm mouth fastened onto me, licking and sucking until my mind shut down. My legs sapped of strength, I braced myself against the velvet wall. The tight coil of desire unraveled. I grabbed onto his shoulders for support and screamed as a sharp orgasm spiked through me. My body tensed and arched. A mist of sweat bloomed on my skin. My knees turned liquid, buckling beneath me. Boneless, I collapsed in his arms.

As I drifted in a sensual fog, it vaguely registered that a couple had entered the dimly lit room on the other side of the glass. Their masks only obscured the tops of their faces. The man was very muscular. He undid his bowtie and removed his shirt, revealing an enormous expanse of chest with deeply tanned skin and a mat of dark hair covering it. The woman was small with full breasts, rounded hips, and long blond hair that fell down her back.

He moved towards her and unzipped the back of her dress, pushing it off her shoulders roughly while he kissed and bit a path down her neck. I could see where his teeth left a mark. Eyes wide with curiosity and apprehension, they moved from the scene playing out in front of me to Sebastian who was watching me instead. He placed me back on solid ground, facing the dark glass. My hands pushed against it while he covered me from behind.

"Can they see us?"

"No...tell me what you see."

He kissed my neck and caressed my breast, his other hand squeezing and stroking my bottom. "I see why you picked out this dress," I said, laughing, then squeaked when he pinched my rear end.

"That's what you get when you misbehave."

"Yes, Your Highness," I answered, and felt the sting of his hand on my bottom. "Ouch."

"Let's try that again."

The man behind the glass took hold of his lover's elbows and brought them together, binding them with leather cuffs behind her back. Her chest thrust out, her dark nipples erect. He guided her to her knees, unbuttoned his trousers, his enormous erection bobbing as his pants fell to his ankles. It felt like we were in the room with them, sharing a private moment. I was stunned with a mixture of perverse curiosity and shame.

"She's powerless to stop him."

I pushed my rear end back into Sebastian's erection. Impossibly hard, it strained under his tuxedo pants. He hissed out a breath and cupped my sex. I was wet again, ready for him to possess me and fill me up.

"Do you want me as badly as I want you?" His voice was barely a whisper.

"Yes." Sebastian stepped away and unzipped his pants. Cool air swept over the cheeks of my rear end. I missed him already.

Across the glass, the man took a punishing hold of the woman's hair and pulled her head towards his twitching erection. She licked the underside, sucked on the wide, dusky crown hard enough that her cheeks hollowed out. Then, slowly, she began swallowing more and more of him.

I heard the tear of foil, felt Sebastian's body heat burning my back, my rear end. I wanted to melt into him. "Go on."

Reaching one hand around, I squeezed his sac. He dipped his fingers inside of me and spread the welcoming moisture up the seam and in between the cheeks of my rear end. My body shuddered, responding spontaneously to the dark, hot sensation while my unfocused gaze remained on the lovers across the glass. I watched the man roll his hips, grip his lover's hair. In and out, in and out, she took all of him down her throat.

"It's turning me on."

"And..."

"She's at his mercy."

The man threw back his head and thrust his hips,

pumping himself into her mouth; the evidence of his passion dripping out of the corners of her full lips. He unbuckled her restraints, picked her up with ease, and placed her on the bed, tethering each limb to a post with silk ropes. I watched them while Sebastian kissed my spine and placed his forehead on the curve of my neck.

"Tell me where you want me," he murmured.

The man licked his lover's nipples and placed tiny clamps on them while she writhed, tensing off the bed. He was erect again. Grabbing a hold of his penis at the root, he pulled on it roughly while brushing the fringes of a whip up and down his lover's body. She arched and struggled as the biting sting of the whip hit her breasts, the apex at her thighs. He climbed between her legs and with one quick thrust of his powerful hips, shoved himself deep inside of her.

Sebastian placed his hand over my much smaller one splayed on the glass in front of us. His tan fingers nestled in between my pale ones.

"Inside of me," I murmured.

He gripped my hip with his other hand and shunted deep. I gasped at the feeling of fullness, of completion. He was everywhere, filling me up, sheltering me from behind…fused as one. My gaze returned to our joined hands on the glass. He closed his fingers around mine and an overwhelming swell of emotion rose up my throat.

And they will become one flesh. The words swept through me.

"This is where I live," he said, nudging me with his hips. "Where I belong." His voice faded into a hoarse whisper. He held himself perfectly still, buried inside of me until I started to squirm, needing him to move. He began thrusting deep and steady. I pressed back against him, the sound of our skin slamming together holding the constant beat. Sweet relief was in sight. I felt it building within me. But every time I reached for it, Sebastian would ease off his pace, leaving me in an unendurable state of arousal, reminding me who was in control, staking his claim.

"Home," Sebastian mumbled quietly.

He slammed hard one last time and sent me soaring. I broke apart and was put back together as someone else, some elemental part of me transformed. I heard him grunt out my name in between deep surging breaths. Once the tremors subsided, his whole body slackened. I lifted my heavy eyelids and watched the man on the other side of the glass remove the nipple clamps. His lover screamed as she climaxed. Her back arched and her eyes slammed shut. He was still erect when he pulled out. After untying her legs, he flipped her onto her stomach. Her arms were still bound, crossed above her, making it impossible for her to move. He lifted her hips in the air and began rubbing the crown of his shaft, glistening with cum, between the cheeks of her buttocks, around the ring.

Oh...my...God.

I couldn't take anymore. My senses were maxed-out, flooded with too much information and feeling. The man grabbed the base of his thick shaft, positioned himself, and slowly...slowly...inch by inch...sank into her. When he was completely embedded, he began thrusting. The globes of his muscular rear end hardened with each quick, shallow pump until he climaxed, driving his lover halfway up the bed on the final thrust.

Sebastian dragged me backwards, onto his lap as he sat down in the chair. His forehead rested on my back, his body still tucked inside of me. My throat tightened as a meaningful moment stretched between us. "Holy shit," he whispered.

"I never knew it could be like this," I heard myself whisper back.

"Neither did I."

My body was still trembling when he stood me up and pulled out. He was unusually quiet as he fixed his own clothing before smoothing my dress back into place, my limbs being completely useless. A brooding silence hung over us. Had I not been so utterly spent, it would have made me feel awkward. But in the present state, it took all my energy just to put one foot in front of the other.

Handing me my mask, he took me by the hand and dragged me out the door, the scene on the other side of the glass fading into the background. He easily navigated us back to the room with the fireplace, obviously familiar with the layout. Something about that didn't sit right with me. We were headed for the door when a woman with a sleek, black bob and Amazonian proportions placed her hand on Sebastian's arm. He braced subtly.

"Sebastian?"

She was busty. *Fake*, I thought enviously, though couldn't be sure. My thought patterns resembled that of a cadaver at this point in the evening. I had nothing left for research and observation, only a sudden urge to visit the ladies' room.

"I'm going to look for a restroom," I whispered.

"Just around the corner," said the woman with a guttural accent, German perhaps. I left them standing there and found the ladies' room, stepped inside, and removed the mask.

There was an impressive amount of healthy color on my cheeks. I had forgotten what that looked like. The rosy glow made me look younger, less serious…happy. I ran a finger over my swollen lips and turned on the cold water. Cupping it, I drank thirstily in an effort to cool the heat blazing under my skin.

I walked back to the spot where I had left Sebastian and discovered them both missing. My heartbeat faltered. Only slightly at first. It quickly increased to pounding like a jack-hammer as I scanned the area and couldn't locate him. I moved from room to room, searching frantically, anxiety wiping away the heady afterglow of the seismic orgasm I had only minutes ago.

And then I found him...

My heart crashed to the floor and splintered into danger-ously jagged pieces. In a corner, away from the crowd, his mask was tipped up and his lips were locked onto the lips of the woman I had left him with. I'm surprised I didn't faint from the shock. My whole body shook from the pain and sense of loss that gripped me.

When I finally realized I could still move my legs, I turned and fled. I walked as quickly as I could manage on stilettos, propelled by rage and sheer force of will in search of the exit. I heard him calling me softly, trying not to draw too much attention to the barely clothed woman that was leaving a wake of curious stares as she shoved people out of her way. Somehow I found the jewel box chamber and ran down the velvet corridor. I blasted the steel doors open hard enough to startle the hulking bouncer. Without a backward glance, I continued marching towards the street, too enraged to even consider where I was headed.

"Vera, stop." He sounded angry and annoyed. *The nerve...*I didn't look back. I knew he couldn't run after me, but I wasn't running either. Mostly because I had no idea where I was, or where I could run to.

"I said stop, Vera. Goddamn it, you know I can't run after you!" A strong hand encircled the upper part of my arm and spun me around. His face was a mixture of anger and frustration with an undercurrent of fear. He gripped my upper arms painfully and shook me. "Where the hell do you think you're going?! Don't ever run from me again! You know I can't run after you!"

I swung with everything I had, slapping him across the cheek. He dropped his hands, shocked at the force of my blow. "Don't ever touch me again. Go back inside and enjoy yourself."

He grabbed me again, his grip punishing, and pulled me into a deserted alley around the corner. Pushing me up against a cold wall, he caged me with his body, heat and anger burning through our clothes.

"Now you listen to me, you little witch." His voice was raw and low. "I was getting damn good at doing an impression of a dead man until you walked into my life. You don't get to come in and disrupt everything, make me feel things I don't want to feel, and then get to tell me it's just sex!" he shouted, his hand slashing through the air. "You don't get to turn my life upside down, make me want you...make me want things..." He shook his head. "I know you're scared, and don't even think about denying it. Fuck!! I'm..." Breathing heavily, he looked around searching for words he didn't have. "Forget it." His shoulders sagged, the fight leaving him all at once.

Tears funneled down my face unchecked. I blinked repeatedly, trying to push them back, and bit my bottom lip in an attempt to stop it from trembling.

"Tell me. Are we just fucking? Because if that's what this is then I'm done. I'm out." He released me and turned away, then abruptly spun back towards me again. "And I sure as hell never said that before!"

It came tumbling out of him in a tone soaked in rage and

lust and something else, something soft and vulnerable. I launched myself at him. Shaking, I held him tightly. I was a messy heap of raw, exposed nerves. With a few simple words, he had cut me to the quick. I shook my head.

"No...no, it's not just sex," I said with my face buried in his chest. I could feel his heart thumping loudly. His warm hands cupped my face, his thumbs brushed the wet stains off my cheeks. He tilted my chin up and stared down with passion and yearning in those brandy colored eyes. I lost myself in those eyes. Dropping his face onto the curve of my neck, he hugged me tightly, too tightly, as if he were scared that I would get away somehow.

"I had to know. That's why I did it...I had to know." Something around my heart released at the sound of his words, relieved that he felt bound to me. Because he had already reached deep inside of me and attached himself to vital organs.

CHAPTER 24

We were both quiet on the drive back to the apartment. There was too much feeling hanging in the air between us, dense and charged with significance. He parked the Bentley, turned to look at me, and still said nothing. There was an obvious shade of apprehension mixed in with desire in his expression. He looked lost, unsure. His hands were on me the second the elevator doors shut. Touching, gripping, pulling me up against his body with an urgency that I recognized in myself. The brakes he depended on to keep him in check, at a distance, were failing.

He yanked me forward into the apartment, dragged me to his bedroom without pausing. Everything happened quickly after that. His lips came crashing down on mine, much too hard. His hands were all over me. I pushed at his shoulders trying to temper his passion.

"Easy," I whispered.

"I can't. I need you too much. I can't be gentle right now."

He divested me of my dress in seconds, leaving me standing in nothing other than my gladiator heels and the diamond earrings. I didn't even have time to feel shy about it. He stripped himself carelessly, sending buttons flying in the air, never breaking his assault on my mouth as the clothing pooled at our feet. Not bothering to pull back the down duvet, he pushed me down on the bed. His hard, aroused body fell on me. I was actually surprised he paused long enough to reach for a condom. He tore the foil between his teeth, his hands shaking as he rolled it on. Grasping both wrists in one hand, he raised them over my head and pinned them to the bed. Butterflies settled in my stomach even though I knew he would never do anything to harm me. I trusted him implicitly. When had that happened?

The meager remains of his patience finally disintegrated. He slammed into me with enough force to drive us both up the bed. My body was ready for him, in silent correspondence with his. I gasped at the feeling of invasion. Although not unwelcome. A dark thought, a strange euphoric feeling came over me. I liked being taken like this by him, being needed so desperately that reason ceased to exist. His need was so acute he wasn't beyond inflicting a little pain.

"Are you okay?" he gasped.

"Better than okay."

I wrapped my legs around his waist and drew him deeper into my body, ready to lose myself. He started a vicious hammering that left little room for pleasure. I offered myself freely, however, giving him everything he needed. His eyes never left mine, communicating something I couldn't decipher. On the last thrust he released my hands and rose up, came hard. His thick lashes lifted and his eyes, burning brightly, held mine. I watched pure bliss transform into stark vulnerability.

A sudden understanding dawned on me—whatever happened this man would not let me go easily.

Dragging air into his lungs, he collapsed on top of me. His fingers curved around my skull, held me steady while he kissed my neck softly. I stroked his back. He melted into my touch, the subtle tension leaving him at once. His hold on me didn't slacken. He wouldn't let go, like breaking contact would deprive him of something necessary for survival. I recognized it easily now and had grown accustomed to it. I even liked it. I raked my short fingernails against the taut skin of his muscular rear end and he raised his head.

Searching my eyes, he asked, "Did I hurt you?"

"No. Why would you think that?"

"I was rough." His eyes flickered away in a guilty expression.

"I like that you don't treat me like a piece of crystal."

"But you didn't…"

"It's okay. You'll owe me one."

Satisfied with what he found in my eyes, he nodded and scattered lazy, gentle kisses all over my face. When he finally pulled out, I winced at the loss of him. "You're sore. Wait here, I'll run a bath." He removed the condom, and walked around the bed towards the bathroom.

I could never tire of watching him. Naked, he was God's perfect work of art. The elegant lines of his body. The graceful way he moved in spite of his injury. An intensely powerful energy hid beneath the calm surface. He looked over his shoulder and found me stretched out on my side, my head propped up on my hand, and an appreciative smile curving my lips.

"Enjoying the view?"

"Yes, sir," I replied. More than anything I was relieved to see the haunted look gone from his face.

With a shy smile, he murmured, "Give me a minute and you can enjoy it some more."

I listened to him moving around: turning on the water, adjusting the knobs, the tub filling. It was easy for me to recognize that little boy now, the one rescuing small animals. He took such good care of me, made me feel cherished.

Unwanted emotions began crowding me again so I pushed back against them. In an effort to distract myself, I glanced around the room. It was large, decorated in the same style as the rest of the apartment, with a wall of windows that overlooked the lake. Only a few lights twinkled in the dark curtain of night. Again, no pictures, nothing too personal, the environment sanitized of the past. I wanted to ask him about it but I didn't want to ruin the comfortable ease between us. Instead, I picked up his scattered clothes, folded them neatly and placed them on hangers.

When he returned, I was sitting on the edge of the bed, still wearing those absurdly expensive earrings and the high-heeled gladiator sandals that came up to my knees. He stopped abruptly, his eyes brimming with excitement, so vastly different from the apathetic look that was usually there.

You did that, the thought snuck in.

He offered his hand while his eyes traveled from the top of my head to the tips of my toes. "Christ, you're beautiful." His compliments always came at unexpected moments. Caught by surprise, a rosy glow colored my cheeks. His eyes turned sultry, hungry. He pulled me up against his naked body, gently removed the earrings from my lobes and rubbed them. The priceless jewels were tossed on the bedside table carelessly, like they were rhinestones. Next, he dragged me out of the bedroom.

The lights had been dimmed, painting the bathroom with a romantic luminescence. An enormous tub sat in the middle. He pushed me down to sit on the edge of the tub and held my foot up while he unzipped the sandals, throwing one by one aside. Total proficiency born out of practice. In this too. How many others had there been? A pinch of jealousy popped up. *So that's what that feels like.* An echo of words heard not too long ago intruded.

By the time my father married his mother he had moved onto saving larger animals.

How depressing. I sank down to my chin in frothy bubbles. The water was hot. It splashed over the sides as he stepped in and sat behind me, his long legs encasing mine. Not leaving any distance between us, he hugged me tightly and kissed my temple.

"We've made a mess," I giggled.

"It's a wet bath. It'll drain."

The scent of something exotic, deep and earthy, drifted up in the steam. He poured the oil in his large hands, and began massaging my back with deep strokes of his thumbs. Starting around the base of my neck, he worked his way south, a warm flush spreading through my veins the lower he went. I exhaled deeply and closed my eyes. "You're good at this." He was great at it. I could barely keep my head up.

"Not nearly as good as you are."

"I'm glad I can do that for you." He kissed the back of my neck. "Sebastian?"

"Hmm."

"I have a million questions."

I felt his smile on my shoulderblade. He nipped me, soothing it afterwards with a lick that made me shiver. "I thought you would."

"That place—they know you there?"

"Hmm."

"Do you go often?" Silence. I could feel him weighing how much to reveal and what the consequences would be.

"I used to…before the accident."

"While you were married? With your wife?" I couldn't keep the bewilderment out of my voice.

"No, before that." His skilled hands traveled to my breasts, where he teased my nipples into hard peaks. My breath quickened and my eyes fought a losing battle to stay open.

"If you're trying to distract me—"

Chuckling, he whispered seductively, "I didn't think it would be that easy."

"Were you ever in the rooms, while other people watched?" Silence again, except for the swish of the water.

"Yes…does that bother you?"

I wasn't sure how I felt about it yet. My tangled, messy emotions were still too fresh and close to the surface. I needed time to process way too much information. "With that German woman I found you kissing?" I asked hesitantly, my voice holding a bitter edge.

He wrapped his arms around me and squeezed, his lips resting on the curve of my neck. I felt the muffled "yes" on my skin. Leaning forward, I pulled away but he held on tighter.

"Don't."

"I want you to consider how you would feel if you found me kissing someone else."

His body turned to stone. "There would be blood on my hands and you would find yourself standing next to a corpse." Grasping my chin a shade too firmly, he looked into my face. "Don't ever test how seriously I mean that." His eyes were fire and ice, reflecting the indisputable conviction in his words.

"Tell me about that place."

He released my chin and returned to massaging my

shoulders. Did I really want to know? Just hearing about Little Miss Sauerkraut put me in a jealous tailspin. He took a deep breath before he spoke again. "It's a private club that caters to people's...unique tastes. Voyeurism, BDSM, S&M, whatever you're into."

"What are you into?" Incurably curious. It was an affliction. I had to know even though I was scared of the answer.

He shrugged, pausing to carefully choose his words. "I like control—no, that's not true. I need it. Places like that... anonymity is essential. After my accident—the scar, it's too identifiable." That answer only begged a thousand more questions. Did he stop because of his wife? Did he love her that much? "What you saw tonight was pretty tame." I looked over my shoulder and found his eyes shuttered, his thoughts inaccessible.

"Are you trying to scare me off?"

He shook his head slowly. "No...but I want to be honest with you. And I need you to be too."

That was a request I couldn't accommodate. "Are you telling me you're a sadist?" My eyes were wide in anticipation. The thought of him wanting to inflict pain on me...no, it wouldn't work.

"No, pain isn't my thing. At least, not extreme pain."

My brows creased in doubt. "What other kind is there?"

His eyes dancing, alight with mischief, he replied, "We'll save that demonstration for another night."

I pressed backwards against his muscular chest, and his penis twitched and turned hard against the small of my back. His hand skated over my taut abdomen. It moved lower until he was raking through the patch of hair covering my sex. When he parted and stroked me, I gasped. He soothed the sting with his touch, working the oil into my tender skin. In short order he had my body bunching up again, in desperate need of relief.

"I've got you. Let go, Vera," he murmured.

How could I explain that I could never completely let go, that I was incapable of letting myself depend on anyone? My mind screamed to run away—it knew it was in grave danger of relinquishing all control—while my body, addicted and enslaved, raced towards him at Mach speed. His formidable persistence paid off. It started quietly, building momentum until I fell over the edge with a scream that could have woken the neighbors. My head flopped back onto his shoulder.

"I didn't think I had another one in me."

"Don't ever underestimate me, lover."

No. I would be a fool to ever underestimate this man.

———

STRETCHED out on the bed with his hands tucked neatly behind his head, his arms protruding like wings, he looked like a jaded, just recently pleasured sultan. A self-satisfied smile lingered on his lips. His beauty still managed to leave me speechless at times. I lay on my stomach perpendicular to him, my lips charting a path from his navel to his right hipbone. His penis lay long and soft on his thigh. When I licked the space between bone and muscle it twitched, coming to life again.

"You are insatiable," I proclaimed with a filthy smile.

His lids lowered to half-mast. "Your fault." He chuckled at my eye roll.

"Do you know," I said, kissing the dip between his taut abdomen and hipbone, "that I have been dying," another kiss, "to do this," he hissed as I licked him, "since I saw you hanging by those sinister-looking straps in your gym." Come to think of it those straps didn't look so unappealing anymore.

"Really?" His voice was high and tight.

"In fact, I'm certain that this small piece of real estate right here," I licked my index finger and drew a triangle between his navel, his hip bone, and the beginning of his pubic hair, "is the most precious in all the world. I would love to build a home right here." I dropped another soft kiss on the spot, rubbed my nose on it, and watched him grip the sheets tightly. His sex turned dusky and hard, erect.

"Imagine the view," I purred. In a heartbeat, I was lifted and placed astride his lap. I squealed in surprise.

"Enough," he said, laughing, a full-throated laugh I hadn't heard from him before.

Music to my ears. His laughter was so rare I almost didn't recognize the sound. I wiggled against his twitching erection.

"Good Lord, woman, have some mercy," he pleaded in a heavy drawl, "I've abused your sweet body enough tonight."

"That accent makes me crazy."

"Good to know. Have to put it to use at a later date." We were both grinning like idiots. It made my heart swell to see him relaxed and happy. He closed his eyes and kissed me so tenderly that my throat closed. It came to me in a rush, the knowledge that I was way past the point of no return, already fiercely attached to him. So I pulled back, scared of my own feelings, of my weakness for him.

A flicker of disappointment dimmed his eyes before he averted his gaze. Running his fingers through his hair impatiently, he said, "It's late. We should get some rest."

When he turned the lights off, the silence was stifling, a chasm separating us all of a sudden…and then I felt him reach out and pull me closer. Tucking in behind me, he held me like he never intended to let go. I exhaled, relieved because I didn't want him to either.

———

THE ROOM WAS SWADDLED in darkness. I blinked repeatedly as my eyes adjusted slowly to the faint glow of a streetlight pouring in through the wall of windows. His iPhone on the bedside table read 3:50. The smell of sex hung in the air. It invaded my senses, bringing with it a rush of images and feelings of all the things we'd done and shared.

Restless, Sebastian mumbled something I couldn't understand. I adjusted the covers he had kicked clear off the bed. Tucking them around him, I watched him sleep for a while. My very own Sleeping Beauty. I never got the opportunity to really look at him. When he was awake, all that intense energy was blinding, like trying to study the sun. His face was tight, his brow furrowed in discomfort. I felt a pressing need to sift my fingers through his hair but I didn't want to wake him. The pain was probably due to overexertion and he needed the rest to recover.

I crept off the bed slowly. Small twinges of pain lanced through me with every step I took to get to the bathroom, a satisfying reminder of where his body had been. I was staring at my reflection in the bathroom mirror, inspecting the red patch on my collarbone and the hickey on my throat, when I heard a low moan. I stepped back into the bedroom to find him breathing erratically. He wasn't just uncomfortable, he was distressed as well.

It killed me to see him in such a state. He was always so busy taking care of everything and everyone else that he forgot to take care of himself. The protective streak burning inside of me grew wide and angry.

I began massaging his leg, and he quieted almost immediately. The space between his eyebrows relaxed. His breathing turned deep and calm. Beautiful, stubborn man. Any time I tried suggesting he use his cane, he changed the subject. His pride might not allow it, but his body would insist on it or pay the price.

It was taking more and more of the powerful opiates to get him through the day. He was addicted to them and we both knew it. With his resources, I refused to believe that a good orthopedist couldn't alleviate some of the discomfort and made a mental note to do some research on it.

He mumbled again. I could barely make out the whispered words. "Don't leave me...I need you..." I paused, questioning whether I had heard him correctly. "Don't go..."

A great weight was suddenly sitting on my chest, crushing the air from my lungs and destroying a newborn hope that had been steadily growing since we left the club. He was dreaming about his wife...after everything we had shared.

"Love you...don't leave me."

My jaw trembled. Tears stung my eyes. I was dying inside, my heart disintegrating a piece at a time, sucked into a black hole of despair. Then, the realization hit me, earth-shaking in its magnitude. That it was too late to turn back, too late to save myself. Because I had totally, irrevocably fallen in love with him.

CHAPTER 25

I woke at dawn with his sandy head between my thighs. Not the worst way to start the day. Pinned to the mattress, all I could do was surrender as he licked and kissed and worked me up into a state of arousal that had me begging in not one but three languages. Finally taking mercy on me, he planted me astride him and buried himself deep inside of me.

Something was driving him. He was relentless, hell-bent on drowning me in pleasure until every part of me was filled up, touched, and tasted—enslaved by him. It only occurred to me afterwards that it had felt so good because he wasn't wearing a condom. He looked appropriately embarrassed after my scolding.

"I don't have any control when it comes to you," he muttered.

"How about your mind? Do you have any control over that?" His lips twitched, his expression wavering between amusement and challenge. Still, he didn't argue.

"When's your doctor's appointment? I'd rather you see mine."

"Next week, and no, thank you. I'm perfectly capable of choosing my own doctor."

And that's how the morning began...

"They're yours. Why wouldn't you take them?"

He looked like an angry god now, an angry Eros, with his hands on his hips and a sexy scowl on his face. I wanted to kiss that scowl away. Instead, I stared at our reflection in the vanity mirror and continued brushing my hair.

The coach had turned back into a pumpkin. The horses were mice again. I had my old, tired clothes back on while he stood behind me wearing those titillating, snug boxer briefs and nothing else. He was so damn gorgeous— privately I was sighing and ogling like a teenage girl.

"They're not mine. They were on loan for one evening. Thank you for doing that for me, but I don't feel right accepting them. Besides, what would I do with them? I don't need designer clothes. I'm a housekeeper, remember?"

Frowning, he shook his head. "Don't say that. That's a temporary situation." The pained look on his face shifted to determination. "You'll need them when we go out. You need a lot more, but I figured you could pick out what you want yourself."

I had a good cry the night before. I went into the bathroom, crawled into the shower, curled into a fetal position, and sobbed hysterically. I got it all out of my system and felt peacefully resigned about the whole messy situation. Of course he was still in love with his beautiful, dead wife. She had looks, class, and style and ran in the right circles. The only circle I ran in was the one that revolved around his dining room table while I dusted it. There was no contest.

She won by a landslide. If he hadn't been in such a dark place when we met, this affair would never have happened.

I finished gathering my hair in a ponytail, turned around, and walked over to him. I petted his chest, just above his heart. He liked it when I did that. "No hair," I teased, trying to lighten the mood.

His expression turned smug. "Grass doesn't grow on rocks."

I smiled at his adolescent remark. "Sebastian…" Before I could continue, he cupped my face, his thumbs lightly outlining the angles and planes…and I lost my train of thought. The man made me senseless. "Sebastian."

"Hmm."

"I don't see how there will be a lot of going out for us. I rarely have two days off together. And I'm certainly not going to ask Mrs. Arnaud to change other people's schedules to accommodate mine. I just started working there."

"There? You mean my house." His intense gaze locked on mine, an unmistakable argument gaining strength in his eyes. "Am I the only one that finds this bullshit excuse ludicrous? You work for me. Not Marianne."

"That's a valid point," I agreed. Nevertheless, I report to her. And there's no way I want her to think less of me." Standing on my toes, I kissed his stern lips until he softened and kissed me back. "By the way, your language is filthy."

He wrapped his arms around me, steel bands that sealed us together length to length. "The clothes, the earrings—they're yours. You can keep them here and that's all I'm going to say about it. I'm fucking starving. We need breakfast."

"Sebastian—"

He smacked my lips with a quick, loud kiss. Stalling the rest of my words, he turned towards the door and added, "Don't push me. I'm going to get dressed."

Impossible man. When he set his mind to something, he was an unstoppable force. I needed to handle this with care. Otherwise, he would take it as a personal challenge.

———

"How about I cook?"

He looked like I had just confessed to inventing fire, hopeful though mostly disbelieving. I stood in the middle of the immaculate designer kitchen while he sat on the counter stool looking incredibly sexy in a white dress shirt and his old Levi's.

"You want to cook? Breakfast?"

"No, the inauguration dinner for the next U.S. president. Yes, breakfast. Hasn't anyone ever cooked for you?" Actually, the appliances looked unused, just out of the box.

"Marianne…but not in this kitchen. Ruth, at my mother's house," he mumbled.

I tried to cover up my surprise by opening the cupboards and pretending to look for something. My chest felt tight. Nobody other than an employee had ever fed him? Maybe I was old-fashioned, but that didn't sit right with me. "Do you have groceries?" I opened the stainless steel Sub-Zero and found…champagne, champagne, thirty bottles of Fiji water, a jar of capers, and a Red Bull. My eyebrows hitched up. "I'm scared to ask what the capers are for."

His mouth curved into a lazy smile. He walked up behind me and hugged me tightly, resting his chin on the curve of my neck. I felt the erection growing in his jeans. My eyes widened and a burst of laughter bubbled up.

"You can't be serious."

"We better go to the grocery store. I need food if this is going to keep happening every time I'm around you."

The Mercedes SUV crawled next to us as we walked the short distance to the grocery store. He draped his arm around my neck. I swung mine around his waist, hooking a thumb through the belt loop of his jeans. We looked like an ordinary couple, doing ordinary things, on an ordinary sunny Saturday morning. If only.

Inside the store, I searched for a cart, looked over, and found him looking a bit lost. "When was the last time you went food shopping?" He just stared back, unblinking. "Never mind, let's get a cart," I added, not wanting to put him on the spot.

"Let me do that," he said, commandeering the cart. Only this man could turn a shopping cart into a sexy accessory. I schooled my expression, not wanting him to think I was laughing at him. Needless to say, he caused a traffic jam down every aisle we wandered. Women halted their shopping to openly stare as if it were a sighting of the Beatles circa 1960. I might as well have been invisible, the feeling not a pleasant one.

He followed me around, playing the part of the gallant servant. Completely unaware of the uproar he was causing, he waited patiently while I selected fresh vegetables, fruits, eggs, dairy products, and various other items that we needed, even seemed to take pleasure in it. Every time he picked up an item and I inspected it before letting him place it in our cart, he smirked. Twice, I had to put something back and explain where the bruise was, or that it wasn't ripe enough.

"What's wrong with this peach?" He held up said fruit.

"It'll be days before it's ripe enough to eat. And it has no scent. Here, smell." I pushed it under his nose. His eyes danced with mischief.

"I know where to find a peach that smells real good," he

murmured in a low, sexy voice and held me steady for a quick kiss.

"We'd better go before you cause a stampede," I suggested. A happy sigh rose up my throat as I laced my fingers together around his neck.

His brow furrowed in confusion. "A stampede?" I motioned for him to look around and stifled a laugh. Every pair of female eyes in the store was trained on him.

Once we got back to the apartment, the day only got better. I cooked us a hearty breakfast, starting with my signature omelet. Brown, free-range eggs, ripe cherry tomatoes, fresh basil, fresh mozzarella cheese, a dash of freshly grated Parmigiano cheese, a pinch of sea salt, and a nice, fat pat of butter on the skillet. I toasted a brioche for myself, and roasted baby russet potatoes drizzled with olive oil and rosemary for him.

Sitting side by side at the counter, he lifted my leg and draped it over his lap, caressing it as he ate. "Damn, you're a good cook, woman." A moan of satisfaction followed every time he took a bite.

"Don't you think you're overdoing it a bit?"

His eyes grew sulky, scheming. "I'm 'bout to show you how grateful I am for this meal."

Shrieking, I tried to evade his playful grab, but he caught me easily, kissed me soundly, and proceeded to make love to me on every available surface of the apartment.

"I'm going to get hard every time I walk in the door now," he said on the drive back to the estate.

I met his happy, sparkling gaze and smiled. *I love you*, I thought, words I could never say out loud. "Poor baby, you'll just have to grin and bear it."

He shook his head slowly. "Darlin'," he drawled, reaching over to tuck his hand between my knees, "you're the one who's going to have to bear it." Then he unleashed one of his megawatt smiles. "But I'll make damn sure you're grinnin'."

———

IT TOOK me a week to come down from the residual high of those two fairytale days at the apartment. I was blending his unsavory protein drink when Isabelle stalked into the kitchen. She eyeballed me with a suspicious look on her face. Annoyed with her scrutiny, I turned off the blender and returned a blank stare.

"I think it's funny how he always asks for you even though you two supposedly hate each other. Funny how I haven't seen any evidence of that legendary hatred for weeks now. What were the two of you doing in the woods that day anyway?" Her cold eyes narrowed.

"Maybe he appreciates the fact that I don't push a pair of big, fat breasts in his face any chance I get. Maybe he finds it refreshing when I don't bat my eyelashes, pant and moan, and generally make a fool of myself every time the man takes a breath."

I completely ignored her last question and prayed she wouldn't notice. I knew I shouldn't be snippy with her, that any show of emotion would say too much, but I couldn't help myself. I had to endure watching her bend over to serve him breakfast and practically fall into his lap on three separate occasions! She was becoming more and more brazen while he responded with a small polite smile and carried on as if nothing awkward had occurred. I don't even think he noticed.

A number of the employees had remarked on his change of mood lately. I feigned complete ignorance whenever they mentioned it. Poor old Betty almost fell over in shock two mornings ago when she passed him in the kitchen, and he stopped to inquired about her husband's health.

"Some of us aren't frigid," she shouted before walking out.

By the time I reached the gym, Yvette had cornered him into a private conversation. I was greeted by one raised eyebrow. "Vera, my drink, please."

I bit the inside of my cheek to stifle a grin. Yvette's dark head whipped around, her sculpted face dropping at the sight of me. I couldn't help but feel some sympathy for her. I knew how irresistible he was. Maybe better than anyone. Sensing her window of opportunity had closed, Yvette begrudgingly grabbed her bag and began to walk out. Her eyes narrowed in my direction as she bid him goodbye.

"You're late."

"I can't protect you from every woman that's attracted to you. That's a full-time job and an impossible task," I snickered.

"Very funny. Maybe I'll hire you to guard by body." He reached out but I leaned away in time to avoid his grasp. Looking over my shoulder, I checked the open doorway.

"You already have three bodyguards. Besides, you can't afford me."

"Darlin', I may be the only man that can."

That lazy drawl never failed to turn me on. That's what too many reruns of Dallas will do to you. I slapped his hand away as he stroked my breast through the wool of the uniform, then laughed at his adorable frown. I had it bad.

"Hitting an injured man, Dr. Sava? Your bedside manner needs polish."

"I need to check the stitches after you shower."

"I think I'll need your assistance in the shower, Doc, wouldn't want to re-injure myself." Grabbing my wrists, he clasped them to my lower back. My giggle turned into a moan when I felt his lips, then his teeth on the curve of my neck.

"I love that sound," he mumbled between kisses.

"What sound?" I asked, panting.

"Your laugh." His unabashed sweetness left me raw, exposed. The urge to shrink back was overwhelming. My gaze moved to a spot beyond him.

"Why do you train with her if she makes you uncomfortable?"

"Because she's the best available trainer around here."

"She really likes you. You're very popular with the brunettes."

"It's because I'm blond."

I wriggled my wrists and couldn't pry loose. He was always so careful with me that I often forgot how large and powerful he was.

"You're not that blond—mostly dark blond."

Releasing my wrists, he placed my hand on his erection and pushed it down its swollen length. "Let me remind you where I'm real blond," he purred, while I squirmed and laughed.

"I almost feel bad for her."

"Don't. She doesn't like me, she wants me...like a stag head on the wall."

"My goodness, you don't like being objectified, huh? What about me? I want you."

He walked forward, backing me up in an awkward dance towards the wall. "Then I'll make you like me." His sweaty chest pushed against my wool gabardine uniform. He cupped the back of my head. His hooded eyes filled with lust and need.

"Stop, you're all sweaty." My breathy voice held not an ounce of conviction. That scent that was distinctly him: full-grown male, soap, and God knows what else was a powerful cocktail. Heat shot right between my thighs.

"I'm getting some very good ideas about these straps and what we could do with them. Besides, you're going to be sweaty in a minute, too."

I was trapped between the hard curves of his body and the wall. His shaft pressed against my belly as he raised my wrists over my head, to where the straps hung down. "Yes, but not here...and definitely not now. Anybody can walk in."

"I'm done sneaking around like a fifteen-year-old at boarding school. I'm a grown-ass man in my own fucking house. I will make love to my woman when and where I want."

Make love? I pretended not to hear that. "First of all, your language is atrocious. Second, I will not permit you to out me. And since when am I your woman?" It was close to impossible to sound determined when he kissed my neck and nudged his erection into my sweet spot with the accuracy of a world class marksman.

"First, get used to it," he murmured in my ear. "And lastly, you've been mine since the day I found out you existed."

The last few words bounced around my brain. Then we both heard it—the gasp coming from the doorway. Our heads popped up in unison to find Charlotte standing there with her fingers resting like the bars of a prison over her full lips, her eyes as large as a cartoon character's. She turned on her heels and fled. Sebastian's body sagged against mine.

"Let go. I have to speak to her." I struggled in his firm grip, anxious to get going.

"Wait a second. This gives us the perfect opportunity to stop this cloak and dagger bullshit. I'm fed up. I want everybody to know we're together."

"Absolutely not. We agreed. I need to convince her to keep this quiet."

He flinched, releasing me instantly. "We never agreed. You insisted. And what are you saying? That you're embarrassed to be with me?" The set of his shoulders was rigid, his hands sat on his hips in a defiant stance.

"I can't discuss this with you now. I have to find Charlotte." I stood on my toes and kissed his stern lips.

"Be in my room by ten."

"Not tonight."

His eyebrows shot up. "Be there by ten or I'll come looking for you." He may have said, *looking*. However, his eyes clearly meant *hunting*. I knew arguing would get me nowhere, he was relentless when he wanted something, so I nodded and left to chase after Charlotte.

CHAPTER 26

I found her in the vegetable garden with a cigarette in her hand, her thumbnail worrying the nail of her pinky finger. I was mortified. Unsure of how to begin, I walked up quietly and stood there fidgeting with my apron as I searched for the right words to break the uncomfortable silence.

"I'm so sorry, Charlotte."

She looked over her shoulder for only a moment before returning her absent gaze to the dusky horizon. "There's no need to apologize to me."

"Yes, there is. You've been a terrific friend to me and I...I haven't been to you. Trusting people is difficult for me. I've been burned before. It's no reflection on you. I just didn't know what to say."

"I know what that feels like, Vera, believe me," she said, a weary understanding present in both her voice and expression.

Next to her, I leaned against the brick wall and watched the early evening fog roll in. The words came out before I realized what was happening. "I was engaged six and a half years ago. Before we could be married, my father was caught up...there was a scandal." Her brows were knit, her eyes patient. I took a deep breath before continuing. "Before the trial, Aleksander, my fiancé, decided that we should move to Belgium, that the stress of the trial would be too much to deal with. He wanted a fresh start. I couldn't leave my father, of course...the last time I saw him, he was boarding a train for Brussels and promised to send for me once the trial was over...I never heard from him again."

"Bloody bastard!" She threw down the cigarette and stomped it out under her foot.

"My thoughts exactly," I stated, smiling at her dramatics. I felt lighter. Having unburdened myself a little bit of the load felt good. "Anyway, I'm over it. Nobody knows, Charlotte, not Sebastian, not anybody."

"Your secrets are safe with me...are you in love with him?" I knew she was dying to talk about him. Her face gave away every thought and emotion.

"It's...we're both lonely. It's just sex."

"That doesn't seem to be true," she murmured. Crafty Charlotte. She was on to me. I turned to her with a resigned look.

"It has to be. I can't afford to be wrong again."

"You can do that? Stop yourself from falling in love?"

"I'm not sure," I admitted, my convictions as ambiguous as the gray mist that marked the horizon. "But I do know one thing—if I don't fly too high, I'll survive the crash landing."

She reached for my hand, laced her fingers through mine, and gave me a gentle squeeze in sisterly support.

———

IT WAS after eleven when I stepped into his bedroom. He was sitting in his oversized armchair near the fireplace, wearing a pair of ancient-looking jeans and an optic white t-shirt that made the tan on his face look deeper. His injured leg lay straight on the ottoman. With his elbow resting on the arm of the chair, he leaned his handsome face on the triangle of his thumb and index finger. His eyes were sulky and irritated, promising retribution.

If you asked me, he was even more irresistible when he was dressed casually, a little unkempt. He had so much natural sex appeal that he didn't need all the gadgets and expensive clothes. Sebastian didn't have a vain bone in his body. Even when he dressed, it seemed he played a part for business, for everybody but himself. And there was no question he was much more comfortable naked. If the servants didn't live in the house, I was certain he would've roamed around as naked as the day he was born all the time.

That he didn't like being pursued by women had been an unexpected discovery. There was no hope for him unless he wanted to wear a paper bag over his head. But there's no accounting for how people view themselves. When I looked in the mirror, I saw someone strong and resilient. Not fragile, not in need of rescuing. I guess when he looked in the mirror, he saw an inconvenience.

"Charlotte promised she'd keep quiet."

His eyes narrowed at the declaration. He threw his head back against the chair cushion and stared at the ceiling. "Why are you dressed?"

"Because we need to speak, and I can't do that wearing my nightgown."

"I'm going to take every piece of your God-awful wardrobe and incinerate it first thing tomorrow."

My whole body stiffened in embarrassment. I knew my

clothes were pitiful, but to hear it from his lips was some-thing else altogether. I was too tired to quibble with him. "I don't even know how to respond to that ridiculously rude comment. You know I can't afford to buy clothes right now."

"And then I'm going to call every fucking store from London to Paris and have them send me everything in your size...I hope they bankrupt me."

The low simmer of anger in his voice warned me to tread lightly. I sat down on the ottoman, next to his leg. His expression didn't change—until I rubbed his kneecap. Then his thick lashes fluttered. We could read each other so easily. I don't know when that happened. That mastery over each other. He knew exactly where to touch me to render me speechless, which words would cut deep and which would spark my temper. I learned quickly when to back off, how to soothe him, where to touch him to bring him to ecstasy.

"Lover, listen to me. I know why you want to do that, but it wouldn't be right. It makes me feel...beholden. Do you understand why?"

He brushed my cheek with the back of his fingers, a note of...was that pity in his expression? I pushed his hand away.

"I understand how you came up with that absurd idea. Why can't you let me take care of you? Why would you deny me that? Because your pride will suffer?"

A restless discomfort coursed through me because he may have had a point. Was it about my pride? Was I doing it so I could look in the mirror one day and say I gave pleasure and took pleasure equally, and nothing else? If I let my guard down, he would trample me into letting him have his way. I was already perilously close, incapable of resisting him when he put his mind to something. And what would happen when it ended? And it had to end sooner or later. He could never know what had happened in Tirana. What would Cinderella's new wardrobe mean then? A reminder of dashed hopes? Payment for services rendered? I didn't dare contemplate where my dark thoughts could lead me.

"This isn't about money."

"The hell it isn't."

"I don't want to argue about this. Can't you just respect my wishes?"

The focused intensity was steadily building in his eyes. He was digging in for a fight. This did not bode well for me. "Let me ask you something, do you remember when I found you under the wisteria tree?"

"Yes, of course."

"Why did you touch me? Why did you touch my leg?" I stalled, trying to discern where this train of thought was headed. "Answer me, damn it!"

"Because you were in a great deal of pain, and I wanted to help you. I wanted to take away your suffering."

His breathing was deep and quick, emotions raw and on the surface. "How would you feel if I had denied you? If I wouldn't let you touch me?"

"It would bother me," I said, frowning at the thought. I would feel frustrated and helpless."

He stood up and quickly closed the distance between us. Wrapping his powerful arms around me, he pressed me to him as if he could absorb my body into his. "Let me take care of you," he pleaded, his amber eyes determined and serious. "I've given a great deal of thought to this. I want you to hear me out before you say anything else. I don't want you working here anymore. I want you living here, with me..." He paused at the look of shock on my face. "Be with me."

"You can't be serious. We've known each other barely two months, and half that time we've spent fighting."

A flash of pain appeared in his eyes. Tucking it away, he

pressed his case. "We can stay at the apartment during the week and come here on weekends."

I was beyond shocked. I didn't want it to end yet, but I didn't know how to slow him down, how to make him back off. I was in uncharted waters, drowning in anxiety. "Let me go."

"That won't ever happen," he stated tenderly. Ruthless man. He knew what it did to me when he spoke like that.

I felt split in two and fought back tears spilling from my heart. Part of me wanted desperately to believe this could work. However, the small part of me that could still reason knew better. I pushed against his shoulders, and he released me. "You don't know me! You don't know anything about me! You don't know what you're asking. I can't afford to rely on anyone!"

I had never raised my voice to him like that before. It surprised him. He reached out to grab my wrist, and I stepped away just in time to evade him. Raising his hands in surrender, he begged softly, "Okay, easy...please let me hold you, please. You're killing me, lover." His face was a mixture of fear, affection, and intense awareness.

I ran into his open arms, the only place I wanted to be, and let him hold me, let him chase away the fear and sadness with his magic touch. Closing my eyes, I soaked in the feeling, burning it in my memory so I could look back on it one day and treasure it. "It's okay, we'll work it out. We'll take it slow," he murmured in my ear.

Laying me down on the bed, he fitted himself snuggly between my thighs. My hips, as if summoned by their master, hitched up to meet his. He teased my mouth with his own, nibbled, licked, and petted until I was clay in his hands. I kissed him back passionately, pouring all the love I had for him into that connection.

Would this heat between us ever recede? Would we ever get enough of each other?

His expression was worshipful when he broke the kiss and stroked the hair off my forehead. "I want you to let me in. I want you to trust me."

The weight of all the words I couldn't say pressed down painfully on my chest. How could I tell him that was an impossible request? I didn't have the heart to drive the stake through his fragile hopes. I couldn't respond, so I did the only thing I could—I kissed him until all thought ceased and only pleasure existed between the two of us.

My hands stroked the silky skin of his well-muscled back and traveled lower, over the dip at the base of his spine and underneath his jeans, where I discovered that he was naked. His lips kicked up on one side. I squeezed the globes of his backside, and he nudged me in answer with his aroused body.

"Let me in," he whispered, as he made love to me. Those expressive, liquid pools of fire trained on every sigh, every twitch. I didn't know how to respond because he was already there, fastened onto my heart.

———

"WHAT DOES THAT MEAN? Now that Argentina defaulted."

We fell into a comfortable routine, meeting in his bedroom after eleven. We spoke for hours at night, in between wild sex and gentle lovemaking. Sometimes, I didn't know what was better, the mind-blowing orgasms or the mind-blowing conversations. I wouldn't have wanted to do without either one.

"It's not the first time they've defaulted," he said as he loosened his tie. Work had kept him at the office late all week. It was costing him. I could tell from the shade under his eyes that his leg was bothering him.

"It's just crazy that one hedge fund can hold so much Argentine debt that they can decide to sink an entire country. It sounds like extortion."

"Negotiations broke down when the hedge fund refused to take pennies on the dollar," he explained. "It's getting ugly. They've been shut out of foreign capital markets for too long. Inflation is over twenty-five percent."

When he sat on the bed to remove his pants, I instinctively reached for him and raked my fingers through his hair. A weary sigh escaped his lips, and his eyelids grew heavy, fluttering shut.

"This sounds like some far-fetched Hollywood thriller. Can't the American government do something? Isn't that what they do? Save the world from all villains?"

"You don't have anything against Americans, do you?" he asked, smirking.

"I happen to love all things American." Immediately, I stiffened, realizing I had inadvertently used the word "love." He stood up and wrapped me in his arms as if he sensed my impulse to retreat.

"So what is there to do for poor Argentina?" I asked, trying to pivot away from the serious moment.

"The president can bail Argentina out under a principle known as *comity*. He needs to inform the federal judge handling the case that the suit brought by the hedge fund against the Argentine government interferes with his ability to conduct foreign policy, and the judge will dismiss the suit." He placed a delicate kiss on the tip of my nose, released me, and continued undressing.

"I told Marianne that I'm going to dry out this weekend...I told her that I need you with me," he said, without making eye contact. He threw his navy trousers onto the chair next to the fireplace. Without thought, I picked them up and hung them neatly on a wooded hanger. When I turned towards him, he was staring with a spark of amusement in his eyes.

"What did she say?" I wanted to be there for him, but Mrs. Arnaud had a keen mind. She would find it suspicious.

"She said it was a good idea. Unless I wanted to go do it at a clinic, and I have absolutely no intention of doing that."

"Did you speak to your orthopedist?"

"Yeah, he said the NSAIDs should be enough and to make an appointment to see him soon." He removed his dress shirt and threw it on the floor. I walked over, picked it up, and placed it in the hamper.

"What's so funny?"

"Nothing," he answered, his voice on the verge of breaking out in laughter.

He stripped his boxer briefs off and handed them to me. I took them from him and placed them in the hamper as well.

"Are you laughing at me?"

He lifted his chin, and a blinding grin stretched across his face. "Do you realize that you do that all the time?"

"Do what?"

"Follow me around, picking up my mess." His face fell, grave, all of a sudden. His dark lashes lowered over his eyes. "No one's ever picked up my mess before. It's usually the other way around."

He rarely opened up about himself. He played his cards close to the vest, and I didn't want to say anything to discourage him. I knew he had revealed more than he intended so I tried to lighten the mood. "That's because you're a slob."

His lips quirked. Clasping my wrist, he brought me gently

against the warm shelter of his chest. "Your slob," he said seductively, prompting a smile on my face too.

While his fingers smoothly unbuttoned my uniform, he made love to the delicate skin of my neck below my ear. He hardened against my stomach as he began licking and biting the exposed skin of my bare shoulders.

"So...about this weekend?" The hint of something vulnerable in his voice didn't escape me. His gaze caught mine. Apprehension and hope took turns flashing in his eyes.

"I'm here for you," I whispered. Because I was. And I was done denying it to myself and to him.

It was chilly that night, even though it was already the end of June. He lit a fire, and we made love on the rug in front of the fireplace. Relaxed and replete, I stretched every limb like a cat sunning itself on a hot pavement in summer. He rose up on an elbow and picked up a ripe strawberry from the bowl we had stolen from the kitchen.

"Those were supposed to be for the tart Marianne was baking tomorrow."

With a seductive spark in his eye, he bent his head and kissed my nipple. "I'm having a tart right now." I giggled when he raised his eyebrows playfully. I hadn't laughed this much since I was a child. He had a gift for breaking through the stiffness, the formality I wore as a shield. He teased me mercilessly until I was loose and easy and putty in his hands.

"You're completely incorrigible."

"Damn right," he purred, placing a string of lazy kisses on my breasts. "Whatever that means." Then he bit the tip of a ripe strawberry and let the sugary juice spill onto my stomach, pooling in my navel.

"What are you doing?"

"You asked about my work. This is your first lesson: How to recognize a pattern on a trading chart." He took the juicy strawberry and ran it along my feverish skin. "This is called a head and shoulders pattern." He drew on my body, up and over one breast, down the valley in between, then over the other breast. I giggled and squirmed.

"Sit still," he crooned, licking the sticky juice off. "Or I'll give you an F."

After his expert demonstration, we crawled onto the chaise lounge and watched the fire's dull roar turn into a moan until it extinguished. Gloriously naked, he lay back in the chaise while I straddled his lap, the dying flames highlighting the perfect angles of his face. "I haven't read that one," he admitted, pushing the silk curtain of my hair back off my shoulder. I caught his hand and kissed the pale, pointy scars one by one, his gaze softening as he watched me.

"You haven't read *Jane Eyre*? You haven't read much," I said between kisses.

His sultry lips curved up. "Jesus, you're like one of those stern Catholic school teachers. Are you going to paddle me?"

"Would you like me to?"

A wicked glint flashed in his eyes before he kissed me, devouring my mouth. When his lips lifted, the space between his brows creased and his expression turned solemn. "I never did much reading until the accident. I was bedridden for a long time. Then it was all I could do."

The previously light mood turned to lead. I caressed his beloved face. He closed his eyes and turned to kiss my hand, then covered it with his own, keeping it in place on his cheek. "I'm so sorry," I whispered softly.

"All that time to think—that was the hardest part."

"Tell me."

"There isn't much to tell." His eyes darted away, his voice flat. "I killed my wife."

"That's not true," I argued quietly.

"I was driving, wasn't I? I'm the one who drove the car off the side of the road. She died because of me."

I had to tread this scarred territory lightly. I didn't want to discourage him from opening up, and the emotional wound was still tender.

"Darling, look at me, it was an accident. You didn't cause anything. And you certainly didn't kill her. There nothing you, nor anybody else, could've done to prevent it from happening. As powerful and capable as you are, you are still just a man. And I'm so grateful you were spared."

His eyes flared. I watched my words sink in, watched his expression transform from tortured to thoughtful. I had succeeded in reaching his intellect, cutting through the smothering blanket of pain. He wrapped his arms around me, binding us together skin to skin, and hid his face in the curve of my neck. "Don't ever leave me, Vera."

I swallowed the angst rising up my throat because I couldn't tell him what we both wanted to hear, and I wouldn't make promises I couldn't keep.

CHAPTER 27

Unexpectedly, something wonderful happened the next day. I received a letter from one of the hospitals in Geneva informing me that interviews for their residency programs would begin in December and that I had been scheduled in.

My heart almost exploded with joy. I read and reread it several times to reassure myself that I wasn't imagining it. The first thought that came to mind was that I couldn't wait to tell Sebastian. This was awful. I was slipping and sliding deeper and deeper into love, and there wasn't a damn thing I could do about it. Except make sure that he didn't know. That was the only way my heart would survive the aftermath of having to let him go.

"I have news." I leaned forward while he squirted soap on his hands and cleaned my back with languid, sensual strokes, rubbing the sore muscles of my shoulders.

It was midnight. He'd insisted we take a bath after gifting me with not one, but two excruciating climaxes, each time drawing the pleasure out, prolonging it until I was begging him for relief. I wasn't sure if it was the begging he wanted from me, or something else. Something drove him, something he hadn't gotten yet.

"Is it good?" His voice was husky. He kissed the top of my spine and nibbled on my earlobe, making me shiver and want him again. I was no expert, but it just didn't seem normal. My head fell forward, and water splashed up as he rinsed my back.

"Don't get your dressing wet," I ordered. Although the effect was ruined by my breathy voice.

"Yes, ma'am, what's the news?" His wicked hand snaked around to the front of my body, inside my thigh, up to…

"I can't speak when you do that. I can barely think after what you did an hour ago."

"Hmm, is that a bad thing?"

"No. Yes. I mean…do you see what I mean?"

His gentle massage had moved on to my eager breasts. I could feel his shaft getting hard against my rear end, and any blood left in my head swiftly traveled below my waist. "Oh my God," I gasped. "How is this even possible?"

"Let me get this straight—you don't want to want me?" Even though his voice was steady, there was a hint of something wounded in it.

"I couldn't stop wanting you if my life depended on it." I felt his satisfied smile on my skin as he kissed my shoulder. "Sebastian, has this ever happened to you before?"

"No," he answered without hesitation.

"Me neither." I sank back against his chest and his arms wrapped around me protectively, both of us quiet as we absorbed the enormity of that truth. "I received a letter from one of the hospitals today. I have an interview for their residency program in December."

He guided my chin around to face him. His eyes were

bright and happy for me. Sweet, beautiful man. "That's great news. François can drive you in."

My brows lowered over my questioning gaze. "Drive me? How do you know it's not in Zurich?" Something flared in his eyes. "Did you have anything to do with this?" He blew out a deep breath and looked away from me. "Look at me," I ordered softly.

"Okay, I put in a good word. That's all."

I was stunned, angry, and grateful at the same time—a strange mix of emotions that left me feeling awkward. "I guess I should thank you."

"You don't look like you mean it."

The water was suddenly cold. I stood up, dripping into the tub in front of him while he looked up at me with supplicating eyes. He ran his hand around my calf, caressing it, the only place left on my body that was warm. His hand slipped away as I stepped out and wrapped myself in one of his decadently luxurious towels.

"Vera, don't be mad."

When I turned towards him, I found him standing in the tub, water sliding down the utter physical perfection of his body, and almost got distracted. Almost. Stepping out of the tub, he grabbed a towel and began drying his hair...his hair. He stood there deliciously dripping wet...drying his hair. The shameless sex god knew the effect he had on me and was prepared to use every weapon in his arsenal.

I crossed my arms over my chest. "I know what you're doing," I warned, punctuating the seriousness of the situation with a raised eyebrow. He continued to towel dry his hair while he inched his way closer to me.

"What am I doing?" he asked with poorly feigned innocence.

"I just...it's just that I thought I did it all on my own.

Don't you understand? And now, I know I didn't, even though I'm unbelievably grateful for your help."

Dropping the towel, he brought me up against his warm, wet body, and hugged me tightly, his cheek resting on the top of my head. "Vera, you've done everything in the last six years on your own. You've done more on your own than most people accomplish in a lifetime." The comforting sound of his deep voice reverberated off his chest as he spoke. "Let somebody help you for once."

I hated it when he made perfect sense.

————

"I DON'T...KNOW...IF I can...do this."

It was midnight, twenty-six hours since his last pill of oxycodone. Alternating between cold chills and burning sweats, he was in full-blown withdrawal, shaking so violently that I had to get on the bed and press the entire weight of my body on top of him just to give him some relief.

I did anything and everything I could to ease his suffering. I rubbed his back while he threw up. The last few times were painful to watch as he dry heaved until he almost passed out. I held him when he shivered; it seemed to make him feel marginally better. I tried to keep him hydrated but it was difficult because of the nausea.

Sifting my short nails through his hair and scratching his scalp, I murmured, "You can do this. The worst is almost over, I promise."

That was a major lie. It wasn't anywhere near being over.

"Keep...doing...that...pleeeeze."

Heartbreaking. In the midst of excruciating suffering he was grateful for every little thing I did for him. There was always a "please" and a "thank you" after I emptied the bucket with his vomit, or rubbed his leg, or changed his sweat-soaked t-shirt. He seemed surprised that I would do that for him.

It was bad enough finding out that no woman had ever cooked him a lousy meal, other than an employee, but I was beginning to wonder if anybody had ever done anything for him ever. It seemed preposterous that a man that was so generous, so kind, never had a woman want to take care of him. Specifically, this supposed *angel* he had married and was still in love with. It didn't make sense, and frankly it made me furious.

"Talk…to…me."

"Okay, let's see…" I struggled for a neutral topic, my mind lazy from lack of sleep. "I'm really scared of pigeons. I never even got to see the inside of the Duomo, the cathedral in Milan, because I could never get past the army of pigeons. Umm, what else? Oh! I love how quiet it gets when snow falls."

I glanced down and discovered his face had softened. His thick lashes cast shadows on his high cheekbones. He had fallen asleep. Thank God. He needed some relief. My dissertation on pigeons and snow proved to be a powerful sedative.

Sweet dreams, my love, I thought, while I stroked the hair off his forehead.

The door cracked open and Mrs. Arnaud peeked her head in. I crept off the bed quietly and tiptoed into the hall. "Vera, you look terrible. You need to eat and rest. You've been going for over a day."

She was right. Even though my mind was racing, my body was spent. "I'm fine, really. He's finally asleep. The last few hours have been…difficult."

"Let me sit with him." I shook my head but she wouldn't

take no for an answer. "I insist. Now go, or you won't be any good to him tomorrow."

Exhaustion finally caught up with me. I ate and showered in a listless fog. When my head hit the pillow, I fell into a coma, sleeping like the dead through the night. The light filtering in at dawn woke me. Jumping out of bed, I dressed in a hurry, mindful that poor Mrs. Arnaud had been there all night and was probably ready for some sleep herself. As I was taking the stairs two at a time, I crashed right into Isabelle. "Sorry!" I shouted.

She narrowed her eyes as I hurried past her. A cold sense of foreboding followed me up the stairs. Undoubtedly, I would have to deal with her later.

In Sebastian's bedroom, I found Mrs. Arnaud snuggled into the oversized armchair near the fireplace with her legs up, snoring at a high decibel. Sebastian was still asleep. Restless and fidgety, but asleep. I placed my hand on Mrs. Arnaud's arm and she jerked awake. "Go to bed," I whispered.

Nodding weakly, she pushed out of the chair and left. I dropped into the empty space she had occupied only moments ago and watched him sleep for hours, watched him struggle for some peace. *My very own Sleeping Beauty*, I thought. If only.

———

"I NEED A SHOWER," he said, when he woke from a nap.

Day three. His face still looked drawn, dark circles were painted under his eyes. At least the tremors and hot flashes had subsided. He was weak, standing under a hot shower wasn't a good idea. "I'm running the water for your bath right now. But I want you to have some broth first." I fluffed his pillows and placed them behind his back so he could sit up in bed more comfortably.

"I can't." He made a feeble attempt to turn his head away as I drew closer with the cup of steaming liquid.

"Sebastian, please, you need nutrients. You've already lost weight, and you're probably dehydrated...just a cup." I brought the cup to his lips and he sipped it slowly, watching me the whole time. His expression was a mixture of fascination and caution, as if he were expecting me to peel back my skin and reveal something alien.

When he was done, he closed his eyes and his head fell back against the padded headboard. Utterly beautiful in the midst of his struggle. So vulnerable and yet so brave. I knew how difficult it was for him to appear defenseless in front of anyone, and the fact that he wanted me here made me love him even more.

"You're right. I feel better." He cracked one eye open, then the other. "You never talk about yourself."

"There's not much to say. I'm not the handsome, rich bachelor traveling the globe and dating supermodels." My childish attempt to distract him didn't work. His eyes filled with sympathy instead of disapproval.

"How did you get to Milan?" The silence was heavy. He waited patiently for me to respond.

How could I deny him? He had placed himself in my care, trusting me so completely that I felt compelled to take at least a tiny step forward. "A friend of mine from university— his father ran a ferry from Durres to Otranto, near Bari, Italy. I packed as much as I could carry and met him at the docks at midnight...it was so cold that night." Lost in thought, the edge of my vision bled, a rush of memories hitting me all at once.

"There were seventeen of us on board. The water was

choppy, and the boat was old. I was scared—you know I'm a terrible swimmer—but there was a little boy, maybe six, traveling with his father. So I pretended the swaying of the boat was fun." I turned to look at him and found his soft eyes unblinking. He squeezed my hand—the hand I hadn't even realized he'd been holding the entire time. "The boat crashed on the rocks in Otranto. I can still smell the gasoline in the water... The Italians caught two others who were with us, but the boy and his father made it. We were lucky. I heard another ferry sank a week later."

The conversation left me feeling raw and exposed. I shrugged, trying to mask my discomfort. "The rest was easy. I took the train when I could and walked the rest of the way."

"You walked from Bari all the way to northern Italy?" His bewilderment made me smile. It didn't sound extraordinary to me at all. Somewhere deep inside of me, an impenetrable core existed, a force of will that would never allow me to surrender, to be swallowed up by despair. I had always been aware of it.

"It sounds crazy now, but it was easy at the time. I guess we don't know what we're capable of accomplishing until tested." I bent forward and caressed his jaw, ran a finger down the gentle slope of his nose, and kissed the tiny scar on his top lip. His lips parted, and a soft sigh slipped out. "Your bath awaits you, Your Highness." His eyes were filled with an indescribable emotion. I stared back as something big passed between us, something meaningful. *I love you,* I thought. And this time, I didn't look away.

In the tub, he laid back and shut his eyes. He hadn't shaved in days and his dark golden scruff had fully grown in. He looked like a disreputable rake in a Victorian melodrama and outrageously sexy for a man who'd recently been to hell and back.

"Would you like me to shave you?"

His lashes lifted lazily. "Depends where," he answered with a one-sided grin.

"You must be feeling better. I see your wicked sense of humor is back. I vote for leaving the scruff. I like it."

His eyebrows lifted a fraction, mischief lurking in his expressive eyes. "If you like it, then it stays."

I sat on the edge of the tub and began washing him. His head fell back in surrender. The fatigue stamped on his face softened, a content expression growing on his face as I lathered his arms, his shoulders, and in between each finger before moving on to his chest and corrugated abdomen. I tipped him forward and washed his back, the nape of his neck, down his legs and toes. When I skimmed the sponge between his thighs and over his sex, I heard him moan. I almost couldn't believe my eyes when his penis stood erect underwater, evidence of the man's considerable virility.

"How could you possibly get hard at a time like this?"

The sensual creature that he was, a lazy smile curved his lips. I dropped the sponge and poured more gel on my hands. Alertness entered his eyes as I grabbed his erection firmly at the base and began stroking him, pressing my thumb on the ridge under the crown. His eyelids turned heavy, his breathing harsh. His grip on the edge of the tub tightened. Lost in arousal, he was simply stunning. I loved watching him lose control. It was always the other way around. I was always the one moaning and begging for his mercy. I dipped my other hand below the water and squeezed his sac. Groaning loudly, he arched into my hands, pumping his hips. I kept stroking him until he climaxed and a primal cry from somewhere deep and dark erupted out of him. He sounded wounded, full of pained emotion.

He was just a man, after all. Often in control and dominating but not impervious. It was easy to forget when confronted with the beautiful ruse. And I was so caught up in my own problems that I hadn't stopped to consider how deep his pain still ran. He had lost a woman he loved very much.

Grabbing my hand, he placed it on his chest and covered it with his own. The heavy thumping under my palm felt like I held his heart in my hand. My gaze traveled up to his solemn eyes.

"Thank you...I..." he murmured, struggling for words. "Thank you."

I swallowed the lump of love and sympathy stuck in my throat. "You don't have to thank me. I want to do this for you." Then he pulled me down for a sweet, heartfelt kiss.

CHAPTER 28

The shrill of the kitchen phone interrupted my daydreaming. My nails were bright green from cracking open pea pods and robbing them of their carefully protected cargo. I inspected the stain that seemed determined to stay under my fingernails, undiminished by a vigorous scrubbing.

Mrs. Arnaud turned off the kitchen sink and dried her wet hands on her embroidered apron. "*Allo*," she answered in French, switching to English immediately afterwards. "Vera, it's for you."

My head snapped up. Anxiously, I reached for the phone.

"Vera?" Emilia's voice was shaky, weak.

"Emilia, what's wrong?!"

"Can you come? I need you."

"Give me your address." Glancing up at the antique clock on the wall, I said, "It should only take me an hour by taxi."

"Okay," she responded with an unsteady sigh. "Thank you."

"See you soon, Em."

Her address in Eaux-Vives on the Rive Gauche had me suspecting that I was probably meeting her at Yuri's apartment. She couldn't possibly afford the rent in that neighborhood on her inconsistent salary. Mrs. Arnaud insisted that Theo drive me instead of calling a taxi. I didn't have time to debate the matter and agreed.

Theo's car made slow progress down the country roads. I stared out the window at the passing scenery. Dusk fell reluctantly, airbrushing the sky a pretty ombre from orange to lavender before it descended into darkness.

In my rush to get to Emilia I hadn't mentioned it to Sebastian that I was going out. I had every intension of sending him an email when I ran to my room to change, but something stopped me. Because what would that say about us? That we had some kind of obligation to each other? It was a slippery slope.

By the time we pulled up to the address, it was already late. Her building was located on a beautiful tree-lined street, seated in between quaint shops and trendy cafés. I scanned the directory and rang the button next to a familiar name. Yuri Skilenski. After she buzzed me in, I climbed the steps to the second floor with my heart thumping loudly, dreading what I would find on the other side of the steel door.

The door opened abruptly. It only took a few seconds to assess the bloody lip, the messy hair, the ruddy cheeks. Fresh tears slipped down her face. I wrapped her gently in my arms, unsure if there were any broken bones. She leaned on me, her knees giving out. I rubbed her thin back as I kicked the door shut. Small sobbing sounds burst out of her in between choppy breaths. I pulled away only long enough to take a more thorough inventory of her injuries.

"Emilia, where are you hurt?"

She dipped her head and turned away in embarrassment.

Lifting her cotton shirt slowly, she revealed a cluster of bruises on her ribs. I touched the swollen, darkening mark gingerly, and stopped when she winced.

"It looks like you may have a cracked rib."

"Can you do something for it?" she asked, watching me with sad, worried eyes.

"Not really. You should x-ray it to make sure. But it has to heal on its own. It takes time."

"What about pain medication?"

I didn't like the sound of that. Painkillers and distraught people generally aren't a good mix.

"The hospital could probably prescribe them, but you could re-injure yourself more easily by dulling the pain."

Hunched over, she walked away and sat at the kitchen table with her head in her hands. I followed her into the apartment. It was expensively decorated in modern Italian furniture. Mostly in white, and about as cozy as the inside of a refrigerator. Sitting in the chair next to her, I took hold of her hand and squeezed it in comfort.

"Emilia, where is he now? Will he be coming home soon?"

"No. He'll be at the club all night." She grimaced, pain tugging at her side.

"Let's put something on that." My search of the freezer turned up a bag of frozen peas.

"Is this the first time? Here, place these on your ribs." She shook her head, wincing when the cold hit her skin. Suspicion confirmed. A deep sigh rose up my throat. "What happened?"

Her anxious gaze darted away from mine. "We had a fight...about one of the girls at the club. I think he's sleeping with her."

Again, no surprise there. I needed to handle the confession with care, fought the urge to rail knowing her proclivity to argue to her very last breath if she felt cornered.

"He's hurt you before," I stated very gently. "He'll do it again."

"Maybe." My heart broke for her. She sounded so small, belittled. "But I love him," she added, as if that was all the justification that was necessary.

How could I respond to that? I was in love, too. I was in an untenable situation, also. I wouldn't ever allow a man to lay a hand on me, though I could sympathize. In my own way love made me weak.

"I understand you better than you think." I rubbed the space in between by brows where all my heavy thoughts seemed to settle lately. Her head whipped around and her pale green eyes searched mine. "I'm in love with my employer." I rolled my eyes and hid my face in my hands. "What an ugly cliché, right? The housekeeper has an affair with her boss." Her mouth fell open, literally fell open. "I've shocked you? Well, I've shocked myself."

"It's just that…it's just…you always do the right thing. Nothing ever seems to distract you," she stated, her tone incredulous.

"I assure you, I'm distracted."

"How did it happen?!" she asked, smiling, the sadness momentarily replaced by curiosity.

"I'm human, Em. I'm not sure how. We were awful to each other at first. Maybe because we both felt it and were scared of where it would lead." I shrugged at the admission, the truth so clear in hindsight.

"Sebastian Horn is one of the most eligible bachelors in the world, and he's in love with you!"

"I didn't say that. I said I'm in love with him."

Her smile faltered. "Oh. Do you think he is?"

"It doesn't matter. It can't go anywhere. I could never tell him about my past. I can't involve him in any of that."

"Maybe he could help?"

"No. Absolutely not."

"I see."

"Come back with me, Emi. Let's pack your things and leave here. He's the most generous person I've ever met. I'm sure he would let you stay at the house until you can get a place of your own."

She shook her head. "I can't. I love him. And I know you think he's trash, but you don't know him like I do."

Classic battered woman syndrome.

"And what about the next time? When he breaks your arm or your face, and you can't work?" It came out harsher than I intended, my concern for her overruling my intention to handle the matter delicately. She stood up, her face hardening into an implacable mask.

"Thank you for coming, Vera, but I can handle this on my own."

"Emi, I didn't mean—I'm really worried about you."

"It's fine," she interrupted. "I'll go to a clinic tomorrow and see about getting an x-ray. I'll call you in a couple of weeks. Maybe we can meet for lunch."

I nodded. It was useless arguing. She was as stubborn as an ox when she was like this. As we stood hugging at the door, I made her promise to call me as soon as she saw a doctor.

———

I took a taxi back to the estate. It was one by the time it pulled up to the front door. On the steps, Gideon Hirsch stood with his arms crossed, looking like the instrument of God's vengeance.

"I thought I told you to let us know when you're leaving the premises?"

Being scolded like an errant child by the security detail was a new low. "I was in a hurry. I didn't think it mattered since Theo drove me."

"Sebastian was worried." As if that required no further explanation. Truth was, I understood the subtext perfectly. "It matters—don't do it again," he added with a cold, hard look in his eyes and stalked off.

I was definitely not Gideon's favorite person. I'm not sure he trusted me. Clever man.

I padded silently up the marble staircase and down the hall towards Sebastian's bedroom. I figured I might as well get all the scolding out of the way. His door was cracked open, a slice of faint light pouring out. I pushed it open wider and quietly stepped inside. He sat slouched in his stuffed chair next to the empty fireplace, his head tipped back on the seat cushion, his eyes fixed on the ceiling. The dim light of the lamp outlined his perfect profile in gold. An empty bottle dangled carelessly from his large hand over the armrest.

Oh crap...

His head swiveled towards me at the clicking sound of the door closing. At first he was very still, his expression blank. I watched his mind registering my presence. It took only a minute for the storm to gather in his eyes and skewer me with out-and-out fury. I squirmed under his heated gaze. My heart skipped a full beat.

"You're back." His voice was clipped. He didn't sound drunk at all, only mad.

I love you. I did. I loved him madly. I just couldn't say it.

I marshaled my strength and walked over to him, his fiery eyes following me the entire distance. His chest rose and fell in deep, agitated breaths. He hadn't had a drink in weeks. I should have been scared, petrified, to find myself alone with him in such an unpredictable state, and yet I knew he would never do anything to hurt me intentionally. He'd more likely hurt himself.

"At least I got two words out of you. When you're stewing about something, you turn monosyllabic."

"Oh, I have plenty of words for you," he growled, hostility rippling off of him.

I walked over to him and gently took the bottle out of his hand. Macallan 39. "This will be an expensive hangover."

Moving with remarkable speed, he trapped me between the unyielding solid mass of his chest and the cold wall in seconds. I could feel the raging beat of his heart through my clothes. His hands curved around my skull, gripped my hair tightly, and held me still for a vicious kiss. Instinctively, I knew yielding completely was the only way to get through to him, to bring him back to rational thought. When he realized I wasn't resisting his assault, his touch gentled, his lips softened. The anger and desperation remained, though.

I reached up and cupped his face, stroking him, soothing the wildness away. He pressed his cheek into my palm. His gaze was filled with a mix of apprehension and longing. I kept petting his stiff shoulders and his chest until his frown eased, and he shivered and held me close, his hard shaft pressed between us.

"Where were you?"

"Geneva. I went to see my friend, Emilia. She needed me."

He exhaled a deep breath. "Why didn't you tell me? I have no way of reaching you—and you didn't tell Gideon!"

That's when it hit me—why I hadn't told him. I had

purposely left without a word to see exactly what kind of reaction I would get. What a coward I was, playing games with his feelings instead of confessing mine. He'd been honest with me from the start. Shame and regret rolled up on me quickly as I stared into his wounded eyes.

He gathered me in his arms, picked me up with ease, and threw me on the bed. His eyes reflected a turbulent mix of emotions, transforming like a mood ring from amber to green and back again. Without another word, he painstakingly undressed me and himself and joined me on the bed.

Starting at my feet, he placed delicate butterfly kisses on the insides of my ankles, charting a course up my thigh, navigating around my navel, and further north until he reached my hairline. I was drunk on lust and the sweet sensation of his mouth worshiping my body. I wanted to touch him, give him back the pleasure he gave me. As I reached for him, he clasped my wrists and brought them over my head.

"Keep them there," he ordered. A drawer banged shut. I opened my eyes and realized that he had tied a silk scarf around one wrist, worked it around the slender post of his mahogany bed, and was now securing my other wrist. My mother's scarf—the one I had left in the kitchen. My eyes flew to his. His razor-sharp stare dared me to argue. I didn't. This was my apology to him. I couldn't put it in words. All I could do was surrender my body to him without reserve.

I love you. I'm sorry for worrying you.

When he finished securing the knot, he reared up and studied his work. I shivered under his intense scrutiny, an erotic flush staining my pale skin. His nostrils flared and a dark, predatory glint entered his eyes. He ran his large hands assertively up and down my body, branding me with blazing heat and ownership. God, I loved this man. I loved him fiercely, with all my heart. That well of emotion ran so deep in me that I still hadn't reached the bottom of it. It had been so different with Aleksander. My love for him had been mild-mannered and economical. My love for Sebastian was a wild thing—beautiful and rare, and totally unmanageable.

He orchestrated an assault on my senses with the tactical dexterity of a five-star general, breaking me down a little at a time with his tongue and hands and teeth. He moved lower, circling around my sex and never quite reaching it. A mist of nervous sweat covered me from head to toe. I writhed and strained against the silk bindings. Widening my legs, I tried to urge him closer, but he ignored me. His tongue grazed my sweet spot, and I screamed in encouragement. My toes flexed, my body bucked off the bed chasing the feeling, my need so acute that begging was not beneath me.

"Sebastian, please."

"Quiet." He sounded detached, chilly. Something was off. He continued torturing me, caressing, dipping inside, and quickly retreating as soon as he realized I was building.

"I need you, please, please, please. I need you now," I panted.

"I'm not concerned with what you need," he answered in a deceptively calm voice. "It's pretty clear you're not concerned with what I need."

My head snapped up. Then he covered my clit with his mouth and it dropped right back down on the pillow. He bent me to his will with his mouth and his hands. The strain of being kept unsatisfied broke me. I was being punished and we both knew it. "How does it feel, Vera? Are you frustrated? Angry? Do you feel powerless?" he said quietly, his voice laced with bitterness. Exhausted and scared of my own feelings, it didn't take much for tears to fill my eyes.

"Yes! Go ahead and punish me if it'll make you feel better." My body went limp in defeat, a tear escaping down my temple. He sat up and scrutinized me, the hardness in his eyes fading away as his expression shifted to concern. As he untied the silk, his gaze never left my face. I turned on my side, away from him, and curled into a ball. I couldn't look at him. I would burst out sobbing if I did. Lying down behind me, he curved his body around mine.

"I'm sorry." His low, raspy voice expressed genuine remorse. He stroked the hair off my face. His lips dropped to my throat, licking the salty tears away. "I'll make it up to you. Let me make love to you, Vera, please...I'm begging you."

I turned and raised my swollen lips to his, allowing him to kiss me, sweetly, tenderly. He began stroking my body in earnest, brushing his skilled fingers through my dark curls and slipping inside of me, all his attention focused on my pleasure. Fueled by the remains of all the tension that had built up, desire exploded between us. In a flurry of impatience, I fumbled with the condom and he almost ripped it. He positioned himself in the cradle of my thighs and our eyes locked. An unspoken apology passed between us, the moment expanding into something of greater consequence than either one of us had anticipated.

This feels so right.

I held him with my arms and legs and everything else I had to give—all my love and desire. He rocked his hips, and as his hard body drove into mine, my mind and heart screamed out all the words that my lips couldn't.

"Home," he whispered, wonder shining in those brilliant amber eyes. He made love to me like he promised he would, every thrust driving out pain and anger, every thrust pushing me closer to ecstasy. He tilted my hips up and slid so deep I could feel him in my womb, part of me forever, engraved on my soul. I let go and raced towards oblivion.

My muscles contracted and pulsed, insisting that he join

me. And he did, reared up on a final thrust and shouted my name while his beautiful face twisted in rapture. When the aftershocks faded, he sagged back down and tucked his face into the curve of my neck, the full weight of him pressing me down into the mattress. I held him and stroked his back, ran my nails lightly over his skin, relishing the feel of him. The exquisite moment.

"I love you."

It came out on a deep exhale but I heard it as if he had shouted it at the top of his lungs. My heart sped up. My hands slowed down. Tears pooled in my eyes, tears of love and surrender. "I can't stop...I can't stop myself from loving you." I swallowed hard. He said it with such unabashed sincerity that it made my conscience hurt. His thick fan of lashes lifted and his eyes met mine. Undiluted love and hope stared back at me.

"I love you, too." Gripped with fear, I wasn't even certain that sound came out of my mouth. His face relaxed as he released the breath he was holding.

"Thank God...thank God," he whispered repeatedly. And then the dam broke, unleashing a surge of emotion so powerful he couldn't manage it. His mouth crashed into mine. He murmured *"I love you"* in between every feverish kiss, touch, and stroke. His infectious, unbridled excitement transformed my worries into giggles. After discarding the condom, he climbed back into bed and held me, pressing me to him as if he couldn't get close enough. We were both quiet as we discovered each other all over again.

"Tired?" he asked.

I traced the contours of his lips with my finger and nodded. "It's been an eventful day. You look...perky. How are you not tired after drinking a bottle of whiskey?"

The side of his mouth crept up slowly. "No one's ever had the balls to call me perky to my face."

"Until I came along," I said, laughing.

"There was nothing before you," he mumbled, his expression turning so serious my smile faded. "I had half a glass. There was barely any left. Charles must have gone through an entire case when he was here. Tell me about your friend."

That didn't take long. Only I could find that commanding tone endearing.

"Emilia is more than a friend, she's practically family. We grew up together. Unfortunately, she's been dating a nightclub owner named Yuri Skilenski."

"I've heard of him," he said, deep thought marking his brow. "Doesn't he have ties to the Russian Mob?"

"The very one. We've argued about it, but she won't listen. She called me this afternoon in tears. He beat her up pretty badly. Broke a rib, I think."

Turning onto his back, he blew out a deep breath. "Are you telling me...that you went to that fucker's place alone?" Oh no. I knew that look. "Do you have any idea how incredibly stupid and dangerous that was?"

"Sebastian—"

"No! Don't say another fucking word," he interrupted. "What if he'd been there? What if..." Pinning me with a furious glare, he shoved his fingers in his hair and left some pieces standing straight. I sighed audibly as I stared at those wisps of hair sticking up. Apparently, he wasn't satisfied because he kicked off the covers, stormed out of bed, and dialed his cell phone. "Don't let Vera out of your sight for a minute. Yeah, she's sneaky. I want someone watching her every move from now on. I don't care if you have to follow her into the toilet, okay."

Click.

I glared back. "Don't you think you're overreacting just a bit?"

"I want you to listen closely," he said in a low, steady voice. "I love you."

The sweetly vulnerable look on his face made my heart hurt. "I love you, too."

"But I've never been in love before." His tone managed to encompass the magnitude of that confession. Had I been standing, I would've crumpled to my knees. My mind was still in neutral, processing what he had revealed when he continued. "I won't have you risking your safety because of some misplaced loyalty to a friend. She's in a relationship with a fucking criminal that likes to use her as a punching bag."

He had a point. He looked truly worried, and I didn't want to do that to him. I hated it when he made sense. "Can you come back to bed, please?"

He stood splendidly naked with his hands on his hips, all six foot three of him, glaring. I wanted to kiss him everywhere. "Are we going to argue about this?"

"No."

He climbed back into bed and pushed me down on my back, caging me with his big, warm body. After searching my eyes, he dropped a soft kiss on my nose. "I love you, damn it. There isn't anything I won't do to keep you safe and smiling."

I drank his words in, soaked them up like parched earth and spring rain. And then I remembered...

"I have to ask you something."

His gaze sharpened. "Anything." I hesitated, not knowing how to begin. The words got caught on my lips. "What is it, lover?" he said, coaxing gently.

"The night we stayed over at your apartment, you were talking in your sleep."

His head cocked. "I did?"

"It sounded like you were dreaming...about your wife." We never spoke about her and I liked it that way. It was even hard for me to say the word.

"I don't remember dreaming about India. What exactly did I say?"

"You said...don't go. You said," I took a deep breath, "love you...don't leave me."

His brow furrowed. Then he flushed as a spark of recollection entered his eyes. "Vera––that was the night you ran from me. I was dreaming about you. It was a nightmare, actually. You kept running and I couldn't reach you."

I inhaled sharply. "I love you," I said, much louder this time. And he proceeded to convince me with his words and his body that he felt the same way.

CHAPTER 29

François came in to pick up his dinner after one of his long bicycle rides. The rest of the staff had already eaten. I sensed that he was lonely, needed someone to talk to, so I poured him a tall glass of water and invited him to sit on the kitchen stool while I peeled green apples for Mrs. Arnaud's famous apple tarte Tatin.

"How's the training going, Lance Armstrong?" I teased.

"*Mon Dieu,* don't mention that name to a cyclist. You know they are considering stripping him of his championship titles."

"Really?"

"He was doping. His entire career apparently. Bloody shame. Do you ever watch television?" he replied, teasing me for a change.

"No. Medical school and life in general."

"Good excuse." His friendly face split with a broad grin. "Training is going well. I'm up to riding fifty kilometers a workout and taking three days off in between."

I looked up in the silent pause and found him staring at my lips. He quickly averted his eyes, but it still managed to embarrass me, a faint flush prickling my collarbone. François had always been a gentleman and I didn't want to give him the wrong impression, lead him on in any way. I cherished his friendship.

Of course, Mr. Impeccable Timing walked in, took in the scene, and came to an abrupt halt. His gaze turned glacial when it settled on poor, unsuspecting François. Recognizing the death stare for what it was, François stood up quickly.

Sebastian's attention slid to me. "Vera, you can bring dinner to my office."

"Yes, sir." Had to keep up appearances. Although it galled me to address him in that manner.

The awkwardness increased times ten when Sebastian didn't leave the kitchen right away, as he should have. Instead, he stood with his hands on his hips, glaring at François, and bullied him into leaving first. It didn't take much. François needed the job. He had a three-year-old daughter to support. As a good father, he wouldn't jeopardize his salary for the sake of a pissing contest. After thanking me profusely for packing up his dinner, François left through the kitchen door. As soon as the door shut behind him, I turned towards Sebastian with a withering scowl.

"What?" His innocent expression made my blood boil.

"You know what."

"You're mad?"

"I'm not having this discussion when anybody can walk in. I'll be in your office in twenty minutes."

In no mood for a debate, I turned away, essentially dismissing him. He stood there for a while, lingering, unaccustomed to being told what to do. But eventually, he left, albeit reluctantly. His answer to any problem was to bully it, buy it, or run it over, and I wasn't going to allow him to do any of those things to me.

I arranged the Scottish salmon on a dish with some grilled vegetables from the garden and roasted potatoes and headed to his office. The door was wide open.

"Twelve million…"

The booming voice belonged to a woman and held a hard edge. I was pretty certain this woman wouldn't whisper under any circumstance. "And there's more—look at this… knew there was something irregular about these deposits but —" An employee of the bank, I surmised. "Well, I figured you already knew about them and had okayed it with accounting."

"I didn't know shit about this," Sebastian responded, "When are the auditors coming in?" His worry was palpable. Whatever was being discussed must've been significant to get him so distressed.

"In ten days. There's still time. Don't freak out yet. That's my job. You're the one that's supposed to play it cool, ride in, and fix this if I can't."

"This isn't funny, Shay. Where did the wires originate from?"

"That's the shady part. A Panamanian bank. They keep taking messages and not calling me back. I haven't been able to get any information out of them."

"Fuck!! Fuck, how long has this been going on? Have you spoken to Charles?"

"No way. I figured you would want to do that."

His food was getting cold. I knocked on the door.

"Come in."

He stood with his fists planted on the desk, hovering over some papers while she looked over his shoulder. They both glanced up when I entered. She was very tall with a sleek mane of red hair that looked natural and she wore a sophisticated, camel-colored suit with a feminine cut that accentuated her voluptuous figure. Her porcelain skin was line-free, even though she was probably around forty. Her intelligent, brown eyes followed me as I crossed the room.

The distance between the door and the desk seemed to have suddenly tripled. I started sweating under her scrutiny. You could hear a pin drop as I placed the tray on the desk. I turned to leave, but Sebastian caught my wrist. "Stay... please." His voice was low and intimate. I stood frozen in place. My eyes darted to the redhead. There was an almost imperceptible lift of her elegant eyebrows, and then a genuine smile stretched across her face.

"Longhorn, is this who's been putting a smile on your face?"

Needless to say, my face burst into flames. Sebastian smiled reluctantly. He hooked his arm around my waist and pulled me closer. "Yes, and, Buckeye, if you give me shit about this—"

She raised her hand as if swearing. "My lips are sealed." Then she shoved her arm right under Sebastian's nose and offered me an extended hand. I shook it. She had a very firm grip.

"It is so nice to meet you. I was getting so tired of the moping and the shitty moods. In fact, I was ready to start slipping some anti-depressants into his morning coffee. You came along just in time."

Brazen, definitely brazen.

"Vera, Shay. Shay, Vera," Sebastian said in an annoyed, but

I love her anyway tone. "Try not to scare the living shit out of her in the first five minutes," he said to Shay.

"I'm not scaring her. The girl's got grit. I can tell. She's taken you on. That says more than enough about her." I instantly adored her, especially for giving Sebastian a hard time. "Well, I'm going to get going. We'll talk about this tomorrow." She gathered her purse and briefcase and walked around the desk. Throwing her arms around me, she engulfed me in a warm hug. "Thank you. Thank you, Vera, for making my life bearable again. I can't wait to get to know you better."

I looked over at Sebastian and resisted the impulse to laugh. His eyes were sulky, and yet he was fighting a grin too. A moment later she walked out with her hips swinging and the faint scent of Givenchy's *Amarige* following her out. He sat down and watched while I arranged his dinner on the desk, wisely remaining quiet.

"Are you still mad?"

"Of course, I'm still mad," I snapped. "How could you do that to him? Shay seems wonderful, by the way."

"To him?! I walked in and found him undressing you with his eyes."

"Sebastian, he is lonely. We were just talking. He's been a complete gentleman since the day we met—unlike other individuals who shall remain nameless—and he's your employee. He's in no position to defend himself. He can't lose this job. He has a daughter to support." I crossed my arms like a sour Sunday schoolteacher. He had the good sense to look remorseful.

"I'm sorry," he said quietly, grabbed my hand and played with my fingers.

"Your dinner is getting cold."

"Stay with me while I eat." It was beyond my capacity to

deny this man anything. Only he could never know that. It scared me; the power he had over me. He wouldn't let me pull away, so I half-sat on the corner of the desk and watched him take a bite of the salmon. "Where did you learn to cook like this?" he asked, smiling.

"I worked in a restaurant in Milan for six years. And at home, I had to cook. Otherwise, I would've been forced to eat my father's cooking," I told him, my nose wrinkling.

"What's Albanian cuisine like?"

"Pretty regular Mediterranean with a Turkish influence. Lots of vegetables, fish. Rather simple."

"I really am sorry...about François. I lost it when I walked in and found him looking at you like that."

He tossed his linen napkin over the empty dish. When I moved to grab the plate, he took hold of my wrist and gently pulled me in between his thighs. His touch disarmed me completely, dispelling the aftertaste of chagrin. I pushed the hair off his forehead, raking my short fingernails through it. Exhaling deeply, he wrapped his arms around my waist and placed his cheek over my heart.

"You can't keep jumping to the worst possible conclusion every time some man speaks to me. And you seem to be under the false impression that I'm some sort of femme fatale."

He looked up and searched my face while I continued stroking his hair. "It's not you I'm worried about, it's them. And you're too damn modest to understand what men see when they look at you. I love you, and I...I..." He was editing his thoughts, keeping the words from spilling out.

"What is it, lover?"

"I have something for you." He opened a drawer and pulled out a brand-new iPhone.

I held it up and inspected it. "What's this?"

"It's called an iPhone. Nifty gadget. You can make calls, write text messages, even emails."

My lids lowered over annoyed eyes. "Hilarious, but I still don't understand why I need one."

The soft look on his face vanished and his eyes narrowed. "Because I need to be able to get a hold of you whenever I need to. I won't go through that again. Not to mention it's safer for you." There wasn't anything I could say or do to dissuade him. Resolve was splashed across his handsome face. I looked at my new iPhone suspiciously. "My cell phone, my office, and my email are already programmed in there."

"I hope you plan on being judicious when you say 'get a hold of me when you need to.'" Looking at the screen, I scrolled through the contacts.

Your Highness...iPhone
Your Highness...Email
Your Highness...Office

I didn't fight the smile growing on my face. Then he held up his phone. My gaze swept over the screen and there, in bright, shiny letters.

Her Majesty...iPhone
Her Majesty...Email

He caught me by the waist and wrapped me in his arms. He sprinkled teasing kisses on my throat, my temple, and my nose while I laughed at his playfulness. Sighing happily, I pulled back and gazed into his warm eyes, where adoration gave way to awe. It was still new, seeing his emotions shining openly there. I wrapped my hands around his cherished face and ran my thumbs lightly over the planes of his features, committing every subtle nuance to memory.

"Do you know how much I love you?" It rushed out of me. It didn't often. I still felt the heavy burden of my past, of what I hadn't told him. I abhorred dishonesty and it troubled me that I was as guilty of it as a thief at confession. He said it freely though. Unencumbered by shame or secrets, once he had spoken the words, he couldn't say them enough.

He pushed me up onto his desk and stepped in between my legs. His warm hands spread on my knees and skimmed wickedly over my stockings, up my thighs. When I cupped his erection, his hips hitched up, pressing harder into my hand.

"I love you more," he crooned between unhurried kisses. "I need you."

The heat in the room turned up by a hundred degrees. In short order, he had me panting and writhing, begging for him. I stepped back, outside of myself, and watched the scene from a distance. The woman with legs spread apart invitingly, the one gripping the edge of the desk for leverage with her head thrown back in abandon...that woman wasn't me. I didn't recognize her. Anybody could have walked in. When had I become so reckless?

The day you met him, whispered that tiny voice of reason. This is who I had become. He had irrevocably changed me. Which only begged the question: Who was I going to be after him?

His restless hands ruched up the skirt of my uniform and discovered the lacy tops of my new thigh-high stockings. The question mark in his eyes turned into a playful smirk. "You destroyed four pairs of perfectly good hose last week alone. I thought these might work better if you're going to keep accosting me in dark corners."

His smile opened up into one of his mind-numbing, thousand-watt stunners. "Are you being sexually harassed in the workplace, Miss Sava?"

My head fell back to give him better access to my neck. I

grabbed the hard globes of his beautiful derrière and pulled him closer. "Yes, thank God."

The pleasant sound of his laughter filled the room before he returned to skillfully seducing me.

CHAPTER 30

"This event is really important."

I scanned the open bedroom door, then glanced at him. A crease appeared between his brows, disrupting the flawlessness of his face. It only succeeded in highlighting his spectacular looks, making him real, not a figment of my imagination.

"It's seven, shouldn't you be on your way to the office?" I kept the tone casual. The determined look on his face warned me that something was brewing. I concentrated on making his bed. It was my only defense.

He was wearing one of his pale gray gabardine suits, the narrow one that made him look impossibly tall and broad-shouldered. He stalked into my line of sight and stood in front of the French doors of his bedroom with his hands on his hips. With that halo of soft morning light glowing around him, he looked like an irritable archangel sent down from the heavens to remind me just how mortal and flawed I was. My desire for him was raging out of control, growing stronger each day. So much for the theory that we could slake this lust and be done with it.

"Most of the important bank clients will be attending. It's my father's foundation. I have to be there."

I carefully folded the Pratesi sheets back so that the intricate scrollwork on the edge faced up, anything to avoid his perceptive gaze. "What kind of charitable work does the foundation support?"

"It funds a number of programs in Africa." My gaze locked onto the graceful movement of his long fingers as he went down the list. "Sustainable farming, clean water, literacy."

"How wonderful. Do you run it?" I asked distractedly, my attention still focused on those skilled fingers, fingers that had done unspeakably wonderful things to me the night before.

"Partly, I also have some great people working for me." His hands came to rest on his hips again, two fingers tapping anxiously. "I need you with me." I looked up and found his expression resolute, tense. His jaw twitched. Need was waging war with his vaunted self-control, and need was winning. I tucked the silk blanket neatly under the mattress.

"You know that's impossible," I replied as gently as possible, trying to stave off a potential argument.

He raked the silky hair that had fallen over his eye back in an exasperated gesture. "No, it's not fucking impossible," he snapped. Glancing at his Rolex, he added, "I have to go, but this discussion is far from over."

Out of prudence, I didn't respond. His patience with the situation was unraveling by the day. It was wearing on him, and I didn't blame him. It must have been difficult for a man who was used to getting his way, without question, to be denied something he seemed to want badly. But we were at an impasse. He was chivalrous to a fault. I couldn't confide in him about my past because he would insist on getting involved. And I couldn't risk that. He was too high-profile a person. It could hurt him in a million different ways, and I would've rather faced the vultures in Tirana alone than cause him a moment of trouble. I was just as fiercely protective of him, as he was of me.

Isabelle stepped into the bedroom as I was fluffing up the last of the pillows. It was obvious she was on a mission to catch us in a compromising position. I almost laughed when a disappointed frown appeared on her face.

"Mr. Horn, Mrs. Arnaud would like to know if you'll be here for dinner this evening, or if you're staying in town?"

He pinned her with one of his lethal stares. He was in a really bad mood. "I'll be here this evening like I have been for the past few weeks. Tell Marianne to cook whatever she wants," he answered brusquely and departed.

"What's his problem?"

We watched him disappear down the hall.

"He must be in one of his moods again," I replied with a smirk and left her standing alone in the bedroom.

———

HE MADE love to me passionately that night, withholding his own release until I was begging him to stop from exhaustion, having climaxed enough times to actually make me sore. My hair was soaked in sweat, plastered to my throat and face. Barely able to lift my arms, I made a feeble attempt to push it aside.

"I think you're trying to kill me with sex," I said, panting and wheezing.

I looked over and found his arm lying over his eyes, his

nostrils flaring, his chest rising and falling rapidly. His lips didn't move. He wasn't amused by my attempt to lighten the mood. I placed my hand on his chest, over his heart. "It's two. I should get back to my room."

He lowered his arm and scowled at me. "It doesn't bother you that we can't sleep in the same bed? That you can't wake up in my arms?"

I knew that tone. He was angry and itching for a fight. "Of course, it does. I love you. Every minute that you're not with me, I miss you." His face softened. He turned on his side and caressed my face, running his thumb over my kiss-swollen lips. "But this is how it has to be."

His face hardened instantly. "Tell me what it is that you think I can't handle. And don't you fucking lie to me and tell me it's about Marianne because I will fucking wake up the whole damn house if you do."

My blood froze. I was no match for him in a battle of wills.

"I can't. Don't ask me to, please, I beg you. You're right, it's not about Marianne anymore. In the beginning, it was, but that was before—"

"Before what?" he interrupted.

"Before I realized how much I love you."

His anger didn't abate while he searched my face, his eyes remaining confidently cool. "When I get back from London, I'm going to tell anybody that will listen that we're in love."

"Darling..." My plea was tentative. I knew him too well by now to pose anything that resembled a challenge.

Speaking over me, his voice grew louder. "That gives you three days to acclimate yourself to the idea. Whatever it is that you won't tell me—I don't give a hot shit about it. I don't care if you were on the grassy knoll and murdered John F. Kennedy. I love you. I want to share my life with you, and no amount of bullshit will prevent me from doing that."

I swallowed hard. This man never threatened, he promised and followed through. Nothing I could say or do would dissuade him. I walked back to my room in a state of silent panic. Three days to make a decision. Three days to decide to stay or flee...flee? I couldn't do it. I had fashioned this prison with my own hands. I was trapped, bound to him by silken manacles of love. A sense of inevitability swept through me, filling me with dread. I had only three days to come up with a plan. And it had to be a good one.

———

HE DEPARTED at dawn the next day with Gideon and Bear, leaving me in the tender care of Mr. Bored and Unflappable, Justin Luck. I got an earful about keeping my phone on me at all times. He repeated and repeated it until he was certain I understood not to "disobey" direct orders. I kissed him hard and told him I would miss him. Because it was the truth. I would miss him desperately. It was the first time we would be apart since we started sleeping together. Not that we ever actually slept together. That was the bone of contention, and he planned on getting his way.

Ben Winters had recently returned after a short trip home. I was in the kitchen, cleaning up after breakfast, when Ben entered after one of his early morning workouts. Soaked in sweat, his gray t-shirt stuck to his muscular torso like he had just won a wet t-shirt contest. He was quite a specimen.

"Let me make you an omelet." I reached into the basket of freshly-laid eggs and began counting. "How many eggs?"

"Twelve."

My eyebrows rose up my forehead. I glance up at him and

he shrugged, an optic white smile taking up half of his face. Ben took a seat at the kitchen counter and drank his water while I began to crack the eggs and beat them. I watched him scan the kitchen.

"How come you didn't go to London with Sebastian?"

"I couldn't."

"Why not?"

I shook my head. "It's complicated," I dissembled, while I stared at the blue flecks on the cracked eggshells.

"Looks pretty simple from where I'm standing. Vera, I haven't seen him like this ever."

My gaze lifted swiftly to his and found the indisputable truth of his words. An unspoken understanding passed between us. Ben loved Sebastian as much as I did. I didn't fault him for not wanting to see his best friend hurt.

"Where's home?" Deflect and redirect—I had become remarkably good at it. I resumed chopping the baby spinach for the omelet.

"Colorado, for now."

I diced baby heirloom tomatoes and dumped them in the bowl with the eggs and the spinach. "Do you like it? I've seen pictures. It looks very beautiful."

"My business is based there."

I sprinkled a few pieces of fresh mozzarella cheese in the bowl, added the mushrooms, and poured the contents onto the hot skillet, infusing the room with the perfume of fresh garden vegetables.

"That smells amazing." His stomach agreed with a growl.

"Why is your business based there?" I asked curiously as I flipped the golden fan onto a porcelain dish and placed it in front of him. He closed his eyes for a moment, breathing in the aroma wafting up from the plate, then dug into the omelet with enthusiasm.

"With the new marijuana laws on the books, businesses can sell it but can't deposit the profits in banks, they have to store the money elsewhere. My guys protect the money as it's being transferred from location to location. We're talkin' hundreds of thousands so you can imagine how tempting it would be to anyone skilled in armed robbery."

"So basically, you're a drug dealer?" Charlotte's clipped British voice rang out as she entered the kitchen. I noticed the brief stiffening of Ben's body. His eyes narrowed as his head swung around to meet Charlotte's smug expression.

"Charlotte, be nice," I warned in a motherly tone.

"I'm a businessman, Miz Beckwith. I provide a needed service and my guys happen to be the best."

"At being thugs for the drug trade?" Her voice was sticky sweet, without an ounce of remorse.

"Charlotte!"

Ben's charming demeanor vanished. His jaw pulsed with pent-up emotion. "Are you a lesbian, Beckwith?"

"Ben!" I shouted.

Charlotte's eyes were as round as dinner plates, an angry twitch visible at the corner of her pursed mouth.

"Is it all men you find repulsive, or just me?"

Thankfully, just as things were spiraling out of control, Mrs. Arnaud entered the kitchen in her usual jovial mood.

"Good morning, Ben. I see that Vera has already taken very good care of you."

"Mornin', ma'am. Yes, she has. Thanks, Vera, this was... amazing. You're amazing."

A deep flush the color of beets rose up my neck at his high praise. I looked over and found a quirky smile playing on Marianne's lips, and Charlotte...well, Charlotte looked like she was about to spontaneously combust. Her face was turning from shades of pink to purple. The vein in between her brows was throbbing. I could see it from a distance as he continued to talk.

"Kind, beautiful, can cook, knows how to treat a man," he said in his low, sexy baritone. "Not a man hatin', shit talkin', lesbian with a grudge," he muttered.

What the hell happened between these two to inspire such animosity? Just then Isabelle walked into the kitchen, disrupting the uncomfortable moment. She waved a newspaper in the air. "Guess what I have," she practically sang, a pernicious smile on her lips.

She slapped the tabloid paper down in the middle of the counter. On the front page, for everyone to see, was Sebastian with his arm hooked around the waist of a stunning young woman. He was kissing her cheek while she smiled into the camera. They made a striking couple, his golden magnificence complementing her dark elegance. He looked relaxed...happy.

My heart sank.

"Is that Joan Smalls?"

Charlotte's voice sounded underwater, dampened by the rush of blood in my ears. I tried to remain as still as possible, careful not to give anything away, but my stomach was churning.

"No, that's the new Ethiopian model everyone's talking about. Don't they make a spectacular couple?" That was Isabelle's voice. I was sure of it.

"You're such a bitch, Isabelle. They're not together. It's probably just for publicity," Charlotte argued.

"She's very beautiful," a remote voice interjected. Then I realized it was me who had spoken. Everyone else was dead silent. "I need to check on the laundry."

I started moving before anyone could stop me and marched to the far end of the manor with Mr. Luck tagging closely behind. When I looked over my shoulder, he stopped and leaned against the wall, too lazy to remain standing under his own power.

"Are you planning on doing this all day?"

"Yes, ma'am." I skewered him with an annoyed glare and the side of his mouth curved up, amused at my reaction. "Strict orders, ma'am."

Breathing an exasperated sigh, I continued to the laundry room. The iPhone rang. I took it out and stared at the screen while tears blurred my vision. Never one to succumb to crying spells in the past, it seemed I was on a hair trigger now and it bugged me. It made me feel overemotional and immature. Two traits I detested.

"I love you. I miss you. I wish you were here," the text read.

In the laundry room, I folded and refolded the same towel three times. My emotions raced to the worst possible conclusion while my intellect tried to reason with them. *There's a perfectly good explanation.* The mantra played on repeat in my head in the hope that it would sink into my subconscious and I would begin to believe it.

An irrational stain of jealousy spread in my chest. Not once in my entire life could I recall ever feeling like this. But somewhere in the dark recess of my soul, I knew this would happen eventually. It was so easy to get wrapped up in romantic notions inside the bubble we had created, but life couldn't exist solely between these walls. The outside had finally caught up to us, remembered that a poor immigrant and a wealthy playboy did not belong together in this unforgiving world.

As I lay in bed that night, contemplating the ceiling, my phone rang about thirty times. It was hard to breathe, tears constantly on the edge of my fragile emotions. I turned to look at it, finally got up, and shut it off.

CHAPTER 31

I overslept the next morning. The extra hour of sleep seemed to have the opposite effect. I was uncommonly irritable and moody. I even snapped at François when he asked if I had anything to do with his salary being doubled.

"How could I possibly have anything to do with that?"

He was taken aback by my thorny response. "I don't know...I thought, maybe—"

"Thought what?" I interrupted.

He had an appropriately apologetic look on his face. "Nothing," he said with a slightly embarrassed smile. "Forgive me."

I worked furiously, hell bent on exhausting myself until my brain ceased functioning. It didn't take much. I felt listless by late afternoon and crawled into bed earlier than usual. Reading was out of the question; I couldn't concentrate. I tried sleeping, but after tossing and turning for hours I finally gave up and stared at the shadows the moon cast on the ceiling as if they held the answers to all my problems. By eleven I had made a decision and worked up enough courage to do something about it.

Hoping to find her still awake, I went to Mrs. Arnaud's bedroom and knocked quietly. It was *not* a relief to hear the shuffle of footsteps on the other side. Vibrating with nervous energy, I unconsciously wiped my sweaty hand on my nightgown and left a trail of blue across my chest, the outline of the speech I had written on my palm. Then the door cracked open and Mr. Bentifourt stepped out, wearing pajamas. There was no backing out now.

"I'm...sorry. I must have the wrong room," I apologized, looking around awkwardly. He examined me as if I was the strange part of this picture.

His lips pinched. "No. You don't."

"Who's at the door, Olivier?"

He turned his bristly, white head towards the jovial voice. "It's Vera." The way he said my name made me acutely aware that I may have interrupted something.

"Well, let her in, *chérie*," she said as she opened the door wider. Pushing him out of the way, she greeted me with a warm smile. I shifted from foot to foot self-consciously.

"Mrs. Arnaud, umm, may we speak privately?"

"Of course, let's go to the kitchen." She turned her attention to the man in the room. "Olivier, you can watch your show. I need to speak to Vera."

I bit my lip, fighting a smile, when I heard him whisper in French, "Hurry up."

She wrapped a motherly arm around my slim shoulders and together we made our way to the kitchen, both choosing to remain quiet. Once there, she went directly to the stove.

"I'll make some tea," she announced.

I sat at the oak table and fought for courage to begin, words deserting me when I needed them most. Consumed by shame, I fidgeted with my nightgown, twisting the fabric until I heard a rip. She placed a cup in front of me and poured hot water from the kettle. Her soft eyes searched my face as she took the seat at my elbow.

"It's chamomile, drink all of it," she ordered gently. I took a sip and looked into her patient eyes.

"I have something to tell you that I am deeply ashamed about...I don't know where to begin."

She took my hand in hers and rubbed it. "Do you love him?" Her voice was sweet and comforting. The dam broke. Tears gushed out of my eyes. My jaw trembled with the strain of fighting the emotion from exploding out of me.

"You know?"

"*Chérie*, nothing goes on under my roof that I don't know about."

"And the others?"

She shook her head. "Just Olivier."

An avalanche of words rolled out of me. "I'm sorry. I am so sorry. You have been nothing but kind to me and I betrayed you. I never meant to lie, but the situation is so complicated and unexpected...and..."

"Vera...Vera, stop. Listen to me, there is nothing for you to be sorry about. I'm not sorry that Sebastian is himself again. He's happier than I've ever seen him. I'm not sorry that he stopped taking those damn pills, or that he stopped getting drunk. I'm definitely not sorry that he stopped sleeping with that viper." My eyes grew even wider. She knew about Paisley. Of course. "And I'm definitely not sorry that he finally has someone that really cares for him. Not the money, or the social status." Aching sobs bullied their way up my throat. "Don't worry about the picture. He loves you. I'm certain of it," she continued.

"You're so good to me and I..."

"Are you in love with him?"

"Yes, but my past. I wish I could explain...I don't want to hurt him with it."

"The only way you can hurt him is if you leave him. I'm reluctant to say this, but it may just be worse than when his wife died." There wasn't the smallest evidence of exaggeration in her expression. She believed it.

"He wants us to go public and I'm petrified of what that may do to him, to the bank."

"Tell him everything. He'll fix it."

I shook my head vigorously. "I can't."

"Can't, or won't? Vera, listen to me, one virtue that Sebastian is lacking is forgiveness. If you deceive him in any way, he may never forgive you. His mother made sure of that. She taught him too many painful lessons about women being lying manipulators." The conviction in her words made me pause. Food for thought. There was so much to consider my head felt like it was going to explode.

"I don't know how I could ever repay your kindness. I don't know where I would be without all your help." She smiled tenderly before wrapping me in her soft arms, her comfort and encouragement seeping into my bones. "Make him happy. Make yourself happy. That's how you can repay me."

––––––––

SOMETHING TICKLED MY NOSE. I cracked open my eyes and was met by a dense wall of black. Overcome with exhaustion, they drifted closed again. I felt a hand brush my hair and alarm bells went off. I jerked awake.

"Easy, it's me."

I sighed in relief at the sound of that sexy, raspy voice and sat up. I could scarcely make out the outline of his features. Feeling around, my hand collided with the immovable mass of his chest. He was sitting on the edge of my bed, close enough that I could feel his breath on my temple and cheek, as he sought my lips. His hand reached out and cupped my face.

"What are you doing here?" I whispered in a sleepy voice.

"I came back early." He didn't kiss me, just hovered his lips over mine while our breath mingled.

"What time is it?" My hands moved of their own free will up the swells of his chest, over his shoulders, and around his neck. A shiver rocked his large frame.

"Four thirty."

"Who flies at this hour?"

"Someone who owns a jet."

"Oh." My heart sank a little. Most of the time I managed to forget how truly wealthy he was.

"Why is your phone turned off?" I knew him too well to be deceived by the bland tone in his voice. He was annoyed.

"Because I was mad at you, that's why."

"Mad?" He chuckled. "At what?"

"Isabelle showed everyone the tabloids yesterday. There's a very nice picture of you with that Ethiopian model. Everyone thought you made a very striking couple." I sounded petulant, even to myself.

"You know that's strictly publicity. She's eighteen years old for fuck's sake."

"So?"

"So, I was discussing the futures markets with a colleague and she asked me the name of the psychic I use," he explained.

I bit my lip trying to suppress a bubble of laughter. "She's young."

"Yes, she is."

"She should probably get an education," I added.

"Probably."

"I love you."

"I missed you," he murmured tenderly, the words smothered by his kiss.

His hands were all over me, as if he suddenly had more than two. I fumbled with his belt, his zipper, while he ripped the covers back and pushed me down on the bed. It was unbelievably erotic, not being able to see anything, having to feel our way. All my other senses heightened to HD quality in the absence of sight. I could literally smell the pheromones pouring out of him. My skin was so hypersensitive feeling his breath on it sent sharp electrical impulses directly to my female parts. He kicked off his pants, pulled his shirt over his head, and in his haste ripped something. I giggled as he clumsily tried to get his large body on my tiny twin bed. We banged knees. He swore. I laughed. And when we were finally both naked, facing each other, plastered to one another, he paused.

"I love you so much," he said in a voice filled with raw passion. "I don't...I don't ever want to be apart from you. I was counting the minutes 'til I got home."

Hearing those words spoken with such conviction gave me the courage to tell him everything. He kissed me, worshipped my body, and made love to me by stealth. I cried the whole time. Don't know why. I guess it felt different, like we were about to take a giant step into the unknown. He wiped the silent tears from my face after coming with deep, powerful thrusts.

"What's wrong, baby? Why the tears?"

Baby? He was going to make me cry again. Sweet man.

"I'm sorry. I've been hysterical lately. I don't know why,

maybe stress. I'm never this emotional." He peppered my mouth with his sweet, fortifying kisses. "I have to tell you something, and I…I think I should do it now. Maybe it will be easier in the dark, without you looking at me."

"Nothing you say could ever change the way I feel about you." The deep rumble of his voice soothed me. Everything about him soothed me.

"Let's save that edict until after you've heard the story." I took a deep breath and began. "My father killed himself six and a half years ago. I'm the one that found him. He hung himself in his office at the University of Tirana, with a lamp extension cord."

"I'm sorry, baby." He stroked my face reassuringly, encouraging me to continue.

"My father was the dean of the university for many years. He was very well respected for most of them…until the scandal."

A vision of my father stole through my mind. His lean form behind the simple, steel desk in his office, the glasses slipping down his nose, the gray streaks at his temple highlighting his high cheekbones. I missed him.

Sebastian didn't stir, so I continued. "Someone tipped the minister of finance that funds being issued to the university were being redirected."

"Embezzled?"

"Yes. The only person capable of that was my father. He had access to the money and was responsible for allocating the funds to the various departments. A trial date was set, but he killed himself shortly before it began."

There was a weighty moment of silence before he spoke. "I'm really sorry about your father but—"

"There's more. The money was wired to an offshore account in my name." Silence, not even an intake of breath. I rushed through the rest of it, anxious to rip the scab off quickly. "I fled before they could investigate me. I had already applied for and received a student visa from Italy. I had planned on getting my medical degree there for a long time. Things were escalating quickly, and I couldn't risk a trial, so I fled...in the middle of the night...like a thief." My heart was pounding viciously. He must have heard it because he placed his large, warm hand on my chest and rubbed. "I can't risk you getting caught up in this mess. You're too high profile, too important to the bank. That's why we can't let anybody know we're together. It could hurt you in a million different ways."

"How much money?"

"Almost three million U.S. dollars." I held my breath and waited for his verdict.

"Thank you for telling me," he murmured, stroking my hair back.

"That's all you have to say? After everything I just told you."

"I knew already. But I wanted to hear it from you."

I sprang up so quickly the bed bounced. "What??!"

He pulled me back down and nestled me in his arms. "You'll wake the house."

"What...I...how long have you known??" I asked in fits and starts.

"It took a while to get all the details. About three days after I found you crawling around my floor."

"Three days?" I was repeating everything like an idiot again. If I could have melted into a puddle of humiliation, shock, and relief, I would have. Apparently I had grossly overestimated my ability to keep a secret. First, Mrs. Arnaud. Now, this. Clearly, I wasn't cut out for a life of crime. "You've known all this time?"

"Yes. I run a full background check on anyone I'm involved with. I have to protect the bank."

Involved with? Three days after meeting me?

"Aren't you going to ask me if I know where the money is? If I was involved?"

"I don't have to. I know you didn't have anything to do with it."

"Why are you so certain?"

"Because I know you."

"I didn't. Thank you for that." I took a deep breath and something warm and peaceful spread through me. "I feel better now that I've told you. But it doesn't change the fact that we can't be seen in public. I won't be responsible for hurting a hair on your head," I said, yawning. "So tired..." My eyes drifted closed. I felt the brush of his fingers on my cheek.

"Sleep, baby. We'll figure it out together," I heard him murmur before I slipped into a dreamless void.

CHAPTER 32

T he next day I floated around like the weight of the world had been lifted from my shoulders. I hadn't even noticed how much anxiety I was carrying around until it was gone. I slept like the dead, didn't even stir when he left to return to his bedroom.

It was my day off and I had to be in Geneva for my doctor's appointment by noon. It was unusually humid for July. I dressed in a simple white silk shell, a navy linen pencil skirt, and a great pair of silver thong sandals I had found on sale in Italy. Sebastian insisted that Bear drive us in. He would get dropped off at the office and I would go on to my appointment. I didn't have the energy to argue. I didn't have much energy, period. It felt like I was coming down with something. It was a good time for a doctor's visit.

There was an awkward moment when François pulled the Mercedes GL out front. He held the car door open as I stepped inside and sat beside Sebastian. I blushed, of course. Sebastian slipped his hand between my clenched knees, inside my thigh, and left it there. Then he leaned closer and placed a kiss on my neck, marking his territory like a junk-yard dog. He was gloating a little too much if you asked me, but I wasn't going to be a shrew about it.

Isabelle came running out to tell him that his mother had been trying to get a hold of him—he hadn't been returning her calls, it seems—and witnessed the scene. She glared at me, wearing an expression that could only be described as a cross between Elmer Fudd and the Tasmanian devil. When I tried to put a respectable distance between us, Sebastian only pulled me closer with a shade of smugness on his features. That aura of invincibility had increased tenfold lately. Like neglected, tarnished silver, all he needed was some tender, loving care to bring back the sparkle.

My gaze swung out the window, the landscape passing before my eyes as random streaks of color. As much as I wanted to marinate in the groovy feelings that had developed between us overnight, the pragmatist in me still clung to doubt and concern. My past, his past, our present, our future. It was still all so unsettled. I did my best not to over-analyze it into ashes. Who knew what the future held? What I did know, however, was that I wasn't going to let it keep me from enjoying the present.

His phone rang. Scowling at the screen, he answered and jumped right into rapid-fire trade talk. "Hi...how big a position do we have? The exact figure...and he wants how much more? That would push us over a billion—remind him his last name isn't fucking Soros. Yeah, in exactly those words..."

I loved watching him when he spoke of margin calls, futures, QE's, what the Fed was doing. He was lit from within, a predatory glint sparking in his intelligent eyes. It was an incredibly sexy contrast—his voice full of authority and power while his splayed fingers gripped my thigh and his thumb idly stroked my knee tenderly.

"If they want to go through every account with a fine-tooth comb, then we are going to let them. Is that clear? I'm not getting into a pissing contest with the Department of Justice just to make a point...the clients will be fine about it. I don't want anybody sandbagging this shit. Listen, I'm here—downstairs." He caught my absorbed expression and graced me with one of his platinum smiles.

"I'll say hello to her for you. Yes, we'll go out to dinner soon. Only if you promise not to scare her with any of your stories...okay, tell Tim not to do a fucking thing 'til I speak to him." He dropped the phone in his jacket pocket and turned to me as Bear pulled the truck in front of the elegant marble building and parked.

"I'm sorry. I was lousy company on the ride over." He leaned over and kissed me, pulled away, looked at me, then kissed me again.

"It's fine. I like to listen when you talk about work."

"You do?"

"Yes," I confessed between a bubble of laughter and his kisses.

Heavy lids lowered over smoldering amber eyes, his voice a seductive purr. "Then I'll seduce you with talk of the VIX and double-dip recessions later."

"Can I ask you something?" I whispered, aware that Bear could hear everything.

"Anything." He wrapped a lock of my hair around his finger. "You know that."

"Have you and Shay..."

"No, never," he stated firmly. Studying my reaction, surprise and uncertainty flickered in his eyes. "You don't believe me?"

"It's just that...in your office..." My voice dropped lower. She called you longhorn.

His expression went totally blank, unreadable. He blinked twice. Then an explosion of laughter so loud burst out of him that both Bear and I jumped in our seats.

"Sebastian?"

He waved a hand, his shoulders still shaking with laughter. Then he grabbed my face and kissed me hard and fast.

"Texas Longhorn. It's a steer," he struggled to explain, in between deep, jagged breaths. I stared in confusion. "It's a type of cow. It's also the University of Texas' mascot. Where I got my undergrad degree...I call her Buckeye. She went to Ohio State University."

Then it dawned on me. "You are not to breathe a word of this to anyone, is that clear."

"Scout's honor," he promised, chuckling. "Wish I didn't have to go in today, but there's too much volatility with the markets right now."

"Go," I ordered, smiling, and pushed at his shoulders.

"I love you. Call me as soon as you're out of the doctor's office." He raked me with a salacious gleam in his eyes before he stepped out of the SUV

"I love you," I whispered, still too bashful to be out and proud like he was. I had to adjust to things by small degrees. He, on the other hand, dove in head first.

He threw a smile over his shoulder before entering the building through the heavily adorned glass and brass doors. As I watched his broad shoulders fade away, a prickling sensation on the back of my neck drew my eyes towards the street corner. And there she was, wearing a stunned look on her plastic face. Paisley. The shock and awe on her features reconfigured into burning outrage. I pulled back from the open window and slid the dark, tinted glass back up, my heart racing. That sinister expression on her face did not bode well for me, and I made a mental note to warn Sebastian about it later.

———

WE DETOURED TO MY BANK, before heading to the clinic. I had to deposit my salary and check to see if I could afford to buy a few new articles of clothing so that His Highness could stop complaining about my "God-awful" wardrobe. I handed the teller my check, and she returned the receipt with my balance printed on the bottom.

"There's been some mistake, miss," I said in French. "This isn't my balance."

The stiff-faced young woman took the receipt from me and checked it against her computer screen.

"There's been no mistake. I double-checked your account number," she rudely replied.

"This says a hundred and five thousand euros," I whispered, looking around furtively. "That's a hundred thousand euros more than I should have. Can you please check again?"

I couldn't help sounding agitated. After being investigated for embezzlement, the last thing I wanted to hear was that there was an enormous chunk of money sitting in my bank account that I didn't know about. She narrowed her annoyed eyes at the computer screen. The man behind me started making impatient sounds, craning his neck to see what the holdup was about.

"Here it is, two weeks ago, a wire transfer from Horn & Cie. to UniCredit in the amount of a hundred thousand euros into your account."

My knees turned liquid, strength deserting me. "Does it say who specifically sent the money?"

The woman typed something into her computer. "It came

from a personal account...Sebastian Horn." Her eyes widened, then her gaze returned to me with a newfound alertness. Suddenly, she smiled. "Is there anything else I can do for you, Miss Sava?" she asked in a sweet voice.

Wow, that was a rude awakening. In the time it took her to read a name, I went from annoying nuisance to Miss Sava. She handed me the cash I had requested. "No, thank you," I answered absently.

I walked back to the Mercedes on autopilot, still processing the information. *A hundred thousand euros.* Impossible man. And sighed. I knew what was coming next— another argument. Knowing him well enough by now, he would rather burn it than let me return it. I stepped into the Mercedes and texted him.

Do you have a moment to talk?

His Highness: Always, for you.

My heart beat rapidly as I dialed his number. "Darling."

"Hmm, I like the sound of that."

"You won't like the sound of this. I just went to my bank."

Silence. *Here we go*, I thought.

"There will be no discussion about this. I want you to go shopping. Tell them I'll call with my credit card if it's not enough," he said in his most "Your Highness" voice.

Not enough? "Sebastian, I..."

"I don't give a shit if you burn it in a bonfire. It's yours. Don't push me. I'll talk to you after your appointment." CLICK. He even hung up angry.

Well, just as expected. Bear looked into the rearview mirror and smirked. I had forgotten that he could hear everything. How embarrassing. "Dropped call," I lied, my cheeks as pink as an English rose, no doubt. He responded with a short nod and smiled.

———

I SAT in the waiting room with my nose buried in an Italian translation of *Pride and Prejudice* I had borrowed from the library. I liked reading in different languages. It kept my language skills sharp and I found it entertaining how different cultures translated the subtle nuances in the classics.

A quick inventory of the room spoke volumes about Dr. Maria Rossetti. The oak floor was old but scrubbed clean, the walls were freshly painted but unadorned, and the reception area modest. The patients, old and young, were poor. With the list of commendations and awards this woman received, she could have easily set up a slick, expensive office off the Rue du Rhone. Instead, she had chosen to use her considerable talents to help the most needy.

A baby's hysterical shrieks drew my attention to the far end of the waiting room. The child looked to be around one. Her face was ruddy and tear-streaked, a few teeth visible in her wailing mouth as she bounced on her exasperated mother's lap. Her mother was young, no older than eighteen, too young. She was losing her patience with the baby and seemed close to tears herself. I heard the mother pleading with the child in a language I couldn't understand. Portuguese, I think. I was about to go over to them and offer some assistance when a nurse appeared in the doorway and called my name. I followed her to an examination room, where she left me to change into a gown.

Dr. Rossetti knocked before entering. A handsome woman with thick lips, wavy mahogany hair, and hazel eyes that tilted up at the ends, she wore her age with grace. Early fifties, I estimated.

"Miss Sava, it's a pleasure to meet you, I'm Maria Rossetti." She smiled pleasantly while she studied my chart. "Sei Albanese?" she asked in Italian.

"Yes, I'm Albanian," I replied in the same language.

"Your Italian is impeccable. You sound like a real Milanese."

"I lived there for six years. I studied medicine at the University of Milan."

Her shapely, dark eyebrows rose. "Did you graduate?"

"With honors."

"Congratulations." She smiled warmly as she put on a pair of surgical gloves. "Are we doing a full physical today?"

"Yes. I'm interested in getting on birth control, but I've also been feeling tired and weak lately."

"Let's weigh you first."

I was surprised to learn that I had gained six pounds. I knew the rawboned look was gone. However, six pounds for me was like a normal human gaining twice that amount. She took my temperature and blood pressure and ran other diagnostic tests before she pulled my blood. I was getting dressed, zipping up my skirt when she stepped back into the examination room.

"Here's a prescription for the pill," she said, handing it to me. "Don't start taking it until I call you with the lab results, just to be safe. It shouldn't take more than a day."

"Of course, and the lethargy?"

"Doesn't seem to be bacterial. I'll get a better idea once we get the test results. It could be a degree of anemia." I nodded. I had considered that as well. "Where are you doing your residency?"

"I have an interview this winter with a hospital here in town."

"Why don't you email me your file? My husband could probably arrange an interview at the University Hospital in Zurich."

My eyes lit up. "That would be...thank you so much, Dr. Rossetti."

"Don't thank me yet. I'll see what I can do," she said with a reassuring smile.

I left her office with a new prescription and a huge smile on my face. I couldn't believe this stroke of luck. And I got the distinct impression that Dr. Rossetti was a no-nonsense type. She wouldn't offer if there wasn't a good chance she could get me an interview.

Zurich. Sebastian wouldn't like it. It was probably a good idea not to mention it until I had an interview scheduled. No point in arguing with him over hypotheticals.

I stepped back into the Mercedes and Bear's eyes connected with mine in the rearview mirror. I had to admit traveling around town with a driver waiting for me was a luxury I could really get used to.

"Where to, ma'am?"

"Just one more stop, Mr. Mahoney," I replied with a sly grin.

———

IT WAS LATE, around midnight. I was in Sebastian's bathroom when I heard him walk into the bedroom. He had stayed later than expected at the office, something about overseas markets and earning reports coming out worse than forecasted.

"Honey, I'm home," he announced cheerfully.

I smiled into the soft towel I was drying my face with. He stepped into the bathroom, yanking on his tie, his suit jacket already dispensed with. His hand stalled when he saw me. I watched in the bathroom mirror as his eyes roamed over me with a licentious promise in them. Turning to face him, I leaned back against the counter, openly appreciating the standard of masculine perfection standing before me.

"Did you go shopping?"

Smiling, I nodded. Then, slowly, I untied the sash of the nude-colored silk robe I was wearing. His expression turned comical when he saw what I had on underneath.

"Holy fuck."

My brows rose up my forehead. "I should wash your mouth out with soap."

"I don't care what you do to me as long as you do it wearing that." Moving swiftly, he pinned me hard against the bathroom countertop and devoured my mouth.

After my doctor's appointment, I went to the La Perla shop on the Rue du Rhone and splurged. I was wearing a black babydoll nightgown made entirely of Chantilly lace with a matching thong. It really was a masterpiece, tasteful and sexy at the same time. The only reason I didn't get sick when I went to pay for the items was that I rationalized it as a gift for Sebastian, a gift he clearly appreciated.

I was assaulted with kisses. His hands cruised over every inch of me, squeezing my breasts, and butt cheeks, pressing my hips against his straining erection. "I'm glad you're eating. There's more of you to squeeze," he muttered between kisses.

"I guess you...like it," I said, the remark interrupted by bubbles of laughter.

Pulling back, he looked down with a carefree grin. The

contented look on his face was worth every franc I'd spent and more. "I can't wait to see what else you bought."

"You're looking at it, darling. I almost fainted at the figure I spent on this."

The smile turned into a frown, then his lips twitched in silent mirth. "I see I'm going to have to take matters in hand. We're going shopping tomorrow afternoon."

I removed his tie and unbuttoned his shirt—now something of a habit—and glanced up to find him watching me with unambiguous love and wonder shining in his eyes. He still seemed visibly surprised and grateful every time I did the smallest thing for him. It broke my heart. And I couldn't help but wonder if anyone had ever done anything for him purely out of love, without benefit to himself or herself— more specifically, herself.

"I love you," he whispered. The weight in his voice caused me to look up. His expression had turned grave, his eyes unblinking, as if he were expecting me to disappear into thin air somehow.

I ran my index finger down the gentle slope of his nose, traced his sculpted lips, found the soft dip in his chin, and proceeded to place kisses where my finger had been. "I love you more," I whispered back.

We were always so attuned to each other's needs that he could tell I was tired. He undressed me with tender care and made love to me selflessly.

"I can't believe I get to hold you all night. No more sneaking around." Wrapping his arms around me, he snuggled his face in the curve of my neck.

"You always get what you want, don't you?"

"Not always," he said with a crooked grin. "But hopefully, with you, I will."

Over his shoulder, the Gerhardt Richter painting of the mother and child hanging over the dresser stared back at me.

"I love that painting. Why did you buy it?"

He looked at it before his pointed gaze met mine briefly. "A good investment." A shrug off if ever I'd heard one. I didn't believe that for a minute. "How was the doctor's visit?"

Yeah, I knew that trick, too.

"Good. I got a prescription for the pill. You'll have to suffer through a little while longer, though. I can't start until we get the results of the blood test."

"Hallelujah, and the fatigue?"

"Most likely anemia. She can't be sure until she sees the results."

With his magic fingers sifting through my hair, I was losing a battle to stay awake. A fuzzy memory of Paisley's face drifted in. "I have to tell you something else…" My voice trailed off as he tucked my body against his chest and sighed deeply.

"Tomorrow," he murmured. And just as I was about to fall asleep, I heard him mumble one last word, "Finally," followed by a gentle snore.

CHAPTER 33

I was in the middle of the most erotic dream since creation. I heard myself moan. A mirage of golden eyes stared back at me, heavy-lidded, sullen…

A tiger. I was making love to a great, big tiger.

Tyger, tyger burning bright…Who wrote that?…Blake…Dunn… Blake?

My body was painfully aroused, all my female parts throbbing with need. My nipples were erect and hypersensitive. A scrape of something wet and rough. A tongue. *Oh God…yes.* My body turned hungry and willing. Then a bite that had me bowing off the bed and nonsense spilling from my lips.

I was climbing. But the tiger taunted me, kept me mercilessly on the razor's edge.

"Not yet," he commanded.

Moving languidly, the jungle cat rose over me. I felt the head of his hard shaft against the soft mound at the top of my thighs, nudging me in a steady rhythm until I was breathless and needy and spewing words of supplication. My hips tilted up of their own accord, meeting him stroke for stroke until he pushed inside of me. A slow, heavy slide. I dug my fingers into the muscles of his back and tried to pull him deeper, but he withdrew completely. The tiger was in control and made damn sure I knew it.

I was on the verge of shedding tears of frustration when he rocked into me again, with force and certainty. His mouth fastened onto my breast, sucking and biting my nipples. The pain dissolved into hot pleasure. His thrusts turned relentless, deep and fast. And then I came in a rush so powerful that my hips lifted off the bed, clenched his body like a fist, and sent us both in a downward spiral towards ecstasy.

"What the fuck was that?" he asked, breathing heavily. I rubbed my eyes, cracked one open, then the other. The tiger stared in shocked amusement.

In what distant deeps or skies, burnt the fire of thine eyes?

"I was having the most unbelievable dream," I croaked. My body's satisfied state finally began to register. I looked down and found myself naked, with abrasions on my breasts and thighs, everything tingling pleasurably.

"That was no dream, baby," he said, chuckling. "You came so hard you lifted me off the bed."

I blinked in sudden comprehension, blinked again and turned towards him. He curved his large hands around my head, buried his fingers in my hair, and peppered my mouth with soft kisses.

"If I'd known morning sex was going to be like this, I would've tied you to my bed the minute I laid eyes on you."

Pushing the sweat-soaked hair off his forehead, he smacked a quick kiss on my lips and wobbled out of bed. He grinned over his shoulder. "I'm not going to be able to walk today," he muttered as he walked into the bathroom, provoking a smile on my face, too.

We showered together a short while later, taking turns running the sponge over each other's bodies. I was efficient and workmanlike. He was slow and sensual.

"We'll never be done if you continue at this pace," I scolded and ruined the effect by giggling afterwards. I squeaked as his hand connected with a sting on my rear end, the sound bouncing off the marble walls of his cavernous shower.

"You'll just have to stand there and take it," he stated in a low, sexy voice. "I've waited far too long to be able to do this, and I'll be damned if I let you hurry me now." The distinct shade of triumph in that declaration caused my smile to fade. I looked up into his possessive expression and knew something of consequence was about to be said. "I don't want you working here anymore. Just be with me...until you start your residency."

I stared into his expectant eyes and searched for words to make him understand that this was moving too quickly for me. I needed time to think, to sort out my feelings—to measure the costs. Inexorably, he was pulling me into waters I had no idea how to navigate. So I did the only thing I knew was right, taking his beautiful face into my hands, I told him how I felt.

"I love you."

"Which part?"

His voice was so quiet it took me a moment to realize what he was asking. Something soft and vulnerable flashed in his eyes. He waited patiently for me to answer, the value of which was apparent in his expression.

"I love the part that's kind, and gentle, and selfless. The part that's cool, and commanding, and capable. The part that's burning with intelligence. The part that's thoughtful and funny. I also love the part that's rash, and high handed, and rude sometimes. I love every part of you...in a million different ways."

A dark flush stretched across his high cheekbones.

"So much has changed so quickly," I added, forging ahead. "I need some time to adjust. Please, Sebastian."

Even though the water coming down in buckets from the pan-shaped showerhead was steaming hot, my entire body trembled. The sight of me wrapping my arms around myself snapped him out of deep thought. He turned the water off and pulled me out of the shower. His love-filled eyes didn't leave mine for a second while he covered me in a robe that was much too big.

"Okay," he replied in that raspy timbre that had become an addiction.

I exhaled a major sigh of relief. This was progress. He rarely conceded anything. He rubbed my back, my arms, while he stood before me dripping wet and looking absurdly sexy.

"I'll give you a week to come to terms with it."

Well, baby steps. It was four more days than I had gotten last time.

————

THE REST of the staff was already treating me differently and it rankled. Everyone except Mrs. Arnaud, Charlotte, and Bentifourt who particularly never missed an opportunity to dispense a heavy dose of condescension and snobbery. Things were changing quickly and it seemed that there wasn't anything I could do to slow it down to a speed I was comfortable with. There was still so much unsettled, so much at stake.

I was in the middle of scrubbing a particularly stubborn

scuff mark on the walnut floors when the image of Sebastian in the shower skipped through my mind. I schooled the grin that seemed to spread easily on my face lately. Coupled with the stars in my eyes, I looked like I was suffering from either a concussion or a bad case of idiocy. The possessiveness in Sebastian's expression wasn't about ego. It was born out of fear. He guarded me as he would guard his own heart. I couldn't blame him. Love made me feel vulnerable, too.

It was no mystery that his insecurities were a result of being raised by a woman that did worse than neglect her only child. She was around just long enough to teach him that love was painful and nothing good came out of trusting women. However, I still couldn't figure out his relationship with his dead wife. His confession about never having been in love before had shocked me. I was still grappling with it. So why did he marry her? Sebastian was not a social creature by nature. Like the tiger he resembled, he was solitary, self-contained. Something about it bothered me, though I was too much of a coward to ask him about it. I was afraid of what I might discover.

By early afternoon he had texted, informing me that he had arranged for Gideon to drive me in so he could take me shopping, adding in the text not to waste his time objecting or I would get spanked for it later.

I was sitting in the Mercedes, outside his building, when Gideon received a phone call. "What do you have for me?" he asked in French, his clipped voice indicating it was important. "Is he willing to deal? I can send a man to Lyon first thing tomorrow."

Sebastian opened the door, and for a brief moment a flicker of something that resembled doubt appeared on his face. *I love you desperately... you sweet, beautiful man.* He slid in next to me and my body succumbed to the gravitational pull of his. A moment later I was being kissed senseless.

"I just heard from my contact." Gideon's unique accent pierced the lust-filled bubble surrounding us. Sebastian's eyes narrowed as they connected with Gideon's in the rearview mirror. "We have a lead," Gideon added.

"When?"

"Soon."

"Is it about the shooting?" I asked, my voice loaded with concern.

"Yes." Sebastian's remote gaze swung away, directed absently at the passing scenery. Just as suddenly, it returned to me warm and affectionate. "Don't think about that now. Ready to have some fun?"

"Not really."

Smiling, he gave me a sideways glance. "I'll pretend I didn't hear that."

When we walked into Akris, I was surprised to find the store empty. There were two perfectly groomed shop girls that looked ready to swoon over my man, and an older woman, the manager, who I was certain wouldn't swoon under any circumstance. Not even mortal injury.

"It's empty," I whispered.

"Because the store is closed," he clarified with a mischievous wink. Gripped by self-consciousness, my steps slowed to a stiff crawl. Being the center of attention is not my thing, never has been. Sebastian looked over his shoulder when he realized I was no longer walking beside him, a query in his eyes. I stared back with a blank expression, too proud to articulate my discomfort. He read me perfectly, however. He tilted my chin up and brushed his lips on mine, running his warm hands up and down the sides of my arms, soothing me into compliance.

"Come on, lover," he softly urged, pulling me further into the store, the shop girls now staring bullet holes through me.

The clothes hung from neat racks, color coordinated and perfectly spaced apart. I had to admit they were to die for. The richness of the fabrics. The stunning simplicity of the design. I was scared to touch anything. All of a sudden what I was wearing embarrassed me. I turned to Sebastian and realized he was busy on a phone call. He must have noticed the lost look on my face, however, because he motioned to the manager and whispered something in her ear. She nodded, beaming up at him.

Another one falls. Scratch that about her not swooning. Note to self: never underestimate this man's charms.

The warmth remained on her features as she turned and addressed me. "Mademoiselle, let me show you some pieces you may like," she said, throwing a motherly arm around my shoulders.

Sebastian sat in a leather armchair, watching me parade in and out of the dressing room, while the shop girls tripped over each other to please him. A slow trickle of possessiveness started to seep into my blood. He was polite though barely spared them a glance. Every suggestion they made met with a dismissive head shake. God, I loved him.

I chose two pieces. A cotton shirt that crossed over the front and a pair of light wool, skinny, ankle-length pants. Utterly elegant and completely practical. That didn't satisfy His Highness who frowned and shook his head at the manager when I said that's all I needed, then took it upon himself to choose a lot more.

A black, pencil skirt and a cream one.

A short, pleated navy skirt.

A sunflower yellow Dolman sleeve silk shirt that looked amazing with my coloring.

An emerald, crêpe silk dress with cap sleeves.

A white cotton shirtdress with a wide, cognac crocodile belt. On and on it went. An entire wardrobe. More clothes than I had owned in total in the last ten years. Looking over the clothes he had chosen, I added "impeccable taste" to the long list of his virtues.

"If I didn't know firsthand what an insatiable lover you are, I would think you were gay. You have a knack for women's fashion. I love everything you chose." He stepped inside the narrow dressing room. "What are you doing?"

"I'm about to prove what an insatiable lover I am," he answered, grabbing my hand and pressing it against his impossibly hard erection.

"Sebastian—" I giggled, trying to push him away as his arms snaked around me. "Stop that this instant. I have expended a great deal of energy satisfying your baser needs." He held on, rubbing himself against me and fumbling with the zipper of my new skirt as I tried in vain to dress. "No... wait...this is...they can hear us. How embarrassing!" I finally got the words out between bursts of laughter.

He ducked his head out the curtain of the dressing room and said, "Some privacy, ladies," to the shop girls. I felt a small stirring of triumph that really was beneath me.

Spinning me around, he placed my hands against the wall of the dressing room and pushed my back down so that my rear end arched up, seeking him. "You're not doing what I think you're doing," I said, breathless. He flipped up my short skirt and hooked the lace thong with his fingers, exposing my feminine folds to the cool air conditioning. Gently, he skated around my clitoris in a taunting rhythm that had me pushing back for more. My mind went silent while every nerve ending in my body was wide awake. As my eyes fluttered shut, a sudden realization hit me...

This man owned me. I would do anything, be anything for him.

"I want you to watch in the mirror," he purred. Then proceeded to drive me insane by rubbing the soft wool of his trousers against my primed body. In the mirror, the woman I had become stared back at me. Eyes heavy-lidded, cheekbones rosy, hair a curtain of dark silk around pale shoulders. Completely wanton. My lips parted as he pushed his thumb inside my mouth, withdrew it, and found my clit. I bit my bottom lip to stifle a moan. Pushing back against him, I heard a sharp intake of breath. He was just as affected as I was.

"Goddamn, you're beautiful," he murmured. "I'm going to fuck you hard, baby."

*Yes...*I begged silently, shocking myself once again. I couldn't believe how erotic it was, seeing him standing in the dressing room with his legs spread apart, bent over me, all that testosterone crowded into that small feminine space.

He unzipped his pants, and his body sprang free, jutting up provokingly towards his stomach. As he rolled on a condom, our eyes locked in the mirror. Pure love stared back at me, the connection so profound I was on the verge of tears. I knew then that I could never leave him, even if it cost me everything.

He entered me slowly. His long lashes fluttered as he pushed in all the way. I loved watching him, loved seeing that unguarded look of unbelievable relief growing on his face when he was fully fitted inside of me. His head dropped, his forehead resting between my shoulder blades. "How much do you want me?" His voice was raw and needy, with a pronounced rasp.

"More than anything," I answered truthfully, way past the ability to guard my thoughts.

Pressing his fingers into newfound softness, he gripped me tightly and began pumping his hips. Momentum built quickly, sharply surging before crashing. He pinched my nipple, and a lush orgasm hit me. I caught only every other word of praise and encouragement whispered in my ear. A few muffled curses followed, and then he exploded into my yielding body.

I don't even know how we managed to get dressed and not stumble out of the small dressing room. But as always, he seemed much more in command of himself than I was. Naturally, I was embarrassed. Adding to my mortification, Sebastian was wearing an indecent grin on his face. I could've even sworn I heard him whistling at one point. The manager wouldn't look at me when Sebastian handed her his black Amex.

Outside the store, I stood with my arms crossed while he carried armloads of garment bags to the car. "A little subtlety wouldn't kill you," I said, narrowing my eyes.

There was a brief quirk of his lips. "I don't know what you're talking about."

"That ridiculously smug look on your arrogant face."

Gideon took the bags from him and loaded them in the trunk. When he turned to face me, I noticed the mischief in Sebastian's expression had extinguished, changing into something softer.

"I'm happy," he said quietly, "let me enjoy it, please...let me enjoy you," and dropped a sweet peck on my swollen lips. My fit of pique quelled instantly. He sliced me open with a couple of words, and he didn't even know that he was doing it.

I love you, please be happy. I want you to be happy. My heart sang while my lips stayed silent. I nodded and kissed him back.

We stopped by Chanel and Lanvin before heading home. After the workout I had gotten in Akris, I was too spent to argue when he started pointing at items and looking at me for approval or rejection. Yes, to the tiny quilted handbag in black and one in a larger size in nude at Chanel. Yes, to a couple of pairs of flats in different colors at Lanvin. Who knew shopping could be so exhausting? In the end, I begged him to stop.

We drove home without uttering a word. I crawled onto his lap and tucked my face into the curve of his neck, inhaling the comforting scent of him while he stroked my back. A small, satisfied smile played on his lips as he stared out the window. My gaze drew his attention.

"I love you," I mouthed.

"I love you more."

Wrapped in each other's arms, we fell asleep quickly that night. All was right in the world for once. The moment unmarred by reason, regret, or worse yet, reality. But it wouldn't last long. A ribbon of gray, pink and orange marked the horizon. A storm was brewing and neither one us noticed, too blinded by love to see it coming.

THE NEXT DAY, Charlotte and I tackled polishing the silver flatware. No small task, we sat at the kitchen counter with what seemed like thousands of pounds of silver.

"So what will you do? When you're not working. Have you thought about it?" Charlotte's face was a funny mix of curiosity and apprehension. She kept watching the open doorway for Mr. Bentifourt.

"I don't know," I answered, uncertainty written all over my face.

"Will you live here with him?"

"I don't know."

"Does his mother know?"

"I don't know," I repeated with a pinch of my brow.

His mother...crap. I had studiously avoided thinking about her.

"What do you know?" she asked, two apostrophes marking the confusion on her brow.

"I don't know anything, Charlotte. Except that I love him, and I don't want anything to harm or embarrass him in any way. But Sebastian is as stubborn as a mule and won't listen to reason."

Charlotte's frown melted into a wistful smile. "You love each other. That's all that matters."

"You sound as impractically romantic as Sebastian."

"Who the hell would have thought that that man was a romantic." She shook her head, muttering, "Never in a million years."

"I asked him about that," I said, a smile threatening to bust wide open.

"About what?"

"About why he's so standoffish with you."

"And?"

"And he said...his words exactly, 'because every time she sees me, she looks at me like I just took a shit on her favorite shoes.'"

One look at Charlotte's shocked expression and I erupted in laughter.

"That's not true!" She stood up and slammed the counter with her fist, the silverware jangling. I remained silent while her mind chewed on that for a while. "Well, maybe it's a little bit true. Just a tiny amount." I said nothing. "Okay, maybe he's right," she finally admitted and sat back down.

"I suggest you both make an effort to know each other better since you'll probably be in each other's company more often."

Her gaze caught mine. "We can still be friends then?" she asked, a sweet, shy uncertainty in her voice.

"Don't be ridiculous. Of course, we're still friends. Nothing has changed between us, Charlotte. The only thing that's changed is the room I'm sleeping in," I answered, squeezing her hand in reassurance. "Speaking of change, Ben will be back this weekend."

She stiffened instantly.

"Would you please explain why you two can't be in the same room without scratching each other's eyes out? What the hell is going on?"

Charlotte's lips pursed. "I just don't like him."

"You're sticking with that excuse?"

"Yes."

"Okay, let me know when you're ready to talk about it."

Tipping her face down, she inspected a silver fork as if it were the long lost eighth wonder of the world.

CHAPTER 34

By midnight I was seriously worried. I hadn't heard from him since he had texted me at six saying he would be home late. The text was terse. That was unlike him. Instinctively I knew something was wrong, my mind conjuring a million dreadful scenarios as I lay in his bed staring at the ceiling. For a fleeting moment it crossed my mind that he was playing some stupid, vengeful game. Maybe he was trying to teach me a lesson about how nerve-wracking it is to be kept wondering. But I knew we were past playing games. That's what worried me the most.

Determined to find out more, I put on my silk robe and headed downstairs. I figured Ben would know something. And if he didn't, I was going to throw him out of bed and send him to retrieve my missing lover. As my foot hit the last step of the marble staircase, I noticed a dim light escaping under the door of the library. Once inside, I shut the door quietly behind me and walked towards the windows. There was a funny flutter in the pit of my stomach as I passed the last of the bookcases...and then I found him.

Something was very wrong. His shirt was crumpled, his sleeves rolled up, and his tie hung loose. He was slumped forward with his head in his hands, gripping his hair tightly by the roots. Goosebumps exploded on my skin. The space was filled with a miasma of emotion so dense that I had trouble breathing. He looked up abruptly, his golden eyes locking onto mine, and my heart froze.

His face was ravaged with pain, his eyes haunted. He was that wounded creature again, the one I had met months ago. My gaze shot to the glass of liquor by his feet. I willed my legs to work, to walk over to him. Moving slowly, afraid to startle him, I sat down and reached up to brush the hair near his ear back. He squeezed his eyes shut, his large body shuddering as if it pained him.

"What's wrong, darling? Talk to me," I whispered, then waited for an excruciatingly long amount of time until he spoke in a rough-hewn voice.

"Interpol came to see me at the office today." His hands clenched into tight fists. He looked like he was preparing himself for some imaginary battle. My heart beat viciously. I thought the force of it would split my chest open. "They arrested some guy on a botched robbery attempt in Paris. In exchange for a lesser sentence, he told them…that he was hired to run a car off the road. To stage a murder and make it look like an accident…my murder."

"Your wife…" The words left my lips before I could stop them.

"There's a lot you don't know, Vera. That nobody knows." He swallowed, his throat quivering.

"Let me in."

He placed his head back in his hands and wouldn't look at me. I continued to stroke his hair. The need to touch him, to connect, trumped everything else.

"India and I had been dating a year." His voice was barely audible. "It wasn't serious. I met her at the charity concert U2 gave for my foundation. She traveled a lot for work. I was busy, too. I had only taken on managing the bank a year before, so it worked." He paused and looked up at me. I held his gaze, silently encouraging him to go on. I couldn't and wouldn't push him. He would have to tell me willingly.

"Things were good between us for a while. I wasn't looking for more...then she got pregnant." My eyes widened. My heart stopped. A baby. Sebastian's baby. His gaze returned to the floor. He continued as I sat there reeling from his confession. "We got married. Nobody knew she was pregnant, just us. She wasn't that far along."

I was suddenly falling, dropped from an airplane with no parachute.

"You loved her, though?" Real, unadulterated jealousy burned through me. And not the superficial, frivolous type—the ugly, vicious kind. Of a dead woman who had been pregnant with his child.

He looked up, and his distraught eyes turned soft and warm. "Yes, I loved her. But I wasn't in love with her. You're the only..." Shaking his head, he plunged back into despair. "If it wasn't for the pregnancy, we...we wouldn't have lasted."

"Why do you say that?"

"India was a good person, but she was needy. I was always running home to fix something or deal with her in one way or another. It was exhausting. Before the accident, it got worse—a lot worse," he admitted dejectedly. "I guess I was pulling away. She sensed it and started" —his nostrils flared, and his breathing grew ragged—"making scenes in public. Embarrassing me." He rubbed his face and pressed his fingers to his brow. "We were having a bad fight that day." I stroked his back in encouragement, fighting my own tears and feeling powerless against the depth of his pain.

"Lucinda, that woman who lives in my building, told me...she told me she saw a man coming out of the apartment when I was away for business." His chest rose and sank rapidly as he forced out the words. "I lost it when she didn't deny it. I started shouting. I-I took my eyes off the road for a second—"

I crawled onto his lap and held him, stroking his head and his back. Pushed beyond his ability to cope, he clung to me as if he could absorb my body into his. He buried his face in the curve of my neck and gripped me with a force that could have broken ribs. "I'm sorry, darling. I'm so so sorry," I whispered. I could feel the wetness on my skin, the soft tremble of his muscles as I kissed his throat and murmured words of love and comfort in his ear.

"This is why you tortured yourself with alcohol and pills? Hurting yourself won't bring her back, or the baby. It could've easily been you in her place. You didn't cause it. It wasn't your fault."

"It was my job to keep them safe," he mumbled. I sat back and examined his face. His eyes were wild with anxiety, tears glistening on his thick lashes. "Someone is trying to kill me, and I-I can't put you at risk. I'll die if anything happens to you. I won't survive it. I know I won't."

I needed to draw his attention away from where his thoughts were headed. Cradling his beloved face, I kissed him softly until he kissed me back.

"Nothing is going to happen to me," I stated, holding his gaze as I spoke. "That's what security is for. I trust you with my life. You're the most capable man I have ever met. I've never felt more loved or more protected. You won't let anything happen to us."

I watched the words sink in and grow roots. The lost look in his eyes slowly dissipated, and was replaced by a steely determination I was relieved to see. "I won't let anything happen to you," he promised after finding his bearings.

"I know you won't. Now come upstairs with me so I can make love to you."

Not another word was spoken as I took his hand and led him to our bedroom. I undressed him slowly, his eyes fixed on me as love, uncertainty, and a million other emotions took turns flashing in those gorgeous pools of liquid fire. He seemed uncomfortable letting me lead, taking and not giving. Dear sweet man, so inexperienced at receiving it was a crime. But I wouldn't let him touch me. If I did, I would succumb quickly. This was my way of showing him how loved and treasured he was when he needed it most—when he needed reassurance.

I kissed every square inch of bare, golden flesh on his body, lingered longer over every bump and scar on his injured leg. His strangled whimpers made me bold. I gripped him firmly at the base and took him into my mouth, sucked strongly on the crown until he sighed and moaned and gripped the sheet hard enough to tear it. His body bowed off the bed, every muscle tense. He squeezed his eyes shut and swelled even larger in my mouth when I pressed down on the sweet spot under his sac. He was close, his skin slick from the strain. The perfect symmetry of his face twisted as the pleasure broke through the pain still on the surface. His muscles turned to stone. I lifted my mouth. His eyes opened wide and his seed shot onto my bare breasts, the room resonating with the primal cry of his release.

Breathing harshly, he draped his arm over his eyes while the last tremors left him. I placed a chaste kiss on his open palm and went to the bathroom to clean myself off. When I returned, however, he was staring at me with that broken, conflicted look again. Snuggling up next to him, I pulled the covers around us and created a cocoon where only he and I existed.

"I need you so much it scares me," he confessed. It killed me to hear his voice so small, to see this powerful man so broken down.

"I feel the same way. There's nothing to be scared of."

His eyes fluttered, fighting to stay open, and his breathing turned deep and easy. "Let me do something for you."

"Not tonight, lover. Go to sleep."

I stayed awake for a long time afterwards, contemplating what had gotten lost in all the disclosures. Someone was trying to kill him. The man I loved. The worry lodged near my heart felt like a ticking time bomb. Fighting the anguish that threatened to overwhelm me, I focused on the comforting sound of his gentle snore and prayed for strength.

———

WITH ALL THAT HAD TRANSPIRED, my head was spinning for most of the following day. Sebastian was quiet as he dressed for work, interrupting what he was doing every few minutes to touch me or hold me. I let him, even though I knew he was running late for a business meeting. I needed to touch him as much as he needed it.

Around four o'clock, I glanced at my phone and realized I had ten new messages. My stomach sank when I recognized the number. Dr. Rossetti's office. No doctor's office ever left that many messages unless it was bad news. Stepping out of the kitchen for privacy, I walked to the vegetable garden and dialed her number, my hands shaking so much that I had to clear the screen twice. Her receptionist told me to hold on. The doctor had been trying to reach me for twenty-four hours and absolutely needed to speak to me. By the time I heard Dr. Rossetti's voice, I was already in full-tilt panic.

"Vera?"

"Yes, I'm sorry, Dr. Rossetti, I wasn't able to check my phone yesterday." My voice sounded steadier than I was feeling.

"Never mind. You didn't fill that prescription, did you?"

I could feel my heart pounding in my throat. "No, why?"

"Because you're pregnant."

You're pregnant. You're pregnant. You're pregnant... it was a faraway echo, followed by a high-pitched ringing in my ears.

"Pregnant?" The word sounded foreign on my lips.

"Correct."

"No, I'm not."

"Yes, you most definitely are."

"That's impossible," I said curtly.

"Are you having sex?"

"Yes."

"Well then, I assure you, it's quite possible."

I couldn't breathe, on the verge of hyperventilating.

"But I never get my period! My mother tried to conceive for years and couldn't. And she died in childbirth!"

There was a rustle of movement behind me. I glanced over my shoulder and found nothing.

"You obviously do not take after your mother because you're quite pregnant. I won't know how far along you are until you come in for an ultrasound. I recommend you come soon. Otherwise, you're perfectly healthy. No anemia—it's the pregnancy making you tired...I see this is unexpected.

Let's talk about it when you come in." I nodded, at a loss for words. "Vera?"

"Yes, Doctor, of course. I can come in tomorrow, late afternoon?"

"Perfect, see you then."

You're pregnant. I'm pregnant? Yes, you're pregnant. But I can't be pregnant. I assure you that you are.

Reason and madness took turns screaming at each other in my head. This was an absolute nightmare. *A baby.* Sebastian's baby. *Oh, dear God.* Sebastian would freak out. He hadn't even recovered from the last woman he knocked up, and now he had me to contend with.

I looked down at my belly and felt beneath the apron of my uniform where the intruder was hiding. Flat as always. My hands cupped my breasts. Definitely larger and fuller. And then the puzzle came together slowly, the irrational moodiness, the weight gain, the constant crying. Some doctor I would make. I couldn't even figure out what was going on with my own body.

I thought I heard a noise, looked behind me again, and discovered a small bird perched on the net wrapped around the tomato plants. I suddenly felt drained, tired beyond anything. My entire body sagged, collapsing under the weight of my troubles. I walked back to the kitchen dragging my toes.

Mrs. Arnaud took one look at me and her carefree smile melted into a frown. "*Chérie*, you look tired. Would you like to go lie down?"

"Yes, *madame*," I said in a feeble voice, "just for a little while."

I could feel her scrutiny as I dragged myself through the kitchen, towards my old room. I lay in bed staring at the dust motes dancing in a shaft of sunlight with my hands resting on the complication. It was so hard to imagine that life was growing there. I didn't feel that different, except for a protective streak starting to build within me. Strange how that happens automatically.

I never considered children. A baby never crossed my mind. I had so many plans, so many things I wanted to accomplish. I was never like other women whose sole purpose in life was to raise a family. Thank God they were out there, but I wasn't one of them. A baby was always some faraway, abstract concept for me.

Unbidden, an image of a dark-haired little boy with amber eyes flitted through my mind. *This is how it starts, how one throws away a lifetime of work...for...for love.* Tears welled up. How in the world was I going to tell Sebastian? It seemed like every time we stepped over one insurmountable load of crap, a larger one presented itself.

I sat up at the soft knock at the door. Before I could respond, he entered, looking more settled than he had that morning. I was relieved. I wouldn't be much help to him in the present state. He threw his suit jacket on the chair and sat on the edge of the bed. The shaft of early evening sunlight illuminated his eyes, accentuating the gold and green flecks.

"Why aren't you in our room?" he asked as he stroked my face with aching gentleness. I turned my face into his palm and let the heat of his hand settle my nerves. I melted under his touch, my senses heightened by all the hormones pumping through my blood. Closing my eyes, I planted a kiss there.

"What's wrong, baby? Marianne said you weren't feeling well."

Baby...that endearment more pertinent than ever.

"Did you get any more information from Interpol?"

"Gideon's handling it. I don't want you to worry. Do you

have a temperature?" He placed his large palm on my forehead.

"No, just tired. Dr. Rossetti's office called. I have to go back for more tests tomorrow afternoon. The blood tests were...inconclusive."

Frowning, a new sense of focus entered his eyes. "Anything we need to worry about?"

"No. Nothing to worry about."

He narrowed his eyes skeptically. "I don't like this. Maybe you should see my doctor."

The lack of energy made me irritable. I was in no state to debate him. "Sebastian, I beg you, please, let's not argue. What time is it?"

"Six thirty."

"I'd like to have dinner, take a bath, and go to bed early."

"Anything you want," he said as he raked his fingers through my hair. "Just promise me something."

"What?" I asked guardedly.

"I want everything out of here and moved into our bedroom. And I want to come with you tomorrow and meet this doctor you seem to think so highly of."

Anxiety came rushing back. I still hadn't worked out how I was going to tell him.

"Yes, to the room. No to the doctor's appointment." I swung my legs off the bed and tried to put some distance between us, but he caught me in his arms before I could escape.

"Why not?"

"Because I'm a grown woman, and you have to begin trusting that I know how to take care of myself. We need boundaries." The wounded look on his face made me hate myself for a minute. "I'm sorry. I didn't mean to sound like

such a bitch, but I don't want to argue. If it's anything serious, you'll be the first to know."

His eyes turned suspicious, his voice stern when he said,
"Now I know there's something wrong."

"What do you mean?"

"I've never heard you curse before."

I stroked his chest, desperate to distract him, and said in a
provocative voice, "I'm going to show you how sorry I am."

His expression softened. He smiled and placed a soft kiss
on my nose and taking my hand, led me out of the room.

———

THERE IT WAS on a small monitor, blinking in black and
white. Life. A baby. My baby. It was official. I felt really pregnant. What the hell was I going to do? I started crying for the
millionth time in the past two weeks, trying to make up for
the last six years during which not a single tear was shed. Dr.
Rossetti squinted at the monitor.

"You're further along than I thought. Around six weeks."
Six weeks. When Sebastian was shot. The meadow. You play
Russian roulette often enough, and someone always ends up
getting hurt...or pregnant. "Have you considered termi-
nating the pregnancy?" Her tone was super gentle.

I looked at her sharply and covered my belly in reflex. "I'm
Catholic." Dr. Rossetti drew her gaze away from the monitor
and met mine, then nodded. "But even if I wasn't, I couldn't do
it." My eyes returned to the fuzzy image on the screen. "Not
after seeing this," I explained, a small smile threatening to grow.

A tiny flutter, barely visible to the naked eye, yet there it
undeniably was. For someone as calloused to the basic func-
tions of the human body as I am—cutting open human

cadavers tends to do that—I still couldn't help staring in wonder.

"Is the father involved? Do you have a good support system?"

"He doesn't know yet. I'm not sure how he'll take the news. He's been rather stressed lately."

Our eyes connected in unspoken understanding. A child was a huge responsibility. A child to an unwed mother on her own spelled the end of any aspirations I had of becoming a doctor. I pressed my thumb and index finger to my brow, trying to stave off the dull ache growing there.

She removed the wand from my abdomen and printed out the ultrasound. I pushed down the paper gown. Suddenly the sound of the buzzing air conditioner seemed louder, an annoying distraction in my ear. I locked my muscles as goosebumps crawled all over my body. I never understood why examination rooms had to be kept at sub-zero temperatures. I felt cold, exposed, and very much alone at the moment.

"Get dressed and we can talk in my office."

I nodded, and she stepped out of the room. Dressing slowly, I put on the white cotton blouse and pleated, navy skirt we bought at Akris, slipped on my nude Lanvin flats, and grabbed my Chanel purse, hooking the chain across my body. The word *fraud* kept booming in my head like the distant sound of cannon fire. I looked down at the sonogram, hanging limply between my fingers. What the hell did I know about babies? Absolutely nothing, except for their biology.

I dragged myself to Dr. Rossetti's office, knocked, and entered. She sat behind a contemporary, pale wood desk with a wall of books behind her and a picture window to her left. She took off her wire-rimmed reading glasses and motioned for me to sit in the armchair opposite her.

"From the look on your face, I can assume you're less than thrilled about this turn of events?"

"I'm still in a state of shock. I'll let you know if I ever come out of it. My menstrual cycle has always been irregular, sporadic at best. There were years when I didn't get it at all. And with my family history, I just assumed..."

"You'll learn this quickly when you start practicing medicine. Never make assumptions." I looked up and met her sympathetic gaze.

"Practice medicine? It looks like my lifelong ambition disintegrated with a simple blood test." I held up the sonogram.

"Not necessarily, but we can only deal with the present. And at present, I suggest you start taking your prenatal vitamins. I can also recommend an excellent obstetrician. She's a classmate of mine. You'll like her."

She handed me some paperwork regarding diet, vitamins, and other information that soon-to-be mothers needed. *Soon-to-be mothers...*I suddenly felt queasy. After taking the name of the OBGYN she recommended, I left her office. As I walked out, I couldn't help staring at my stomach. Still deceptively flat, my mind struggled to connect the dots.

On the sidewalk, I looked up and around, confused. It must have been the shock because I felt dislocated, outside of myself, watching life zip by as if looking through binoculars. How did it all come to this? I knew I should be happy, overjoyed even, but I wasn't. I was lost.

"Vera." The voice calling me turned the blood in my veins to ice. I looked over my shoulder and found Paisley staring back at me, her eyes shooting poison arrows. She stood with her arms crossed under her ample breasts, wearing platform espadrille Louboutins that made her look seven feet tall.

"What are you doing here?" I asked in a drone-like voice.

Her eyes assessed me shrewdly, then turned scalding with contempt. "I see he took you shopping."

"What do you want, Paisley?"

The tiny hairs on the back of my neck stood at attention. I turned and caught Bear craning his neck, watching us with pointed interest from the Mercedes. When I turned back around, Paisley stepped forward aggressively, forcing me to look up to meet her virulent gaze.

"This is what's going to happen, you gold-digging whore. You're going to leave Geneva. You're going to go away and stay away. You won't say a word about any of this to Sebastian. And you'll do it by Sunday."

A cruel smile tilted the corners of her mouth up. Blood rose up my neck and spread over my face. A thousand emotions took turns bubbling to the surface.

"And if I don't?" I don't know where I found the strength to measure my words.

"I was hoping you'd say that. In that case, I'll go to the tabloids. Tell them about the dirty, illegal immigrant who got knocked up on purpose and manipulated her way into Sebastian's heart. It's leading him to make poor decisions that put the bank at risk. Investors will jump ship, and you'll be completely responsible for bankrupting one of Switzerland's most prestigious privately owned banks. I'll make sure there's nothing left by the time I'm done."

That was a sucker punch to the gut. She had struck with the precision of a heavyweight champ, right to the solar plexus. And I had walked right into it. She knew I would do anything to protect him.

"How did you find out?" For some reason, I needed to know.

"That dumb redhead that works for him. Ingrid, Irene, whatever. She overheard you talking on the phone with your doctor and couldn't wait to tell his mother."

That was the meaty left hook to the jaw that left me bleeding.

"His mother?"

"Were you under the impression that Diana approved of a filthy peasant like you shacking up with her precious son?"

And the knockout punch.

"I'll be gone by Sunday," I said in a defeated voice.

"Good choice." She smirked and put on her dark Tom Ford sunglasses. "Bon voyage," she said, laughing as she walked away.

I sat in the back seat of the Mercedes arms crossed and chewing on my lower lip while Bear studied me in the rearview mirror. I was doing a lousy job masking the anxiety that gripped me by the throat. He didn't buy my explanation that I had run into Paisley by accident, the suspicion conspicuous in his eyes. The countryside sped by in a blur, time and objects having lost their shape and meaning. I wandered the labyrinthine alleys of my predicament, searching frantically for a way out that would cause the least amount of damage, but everywhere I turned I walked into dead ends. All because of one absolute truth—Paisley was not bluffing. She would destroy him if she couldn't have him.

I couldn't blame Isabelle entirely, the mistake was mine in equal measure. I should have been more careful from the beginning. *I should have left...*No. I wouldn't let that bitch make me regret loving him. Nothing would ever make me regret that. He was the best thing that had ever happened to me.

I won't survive it. I won't.

His words kept echoing. And by the look in his eyes, he had meant it, believed it with all his heart. After I reached Milan, I would write to him, email him, and explain what had happened—that I had to leave to protect him. I couldn't let him believe that I would betray him in any way. I would've rather died than allow him to believe that.

Two nights. That's all I had left. Two nights to say goodbye forever to the man I loved, the only man I would ever love this way again. The father of my child. My best friend. In an attempt to push back the tears glistening in my eyes, I bit my lip hard enough to draw blood. Tears, I suspected, that Bear had already noticed.

CHAPTER 35

"The market slows down at the end of July. I'm planning a long vacation for us."

His bed had become a small island the two of us were marooned on. I only wished it were true.

"Sebastian—"

"Hear me out. We can sail from Cap Ferrat to Sardinia."

We were both lying on our stomachs, facing each other. His fingers traced my shoulder blade and skated down the rungs of my spine, making me shiver and smile.

"What's it like, Sardinia?"

"Wild and beautiful...like you."

"I'm not wild," I argued with a smirk.

His expression transformed from playful to thoughtful, his eyes two bottomless pools of love. "You are when you're making love to me." My smile slipped. "Sometimes I think I'm dreaming," he murmured, speaking so quietly that I had to read his lips. "I wake up just to watch you sleep. Sometimes I think I'm going to wake up, and I'm still in the ICU."

My jaw clenched painfully. The heartfelt confession

killed me. I couldn't even reassure him because I knew I would be disappearing very soon. I wanted to take away all his pain. I had never wanted something so badly. "You're the dream I never allowed myself to have." I didn't realize I had said it out loud until his eyes flashed and squeezed shut, capturing those words forever. He knew what that monumental declaration from me meant. I rarely expressed my feelings verbally. I'm not built that way.

"I don't know what I did to deserve it, but I thank God every day for delivering you to me," he said softly. "Everything makes sense now."

I bit my trembling lip, held his gaze and swallowed back words that wanted to explode out of me. Words like, *Forgive me, I'm sorry. I'll love you forever, my very best friend.*

"You'll love Sardinia. The water runs from emerald green to powder blue. The coastline," he said, drawing a map of it with his finger down my back, "is jagged. I found this small, hidden beach last time I was there." His kiss turned into a smile on my shoulder. "I want to make love to you with the sun on my back and your dark hair spread out on the white sand."

I could picture it in my mind's eye. "Sounds wonderful," I replied, lost in that amber gaze full of love and hope. "Except, need I remind you that if I attempt to leave the country, I will be deported back to Albania so fast my head will spin."

"I'm working on that."

My skin prickled with awareness. My head lifted off the pillow. "What does that mean?"

There was a smile in his eyes when he said, "I wanted to tell you over a nice dinner with a good bottle of champagne, but it appears I'm going to be nagged until I cough up the goods." Chuckling, he turned over onto his back, and I pounced on his chest, unable to contain my excitement. "I think you broke a rib."

"Out with it. What did you mean?" I shrieked.

He held me steady, cupping the cheeks of my rear end while I attempted to shake the information out of him. "My lawyers are in the middle of negotiating with the Albanian Ministry of Justice."

He might as well have dropped a piano on my head. "Will you ever cease to amaze me? Since when?"

"I hope not," he murmured, a shy smile growing on his face. "A couple of weeks. They've been amenable to our attempts to reconcile the situation as expediently as possible."

"In other words?"

"In other words, I'm ready to write them a check as soon as they clear you of any wrongdoing."

My jaw went slack, couldn't feel my own lips as I began speaking. "Are you insane? Write them a check? For how much??"

"The full amount," he replied casually.

"Three million dollars?!!! But—but I had nothing to do with it! This…this is absurd!" He flipped me onto my back, pinning me to the mattress, and licked my nipple before tugging it gently with his teeth. My back arched, my eyes slammed shut. The devil had a better relationship with my body than I did. "You can't do that when we're having a serious conversation. It's not fair," I moaned.

"Darlin', I never fight fair," he drawled in a lazy, seductive voice. "That's a strict rule of mine."

"Now you're really cheating." He gasped when my hips hitched up and pressed into his erection. "There's no way I'm letting you do that. I'll go back before I let you spend that kind of money on me."

Turning serious in a heartbeat, he grabbed my face and tilted it so we were nose to nose. "Listen to me, baby," he said, his eyes boring into mine. "That's pocket change for me. I won't even know it's gone. I'd give everything I have to protect you." That was the thing with Sebastian—he never boasted or exaggerated. He said what he meant, and he meant what he said.

I bit my lower lip in a feeble attempt to stop it from trembling. "I love you so much. It scares me that you don't have an ounce of self-preservation sometimes. Do you know what this could do to you if it ever got out? I won't be responsible for harming one hair on your precious head."

His eyes softened, love and awe shining openly back at me. "Without you, nothing else matters." He placed a brief kiss on my nose. "I have a team of lawyers that will protect the bank and ensure total anonymity. I want this to go away. There are so many things I want to share with you. Besides, I didn't get to where I am today by being careless."

"I didn't mean to imply that. I'm embarrassed...and worried for you...and it's a lot of money."

"There's nothing for you to worry about. Trust me when I say that it's the best money I will ever spend."

A tear ran down my temple as I swallowed the guilt choking me. I was going to hurt this wonderful man, maybe irrevocably. How was I going to live with myself? I understood him better than ever at that moment, understood what had led him down that dark path of self-destruction for so many years. I kissed him, pouring all the love in my heart into that one tender touch, and whispered *I love you* over and over again, in the hope that when he was hurting the most, he would remember this moment.

————

I FOLDED some of my old clothes and placed them in a plastic bag. I certainly couldn't walk out of the house with my valise when I had Gideon watching me as attentively as a prison warden. I mentioned to Sebastian that I was going to Sunday mass that morning after he woke me at dawn and made love to me until I begged him to stop, soaked in pleasure and sated beyond imagination. He smirked and said he would join me but he didn't want the church to catch on fire, said he would go for a swim instead.

There was a new level of abandon in his lovemaking. I saw it in his eyes, felt it in the way he touched me. He had taken down the last brick of his protective wall. He was all in. His heart placed in my safekeeping. And I was going to break it.

I was in a state of high anxiety all morning. I turned on every faucet in the bathroom while I puked my guts out, praying he wouldn't suspect anything. When he went downstairs for breakfast, I did my best to pretend it was a routine morning on my day off. Even dressed for church in my new clothes, the cropped pants and white shirt. I was brushing my hair when he snuck up behind me and wrapped his arms around my waist. Curving his tall, muscular body around mine, he pressed his hips against my rear end. I closed my eyes and rocked back into him, committing everything about that moment to memory.

This was it. This was the last time I would touch him, see him, hear his voice.

"What time will you be back?" he asked, placing a string of kisses on my throat. I leaned my head to the side, giving him unfettered access, and watched in the mirror with a sense of detachment, my mind shutting out the pain threatening to crush me.

"Around noon."

"I want to take the boat out on the lake. Marianne is packing lunch for us."

When I didn't respond, his warm, inquiring eyes met mine in the mirror. "Do you feel up to it?"

"I'd like that," I replied, smiling weakly. I turned in his embrace and threw my arms around his neck, urging him to lower his head.

"I love you more than anything. Always remember that. Promise me you'll never forget." His mouth perked up, amusement appeared in his eyes. "Promise me," I repeated, more sternly this time.

"Okay, I promise." He smacked my lips with a loud kiss and slapped my rear end. "If I don't get going, I'm gonna have to take a cold shower."

He threw a sexy smile over his bare shoulder as he walked away. I held onto the edge of the counter for dear life, my willpower disintegrating under pressure as I battled the impulse to run after him and confess everything.

"I love you," I called out.

"Back at you, lover," he shouted, his voice fading away.

And just like that he was gone.

Gideon was sitting at the counter drinking his coffee when I walked into the kitchen. His eyes immediately snapped to the plastic bag in my hand.

"Oh. If I'd known you were taking clothes to church for the poor, I would have asked the others if they had anything they wished to donate. Next time, let me know," Marianne said, handing me a freshly made cappuccino in a tall mug. That seemed to appease Gideon's suspicions. His face relaxed.

Thank you, Marianne.

"That smells delicious. Thank you, *madame*."

I walked around the counter and hugged her. Surprised

by my display of affection, her doughy arms flapped before they came to rest on my back. Another betrayal. I would miss her terribly.

"You're welcome, *chérie*," she said, smiling.

The silence in the car was smothering, and the tension was palpable. I had the distinct feeling that Gideon didn't trust me. I just hoped I could distract him long enough to make my escape.

"What time does the service end?" he asked in a cold, businesslike tone.

"In an hour." Our gazes connected in the rearview mirror.

"Do you believe in God, Mr. Hirsch?"

He didn't answer right away, taking his time assessing me in the mirror. "I'm Israeli. I was raised Jewish, but I don't practice."

"You didn't answer my question."

Another long pause.

"I believe in human nature, Miss Sava. And what I've seen of it is vile and selfish. And, as they say, we are created in his image."

"He also gave us free will to muck around and figure it out for ourselves."

He shot me a long, hard stare. "That makes him a slum-lord at best, a negligent father at worst—and still unworthy of all the worship."

The acid undertone in his voice could have melted paint off a car. I finally recognized the shadows in his eyes. I had seen them before, in the eyes of the people in my country, the ones that had survived decades of deprivation or war. Something terrible had happened to Gideon Hirsch.

"You won't hold it against me if I wait out here," he said with a cynical smile.

He parked the Mercedes SUV across the street from the

quaint little church. I watched people shuffle in, greeted at the door by a white-haired priest in his seventies. He smiled warmly and shook hands with a young lady in a wheelchair, then ushered the last of his parishioners inside and closed the door behind him.

I stepped out of the car and looked around absently. I was about to enter the church when my eyes landed on *Inspecteur* Tribolet. He stood a block away, staring directly at me. His hand was suspended in midair, holding a croissant, his mouth full. An insidious unease raced up my spine. I banged on the passenger side window, and it slid open.

"Gideon, it's that detective that was asking too many questions. You deal with him."

Gideon jumped out of the Mercedes and jogged to intercept Tribolet. Having memorized the bus schedule, I knew I was cutting it close, and this was a complication that could have blown my plans sky-high. My pulse jumped around nervously while I watched to make sure Gideon was in control of the situation before I closed the church door. Inside, I lit a candle in front of the statue of the Blessed Virgin Mary and begged her to forgive me for the sins I had committed and the ones I was about to commit. Mostly, I prayed for Sebastian, prayed for her to heal his wounded heart, to watch over him. Then I slipped a donation in the box and headed straight for the priest. Service was about to begin.

"Father, may I speak to you for a moment?" I asked in French. His gentle, blue eyes searched my face. He stepped down from the altar and met me behind one of the carved stone pillars. His gaze lowered, falling upon my hand, the one that rubbed the tiny gold cross around my neck for reassurance. "I need your help, Father. There are two dark-haired men outside...standing next to a Mercedes. They've been following me all day. I'm frightened. My husband is a diplomat, and I was doing some sightseeing..." My voice trailed off, hoping he would understand the implication. He nodded, a concerned frown hardening his gentle features. I didn't have to fabricate the anxiety, it was all over me, as dense and dark as mud.

"What can I do, child?"

"I need to get to Geneva without them following. Is there a back door out of here?"

"Yes, and the bus stop is a block away. There should be a bus," he glanced at his watch, "leaving in fifteen minutes. You must hurry."

Quickly, he guided me to a small door that led to the church office and opened up into a back alley. Stepping out onto the cobblestone street, I thanked him profusely.

"I'll contact the police. Good luck, *madame*." He waved in encouragement.

I had just lied to a priest...*may God forgive me.*

Down the narrow street, a bus pulled up to a stop. With my plastic bag in hand I sprinted to catch it in time before the doors closed.

"You made it," said the smiling bus driver in French. I deposited the coins in the machine, walked to the back, and threw myself down in an empty row. Slouching down in my seat, I closed my eyes and wiped the nervous sweat from my brow with the back of my hand. As I stared out the window, trying to gain control of my breathing, a profound sense of loss was already settling into my bones. And yet, like most of the significant choices I had made in my life, walking away had been easier than I had anticipated.

CHAPTER 36

"Five hundred francs a week. You pay now cash," she said, her Russian accent thick and heavy. Mrs. Orloff held out her fat little hand palm up. The other was resting on her well-padded hip. I looked down at her with a vexed, disbelieving expression. I looked down because she was no taller than a gnome.

"Explain to me how the rent could have gone up a hundred francs a week in a little over two months. Did you paint? Did you replace the broken refrigerator? Because the chipped ceiling doesn't classify as shabby chic."

She frowned. Her droopy jowls made her look like a perpetually sad hound dog. Then her wily, black eyes took in my Chanel bag and the expensive clothes.

"We have waiting list. You don't want apartment? I have Brazilian girl will take it."

I was in no position to quibble. I needed a place to regroup before deciding what to do next. I took the cash out of my purse and begrudgingly slapped it in her hand. "I told you," she cackled. Ignoring her, I threw the plastic bag holding my meager belongings over my shoulder and turned up the stairs. "You make good money becoming...as Americans say—sugar baby. In Russia, we call them whore. I don't know what you did to lose sugar papa, but now that you not skinny, we find new one."

I cranked my head around and pinned her with a searing scowl. "I was not...I was working as a housekeeper!"

Her crooked smile revealed a mouthful of gold fillings. "Let me know when you are ready for new papa." I was too exhausted to try to reason with her. Robbed of my will to fight, I watched her waddle into her apartment without another word of protest from me.

Inside my room, I dropped my belongings on the floor and sat on the small twin bed to sulk. Not much had changed. It was still dingy and depressing. It didn't even smell as clean as I had left it. I made a mental note to bleach the sheets and every surface in the place. I got up and checked the refrigerator. The loud buzz emanating from it was strangely comforting. At least it was working.

The bottomless sadness that had been steadily growing since I had boarded the bus felt like a dead weight strapped to my ankles. I didn't even have the energy to cry about it. But as tired as I was, I needed to go to the grocery store. It wasn't just my own health I was responsible for anymore.

I undressed and hung the expensive clothes back in the closet. I needed to start blending in with the locals again. A pathetic memory crossed my mind. The argument I had with Sebastian about him not buying me anything because I wanted to salvage my pride and leave the relationship having given and taken in equal measure. Pleasure for pleasure. I looked down at my flat stomach, where a child was safely tucked away, and smiled to myself. I had definitely gotten more than I bargained for.

I took three pairs of jeans, a sweater, a couple of shirts, and sneakers out of the bag. My medical books, the computer, and my underwear were all gone. The hundred thousand euros was still sitting in my checking account. I needed that money for the baby. I wasn't about to let my pride get in the way of caring for him or her.

I put on my old jeans, a t-shirt, and sneakers. Strangely the old clothes didn't feel right anymore. The worst of it was that it didn't feel like I was returning to my old reality. It felt more like I was suspended between two different ones. I belonged nowhere—except with Sebastian.

When I reached into the Chanel purse to pull out my wallet, I felt a cold, hard object. Unknowingly, I had taken the iPhone with me. I stared at it a long time before sitting back down on the bed and turning it on. As soon as it powered up, a long list of texts and messages started to signal. Twenty-five voicemails and thirty text messages, to be exact.

They began as terse questions, progressively growing more frantic with worry. As I read each one, my anxiety paralleled the rising agony in his written words, the guilt unbearable. Tears stung my eyes and tunneled down my cheeks. For the first time in my life, I wasn't certain if my faith was strong enough to sustain me.

His Highness: Come back to me. Please. I don't know what will become of me if you don't.

That was the final text. I couldn't listen to the messages. I wasn't strong enough. I told myself that letting him go was an act of love, an act of compassion, but I was having a hard time believing it. Even worse, the alternative was unthink-able. I would hurt him more if I stayed. Paisley wouldn't hesitate to carry out her threat. She had that Attila the Hun, scorched-earth look about her. And I would be directly responsible for destroying his livelihood and his reputation, his family name. He would come to resent me eventually. I couldn't live with myself if that ever happened.

I placed the phone on the kitchen table and grabbed my wallet. Anyone could spot the Chanel bag from twenty paces, and there were enough pickpockets in this neighborhood to make the bag an appealing target. Locking the apartment door, I walked past the kids playing in the corridor and made my way down the stairs. The symmetry was not lost on me. The sight, the smells—everything was the same. Everything but me.

A dirty soccer ball rolled in front of my feet. I picked it up and held it out for the two seven-year-old boys it belonged to. *"Falemenderit,"* they shouted in Albanian as they ran back to their game.

"You're welcome," I replied and kept walking. Walking away, but never leaving this place behind.

———

As I entered the grocery store, I was instantly overcome by a strange déjà vu. Had the last few months been a dream? In need of a diversion, I picked up a cantaloupe and pressed my thumbs into the soft navel at the bottom. The sweet perfume of the ripened fruit drifted up. The laugh of a small child tugged at my attention, caused me to glance up. He sat in a shopping cart, gnawing on a slice of tangerine while his young mother wiped the tiny, sticky fingers with a wet nap.

A little boy: dark hair, light brown eyes, long, thick lashes. I stared in morbid fascination. The child's father appeared from around the corner, and the little boy shrieked in joy upon seeing him. My stomach twisted in agony as the melody of the child's giggles hung in the air. In the meantime, I marched to the other end of the store, needing to get as far away from them as possible.

Saving money on food wasn't an option anymore. I needed nutrition. I picked out a nice chicken to roast that would last me a couple of days, fresh fruits and vegetables, and a freshly baked French baguette. I couldn't manage more than two bottles of water. The lethargy was back with a vengeance. I would have had no trouble whatsoever sleeping like the dead on a bed of nails. I could have slept standing if I had to. It was a dangerous new habit.

The little boy and his parents were two spots ahead of me in line to pay for the groceries. The little boy's large, amber eyes found me. He stared as if he were stealing my thoughts. I smiled and turned away, on the brink of tears again. I couldn't shake the feeling that something was wrong, that something bad was about to happen, and I prayed to God that it was simply the result of stress mixed with the surplus of hormones running in my blood.

———

I TOOK my time walking back to the apartment, engrossed in the sights and sounds in spite of the circumstances. Tiny birds chirping madly at each other competed for a few scraps of bread on the sidewalk. Men on bicycles raced past me in a blur of color. Teenage lovers crossed the street, their fingers laced together. The warm sunshine on my clammy skin dissolved the lingering aftertaste of concern.

I closed my eyes for a moment and heard the sound of sirens approaching. When I opened them, police cars zipped by me, lights flashing, sirens blaring. They turned down my street. By the time I reached my corner, the whole block was congested with dark SUVs and regularly marked police vehicles. It looked like a motorcade of an important political figure.

Two small boys, no older than twelve, stood next to me, watching the scene unfold. "Is it a raid?" I asked them in Albanian.

They looked up at me with a cautious expression. "No. They're looking for someone," the taller one replied.

"A drug dealer?" The kids in this neighborhood were wise beyond their years, and often the eyes and ears of the community. Sadly, they knew everything that went on.

"No. Those men are Americans."

My head swiveled in the direction the child was pointing. That's when I saw him emerge from my building, Ben and Gideon following closely behind. My few possessions were in his hand. The other gripped the roots of his hair while his wild eyes scanned the crowd assembled on the sidewalk.

I could have sworn that my heart stopped beating. For as long as I lived, I would never forget the desperation on his face, the anguish. I could feel his pain intensely in every cell of my body, a shock to my system. The blood drained out of my head and pooled at my feet. My trembling knees could no longer hold me up. I knelt down immediately, the grocery bags falling onto the cement sidewalk, and willed myself not to pass out. The cantaloupe rolled away. One of the boys fetched it for me and handed it back.

"Take these groceries to your mother," I told the boys. They looked at each other skeptically. "Take them," I repeated gently.

They took the bags and scurried away. I don't know how, but somehow I found the strength to get up, turn around, and walk away one more time.

———

I STILL HAD MY WALLET. The silver lining, I guess. And that was about it. No passport. No clothes, other than the ones on my back. I walked for hours until I reached Yuri's nightclub, hoping desperately to find Emilia. Darkness had fallen by the time I was standing in front of the locked doors of the club. I burst into tears when I realized it was Sunday night. Exhausted and starving, I found a coffee shop close by, hid in a corner, and ate three stale brioches before I walked back to Pâquis and checked into a hostel.

The man at the front desk handed me a set of sheets and directed me to a room with four beds. There was a tense moment when he asked for identification. Luckily he believed my story about being robbed on the train. One bed was occupied by a young Canadian woman traveling alone, even though she made enough noise for three people, the others were empty.

After washing my face and brushing my teeth with my finger, I crawled into bed fully clothed and stared at the empty blue wall that my bed was smashed up against. I could still see Sebastian's distraught face in my mind's eye, branded there for all eternity. And then I prayed, prayed for God to take away his suffering, to keep him safe. Silent tears soaked my pillow, but eventually, a dreamless sleep stole my anguish away.

It was still dark out when the Canadian girl began packing her things up. My bleary gaze stumbled upon a digital clock in the room that blinked 4:30. I dragged my grief-stricken body to the bathroom. Even though it was clean and empty, I still took the quickest shower since creation, a result of the paranoia I couldn't shake. Breakfast was included in the modest price of the room, so I went downstairs and ate more than my share. I was constantly hungry now. The morning nausea, coming and going, wasn't as bad as I had expected.

I dialed Emilia's number from the lobby payphone. She answered after the third ring. Hearing her voice brought tears to my eyes.

"Em, it's me," I choked.

"Vera! Holy shit! He was here." Those few simple words froze my blood. "You told him about me and Yuri," she continued, a hint of censure in her voice.

My hand flew to my forehead. I had forgotten I had told him. "How was he?"

"He was out of his mind! A fucking maniac! Screaming, threatening us. There was an army of police with him. It scared the shit out of Yuri and nothing scares Yuri—except his mother."

I bit my lower lip as it trembled, licked the salty tear off the corner of my mouth. "I don't know how he found my apartment."

"They tracked your iPhone."

"I didn't know they could do that."

"Have you been living under a rock? Everybody knows that."

I have no criminal instincts!! Unlike some people who are routinely exposed to illegal activities. The words were on the tip of my tongue when I bit them back.

"Yuri said the club is being watched. I'm sure the apartment is, too. You can't come here."

"I need to leave the country and go back to Milan. He has my Italian passport."

"Shit," she mumbled, then sighed deeply. "Let me speak to Yuri. He may have a package traveling there this weekend."

A package? Drugs, or something even more unsavory. "Is it safe, Em?"

"I'll make sure it is. Call me in three days."

"Wait, there's something else, but it has to remain between us."

"What is it?"

"I'm pregnant."

"Holy shit. Does he know?"

"No."

"He looked ready to torture us for information yesterday. I only felt safe because the police were with him. I can't imagine if he'd known. Why are you running?"

"I have to…to protect him. I can't explain now. Make sure it's safe."

"I'll take care of it."

"Thanks, Em. I…" My voice cracked, fear and despair clogging my throat.

"Call me in three days," she repeated and hung up.

———

THE THREE LONGEST days of my life. I stayed close to the hostel. I wasn't certain what lengths Sebastian would go to to find me, what kind of power he could wield. So I stayed out of sight, made myself small, faded into the background. On the third day, I walked by a cyber café and looked through the glass window for a long time before finding the courage to step inside. I bought a cup of tea and fifteen minutes of time on their computer. My hands shaking violently, I typed in the password to my email account. Two hundred and eleven emails from him.

A sharp, stabbing sensation in my stomach made me grimace and hunch over. I felt nauseous, though nothing short of death could have stopped me from opening and reading the last one.

"Whatever I did for you to leave me, I'm sorry. I'm so fucking sorry. Please give me a chance to fix it. I'm begging you. I'll do anything to have you back. Anything. I love you. I'm nothing without you."

Wiping the tears off my face was useless. There were plenty more where those came from. The boy working on his laptop next to me kept glancing over with a mixed expression. I could tell he wanted to say something. My fingers were numb as I typed. *"I will love you forever. Don't ever forget. You promised."* I hit the send button. It was a dangerous move, but I couldn't tolerate him thinking he did anything wrong. I just couldn't allow that.

———

"I GOT YOU A RIDE TO MILAN."

I exhaled a deep sigh of relief at her words. My eyes roamed the lobby. A group of Irish students stood in line, waiting to be checked in. They were laughing about something. Their carefree expressions sparked a bud of resentment that made me ashamed of myself.

"Tonight at ten p.m., meet them in front of L'Usine on Place des Volontaires. They will be in a silver 3 Series BMW."

"Who are they?"

"Sergio and Etienne. They work for Yuri. You can't miss Sergio, he has a pink mohawk."

"Is it safe, Em?"

"As safe as it can be. Call me when you get to Milan. I love you."

"I love you, too."

At exactly ten, I watched the silver BMW drive up. I

pulled the hood of my sweatshirt over my head, dug my hands in the pockets, and walked towards the car. I had timed it perfectly. The last thing I wanted to do was stand around waiting on a street corner, in the middle of the night. I was nervous about leaving so late, but I was in no position to make demands.

The passenger side window rolled down and techno music, pumping loudly, hit me like a blast of hot air. A boy, no older than eighteen and sporting a pink mohawk, bobbed his head to the music. He turned it down and treated me to a thorough inspection.

"You must be Sergio," I stated.

"*Che figa*," Sergio announced, a crass Italian slang word for "beautiful."

The driver bent over Sergio to get a better look, raking me head to toe with bloodshot eyes. "I'm Etienne, get in."

Etienne was older, around early thirties. He was extremely thin with a crooked nose and pale blond hair. As soon as I shut the door, he drove off swiftly and rounded a corner without taking his foot off the gas pedal, the torque sending my body slamming into the door. Then he roughly shifted gears. It practically jarred my teeth loose. I buckled my seatbelt and gazed out the window. The lights from restaurants and street lamps turned into a smear as we sped away.

"If the border police ask, you're my sister, understood?" Etienne stated in a hard tone. I met his gaze in the rearview mirror and nodded once. "Do you speak French?"

"*Parfaitement*," I answered.

"That should make things easier."

"Maybe it would be easier if you didn't speed and bring unnecessary attention to us." I couldn't help it. I was hungry, irritable, and pregnant.

417

His heavy eyelids lowered over dark eyes. "I make this trip on a weekly basis. I would appreciate it if you would leave the driving to me. As a matter of fact, leave everything to me and keep your mouth shut," he cautioned, his voice descending into a growl.

"Vera."

"What?"

"My name is Vera," I repeated.

"That means truth in Italian. Well, Vera, keep your fucking truth to yourself until we get to Milan."

I turned my eyes towards the passing scenery. With every stoplight we passed and every building behind us, Geneva faded away from me. Once a shining city upon a hill—now a reminder of broken dreams.

"Can you turn the music up?" I asked. Sergio granted my request and started bobbing his head to the discordant sound of punk rock. The music gave me a headache. But anything was better than the sound of my thoughts.

CHAPTER 37

"**F**uck, fuck, fuck! Motherfuckers. *Pezzi di merda, cazzo. Putain!!*" Etienne shouted while he pounded the steering wheel with the heel of his hand.

I grimaced. "You've managed to include them all. In every language imaginable outside of Sorani."

"What?!"

"Your cursing. Sorani is a dialect of Kurdish." His shifty eyes connected with mine in the rearview mirror. Nothing—just a vacant expression. "Never mind," I added and turned to stare out the window.

A Christmas tree of taillights snaked across the Mars black night. The line of cars waiting to be inspected by Swiss border patrol stretched for miles. The heavy thump of Sergio's leg nervously beating against the floor of the car kept pace with the sound blasting from the speakers. I dare not call it music.

We had already been driving for two hours and waiting in traffic for three more. A dull ache had slowly developed below my navel. Rubbing it didn't help. I needed food and a bathroom badly. "Etienne, maybe we should find a gas station and get something to eat. This line hasn't moved in an hour."

He turned to look at Sergio and found him cupping his privates like a five-year-old desperate for a toilet. I rolled my eyes. Directing my annoyance at Sergio, I said, "I told you not to drink three cans of Red Bull. Caffeine and B-12 are diuretics."

My critical gaze was met by another blank expression. "What??" Sergio asked.

My patience finally snapped as the dull ache in my stomach spiked. "It makes you piss!"

"She's right, Etienne. Might as well eat and piss," Sergio agreed, shrugging off my anger as if it were commonplace for people to speak to him in that manner.

Etienne pursed his lips. Then he began to make a jarring, three-point turn that had half the cars around us honking their horns. Driving onto the grassy shoulder of the highway, we zipped by the rest of the traffic and made an incredibly illegal maneuver to get back onto the northbound lane. Not too far down the road, we found an Agip station and pulled into the parking lot.

The food court was filled with travelers waiting for the traffic to thin out. We stood in line and ordered. I picked up a vacuum-sealed ham sandwich from the display. As we sat down to eat, Etienne stiffened slightly, his brows lowering over narrowed eyes. My gaze followed the direction of his glare and discovered three Swiss police officers walking in with a German Shepherd.

"What is it?" I asked Etienne.

Ignoring me, he leaned across the table towards Sergio. "Are you sure you locked the trunk?"

Sergio stopped chewing his charred hamburger. His eyes

glazed with indecision. "I think so," he answered, food spilling out from the side of his mouth.

"Why? What's in the trunk?" I asked, anxiety making my voice sharp and high. I was afraid something like this might happen, even though Emilia had assured me that they were driving to Milan for a pick-up, not a delivery.

Etienne's already thin lips disappeared off his face, and his eye twitched nervously. His voice was eerily quiet when he spoke, "You think so, motherfucker?"

Sergio's gaze widened. Under the table, his leg began bouncing rapidly. "I'm sure I did," he replied.

We fell silent as three sets of eyes followed every move the officers made, from where they picked up their bags of food, to when they stepped outside. Suddenly nauseous, I couldn't eat anymore. The pain was a fist pressing on my abdomen. It made my breath catch and my face twist.

"I'm going to the restroom." If either of them heard me, they didn't acknowledge it.

The bathroom was empty and clean. I washed my hands and stared at my reflection in the mirror. What would my father say if he could see what had become of me? After what had happened with Pascal, I wouldn't have believed that things could get any worse. And yet, they had. I didn't want to know what was in that trunk. And I was even more petrified to find out what would happen next.

The cold, fluorescent lights made me look sallow, unwell. This was the worst possible time to be feeling sick. Another hot stab slashed through me, stronger this time. I doubled over and braced myself against the sink, my legs fighting to support me. *Breathe through the pain...breathe through the pain.* I was getting dangerously close to breaking, my willpower slowly ebbing away.

A heavy-set woman walked in, older, around sixty. She

placed a gentle hand on my back and asked, *"Scusi, signorina, hai bisogno d'aiuto?"* I forced myself to stand straight and answered her in the same language, Italian, that I was grateful for her concern, but I didn't need any help. What I needed was to get back to the car as quickly as possible and lie down. I found Etienne and Sergio waiting for me at the entrance, looking through the glass doors.

Etienne nodded in the direction of the officers. "They're right there. Be cool."

Be cool???? I was anything but cool!

We stepped outside, and a gust of warm air greeted us, accompanied by a strong smell. The sweet scent of honeysuckle was mixed with the pungent odor of gasoline and cigarette smoke. My olfactory system was on steroids, heightened because of the pregnancy, and as the smell hit me, so did another wave of nausea.

The police officers were deep in conversation, laughing about something. They flicked the ashes of their cigarettes on the ground, one of them staring intently at Sergio's hair as we walked past them. The one handling the dog ground out his cigarette under his boot and turned in the direction we were headed towards the car. As he passed the BMW, the dog began barking aggressively. All three of us stood frozen.

The officer tried once to tug the barking dog away, but when the dog persisted, he began circling the car. "Hey, you, is this your car?" he asked Etienne in French.

Etienne hesitated a second too long. The police officer's brow wrinkled with suspicion. Another hot stab of pain and my knees were suddenly no longer able to hold me up. A cold sheen of sweat covered me from top to bottom. My breath was shallow and labored, my heart beat as fast as a percussion instrument.

"I'm sorry, Officer. My sister is not feeling well. Yes, this is our car." Etienne made an attempt at looking concerned and walked me over to the curb. I sat down and hugged my knees, hoping and praying the pain would subside.

The tips of Sergio's mohawk danced as he fidgeted nervously with a cigarette. He looked like a nervous rooster. Even to my untrained eye, he looked guilty as hell of something. The other officers, having been alerted by the dog's bark, walked towards the car. Etienne left me on the curb to stand next to Sergio.

A crowd began congregating around me on the sidewalk, finding someone else's misery or misfortune fascinating, no doubt. The raucous bark of the police dog drowned out every other sound. I couldn't hear the conversation transpiring between Etienne and the police. It didn't seem to be going well, however. Sergio's nervous gaze shifted to me, then to the officers, then to the trunk. The situation was escalating. I could tell by the policemen's body language that they were getting ready to search the car.

A disaster was slowly unfolding before my eyes. I knew that if they opened that trunk, we would all be arrested, and I would find myself deported back to Albania to stand trial for grand larceny. I made a calculated decision and willed my legs to move. Backing away slowly, I retreated into the crowd and, as I melted away from the scene, watched the officers open all the car doors, cuff Etienne, and then Sergio. When I was out of sight, I sprinted to the back of the gas station, where it bordered a dense forest.

And then I ran. I ran like the devil was at my heels. Until the pain in my lungs and abdomen was a sharp knife skewering me. This time, there was no place to hide. Nowhere to go and lick my wounds. Nowhere would I be safe.

I could barely see a foot in front of me, the area so rural I couldn't detect any evidence of electricity. I had no idea where I was headed, or in which direction. The adrenaline focused all my energy on making my legs work. I stumbled over tree branches and thick vines of ground covering. My knee banged against a tree trunk. My cheek burned as a tree branch whipped across my face. And still, I kept moving, pushing through the pain.

The distant sound of shouting and the bark of a dog finally registered. The policemen had discovered me missing and were giving chase, hunting me. The voices drew closer. My foot hit a rock and sent me sprawling to the ground. As I scrabbled to my feet, a pain so unbearable tore through me that I collapsed again. My hand accidentally brushed my jeans. It felt damp. The cover of the night made it impossible to see anything except the outline of my fingers. A moment later the clouds parted and a shaft of moonlight fell on it like a spotlight. My pale skin was stained with a thick coating of something black. My fingers trembled. The shouts were getting closer, almost upon me. Fear paralyzed me. Adrenaline forced me to get up.

I began running. In my haste, I never noticed the fallen tree at my feet. My foot was caught under it, and I stumbled to the ground once again. This time, I couldn't manage to break my fall. Pure agony exploded in my head. Unable to go on, I lay there and thought of my father, of Sebastian and the baby. I had failed them all. And then everything went dark.

———

EVERYTHING HURT. My muscles felt like they had been pushed through a meat grinder. My head throbbed. My right hand was numb, clamped down by a prickly vise. I tried wiggling my pinky, though I don't think it worked. I couldn't for the life of me figure out where the hell I was. It took all the strength I had just to crack them open.

In small increments, light poured into the narrow slits of my eyes, flooding my vision, making everything blurry and dream-like. Only this was no dream, more like a nightmare. I was so weak I needed a nap from the effort it took to open my eyes just a fraction. My hearing seemed to be working fine because I heard a deep, steady exhale. That piqued my curiosity. I tried lifting my lids a little bit more, and everything slowly and softly came into focus.

I was in bed. A sandy head was resting on my hand. I tried wiggling my fingers again. The head moved. *Sebastian.* It all came back to me in a tidal wave of thoughts and emotions. My head felt like it might explode. A swell of tears pushed up. With them came an acute pain that made it impossible to cry. They seemed to logjam in my throat, unable to go further.

He stirred and looked up, and when our eyes met, my heart stuttered. His face was ravaged with pain, his cheeks hollow, cheekbones sharper in contrast. He had lost weight, too much of it. Dark circles hung under his eyes, and he had about a week's worth of beard growth on his handsome face. He squeezed his eyes shut, breathing a deep sigh of relief as the thick fan of his lashes lifted again.

I made another half-hearted attempt at wiggling my numb fingers. Realizing what I was trying to do, he began rubbing my hand between his, trying to restore feeling in it. He kissed each finger in between the rubbing. I had to touch him, unsure if this was a sick fantasy I was conjuring. Only I wouldn't be in this much pain if it was a dream. I brushed his sharp cheekbones with my index finger, and his jaw flexed.

A strange croaking sound rose up my throat. I licked my

dry lips and tried to speak again, but I got the same result. His brow creased, his worry palpable. He squeezed my hand.

"Let me get the nurse." His deep, rough-hewed voice cracked as he tried to hold in his emotions.

I squeezed his fingers and mouthed the word "water." Moving anything other than that hurt too much. He stood abruptly, the chair he sat on toppling backwards. The loud sound exploded in my head painfully and bounced down the hall. A stout nurse entered in a hurry.

"You're awake, Miss Sava. Good, I'll get Dr. Rossetti."

"She needs water immediately," Sebastian demanded, his tone overly curt.

If I could have smiled then, I would have—my tender, despotic lover. The nurse raised her thin brows at his high-handedness. She pinned Sebastian with an icy glare. Her expression thawed considerably when her attention returned to me, however. "I'll be right back with some ice water and the doctor," she announced before she walked out.

I squeezed his fingers again, and his gaze, filled with concern, met mine. "How?" I croaked—a small miracle that actual sound came out. A million hows were caught in my throat. *How long have I been here? How did you find me? How's our baby...*

"Let me get you some water first," he said quietly. "Don't try to speak yet." He kissed my hands again before he left my side. The nurse bustled in with a cup and a straw and Sebastian grabbed it from her none too politely. Fiddling with the control button, he elevated my bed, cupped the back of my neck gently, and held the straw to my mouth. The nurse thinned her lips and grumbled in French something about a sense of entitlement and what vaguely sounded like "*American asshole.*"

In the middle of unbelievable lethargy and pain, as I

watched the two of them jockey for position, I had the overwhelming urge to burst out laughing. I had missed this, missed him...desperately. Everything turned blurry as tears slipped down my face. He frowned, his expression pained, while his eyes, burning brightly, absorbed every detail of me.

"It's okay, baby," he murmured. "I got you...you're safe."

I took small sips of water that required more strength than I had. My eyes fluttered shut while he brushed the dampness on my cheeks away with the back of his fingers. I felt his soft kisses on my temple, my eyelids, my lips, assuaging my battered soul. I couldn't hold on much longer. Just before consciousness slipped away, I remembered the blood. I wanted to open my eyes and ask him, but I drifted further into the void. Where nothing existed—except absolute black.

To be continued...

A MILLION DIFFERENT Ways To Lose You... *now available in ebook and paperback.*
A Million Different Ways To Lose You

ABOUT THE AUTHOR

Paola Dangelico loves romance in all forms, pulp fiction, the NY Jets, and to while away the day at the barn (apparently she does her best thinking shoveling horse poop). She was born in Milan Italy, grew up in New Jersey watching her father paint the covers of bestselling romance authors like Danielle Steel and Amanda Quick, and after a long stint on the left coast returned to the right coast to write about finding love in a modern world.

www.pdangelico.com

Mailing List– used only for new releases and promotions.

Facebook Reading Group (P. Dangelico's Mod Squad)